Leigh Smith heads one of the larg___ _____ _____ _____,
Saxon Karate, (*www.saxonkarate.com*.) founded in 1981.
To date his career of almost thirty eight years has seen him become
one of the most successful martial arts instructors. Leigh teaches
worldwide and helped found the official federations, that are
government recognised in: Russia, Latvia and in Sri Lanka for the
people of Tamil Eelam. He is invited many times a year to instruct
not just in Europe but globally.

Leigh has recently been launched onto the after dinner and
motivational speaking circuit and with initial engagements exceeding
all expectations, this enterprise too seems destined for great success.

Leigh Smith lives in West Yorkshire with his wife Laraine and ten
year old daughter Loren. Leigh's grown children and grandchildren
live just over the Pennines, in Lancashire – his son Daniel, his wife
Nicky and their children Kayleigh, Kyle, Emily and Daisy May,
eldest daughter Gemma Leigh and youngest son Gareth.

'Norvern Monkey' is the first in a trilogy of novels. With release dates as follows:

'Norvern Monkey'
October 2007

'Suvvern Fairies'
May 2009

'Monkey's Business'
Autumn 2010

'Norvern Monkey'

FIRST EDITION

Leigh Smith

Bravurex publishing

Bravurex publishing
Copyright © Leigh Smith 2007

A CIP catalogue record for this book
is available from theBritish Library

Edited by Maureen Peacock. B.A. Hons, M.B.A.

ISBN 978 0 9557289 0 7

Printed and bound in Great Britain by
Trade Print Europe
72 New Bond Street. London.
Cover Layout, Jupiter Associates,
Croyden Surrey, UK

Bravurex Publishing
2 Coleman House
Sowerby Bridge
West Yorkshire
HX6 2SH
United Kingdom

www.bravurex.com.

For Maud Ellen, my amazing mother,
who taught me most things are possible.

My suffering but supportive wife Laraine.

My Exceptional Brothers Mick and Alan.
In a different age they would have walked with Kings

My sister Maureen without whose help this novel
would have never been completed.

In most large families there are saints and sinners.
My brother Tony will always be, 'Saint Tone'.

My little sister, Karen.

Though fate has separated us.
We will always be together.

Chapter 1

Whether it was the shock of the freezing contents of the colourful chamber pot, or the child's early introduction to Anglo-Saxon dialogue that brought an end to childish innocence, he would never know.

"You bitch." That statement of affection, plus a feeling of being pissed wet through provided a formal introduction to the tot's dear old dad. Even a mother's protection did nothing to allay fears or to prevent the siren sounds emitting from both ends of a three year old body. The football pitch of a bed, like mother and child, was becoming cold, soggy and stinking.

"Peter, you bastard! Just look what you've done to my eiderdown." Having come second to a hand-stitched heirloom, the event was brought into perspective and even at his tender age, Mark realised, that if his wailing continued, there was every chance that he would follow the Wedgwood masterpiece that his mother had deftly caught and saved. However there were no guarantees that he would be as fortunate as the chamber pot.

"Shut that little bastard up, you stupid cow." How anyone could say such things about a blond-haired, blue-eyed cherub was a puzzle. Besides, his mother had married his father over one and a half decades ago, thankfully sparing the family a cruel stigma that would have invited victimisation in Richton, as it would in most cotton towns in the 1950's.

"If you shut your face for one minute, maybe the little bleeder will shut his." Mark's mother, Helen, had stockpiled some of the best phrases and insults in the English language. This was attributable to the fact that she was more verbally imaginative than most females of her time, and to a hard East London upbringing that had given her a sharp city edge. It also helped that she knew more obscenities than the vast majority of the adult population.

"Don't tell me to shut my fashe, yer bitch, or a'll shmash yer fashe in."

Timber!! Six-foot-two, eyes of blue, drunk as a skunk Daddy, first teetered, then tottered before crashing to the floor. Mother and child watched the immaculate manikin's slow motion progress, his body hitting the ground first, followed immediately by his Brylcreemed head. Finally he became inanimate and oblivious to worldly worries, alcoholically anaesthetized.

"Thank God," muttered Helen. "Come on Mark, let's get cleaned up." With a not unkindly wrench, he was borne aloft, the suddenness caused him to sharply inhale the cold air, and its iciness attacked the saturated, teddy-adorned pyjamas. En route to the bathroom Helen grabbed the clean clothes that had been laid out on an old mirrored dressing table, in readiness for use later that morning. Reaching the bathroom door, Helen paused, turned sharply and returned to her inanimate spouse. "Empty the piss pot on us will ya? You drunken shit. Well 'ave this one on me." It took three vicious kicks from Helen's size fours to Peter's mid-section and one that severely disturbed his perfect parting, to produce even a grunt from him. However, Helen was happy with that result and as the door closed behind them a strange feeling came over Mark. Until that moment in time, he had not been aware of having a mother, a father, brothers' or a sister; in fact he had not been aware of life itself.

Wide awake from the bath he had just received, Mark was studied the person who was vigorously assaulting him with a huge white towel. She was spouting continuous profanities, stopping every now and then to look into her son's eyes, encouraging support for her views. Then, continuing with renewed enthusiasm, she berated her husband and abraded her son, oblivious to his protests against the cotton pummelling. Eventually she paused and gazed at the outcome, a glowing pink, blond, slightly fearful boy.

Mark's Mother, who was now smiling, was an exceptionally good-looking woman with mid-length, bouncy, chestnut hair and bright blue eyes. She exuded a strength of character that exceeded her slight frame and stature, five-foot-four in stocking-feet. Whether it was Mark's reluctance to return the smile of someone who previously had been an incomplete shadow, or his involuntary yawn that caused the maternal smile to disappear, he could not tell. But disappear it had, just like the blue-orange flamed pop of the gas water-heater. The small boy had noticed the contraption earlier, when Helen had stemmed the boiling water from the long, chrome spout once the depth and temperature of the water in the bath had reached a satisfactory level. When Helen had tightened the large, painted, red wheel, Mark had watched the roaring flame through the geyser's lighting aperture. Startled by its explosive demise inside the cream-coloured drum. The roaring flame had been reduced to a pilot light, a tiny dancing flicker that cast cavorting shadows, patiently awaiting the next command to roar into life. Mark was lifted yet again and a faint, pungent smell of coal gas, one of man's most popular inventions of terminal escapism, registered in nostril and brain. Like a first kiss, it was an experience that would be often repeated but which would never again have quite the same impact.

"Terry! Terry!" Helen was softly shaking the bundle in the bed before them.
"Mmmm, nn, whaa, what!" enquired the bundle.
"Peter's sloshed, he's emptied the piss pot on us again. I need to put Mark in with you. If you need me, I'll be next door in your sister's room."
The sleepy head that emerged would always remind Mark of the hedgehog character on a popular TV puppet show of the time.
"Ol right." Terry lifted the blankets with one arm and the boy was lowered gently next to him. Helen stooped and pecked tiredly at her two youngest boys' cheeks and then made her way to the door. As it opened, she paused for a moment framed in the light from the landing.
"Goodnight" she said in hushed tones.

"Night." Terry replied. The door closed and the room blackened for the few moments it takes for eyes to become accustomed to gloom. Becoming aware of the silvery light stabbing through the curtains, providing shape and substance to objects in the room, Mark's attention turned to his bedfellow, who was thoroughly sniffing his head and shoulders.
"What you doing Tel?"
"Seeing if yer smell of pee."
"av' ad a baff!"
"Good job too, otherwise I would av booted yer out."
"av' ad a baff, I av."
"Olright, olright. Be quiet or we'll get done."
The younger boy did not know what this terror of 'getting done' was, and he had no intentions of finding out. So, snuggling into the lumpy flock mattress, he decided to keep silent and still. Still, that was until something stabbed him sharply. "Tell!"
"What."

"It urts."

"Wot does?"

"Pillow does."

Terry sat up and began to search the offending area of the pillow with almost immediate results. Brandishing a small feather by the very quill that had attempted to puncture Mark's cheek, he brought it close enough to the youngster's face for him to identify the offending object in the bedroom's gloom. "Olright, now go to sleep."

There can be surprisingly few moments in life when one can feel secure and loved; this was one such moment for Mark. As his big brother put his arm around him, warmth enveloped the whole of his being; he felt safe. "Tell…. Tell…. Terree!"

"Wot now!"

"I need a wee."

"No you don't, just go to sleep. Night night."

Something in Terry's voice seemed so final that Mark obeyed, soon drifting off. These same slumbers were brought to an abrupt end not many minutes later by Terry's panic-stricken lament, "MARK! You've gone and pissed the bed!", and for the second time that night, the younger boy was wet through, but this time he was going to have his say.

"I told you I needed a wee!"

Life for Mark was extremely confusing in his formative years but he would remember these events as 'Night of the Piss Pot'.

Even at this early age, Mark became acutely aware of the differences between his family and other families in the neighbourhood. Whereas no-one else had a car, they had three, plus a van and a truck. Nobody else had such a large house, and whenever he was privileged enough to be grudgingly dragged along in the company of his brothers' and sister, he became aware of a feeling of superiority, as all the bigger kids legged it at the sight of the Dacey clan on the prowl.

Castaires, a Regency four-storey red-brick building, was a mansion of a home in every way. Outside, at the back of the house, one on each side were two courtyards, housing an outside lavatory and a bin store and large coal shed. These outbuildings were set back, forming a walkway from one yard to the other. There had been a grand washhouse and rockery in one of the yards, but it had been removed to provide further parking space. Several stone steps with an ornate cast-iron hand-rail led to the back door which the family used most of the time. Entering, there was a galley kitchen on the left with a serving hatch to the dining room, in the corner of which was an enclosed sink, not unlike an armoire in appearance when its doors were closed.

To the right was a small store room and three stone steps, which were later to provide Mark with an in-depth experience. The steps led to a double hallway, which was graced by an exquisite terracotta tile, patterned floor, which seemed as big as a park. This masterpiece gave access to four large rooms and a huge front door that was heavily carved and glazed. The hallway was Mark's favourite place. The grand staircase rose, massive and impressive with stone treads and risers, complemented with a complex, scrolled iron balustrade that was capped with a magnificent, gleaming, mahogany hand-rail.

Whether polish and duster or never-ending backsides descending at the speed of light provided this lustre, was of little concern to Mark. Of far greater interest to Mark was the curling pedestal at the stair bottom. During his childhood this thing of beauty would become many things for him; a fort, a castle, a bus, a truck – in fact, anything he could imagine. It would fill those times all children experience, when they are alone but not lonely.

The ascending main staircase formed a square. At the second corner of the square a small flight of steps to the right led to a half-landing and a Juliet balcony, behind the balcony, on the right, was a bathroom and a lavatory, an indoor lavatory! A rarity in Richton houses at that time. A small corridor to the left led to a bedroom. The main staircase continued to rise forming the third side of the square and the fourth side was formed by a magnificent minstrel's gallery, which was accessed through an elaborate wooden gate across the top of the stairway. Five bedrooms and a study were situated off the minstrel's gallery. The main rooms overlooked a sweeping carriage drive, large gardens and grounds which were surrounded by ornate stone walls. These walls were decorated at equal intervals with carved stone heads of medieval knights, ancient busts that had been acquired long ago from the lord of the manor when Richton had been a rotten borough. The Dacey children had used the busts as target practice for air guns and bows and arrows. In the final corner of the square was a small room and a further flight of wooden stairs which led to a massive attic. The extensive and sinister basement, more akin to dungeons than cellars, was reached by descending a long steep flight of stone steps in the back courtyard.

The occupants of Castaires were in descending order of age: Father Peter, Mother Helen, eldest son Jack (sometimes known as young Peter), Karl, Mary, Terry and Mark. These seven were the immediate Dacey family.

Chapter 2

"You look after the little sod."

"It's your bloody turn."

"I'm not looking out for no snot-nose."

"Give him to our Mary."

"Can't… she's gone out with Helen."

It was the unconventional custom of the Dacey children to refer to and address their parents on first-name terms. This practice was not intended to be derogatory or disrespectful, in fact Peter and Helen openly condoned it.

Bickering, as in all large families, was the norm, especially when it concerned who was to care for the youngest child. This particular row between the two eldest brothers', Jack and Karl, was about to erupt into the usual push, shove and punch-up, but rescue came in the form of Mark's favourite brother, Terry. "S olright, al watch im."

With the brat off their hands, the two older boys' were pals again – until the next time.

Walking along in the company of his three brothers', always gave Mark a feeling of safety and well-being. He did not fully understand why, as apart from Terry none of his siblings had ever made much effort to comfort or to reassure him, nevertheless, he shared this brotherly sensation of invincibility. However, the little boy wished that he had longer legs, for although his skinny little limbs were operating at full steam, he was still falling behind the distant trio. Every now and then, Terry ran back, grabbed Mark's arm and dragged him to the front of the group.

Terry told the youngster that if he got left behind a black man would get him. This ruse worked for a while, because in Richton, where few 'non whites' resided, a black man inspired great awe. There was, however, a large community of Ukrainians and Poles, they had settled in the town after the war and had been employed in local cotton mills and factories. These displaced persons presented no mystery to Mark, as his parents owned several large, boarding houses which were used to accommodate the 'D.P.s'. The mills reserved *en bloc* and paid for the rooms in advance to ensure the availability of beds for their prospective employees. In truth, these property's were little more than doss-houses. Just under four years of age, Mark understood that his Father was a man of little conscience when it came to money. However, a black man – that was a different kettle of fish! Fear lent wings and he managed to keep up fairly well as they travelled down Barnham road into the Town Centre, which was a mile's distance from home.

The shops were many and varied, the streets bustled, and although motor vehicles were usually fairly sparse, traffic was brisk on that autumn Saturday in 1957. Occasionally the children stopped to window-shop at the more interesting stores. Jack and Karl were attracted to the clothes shops; 'Teddy boy' gear was a must for sixteen and seventeen year olds. Terry, favoured the model and toy shops and they were Mark's usual choice too. On that day however, he found himself staring at huge bunches of black speckled hoops, rabbits, foul and game, all hung upside down and arranged as attractively as the butcher could present the feathered and furry corpses. These inanimate creatures with crimson ribbons of congealed blood decorating their mouths and beaks, observed life through sad, unblinking eyes.

"Tell, what's them?" Mark pointed a chubby finger at the hoops.

"Black puddins."

"What's black puddins?" Karl recognised an opportunity to assist with his youngest brother's education.

"Black puddins are made from black men."

"Why?"

"Coz they just are." It was obvious that the conversation had ended. Jack emerged from the butchers triumphantly waving a chicken's severed talons.

"Wot you got Jack? Can I'av one? Eh! Eh! Can I?"

Mark had no idea what Jack had, but judging from the reactions and merriment of the other two, it seemed important to possess one.

"No, piss off." The boy was undeterred.

"Wot they gonna do Jack?" Jack responded eagerly, pulling the exposed sinew from the cleaved end of the leg, to restore lifelike movement to the claw. Mark jumped back startled. This was probably the worst mistake he could have made, as his comic expression and fear were seized upon by Jack and Karl who promptly terrified the boy with their impersonations of winged beasties from hell.

"Hiya boys!' Dat's not du way to treets yer liddle brudder."

"Hiya Chalkie!" answered Jack.

"You OK boy?" Mark nodded, transfixed by the brilliance of the black man's smile. "Ere ave sum sweets." A hand shot out to receive the proffered goodies; several gooey humbugs clinging to a paper bag. "See you later boys', be gud now, OK?" Chalkie turned and disappeared into the butcher's shop.

There was no time for contemplation, as Mark was defending the sweets with his life, but to no avail, as he was robbed of all but the two that he had crammed into his mouth.

The journey home was uneventful. When they reached the top of the street leading to Castaires, the youngest boy was forced into one last burst of activity. He hot-footed it for home and safety, all the way screaming entreaties to be saved from the pursuing devils and their dreaded chicken claws.

That night, Mark who was by then a permanent resident in Terry's room, woke his brother with stifled sobs.

"Wots up?"

"Snot fair."

"Wot int?"

"That nice black man."

"Chalkie? Wot about him?"

"He give us them sweets and then went in t' butchers."

There was a brief pause as Terry tried to make sense of the conversation.

"So wot?"

"We dint tell him Terry"

"Tell him wot?"

"Bout black puddins."

When Terry's giggles had subsided, he went to great lengths to alleviate Mark's concern, explaining that it was common knowledge that all black men actually enjoyed being made into black puddings. Mark was not wholly convinced but soon fell asleep. For many months the little boy found himself disturbed by mental pictures of kindly old Chalkie climbing joyfully into the butcher's mincing machine.

Over a period of days, Mark had become aware and had come to terms with a sad, uneasy feeling that permeated daily, family life. It

all came to a head with a visit from two men in blue uniforms.
"Bastard Rozzers." whispered Karl.
All the children, with the exception of Jack, were listening to the conversation from their hiding place in the kitchen behind the closed serving hatch doors. They heard their mother cry out.
"Five bloody years? You bastards. He's just a boy."
"He's a wrong'un Mrs. Dacey and you know it. He's seventeen and already spent most of his life in and out of borstals and remand centres; now we've got him right where he belongs again, in the nick!"
All this was too much for the youngest Dacey. Two grinning giants were making his mum cry. Mark burst through the door and the nearest copper got a small boot in his shin, the second officer screamed shrilly, as needle-sharp teeth sank into the hand that he had outstretched to restrain the toddler. "You little....." CLANG. He was stopped mid-sentence by Helen's well-aimed frying pan,
 "Fuckin' ell! You're a nutter Helen Dacey!" His mate was already out of the door.
"Yeh and you're a cunt, copper. Now fuck off."
"Yeh, fuck off copper!" came the chorus from the Dacey juveniles. Together they slammed the door behind the retreating policemen. Helen gathered Mark into her arms and trying to hold back her tears, she explained that Jack would not be present at Mark's birthday party. Outside, the retreating police officers agreed that to report their ill treatment at the hands of a woman and a child would be to invite ridicule from their colleagues back at the nick.
Understandably no report was ever filed.

Chapter 3

Mark, like all children, was a master of selfish disregard for anyone save himself, especially when he was eagerly awaiting his fourth birthday and party celebrations. Disappointingly and after all the waiting, the event came and went with no lasting fond memories, only memories of another drunken attack on Helen. As a consequence of this, Peter was sent to prison for a short holiday, which did not bother any of the children but which delighted their mother.

Everyone became depressed when they realised that the eldest of the Dacey offspring would be missing from the family circle for a long time. He was destined to be detained at an archaic northern centre for correction. Jack, at seventeen, had taken offence at two older men for, as he put it, 'taking the piss'. This offence had taken place at Richton's famous dancehall, 'The Majestic'. Where Jack had severely thrashed the so-called hard men. A passing police officer had recognized 'that young nutter about town' and in an attempt to stop the fight he had set about Jack with his truncheon, trying to restrain him. The other two assailants were obviously innocent in the eyes of this particular representative of justice. When the older men had decided to enthusiastically assist the officer, Jack had gone berserk. A savage truncheon blow had split Jack's head just above the temple. The vicious, retaliatory head-butt that had loosened teeth and burst both nose and lips, had curtailed the involvement of the uniformed assailant. The sight of an unthinkable retaliation on a police officer and the shriek emitted by that officer had distracted the other two men. In the moment of their distraction, the truncheon had found its way into Jack's hand, and in a few moments it had all been over. It had taken, several, newly arrived burley coppers to drag Jack off the battered forms and only a few minutes more for those brave Boys' in Blue to arrange a reception committee in the cells of the Town Hall. Later, the family had learned how the law's noble ideals had been upheld, by eight burly policemen who had enjoyed kicking a seventeen-year-old boy unconcious.

 With hateful contempt for this cowardly abuse of power, the Dacey family had concurred that all coppers are bastards. Jack's condition had been such that the charge had been amended to resisting arrest and causing bodily harm to the two original bully-boys'.

Over the following few days The Dacey home became a hive of activity, as the clan concentrated on finding ways to help Jack. At the trial, the family were delighted when the charges against Jack were reduced to causing an affray and resisting arrest'. The reason for the lesser charges was that the two 'victims' had refused to give evidence and despite threats of dire consequences from the police, they had remained firm in a newfound belief that the man who had attacked them was not Jack Dacey. Perhaps the concern that had been shown for their future well-being by Karl and his friends had made them see things more clearly.

The police in their wisdom had dropped the charge of assaulting a police officer due to the extent of his injuries, which had not been satisfactorily explained to the visiting police doctor, nor to Jack's solicitor in the cells. So many witnesses had seen only a single cut to Jack's head, caused by a blow from the officer's truncheon, and many were willing to give evidence to that fact. Furthermore had they been called to the stand they would have accused the police of using excessive force during the arrest. Therefore it had been considered more prudent to amend the charges.

The only reliable witness for 'The Crown Prosecution' was the officer who had been involved in the affray. Reluctantly they brought a double charge before the court of 'breaching the peace' and 'resisting arrest'. When the bespectacled beak passed, in the grimmest of tones, a two year sentence of which Jack would have to serve a minimum of eighteen months, Helen gasped. as the large police officer was escorting him to the cells beneath the court, Jack looked back at his Mother and winked. "Don't worry Mum, I can do two years standing on my head!" Then he winced as his escort jerked his handcuffs violently, but quickly recovered, to laugh out loud, not just for his own bravado but also for his mother's benefit. Then he disappeared.

At first Helen was severely depressed, then she settled into a well-rehearsed routine of letter-writing and applying for visiting rights. Life went on, every day bringing something new, courtesy of her wayward brood.

Chapter 4

Jack had been sentenced mid-December, shortly after Mark's fourth birthday. Mark had little idea where his eldest brother was, or what all the fuss was about. The 'coppers' had been round, but that was not an unusual occurance at castaires and since their contact with Mark's teeth and his mother's frying pan, they seemed to prefer standing on the doorstep to entering the premises. When the boy did enquire after Jack, he always received the same reply from his brothers' and sister. "Go and see Helen." It still puzzled him that he was the only one to refer to Helen and Peter as Mum and Dad, while the others addressed them by first names. Eventually, cornered by the little boy's enquiries, Helen said, "Jack is not very well and he's going to be in hospital for a while."

"But why is he not well? As he got chickenpox or somefink?"

"Yes, somefink...I mean something like that. Look, here's threepence, go and get yourself some sweets." This was more like it, three pennies would buy one Arrowbar, two liquorice roots, one Coltsfoot Rock and eight Black Jacks. Helen's generosity would allow her to escape awkward questions and undertake an important errand, alone.

The corner shop was on the adjacent street to Castaires, but traffic was light and it was normal for even very young children to go to nearby shops unaccompanied. Mark was returning from his shopping expedition his pockets and cheeks full of booty bought with coins that had been extorted from his harassed mother. The little boy ran excitedly around a corner and full tilt into Alex. This was the boy who lived across the road at the back of Castaires. At seven years of age and with a marked advantage in size, Alex was an individual whom Mark would have preferred to avoid, having previously witnessed the boy's foul temper and tantrums. For no apparent reason Alex, on a number of occasions, had attacked, smaller playmates, kicking, biting and scratching them.

His mother was a Polish D.P. married to Alex's English dad. She was quite proud of her little Cossack, and being a very large woman tended to frighten other mothers' when they tried to complain about their childrens' injuries. She dismissed all protestations against her little dove, "Eeezz only sticking up for himself. Your kidz iz being cry babies." Well, this was one cry baby who had just run into her not-so-little lovey-dovey and sat him on his podgy arsey-warsey.

Alex's face contorted to scream blue murder. Then, seeing a potential victim who had dared to be on his side of the street, an iniquitous smile crossed his round, pallid face and a strange twinkle entered his piggy eyes. "Twat." Oh dear, that was one of those words that Mark knew was a definite 'no-no'.

"I'm sorry Alex", the smaller boy blurted out in such haste that liquorice juice from tangy black sweets streamed from the corners of his mouth. "Dint see ya Al…." Alex cut him off mid-sentence.

"Shut it Dacey, you fuck." Oh no, not a 'fuck'. Now he was really in trouble.

"Do you want a sweetie Alex?" Did someone say sweets? Now the little porker was interested. Climbing to his feet he demanded "Where did you get those sweets Dacey?"

"Me mum giv me fruppence."

"Huh, is that all? My mum gives me sixpence every day." Sixpence every day, that sort of wealth would normally inspire total envy from every kid in the neighbourhood, even if it was a lie. But at that moment Mark's only concern was to reach his back door safely without sharing his sweets. "Well what you got then?" The youngster opened his mouth exposing the black gooey mass.

"Brack Yacks." he gurgled, almost losing the sticky mess.

"No, I want wots in yer pocket." Alex grabbed Mark by the throat with both hands, making his eyes bulge, and with such force that it caused the ejection of the dark sticky mess from his foaming mouth and into his assailant's contorted face. The permanently staining juice was all over the grey woollen jumper and lighter grey shirt.

"Mi best pully!" "Mi mum'll kill me and it's your fault, you fuck twat!"

'Fuck twat' – that was enough for Mark. As Alex's hands left his throat to smear the mess even more liberally over his Sunday best, young Dacey legged it over the road to safety. Relieved at his escape, he closed and bolted the back door, Alex's fading words striking a chord…."Dacey, you're a dead un."

Still panting, he ran up the three stone steps shouting for the ever present Terry. "Terry, Tel …ah, ahgg." In his headlong flight for the security of his bigger brother, he had misjudged the top step, slipping down the other two and striking his forehead on the topmost edge. Mary shouted to her younger brother. "Terry get some help. Our Mark's cut his head open." Terry stood over his little brother who, as his eyes cleared, looked up. He could hear Mary on the

black Bakelite phone in the hall, "Please come quickly, my mum's gone out and my brother's bleeding all over the place."
Terry was holding a large towel to Mark's head when their sister reappeared.
"The ambulance is coming." They allowed Mark to sit up a little, but not to move any further. Terry occasionally pulled away the make-shift bandage to inspect the wound, each time looking more worried and each time saying to Mary "when is that bloody ambulance going to get here?..."
"It's here, it's here," announced Mary. Mark enjoyed the attention, and as he was stretchered into the waiting ambulance, a crowd gathered, inquisitive children jostled one another to catch sight of the object of their curiosity. Mary and Terry climbed into the back of the ambulance to join Mark, and as the doors were being closed Mark heard one child, "Ooh, did yer see all that blood?"
"Yeh" said another, "Iz ed woz all bashed in." Just a minute – what was all this blood and bashed in business? Suddenly Mark felt pain and fear and then for the second time that day he heard the whining voice of Alex... "Bet he dies."

He did not die, he survived the ordeal of six stitches, petrified but dry eyed. His stoicism gained him the utmost respect from Mary and Terry and the praise for his bravery made the pain almost worthwhile.
None of them, however, was feeling particularly brave when hospital transport kindly dropped them back home. When Helen had returned to find the house empty, she had recieved conflicting stories from neighbours and from their children. She had been in a state of anxiety and panic. When the missing children returned, Helen blamed Terry and Mary for the mishap and ordered her youngest son to bed. "Come on, I'll take you up," and with that Mary took him by the hand. He felt sorry for himself as she tucked him in and as he responded to her. "Goodnight," he spluttered, trying to hold back the tears. "Mary?"
"Yes, Mark"
"What's a fuck twat?"
Feigning shock, his big sister sucked in half a breath and then she answered, "You are, you little shit. You are." With that she turned, flicked the light switch and closed the door behind her.

Chapter 5

Christmas was only three days away and Mark had not given his injured head much thought until that morning, when the district nurse had called in. After inspecting the wound she had removed the stitches and complemented him on his bravery. A while later, when the other family members had seen enough of the new scar to satisfy their curiosity, the boy was allowed to participate in the increasing excitement that anticipation of the festive season causes. During that, time Terry and his younger brother were inseparable. The older boy used every trick in the book to enhance Mark's expectations of December 25th, constantly reminding him of the delights that could be waiting on Christmas morning. "If you don't be good I'll tell Santa." Terry mistakenly believed that his younger brother was convinced by his blackmail routine.

One event contravened the spirit of that season of good will. On the 23rd of December there was a knock at the back door. Terry opened it to find Kevin Fielding standing outside in the cold wetness of the early evening. Kevin was known in the neighbourhood as 'Trouble'. Terry had been told on more than one occasion that this big farmer's lad was more than a match for both his eldest brothers' put together. "I've cum t' see your Karl" said the young man.
"Oh!" exclaimed Terry somewhat taken aback, "Ees in t' gym."
The gym, which was housed in Castaires' infamous cellars, was Karl's pride and joy. Since the age of ten Karl had developed a passion for fighting in general and for boxing in particular. In stature and appearance he strongly contrasted his older brother. Jack was a still-growing six feet, slim with jet-black hair and handsome features, Karl was five-feet-six, just as wiry but with a shock of curly red hair, which would have been unruly had he not worn it so short as to warrant the expression 'shaved to the bone'.
One of Peter's obsessions was that his children were capable of defending themselves. He had been most helpful when Karl had asked for permission to create a boxing style gym in the cellars of Castaires. Peter had bought all the equipment needed from auctions; a rowing machine, punch bags, speed balls, weights and medicine balls, plus gloves and sundries needed for ring and bag work. The result was a very professional set-up and Peter had his heart set on Karl becoming a proficient exponent of the noble art. He had

managed to get Karl into Richton Boxing Club, and in a short time Karl had fought in several amateur bouts, that he had won convincingly. The last match had taken place in Blackpool in front of a large crowd of adult male supporters, many of whom were Peter's cronies. Karl had not disappointed his father nor his father's friends, when he had knocked out the amateur gold coast champion. He was becoming a promising featherweight and was so respected that he had been selected as a sparring partner, by one of England's most promising professional boxers, local born Johnny Bamford. Johnny had voiced his opinion that the young man could go all the way. Amongst Karl's most prized possessions was his boxing licence, which Mark never tired of asking to see.

Before he had joined the boxing club, the junior members of his family would coax Karl into putting on shows in which he would exhibit his boxing prowess and superb level of fitness. On those occasions, if he could find no willing candidate, Karl would use a novel way to aquire sparring partners, to ensure a realistic exhibition of the noble art for his siblings and selected friends. He would seek out some tough youngster who was unafraid of his growing reputation and he would befriend them. Karl could be the perfect charmer when it suited him. When he had gained their confidence, he would tell them that he had in his possession some extremely rare, giant, mutant white rabbits. This claim, which was usually met with disbelief by his latest new pal, was always defended adamantly by an indignant Karl. The invariable outcome was a customary challenge from the tough new friend, "Olright prove it, let's see em then." The following evening the doubter would turn up at Castaires to see the rabbits. With all due ceremony, he would be shown down the steps to the cellars, then led through the first semi-lit room, past the gym equipment into a well lit, white-washed, second room. There he would find Karl who would be busy skipping or shadow boxing. "Where's these rabbits then Dacey?"
"Ee there's no rabbits ere pal, but there might be a chicken."
When the tough youngster had realised that he had been made to appear foolish before the young spectators, he would be more than willing to teach this Dacey a lesson. He would be given the option of gloves or bare fists and almost without fail he would choose gloves. It it was all the same to Karl who would set about the destruction of the unfortunate gladiator, which he would achieve with ease.

After Karl had joined the boxing club the situation had changed. There was no shortage of competitors, though sometimes he had to fight much older men and heavier weights. Mark had observed his brother's training sessions in the cellar gymnasium many times but he had been too young to be privy to the demonstrations of pre-club days. However, he knew by heart and cherished the rabbit stories that he had been often been regaled with. On that evening so close to Christmas, Mary ran on to forewarn Karl of Kevin's arrival. The Dacey boys' slowly escorted Kevin to the cellars, Mark asking on route, "Av you cum t' see our rabbits mister?."

"No I avn't" said the huge Kevin menacingly "Av cum to sort job out once an fer all with yer ginger 'edded little bastard brother."

Mark was spared any further confusion as they had reached the room, where Karl was standing in the centre with Mary. He had been training, so was already suitably attired in vest, long, satin boxing trunks and high laced boots. Mary took up a position with her other brothers' at the far end of the large bare room, "Well, let's get on with it you big useless poof." Mark wanted to ask someone what was a poof, but with the comical sight of the giant and his pint sized opponent circling each other, he turned his attention to the imminent action. There would be no gloves on this occasion. Kevin, at twenty years of age, towered over his adversary and was clear favourite to win. He had been forced to the task of battering this cheeky teenager, because it was common knowledge that he, Kevin Fielding, was the up and coming hard man in Richton. It was doing his credibility no good having this youngster going around, telling everyone that Fielding was a big useless Ox. Karl had claimed that he could sort him out, no problem. It was as if the younger lad had a death wish, taunting him with messages sent via his own friends. Well now it was time for Dacey's first and last lesson in manners, to be delivered from the Fielding book of protocol.

Kevin aimed a scathing right hook at Karl's head and the blow was only just blocked by Karl's left arm which was raised in a conditioned response. Even so, the force of the blow caused him to stagger and he had to use some deft footwork to regain his balance. Then, like a snake's darting tongue, Karl's left fist shot out three times in lightening succession, jabbing into Kevin's face and chin, forcing his head to snap back violently with each contact. Stung into action, the giant tried to grab his smaller opponent. Karl easily evaded the headlong rush and flailing arms with a neat sidestep, releasing a murderous right cross that landed full force on the hulk's left ear, leaving the hulk to pass by clutching fresh air. With surprising agility for a big man, Kevin spun to face his pint-sized tormentor. "Your turn to 'av sum, you clever fuckin' bastard!" raged the infuriated goliath, who was now totally committed to Karl's destruction. The visitor put all his efforts and rage into a straight right aimed at Karl's face. Instinctively a left hand was raised to parry the punch but although it managed to absorb much of the force, a ham of a fist smashed into Karl's forehead then skinned over his skull. For an instant his knees buckled and blood started to seep from the shallow cut across his forehead. Kevin moved forward to take advantage and finish the proceedings.

Mark looked nervously at Terry whom he noticed was also studying the spectacle apprehensively, while rotating an iron bar in his hands. Terry decided that there were no circumstances in which Fielding would leave that room as a winner. The frightened youngster refocused his eyes on the contest just in time to see his pugilistic brother explode into action. The little knee wobble had been a feint to get the heavyweight to drop his guard just sufficiently to give Karl a clean shot. Confidence caused the bigger man to forget caution. As he moved in for the kill, his impetus was met with a screaming uppercut to the chin. At the moment of impact, Karl was clear of the ground, having released the punch like a catapult, with the whole of his body weight behind it. There was a sickening crunch as several of Kevin's teeth broke and crimson rivulets appeared from the corners of his mouth, giving him the appearance of a freshly fed vampire. Karl took advantage, throwing a flurry of hooks, punches and elbows, forcing the giant to try to make sense of the severe pain and confusion he was experiencing. Within seconds Fielding had crumpled to the floor, landing in a mountainous heap. Karl stood over him and unbelievably, Kevin found himself pleading for mercy.

The victor's audience ceased screaming support for their champion, as Karl Dacey set about unmercifully kicking every inch of his vanquished foe. The spectators' blood-lust was replaced with nausea when they witnessed the pain and humiliation inflicted on the defeated man.

"So ginger 'ead am I? You fuckin' poof." Each insult was accompanied by another savage kick, "Admit it - say it, say you're a poof an a wanka." The profanities meant little to Kevin now. A wave of relief swept over the spectators when the battered heap finally whimpered concurrence. The family assisted the loser, as the miserable wretch dragged himself to the top of the stairs. A biting wind brought him more fully round to the misery of defeat and as if on cue, the curtain came down on the evening's performance, with a heavy fall of snow.

Karl stood at the dining room wash cabinet; Mary brought him a clean towel. "Hurry up 'an' get cleaned up before Helen gets back!" urged his sister. "Yeah Ta Mary luv." She went to the kitchen to join Terry in preparations for the evening meal, which would be later than anticipated due to the entertainment. Left alone with his victorious gladiator of a brother, Mark luxuriated in a mixture of pride and fearful respect. He wished that he were closer to his older brother, that their relationship could be as amiable as the relationship that he shared with Terry. He wanted Karl to put his arms around him and tell him that he was his pal; he wanted to tell the whole world that this was his brother. For a few moments more he watched as Karl finished his cleaning up, dabbing gingerly at the cut on his head with the towel. "Karl?" Mark plucked up the courage to address this demigod. Receiving no reply, the youngster repeated his brother's name more loudly.
"What?"
"Are you olright?"
"Yeh, great."
Encouraged by a response from his hero, Mark continued "Karl?"
"What?" Karl took a last look in the plastic framed mirror, turning it to examine his face in the side that magnified the image. "Do you wanna come an' play Batman in my room? You can bounce on my bed if you like." This time the youngster had his heroic brother's full attention. "Mark," the little boy felt a glow as he heard his name pronounced by Karl and his warmth increased as his name was repeated........ "Mark....fuck off!"
The deflated youngster watched Karl disappear to his room. A short time later his mother returned from a shopping trip and he ran to her, hoping to find some warmth in the greeting.

Chapter 6

Mary had taken Karl's tea up to his room, thereby avoiding explanations concerning cuts and bruises. Helen and her three youngest dined simply on baked beans on toast topped with a fried egg. Mark went through his usual ritual with this kind of repast. At first he devoured the egg yolk, then using his knife to slide the egg white and beans off the toast, he piled them to the side of his plate leaving the sticky orange gunge created by the bean juice soaking into the toast. Scraping the goo with the edge of the blade he took each knifeful directly to his mouth, hoping that his atrocious table manners would go unnoticed. Between mouthfuls, he thought that Helen might like to be acquainted with the events that had taken place in the gym. No sooner had he started the narration than his enthusiasm for the story disappeared, as a swift kick delivered under the table by Mary and a stern look from Terry silenced him. Once the meal was over and the dishes had been washed and put away, Helen looked at the trio and made a momentous announcement, "I'll tell you what, let's trim the tree."

With whoops that would have made Geronimo proud, the Dacey children leapt up from the table and followed their mother in single file up to the attic. Five minutes later the raiding party returned to the dining room. Helen was carrying an artificial Christmas tree, while Mary and Terry each carried a medium sized cardboard box. Mark had been draped with several strands of tired looking tinsel. Once the wire and bristle branches had been pulled and twisted into a form that brought agreement from all present that this was the way a Christmas tree should present itself, Helen lifted the four feet of over-sized green pipe-cleaners onto the sideboard under the window, a faded red mat guarding the wooden surface from the tripod's metal feet. Glass baubles were unpacked respectfully and with 'ooh's' and 'ahh's' accompanied by, "Do you remember this one?" The naked tree was adorned in the customary manner; Helen commented that it seemed only a few months since she had been putting the tree away at the end of the previous festive season. Mark's assistance was not required; he had tried to get his hands on some of the decorations but there was always another set of hands to take the delicate piece from him. Deprived thus, he had to be content to mooch about, bumping into one or other of the decorators who, hardly seeming to notice his presence, gently pushed him out of their way. He watched as the tree slowly came alive with shiny glass orbs of green, red, blue and gold, brightly painted wooden figures of angels, Santa, animals and bells. Mark's favourites were the multicoloured glass birds with bushy horse- hair tails and jewelled eyes. There were six of those and they were the oldest and most prized of all Helen's Christmas decorations. They had been very old when she had been given them as a child by her grand mother. It was understandable that when she spotted her youngest son trying to teach one of them to fly, she should be alarmed. She seized the bird and added a half-hearted slap across the back of the birdman's head. Mark gave up his whines of pretended agony, ceasing the exaggerated head rubbing, when he realised that no one was paying him any attention. When they arranged the strand of lights around the tree he soon forgot the slap. The lights were a collection of miniature figures, each one of which would hopefully illuminate, bringing them to life.

At last the workers stood back and Helen rested her hand affectionately on Marks shoulder, as the clan surveyed their handiwork. An odd adjustment to a branch here, an ornament there, a relocation of a strand of tinsel and it was judged to be ready to be switched on. However, Helen rubbed her chin thoughtfully and muttered. "Something's missing." Then in unison Terry and Mary cried out, "The angel!"
Helen grinned, "Well let's put Mark on top then." With that the three of them grabbed the surprised youngster, pinned him to the floor and subjected him to the dreaded tickles, which sent him into fits of giggling screams. When Mark announced he was about to pee his pants, his tormentors left him on the floor, still laughing. Mary stood on a chair and reverently placing the winged angel at the top of the tree, a reminder of the religious significance of an otherwise Pagan display. Terry stood by the light switch waiting for Helen's command to switch off the main light, once she had plugged in the tree lights...... "Now!" For a heartbeat the room plunged into a darkness that was instantly dispelled by the illumination of the multicoloured bulbs. The family stood in respectful awe, as they did every year. "Beautiful," the children agreed with their mother, and in that moment Helen felt like a child again. The main light was turned back on and three of the four got busy, hanging paper garlands and other festive pieces that were taken from the last box.

When the others started singing "Deck the Halls with Boughs of Holly," Mark stood in front of the tree staring at the ornaments which created a fantasy wonderland. He then looked at the small choir. He had never seen them so happy. The shimmering decorations reflected around the room, transforming it into a cheerful abode. The youngest child bringing even more merriment to the proceedings when, his little heart full to bursting with festive joy, he joined in the singing. His rendition of. "Reck your Balls an all be Jolly, lah de dah de dah de dah dah dah," sent the others into purple fits of laughter. Helen had to cuddle her youngest offspring to soothe his deflated ego and the other children tried to convince him that they were only laughing because his singing was so wonderful. Begrudgingly he began to regain his previous demeanour and contemplated singing again, and would have done so had he failed to notice first his mother, then his sister and brother visibly stiffen Communal joy was instantly transformed into apprehension at a sight of the shadowy figure.

Mark had his back to both tree and window and had not witnessed this sight. He had no time to ask the reason for the loss of spirit, as the slamming of the back door made him jump almost out of his skin. He was startled again when the dining room door burst open. "An' wot the fuck are you shower so 'appy about?" Peter Dacey, had been released early from prison to spend the holidays with his loving family. Christmas 1957 had just received a setback. It was at that precise moment that the Christmas tree lights blew a fuse and the room lost all its magic.

Chapter 7

If the fifties were as grey, as they were said to be, then it is difficult to explain how Terry and Mark imagined so many colours on the black and white TV set. As they sat on the floor staring at the small box, at no time did the programme register as anything but colourful. That morning's programme for Christmas Eve was a cowboy. It was one of the brothers' favourites. In a state of stupor they were oblivious to the increasingly frenetic pace of the twenty-fourth of December. In fact the lads could have claimed to posess the first colour TV in Richton, well, the twelve inches of flickering screen might have been monochrome but the cabinet was a beautiful shade of china blue and green and yellow. Several weeks earlier Mark had discovered various tins of oil paint and he had thoughtfully decided to surprise the rest of the family with a display of his artistic prowess. Helen understood that he had only tried to be helpful and of course he should have been supervised, but sitting in front of the vandalised television, Mark could well recall the blows to his legs and backside that tingled in the memory of his mother's understanding. It had only been a few days ago that the budding Rembrandt had been allowed to once again watch TV, Helen had decided that the extra punishment of banishment from the magic box was over. "That's enough telly you two."
"Awe. It aint finished!" Helen stepped over the sprawling boys' to switch off the set, the large dial clunked loudly. "It is now... Terry I need you to run some errands." As usual there were no protests from Helen's fourth born. "Are you cummin Mark?"

Terry was on his feet stretching lazily but his little brother was already standing on a chair grabbing their coats and scarves from the pegs on the back of the door. "Am I cumin?" echoed Mark. It's Christmas Eve and Terry's off to the shops, if he thinks I'm being left behind he's wrong, thought Mark. Standing at the back door, Helen held a large shopping basket. She Noticed Mark struggling with his mittens and placed the bag on the floor so that she could help him. Her rough impatience was brought on by the invasion of cold December weather through the open door. "Urry up and get off, so I can close the bloody door behind you, we are losing all the heat in the soddin house." Terry was knocked through the aperture by the force of the large plastic lined basket being thrust at him. "Awe no, not that basket, its pansy!" moaned Terry. Any protests were useless as Mark and Terry found themselves outside in the cold holding three red-brown ten-shilling notes and the red taffeta, flower covered shopping bag, the usual choice of most old biddies. From behind the closed door Helen's muffled voice issued final invisible commands; "And don't piss about, I want you back as soon as possible! And don't lose the bloody money!" Terry thrust the money deep into one of his short trouser pockets and rearranged his coat. An inspection of the contents of the 'pansy basket', revealed at its bottom a large Hessian potato sack. The older boy cheered up as he led the expedition down Barnham Road towards town the limp Hessian sack slung casually over his right shoulder. Following behind, Mark complained bitterly, having been relegated, to carrying the taffeta, flower covered 'biddy bag'. He whinged that he had been conned into coming on the trip and that he wanted to go home. Terry ignored his whining brother and continued their journey all the while whistling out of tune carols.

"Get a move on Mark, or I'll boot yer up the arse, you donkey!" Insulted by Terry's laughter the youngster sulked and after taking only a few steps more he sat down on the cold stone pavement. "Shan't!" retorted the lad defiantly, hunching even lower into his cross-legged squat to emphasise his dissent. Terry knew that Mark's sulks tended to last for hours. To avoid more time being wasted he would have to suggest a compromise, otherwise the shopping had little chance of being completed before the following Christmas. In soothing tones he addressed his little companion "Look Mark, if Santa sees you being naughty you will get cinders for Christmas instead of toys and sweets." Dragging the boy to his feet he explained fully, while draping an arm around the boy's shoulder, how Santa punished naughty children. On Christmas Day when they excitedly opened their gifts, they found that their presents had been replaced with sooty ash and coal residue, most probably from their own fire's hearth. This horrific threat was enough to galvanise Mark into action and he willingly followed his brother. Terry went on to tell him how Santa was best mates with God. The all-seeing Almighty relayed all relevant information to the portly, old, white-whiskered, red-coated gent. What a turn out for the books thought Mark; the omnipotent Lord above was also a 'Tell Tale Tit'.

For the following half a mile the admonished boy regularly cast cautious glances skywards, sometimes adding a tight lipped smile for good measure, in the hope that God realised how good he would be for ever and ever – well, at least until Boxing Day. As an afterthought, he added a little prayer-like request. Would the Almighty in his report to Santa, not only relay Mark Dacey's new found path to angel's wings but also tell the jolly old man to get his lad Jesus a bike or something nice, as it was his birthday after all.

Now that his younger brother was amenable, Terry elaborated on his efforts to complete his allotted tasks as easily as possible. "Ere Mark, if you put the bag on yer ed and yer arms through the andles you'll be like one of them there robots that fight Flash Gordon." No sooner said than done! Struggling to get his skinny arms through the Raffia reinforced handles, he ignored the potato dust dandruff, then found a flaw in his newly acquired armour. "I can't see Tell." The dilemma was solved by poking fingers through the baskets weave puncturing the plastic lining and allowing limited vision. "Ee you look grand" lied the older Dacey boy. The smaller lad agreed and he strode ahead, arms comically swinging through the handles like an ape, twirling first this way then that, checking the impressed faces of all the other shoppers he met. Of course there was the occasional, minor mishap, for example walking into every other lamp post. There was the old lady, who did not have enough sense to realise that he was practising walking backwards using his radar. When they collided, as she emerged from a shop doorway, he stood on her foot and she went berserk and tried to destroy the steel marauder with her walking stick. Strangely Mark thought that he had felt the blows but of course as the two brothers' made their escape, he knew that was not possible as his armour was impervious to all but a blast from the evil Ming's death ray. Terry was more than a little relieved when they reached the busy junction where Barnham Road met Mallard Street. It was one of the main shopping areas of town, and required the removal of the armour from the valiant machine returning Mark to a normal child; besides they needed the bag for the shopping.

In a whirlwind, the collection of last minute groceries was completed. Most of the time was spent queuing waiting their turn to be served. With both bag and sack bulging, the pair were well on their way home, but had to stop regularly, putting down the bags to

proceeded with prolonged two-handed, two-fingered gestures. Not to be outdone, Mark joined in vigorously with this display of contempt for the attempted hoodwinking. The charge hand set off in enraged pursuit, bellowing threats just short of murder. Waiting until he was half-way across the yard and closing in, Terry called out. "Look out Hopalong there's a bus coming," and with that he grabbed his younger brother's arm, legging it furiously down Briggs Lane towards Barnham Road, Mark's little legs struggling in the effort to keep on his feet.

Bob's attack however had run out of steam at the gates once he had realised that the lies meant to impress the youngsters had been rumbled. He turned and trudged sadly back towards the main building, wishing that the stories he made up were all true. It would be many years before the boys' would realise the pain that cruel words and actions cause. They felt no compassion as they left the corner shop, each with a four pence bar of Fry's Five boys' Chocolate and two one penny toffee bars. The chocolate had been devoured by the time they reached Surrey Street School and as the kids were at afternoon break, Mark hid as best as he could behind his brother until they had passed the gates and they had reached home.

Terry turned the key in the back door lock and leant on the levered handle, opening it with a practised shoulder charge. Looking at Mark, he was about to order him through the doorway when he saw the lad was pulling numerous distorted grimaces, while throwing his arms around. "What are you doin?"

"I'm mill-talking like wot me mum does," announced Mark.

"Well read this...." and Terry silently mouthed a two word profanity. Mark was not yet an expert but knew full well that his brother had just silently communicated the most common of all Anglo Saxon phrases. "No, shan't," then as he squeezed past a laughing Terry and the door continued, "You fuck off!" and with a defiant flourish he shoved a penny toffee bar into his mouth.

A retired family friend was engaged at a reasonable rate to look after Mark, and the boy never returned to Surrey Street School.

In the days that followed he learned that his father had caught up with the headmaster later that evening at the teacher's local pub. Peter had discussed calmly but loudly enough for the details of his little boy's inflicted injuries to be heard by the other drinkers. When all had been said Peter's huge hands seized the petrified bully who, looking about the pub for assistance was met with looks of disgust or faces that were averted. Whatever the drinkers' opinions, none wanted to get involved with Peter Dacey. Yanked off his bar stool, he stumbled and stammered out to the pub's back yard, followed by Peter.

That evening Uncle Frank was punished severely and as a result he spent two days in the town's infirmary. A battered, subdued Frank Bartley informed the police on their appearance at his bedside, that he had fallen down some steps, which although not believed, was duly noted and after all, the coppers were local lads and had heard stories from various sources; their sympathies were inclined to the four-year-old boy.

Several months later the head teacher transferred to another town farther south and was not heard of again, and although he was soon forgotten by the Dacey's, he would remember them every time he looked into a mirror. He was not the first and would definitely not be the last to learn that you touched a Dacey at your peril.

Chapter 10

Mark was trailing through the terraced streets of his home town, behind Terry who was swinging a brown-paper-shopping-bag. However, something was wrong. It was a sunny Tuesday morning. Terry was not at school and they were both off on an adventure to the clinic. Clinic... Mark was not that sure but it had to be better than school, hadn't it? All these big institutional buildings seemed the same to a small boy, green or cream paint, smells of disinfectant and stern faces, especially from the nurses in their starched-white-pinafores.

"Sit here," Terry ordered. Leaving Mark, he made his way to the hatch in the wall where a glass door was slid open before he had chance to ring the bell.

"Yes?" asked the horn- rimmed bespectacled receptionist.

"We was told to come here and give you this", upon which Terry pushed a small sealed brown envelope towards the impatiently waiting hand. "I see," said the woman and peering over the top of her glasses took stock of first the boy in front of her, then the younger sat opposite. "Take a seat next to your brother, nurse will be with you directly."

With that the door closed with a bang. Terry stopped at a low coffee table; at least he thought it was a coffee table. None of the Dacey children had ever seen a cup of coffee, never mind drank one. It was tea, water or alcohol. Stooping down he chose a couple of well-worn, dog-eared comics from the pile, passing one to the youngest Dacey as he sat down. They did not have time to finish the magazines as their names were called and they had to follow the antiseptic figure that beckoned.

They were led into what was a huge bathroom and Mark was horrified when they were ordered to strip, but as his older brother was sheepishly complying he followed suit. They hung their clothes on pegs in a corner of the room then, hiding their future manhood as best as cupped hands could, they climbed into the enormous tiled bath as ordered. The water steamed and smelled of carbolic and was just short of a touch of sulphur to complete the perfect smell of Hell.

In their haste to immerse themselves in the red hot murky liquid and cover their shame, they had not realised how hot the water was and both boys' shot out of the bath again to the amusement of the two nurses who were now watching. Mark and Terry looked at one another, embarrassed by their nakedness, and gingerly slipped back into the water.

Although Terry saw the puzzled look on Mark's face, he failed to fully understand the problem. He was much too busy feeling dejected and miserable, especially when one of the nurses spoke out aloud to her colleague, "Scabies and lice" Terry's head dropped and he started to scrub first himself then his brother all over with a coarse sponge and special stinking, stinging soap. "Terry?"

"What?" replied his brother already expecting to be asked what are scabies and lice?

"Ow come you've got hairs on your willy?"

Terry's disapproving glare conveyed to Mark that what he had just said was never to be repeated if he wanted to see another sunrise.

The misery continued with the nurses further scrubbing, then adding to the water a light-brownish liquid that was pungent and immediately burned. Several more minutes had to be endured before the boys' were ordered out by the gruesome twosome who set about drying both of them with towels that scratched their sore skin. Some pink ointment was used to smother their bodies, ankles to neck. This task was completed and the boys' were told to get dressed in the fresh clothes Terry had brought with him in the brown paper carrier bag, but not before their apparel had been meticulously scrutinised by gruesome number one.

While the boys' hurriedly dressed, gruesome number two produced a pair of scissors and a funny looking comb, then finally she took out of her apron pockets a razor, the kind that Peter Dacey preferred to the more common safety-type. Being fully dressed lessened the humiliation of being man handled and sheared, but it was a sorry pair of almost bald, and in Terry's case shaved, boys' that were eventually released with the final embarrassment of being told to be careful not to touch the clothes they came in, and which were now in the brown paper carrier bag.

They beat a hasty retreat horrified at the prospect of encountering someone who knew them, and anxiously made their way home.

Once thay had reached house and safety, Terry pulled Mark round to face him. "Listen Mark what appened today you don't tell anyone, right?"

"Alright Tell."

"I mean anyone, do you get me?" Terry's tone was more pleading than menacing, but to the nodding Mark it was obvious that conversations about the now hairless willy, lice and scabies were inviolable.

For the next fortnight the two boys' ventured out very little, and when they did so they wore woollen balaclavas. This drew even more attention than shaved heads, as the weather was now warming up. If only Terry had looked around his school and his classmates, he would have noticed, that far from being freaks of nature, they were but two of many. The same predicament had affected huge numbers of the population as the twin scourges of scabies and lice hit epidemic proportions in many Northern towns. He was, however, aware of one piece of good luck. They had been spared the dreaded purple head treatment that was instantly recognised as the treatment for ringworm infestation, and for that Terry thanked God. His little brother, true to his word, had not mentioned any of the unmentionables that day had inflicted on them.

One Thursday morning in June. Mark arrived at breakfast to a hum of excitement shared by Karl, Terry and Mary, eventually he was told that they were going on holiday the next day and that they were leaving at midnight for the most exciting place in the world, 'The New Forest'. Mark had heard of this almost mythical place from the older Dacey's who were always keen to extol its virtues, from the wild ponies, camp fires and adders, which are the only poisonous snake native to the British Isles. Most people would run a mile at the mere thought of encountering the small, brownish vipers, with their distinctive zig-zag markings. However the Dacey kids sought out these timid creatures, hoping to keep their strange new pets a secret from their parents. This was not as difficult as it seemed as the aldults tended to be drunk for most of the vacation. Karl seemed the most excited, saying that with his new air rifle he could shoot a more varied wildlife than could be found in the garden.

Everyone had jobs to do to make sure the big event took place without a hitch, everyone that is except Mark. He was told in turn by each member of his family that his presence was not required. Eventually he decided that the best place to be was in the garden where he would see if any of the early crop strawberries at the bottom of the garden were ripe enough to pinch. He managed to find three medium sized under-ripe ones that were guzzled, then he went on a jungle safari to pass time until someone called him for lunch.

The intrepid explorer heard noises that sent him scurrying to the perimeter, and to enable further investigation, he had to clamber up the footholds, finally sitting astride the wall's bevelled stone top. "Jackdaws," he hissed.

Normally the appearance of the line of nuns on their way to and from the nearby convent signalled action stations for the Dacey clan. This usually resulted in a hail of mud balls being launched at the unfortunates by the unruly lapsed Catholic's. Thinking quickly, Mark realised that by the time the alarm was raised the enemy would have escaped and determined it would be best if he carried out the defence of their lane alone. The first couple of sods hit their marks easily, but getting carried away by the screams and ensuing panic, Mark leant a little too far over and as the third missile was launched it was followed by its launcher. "Ouch!" said Mark on hitting the ground, "Ouch!" He cried again this time it was the kick he received from the irate mother superior, "Ouch!" this time more high pitched as the returning nuns joined their leader in retaliation.

Just when his life was surely over, a storm of stones and clods of earth decimated the flock of pecking jackdaws - the cavalry had arrived. The shock of such a furious onslaught gave the children time to recover their brother and drag him over the wall. Then, howling with laughter the clan ran for home, ignoring the nuns' demands to return and face God's wrath. Not a bloody chance, especially as the youngest Dacey ruled as the hero of the hour and was being treated like one. Sat at lunch, Mark although outwardly revelling in the attention, inwardly did not look forward to coming face to face with that seventy-five year old killer mother penguin ever again. But that meeting was an absolute certainty, as there would be the inevitable visit from the same penguin and the local priest to look forward to, when they came to complain and demand retribution from the unruly brats' parents.

Chapter 11

Christmas apart, this was turning out to be the major event of Mark's year. At a time when he would normally be fast asleep, the whole clan were loading the huge, matt-green Bedford furniture van a former army vehicle that Peter had bought at public auction. Peter had custom-built the body on its original flat bed to suit the second-hand furniture trade, for the next week the van would serve as the families luxury travelling hotel.

"Well that's the lot, get the kids in the van and let's be off," shouted Peter. As usual, Helen was ahead of her semi-inebriated spouse and was handing the last child, blanket wrapped, to Mary.

"Put Mark on the top Mary love, then see if you can get him off to sleep." Mary accepted her allotted task without complaint. As Helen pulled down the roller shutter door, Mark was hurried up the set of wooden ladders that gave access to the Luton top that extended over the cab.

The children were ensconced in that space, made snug with eiderdowns, blankets, and pillows all recently gathered in heaped armfuls from their respective beds. Karl being the eldest was allowed to sit in the cab with his parents, which suited the three younger children fine as Karl was a little too old to appreciate that travelling in a soft furnished aluminium box was tremendously exciting, especially as their father had rigged up a couple of 6-volt bulbs providing the luxury of soft amber illumination. Giving a muted cough the engine rumbled into life. The metallic clang of the passenger door confirmed that Helen had joined Karl and Peter in the cab. In an instant the green monster lurched away to enthusiastic cheers. Peter heaved on the heavy, steel leather-rimmed wheel and pointed the truck towards Manchester. Skirting the city, passing Ancoats, he would pick up the A34 which would take them past Stone. There they followed the A51 to the first of their en route stops, Lichfield. The kids decided a celebratory song was in order.

"We're off, we're off, we're off in a motor car,
Sixty coppers are after us an' we don't know where we are.
Going round a corner eating apple pie,
Along comes a policeman, we smack it in his eye."

Peter indulged his offspring, allowing ten or so repetitions, then banged his fist on the cab roof. "Alright that's enough," which meant of course that the three loft choir members reduced their voices to a whisper and carried on with several more renditions before they too tired of the song and one by one sleep claimed all but the driver.

Several hours later it became suddenly silent, and the wallowing motion ceased. The three youngest family members awoke in a semi-dazed awareness that they had stopped. They could hear muffled voices outside and although some were familiar to Mark, he could not identify the others involved in conversation with Peter and Helen nor the content of the discussion.

The roller shutter was raised, allowing an inrush of chilly early morning air into the truck, "Come on you lot, let's have you out to stretch your legs, and do your business."

The bleary eyed youngsters trooped out of the van to discover their parents had been talking to Peter's older brother uncle Larry and his wife aunt Jenny. "Hiya kids!"

"Hello uncle Larry, hello aunty Jen" Mary replied cheerfully, followed by a similar response from Terry. Mark hid shyly behind Mary, a situation not improved by Larry's robust but friendly tussling of his head. After all, his only contact with the couple confronting him was when they came around to the house for a drinking binge with his parents - and then he was always sent to bed. But the boy thought they were pleasant enough, although he had yet to ascertain what useful purpose an aunty or uncle served.

The adults were enjoying cups of tea poured from striped tinplate flasks and corned beef sandwiches taken from neat waxed paper packets. The meeting was at a familiar rendezvous and pre-arranged.

Uncle Larry and aunty Jenny had arrived with their son Stanley, who was the same age as Terry, and daughter Cathy who was two years younger, both Stanley and Cathy were sound asleep in the smaller, dark blue bull-nosed Austin van that was their transport. Their chosen meeting place was on a narrow B road at Ashmore Brook off the A51 and a little before Lichfield in Staffordshire. Terry explained to a puzzled Mark that even though their relations lived only a few miles from their home in Richton, Dad had set off sooner because the big Bedford was not as fast as the smaller Austin, so they arranged to meet up in Lichfield for a cup of tea and to do their business.

In the 1950's Britain had no plethora of traveller's amenities and as steps were being taken to pack up, Mark was about to find out what 'the business' was. They had pulled off the main road to park next to woods and fields, and into this forest separately and sometimes in pairs, the whole group took turns to disappear, returning a short time later with a little less urgency. "Your turn Terry, take Mark with you and make sure he goes," urged Helen.

Mark was dragged by his brother into the darkness and slightly chilled mist. Although it was only a short distance from the relative civilisation of comforting sounds and waiting transport, it seemed the ends of the earth to Mark. "Ere use this."

Terry thrust a page ripped from one of his comic books.

"But I can't read it Tell, it's dark."

"It's not to read you nit wit; it's to wipe your bum." If there had been enough light, Terry would have seen the look of horror on his younger brother's face as the proverbial penny dropped. There was no toilet and 'the business' consisted of fertilizing the forest.

"But wot about creepy crawlies?"

"There i'nt any, they're all asleep."

Despite Terry's assurances that at 3 am all wildlife slept, it was in a state of great apprehension that Mark undid the s-clasp on his belt, unfastened the top button on his khaki shorts and assumed the crouch that seemed most appropriate. He adjusted his position to avoid the possibility of misjudging aim and filling his pants. He then proceeded to dispatch a rather large steaming turd, the length of which necessitated raising his crouching position to a slight stoop. The sour stench and the thought of his bigger brother rounding the tree to catch him in the act, ensured it became a rather hasty affair, especially as the blades of dew-laden grass had tickled his backside, convincing him that the very legions of insect hell were going to invade his bottom.

Frantically wiping himself with the front page of the Dandy, Mark hoisted up his shorts. He was relieved to be joined by Terry who was returning from the neighbouring bush. The pair beat a hasty retreat, putting as much distance as possible between themselves and the distasteful, smelly event. "Did you wipe your bum properly?" Mark sniffed his fingers "They don't smell of poo Tell." Terry declined to smell the proffered fingers for confirmation.

"I believe you Mark, I believe you."

A few minutes later the vehicles were off in convoy, the Austin leading. The kids were re-established in their mobile penthouse, but it took another twenty minutes for the temperature in the van and that of the bedding to rise sufficiently for the occupants to become comfortable. Mary was first asleep and Terry almost followed but was jolted back by a wail from his young brother, calling to the cab below. "Mum I want a wee."

"For crying out loud Mark, we have only just set off," Helen shouted back through the plywood lined cab roof.

"Yeh, but I want a wee bad."

"Bloody Norah," added his irate father, "you will have to use something to piss in coz I'm not bloody stopping."

At the orders of his mother, Terry descended the ladder and returned with an enamel tin half-pint mug. "Ere pee in that." Silently Mark took the mug thrust at him by an angry Terry.

"Sorry Tell."

"Why din't you av' a pee in the forest?"

"You only told me to av a poo."

In the darkness Terry rolled his eyes upwards. "Hurry up an finish"

"I ave," and to accentuate the fact he held the three quarter full steaming cup in front of Terry's face.

"Ere watch it you stupid git."

Perhaps this was not the best moment to hit a pothole, since the youngster's insecure grip allowed the mug to twist and empty the now lukewarm contents into the corner of the Luton box. It was even more unfortunate that the gap in the boards allowed a steady sream of the liquid to cascade upon Peter's head and neck. This brought profanities from him and almost instantaneous shrieks of laughter from Helen and Karl, the latter squirming across the bench seat away from the unwelcome splashes bouncing off his father's head.

Karl ended up on Helen's lap and the pair hysterically enjoyed Peter's frantic but futile, evasive efforts. Pulling up at the side of the road he shouldered the driver's door open, jumping out in indignation. Thankfully, despite dire threats to murder his youngest son, Peter decided not to open the roller door to carry them out.

Meanwhile, uncle Larry had stopped then reversed to enquire what had caused the impromptu halt. Getting out of the driver's side he was joined by his wife, who on learning the gist of events from Helen, was holding her sides in a fit of laughter, while Larry who was doubled up and leaning against the Bedford's high front offside wing attempted to remain upright. It was Just as well that no vehicle appeared, for Larry, having rolled off the wing, staggered chortling and wheezing across the road and back again in an a helpless condition.

While this merriment delighted all who were dry-headed, the benefits of a good laugh were totally lost on Peter, who was becoming more and more livid. Reaching behind the driver's seat he grabbed a rag, kept there for wiping oil from the dipstick on the frequent checks needed by the leaky diesel engine. He dried himself off as best he could.

"Dun't smell as gud as yur Old Spice Peter," quipped Larry as he and Jenny, in a high state of revelry, returned to the Austin, its engine still running, clouds of smoke billowing from its exhaust pipe.

Stanley and Cathy had been woken by the merriment and as their parents settled themselves in the warm front seats, eagerly enquired as to what had occurred. Jenny explained in-between bouts of choking fit's that uncle Peter was a posh bastard and had a shower in his van. 'While he was driving'! This caused a fresh outburst of laughter from Larry, the van jumped forward stalling, he dipped the clutch again and pressed the start button, the hot engine restarted easily. Larry then accelerated away to rejoin the A51 and resume the journey.

Back in the Bedford at intervals either Helen or Karl would burst out laughing, while a similar state of affairs existed in Larry's motor.

 Peter was becoming more and more vociferous in his condemnation of all mankind, especially his weak bladdered son and the laughing idiots who claimed kinship. In that vague time when you are about to drift into slumber but are still capable of conversation, Mary who was assumed to be sleeping startled the boys' with, "Well I'll tell you one thing….." "What's that Mary?" asked a mildly interested Terry. "That's the last cup of tea I'm 'avin out of that fuckin' tin mug."

It had been said just loud enough to be heard below, launching mother and son once more into uncontrollable fit's and further deepening Peter's black mood. The smile on Mark's face, as he slipped into oblivion, was more due to the fact he had made his mother, sister and brothers' laugh than pissing on his daddy's head.

Chapter 12

Mark awoke to a cacophony of sounds, pots and pans being readied for breakfast and loud advice on the correct way to light Primus stoves by the adults. Looking around and finding no visible family member, Mark proceeded to pummel the heaped bed clothes.

Failing in all attempts to find life, he decided to investigate the disappearances and noise. Finding his plimsolls at the bottom of the steps, Mark wriggled first one then the other over his overstretched baggy woollen socks. It was pointless trying to hoist the grey and green stripe tubes to knee level where they belonged, as his skinny legs had only a fraction of the girth needed to keep them there. In the absence of garters they assumed their usual position, collapsing in folds about his ankles. Jumping the short distance from the rear deck to the ground caused a jolt that, although not painful, served to rouse the youngster fully. Skirting around his uncle, aunt and squabbling cousins, Mark made his way to the central area where the camp fire would be, to a group that were wrestling with a mound of khaki canvas which he was told was a tent. At first the youngster was upset by the way he was pushed and shoved and told to clear off by everyone but he quickly became indifferent. Everything was new and exciting - yep this was going to be a great holiday!

"Oi pissy pants." Mark's heart sank into his floppy socks.

Peter's voice and address reminded him that his earlier mishap had not done him any favours in the terms of endearment stakes regarding his father. He thought of running to his Mother for protection, but could see she was not in the mood to help as she was struggling to erect canvas and poles into a liveable area. "Cum ere."

Dragging leaden feet he approached his father, who had succeeded in lighting the meths stove. "Ere, take this and get some water."

"Where from?"

"End of that field there is a standpipe."

Letting his gaze follow his father's pointing finger, Mark took the kettle and set off in the direction indicated.

Karl was returning from his morning ablutions bare-chested, a towel draped about his neck. He clambered over the wooden stile that bridged the open meadow and the forest area that the Dacey clan preferred to camp in. Without being asked, Karl good-naturedly helped his younger brother over and reiterated that the water tap was that way. Mark's uncertainty on his outward-bound trek was replaced by supreme confidence when he triumphantly filled the kettle, only half-drowning himself in the process.

Humming cheerfully while swinging the kettle, losing water with every swing, Mark Dacey - intrepid explorer, the family's saviour, was returning with water! How fickle is fate. In his moment of triumph he was brought back to reality by the appearance of a savage and malevolent beast. He set off for the fence and escape as fast as his skinny legs could carry him.

Mark had seen such a creature before and had no problem in screaming its name as loudly as he could. "ELP, COW, ELP",

The kettle was abbandoned, the quest for water forgotten; there was serious screaming to be done. Each headlong dive was cushioned by a pancake, its crust hiding a green slimy centre, Mark risked looking back at the bemused beast which was now picking up speed and seemingly intent on trampling the small interloper. They say fear lends wings and Mark seemed to fly, reaching safety just in time. Once over the stile, he carried on running to his father. Breathlessly he stammered " C..C..COW!"

"Cows don't harm, you silly little sod," was the only comfort offered by Peter who, learning that the kettle had been abandoned in the middle of the adjacent field, was fast losing patience.

"I'll get the kettle and water uncle Peter."

Mark was saved by his cousin Stanley's brave offer, but was left in no doubt that it was not made out of kindness, as Stanley pushed roughly past Mark saying "Move you chicken."

Chicken maybe, but stupid? Never! That cow was a killer. Stanley leapt over the fence and almost at once leapt back again resembling an acrobatic starfish - the whole clan witnessed this miracle of flight. "Fuck me!" exclaimed Peter.

"Fuck me!" echoed Larry. Jenny reached her sprawling son offering assistance and comfort, while Karl ran to the stile. Looking over that he turned sharply to face his father and uncle.

"Fuck me! That cow's a BULL!" Luckily this bull had had its horns cut and capped. Stanley's arrival had startled the usually sedate animal and it had decided to send him back as quickly as possible.

Suffering only from hurt pride and a bruised backside, Stanley sullenly accepted the laughter of his family, while Mark became the hero of the hour, as he had outlasted his older cousin in the confrontation with the bull.

Peter chased off the animal, retrieved the kettle, filled it with water and finally put it on the primus to boil. "Well this has to be one of the longest wait's for a cup of tea I've ever had to endure," quipped Peter.

His demeanour improved when his urinating tormentor was stripped naked by his mother and dragged towards the same tap to be cleansed of the green slimy cow pats. Peter sipped his strong brew and listened to the howling of his son in the distance. Smiling to himself he felt justice was being served, the sun was shining, God was in his heaven and all was well.

Scrubbed and glowing, Mark rejoined the others. in the ex-army marquee that Helen had finally managed to sort out. She was busy doling out the bacon and eggs that Larry and Jenny had prepared. A beautiful day had dawned, the food tasted excellent, the banter was carefree and pleasant and it continued this way.

The dishes were washed in a plastic bowl with water from the large jerry cans that the senior males had filled after their first cup of tea. A couple of kettles had been boiled for washing purposes and the adults became a flurry of action as they readied themselves for their afternoon drinking session at the nearest inn, a favourite haunt when they were in the area, and it was only ten minutes walk from the site – well within staggering distance.

Apparently the late breakfast had become lunch, with a promise they would be back in time to cook tea, the four adults waved a cheery goodbye. Far from being despondent at their abandonment, the children, with Karl as leader, organised themselves into a party of explorers and eagerly set off to find adventure. With most of the day taken up with exploring the area, rumbling tummies and a drop in temperature signalled the impending day's end. Mary reminded Karl, who agreed it was time to go back to camp.

They arrived to find that good to their word, Helen and Jenny had returned to prepare the evening meal of sausage, mash and baked beans. After they were satisfied that everyone had had sufficient to eat, they left Mary and Cathy with the washing up and rejoined their other halves who had refused to sacrifice boozing time for a meal.

Unlike home, this remote country pub served beer to any customer still upright and able to pay, therefore licensing laws requiring closure from the lunch time to the evening session were ignored and, as the local bobby was getting drunk with the rest, there was not much chance of legal retribution. The children knew it would be very late when they saw their parents again.

Dusk fell slowly but by 10.30p.m., the campfire Karl had lit with wood foraged by the others, was casting long shadows and welcome light about the campsite. They huddled around the fire, amidst dancing flames and the mood was enhanced with wisps of fragrant smoke. Karl volunteered a ghost story, an idea hailed by all as brilliant.

He commenced with a story of ghostly apparitions, broken promises and murder most foul, elated by the fear he saw in the faces of his audience at the end of the tale. Terry let out a low whistle. "That was the best ghost story ever."

The others were quick to concur. Mark would have added his agreement had he not been suitably scared shitless. That however, was of no consequence as Karl had already launched into another more gruesome masterpiece. Mark was left with only one option, to cuddle up to the nearest family member, which fortunately was Cathy, she put a comforting arm around her young cousin, and in that position they remained staring wide eyed and silent until the sounds of drunken singing and laughter alerted them to the return of the adults.

Their parents had returned fully laden with beer, lemonade, crisps and a surfeit of goodwill. Mark noticed that accompanying the abundance of drunken kisses and outpourings of love maternal, paternal, was the familiar sickly smell of perfume, aftershave, soap and alcohol.

Mary suddenly decided that it was time for bed. She grabbed Mark, and pushed Terry towards the van. Leaving the revellers, she spoke to Stanley "It's time you and Cathy went to bed as well Stanley."

If the petulant youngster considered disagreeing with his cousin, a look in her eyes changed his mind and like Mary they wished the noisy parents a good night. More kisses and drunken cuddles were suffered before they were allowed to go to bed. No conversations and no witticisms this evening, just deep sleep that country fresh air and exercise provides on tap.

The partygoers continued until the early hours, eventually running out of steam. Peter and Helen retired to the marquee while Larry and Jenny squeezed clumsily into the back of the Austin, half-crushing their kids in the process. Karl was the last to remain and was throwing all the remaining brushwood onto the dying flames. He looked intently into the heart of the fire, silently vowing this would be his last trip away with his parents. Giving the fire a last violent poke with the last branch, he tossed it into the crackling centre and headed for the Bedford's cab he had claimed for his own accommodation.

The next morning Mark would discover that the previous nights bonhomie was nowhere to be found.

Chapter 13

A few days into the holiday, Karl had finally succumbed to his younger brothers' pleadings to accompany him on his hunting trips. So it was that the trio were tramping through the forest at 5am, the sun's glow a mere watery orange strip on the horizon while the moon's outline was clearly visible and a damp mist was rising from the forest floor. "Shush!" hissed Karl at intervals, or sometimes he would hold out his arm while dropping to one knee.

After about an hour Terry asked "What is it we are untin?"

"Owt worth eatin" was the reply.

Sounded exciting enough but at that moment Mark would have settled for nothing more wild than a 'Jam butty'. "Down!" snarled Karl.

Terry pulled Mark down with him and put a finger to his lips. The younger boys' looked up and watched as Karl raised his rifle slowly and with purpose. Karl's profile revealed a jutting chin, small nose and shaved skull. For a moment their brother seemed more than a mere mortal.

Thwack, the powerful air rifle snapped and the marksman was running, closely followed by Terry and Mark who, once the initial surprise had faded, soon caught up with him. "Got 'im," he announced triumphantly.

The shock of seeing the struggling rabbit held by its ears made Mark step back a pace; all of a sudden this was not a game anymore, this was a real to goodness bunny-rabbit and it was making the most heart-rending squeals as if beseeching freedom. Mark's mouth made shape to form words, but before he could murmur a thing Karl turned the coney, sharply chopping its vulnerable neck with the edge of his rigid hand. The rabbit convulsed several times and in its final movements slowly stretched and stiffened. Although horrified, the younger boys' jostled to see the dead rabbit, big brother proudly showing where the air pellet had caught the rabbit at the shoulder bringing it down, enabling an easy catch. Mark looked in morbid fascination as fresh blood started to trickle from the rodent's mouth and a smaller streak oozed from the shoulder wound. He was close enough to smell the earthy musk and in the pit of his stomach felt a small knot beginning to grow. He remembered a similar sight he had seen in a butcher's shop window a lifetime ago.

Young master Dacey had been party to his first kill and was discovering the guilt that accompanies the taking of life without provocation or reason.

Terry also felt a little uneasy and said Mark needed his breakfast - the perfect excuse to leave Karl to his search for more victims for the pot. Bidding a cheery farewell the brothers' parted, but with Karl out of sight the bravado vanished, its place taken by melancholy and a sad walk back to camp.

The women spent more time than usual preparing supper.

By midnight the whole family sat eating game stew, remarking how much better it tasted with fresh ingredients. Mark was careful to eat only the chicken that was in his bowl, he could not face eating poor Bugs Bunny. Just before bed-time, Karl sat beside Mark "Did you like the rabbit then?"

Guiltily the embarrassed youngster admitted, "Din't 'av any, I 'ad chicken."

"Chicken! Eh well that's a good un, there weren't no chicken in that stew, only rabbit."

Realising that he had eaten the fluffy bunny. He felt remorse and guilt but was also perplexed. He wanted to understand why rabbit tasted like chicken, and a rather tasty chicken at that.

The following morning he began to wonder where eggs, bacon and other food came from, although he was not sure if he wanted to know. This kind of pondering soon evaporated as the clan wanted to make the most of their last day. For the adults an attempt to drown themselves from the inside out fitted the bill, for Karl it meant leaving his rifle in the van and finding a good forked stick as he was going snake hunting. The other kids were happy reading or making up games.

Mary called to Mark from the tent, "Mark, come and look at this."

Mark skipped across the campsite into the tent where his big sister told him to sit still on a small camping stool and to be silent. Almost as boredom was setting in, he was startled by a fluttering as a little black, yellow and blue bird landed near Mary. It cocked its head inquisitively then pecked gingerly at the crumbs in her outstretched hand, hopping nervously from hand to table and then flying out of the tent to the trees.

"That was neat Mary, really neat." Mary was pleased with her little brother's response and grabbed his hand.

"Here, hold your hand open" and she put a small mound of breadcrumbs in the centre of his tiny palm. "Now sit very still." Mark's heart was pounding but he did not have to wait for long. Back came the cheeky bird landing on the table next to Mary, and then hopping around to face Mark, it fluttered onto his hand. Resisting the temptation to pull his hand away, his face lit up in joy at the gentle pecking that was tickling him. He studied the bird's beautiful form and colours and for a brief moment they looked into each others eyes; the bluetit's bright specks of coal and the boy's pale blue pools of wonderment. The bird chirped a note of farewell and started to beat its wings, raising inches from Mark's hand only to explode in a mass of struggling feathers.

Neither Mark, the bird nor Mary had seen the cat at the tent's entrance, but the cat had seen them.

The violence of the attack terrified Mark. The struggling bird had somehow survived the initial onslaught and was now fluttering frantically in an effort to escape the teeth and claws of the tabby assassin. With Mary trying to kick the cat, Mark had grabbed a stick and intended to brain the animal. This manic melee made escape a possibility for the bluetit, and it finally flew the correct way towards the exit and freedom but in an instant the cat dodged its attackers and leapt acrobatically, snatching the poor distraught bird from the air. The last Mark and Mary saw of their beautiful friend was hanging limply from the tabby's mouth, one delicate wing trailing the ground in a macabre farewell.

Mark was inconsolable, it had trusted him, befriended him and now that evil feline had killed it. Mary meanwhile had gone to one of the caravans further along the site because this was where the cat had come from. Its owners said they were very sorry but that is what cats do. Mark was still hysterical when the grown ups arrived back and even though they were sympathetic and tried to explain it was now with the angels, it was late evening before the young boy stopped sobbing.

That night with Mary and Terry fast asleep, Mark carefully climbed down the ladders from their bunk, made his way outside and surprised Karl who was as usual the last person up and sitting at the camp fire. "Ello, wot you doin out of bed then?"

Mark did not reply but just sat in silence next to his big brother. When he finally looked up he saw Karl was waiting for an explanation. Hard as Karl Dacey was, when he saw the little mite's eyes filling up and his lips pale and trembling, he instinctively threw his arm around the waif that was his flesh and blood. "It killed me bird, it din't do nuffin wrong an' that cat killed me pretty bird."

Karl had of course heard the story earlier that night and not given it much thought. Now however, his heart went out to this sobbing infant and was overwhelmed with a feeling of helplessness. After a few minutes Mark wiped his eyes and nose on his sleeve twice, leaving tell-tale slug trails down his arm. "Karl?"

"Yeh Mark"

"Will you get yer gun an shoot that cat for me?"

He felt the air in his lungs chill and after looking intensely into Mark's face simply said "olright, but you gotta get off to bed now, ok?"

The small boy nodded. "Thanks Karl."

Mark had been back in bed half an hour and Karl was still trying to come to terms with what had happened. He had just negotiated a contract killing, with his four year old brother not for money, but for revenge. With a shake of his head and a soft sigh he picked up his rifle and stalked off to try and make good his promise.

The next morning the clan overslept. As the day dawned, hell had broke loose as they dismantled and packed away ready for the trip home. This done and the site tidied, the vans were checked for the long journey - oil, water, tyres etc.

"Psst, Mark!" It was Karl. "Come on quick before we 'av to go."

Karl grabbed Mark and ran with him to a wooded area about 100 yards from the campsite. Halting abruptly, the bigger boy pointed to a small tree. "Is that it then?"

Mark stared then slowly nodded. The boys' turned away and left the swinging carcass of a tabby cat that had killed its last bluetit.

They reached the cab where Helen was waiting. "You can sit in front with Karl and your Dad if you like Mark."

This fantastic generosity stemmed from his mother's massive hangover, and a nice kip in the penthouse would be just the ticket. Karl even let him sit on his knee to look out of the window to bid farewell to the camp that had been their home for the past week.

As the van lumbered past the other tents and caravans, the boys' could hear one of the campers calling for Tiddles. It was no more than a fleeting glance between the brothers', and the incident was not forgotten but was never mentioned again.

Mark settled back in his place next to his father and the gear stick. A four –year-old boy could not understand the importance of the last two days' events, but with the shooting and eating of the rabbit, the murder of the little bird and the subsequent execution of the cat, innocence had been lost.

The holiday was over, so was June, and the Dacey family's present way of life ticked away to its predetermined conclusion.

Chapter 14

July, August and September came and went. Peter became more of a drunken bully than ever and Helen became more defiant. Uneventful days and unexciting summer breaks interspersed with the odd birthday. Mary spent more time with Helen; Terry seemed unsettled and withdrawn. Jack was midway through his sentence and seemed to be obeying prison rules, keeping out of trouble.

Karl was hardly ever seen now he had reached sixteen, spending most of his time at the boxing gym or socialising with friends after work. He had been working for a local decorator since he was fifteen. In addition he always had sidelines and was never short of money. Karl Dacey was one of the best-dressed young men about town, no longer an adolescent, he was a smart and superbly physically fit young man. He had taken to scowling at enemies, real and imaginary, which added to his aggressive demeanour.

Terry was spending more time with Karl now than at any other time in his life. This had not gone unnoticed by Mark, who added jealousy to his fast growing list of experiences. He had also become aware that Helen, when not seen with Mary, was increasingly absent from his life. He felt more vulnerable in these October days as his parent's arguments became more violent.

Helen had taken to going out with some of the women friends from work at weekends and on occasion arrived home late, sometimes after Peter. This was when the fighting was at its most frightening. Mark would lay in bed, pillow over his head, trying to shut out reality while Mary, Terry and Karl, if he was around, would attempt to reduce the severity of their mother's beatings.

A couple of evenings after such an assault, Helen's closest friend Lucy Byrne, had called round to check on her as she had missed work, the reason was obvious as over the essential cup of tea she inspected the swellings, bruises and cuts to her friend's face. "What a first class bastard!" Lucy said with genuine concern and anger. "Wot a big brave ard man ee must think ee is."

"Ah bollocks to 'im," said Helen, trying to make light of the situation. "E punches like a fairy anyway."

At this the two laughed, and the conversation became more relaxed.

Lucy was a pleasant, pretty woman of twenty-seven, slight frame and two inches taller than Helen's five-feet four-inches, and who had a similarly hard life with an abusive husband every bit as bad as Peter -

a stocky plasterer called Kenny. He was not the brightest of characters and one that most other men evaded in the pub. He was considered a talkative bore when drunk and a morose recluse when sober. Kenny preferred his own company or that of his wife on their infrequent sojourns as a couple to the local boozer. "Well wot av you decided love?"

Helen shot a pensive glance at Mark and Mary sat by the fire, thought for a moment, then reached to the floor for her handbag. "Mary love, nip to the shop for some milk and bread would you? Get a pot of strawberry jam while you're at it."

Lucy was sipping from her bright green mug, her eyes peering over the rim, sparkling with amusement as she anticipated the next words out of Helen's mouth. "Oh and Mary, take Mark with you."

Mary took the red/brown ten shilling note from her mother's hand and the indignation at being 'got rid of' was lessened when she was informed she could have a shilling to share with her brother. That usually meant a fair share of tuppence for Mark and ten pence for Mary. Not exactly fair, but Mark was in a no-win situation.

Once the children were out of earshot, Lucy put down the mug and excitedly asked, "Well wot 'av you decided?" Helen took a breath, held it for a second then exhaled. The words tumbled out in a continuous stream "I can't Lucy, I just can't, not yet, I've got the kids to think of an', where would I go anyway?"

"For Christ's sake girl, if you don't do something soon that evil bastard will do you a serious injury, or worse!"

The last two words sent an involuntary shudder down Helen's spine. "I know you're right love, but I can't leave that piece of shit without sorting things out for me and the kids first."

"Well just do it soon before it's too late love."

Helen nodded agreement but as she sipped at her brew she thought of the futility of escape with young children, nowhere to go and very little money. She was brought out of her reverie by Lucy's voice. "What about the other?"

"Wots that then?" although Helen knew exactly the meaning of the question.

"You know, come on don't be a cow, tell me, what's 'e like?"

Helen took a panicked look about the room.

"For fucks sake Lucy, not so loud."

"Sorry love" said Lucy in a whisper, "go on then."

"Ees olright I suppose, a perfect gentleman in every way."

"Not too perfect I hope."

Lucy laughed, Helen blushed.

"No nothing like that 'appened, we just ad a few drinks and a dance, that's all."

Helen had met a handsome man a few years her junior at a pub in 'Harlsden' where she had gone with friends away from prying eyes. The last thing she and her friends wanted was reports on their nights out reaching the ears of their spouses, though to be fair nothing untoward usually happened. This night however was to be different. Maybe because she was flattered by the attention, or maybe for the first time in years a man was looking at her with desire and not contempt, but whatever the reason she had sidled out of the door to join him, leaving Lucy to cover for her.

Outside she climbed into his car and accompanied him to a quieter pub where they spent some time chatting. Later, they went to a lively little club on the outskirts of Manchester and had a couple of dances. Helen was not comfortable and was in a constant state of anxiety in case she was recognised. Eventually, unable to stand the situation any further, she had asked to be taken home.

Her new friend Barry had helped her on with her coat and obliged. During the trip home neither seemed to find anything meaningful to say and had used up all the irrelevant niceties by the time they pulled up a couple of streets away from the Dacey home where she had asked to be dropped. She had chosen a deserted area where she was as certain as possible she would not be seen. Barry leant across her and opened the door.

"Can I see you again?"

"Dunno, it's very difficult."

"That's not a no then?"

Helen was not given time to answer as Barry closed the door, sat upright, grinned cheekily and drove away. I didn't say no, did I? thought Helen. Looking about the dimly lit deserted back street she satisfied herself as to her safety from discovery and set off at a brisk pace. She wanted to reach home before her husband.

Peter was waiting at the door and his attack was immediate and resulted in Helen's present state. Lucy grinned and screwed her face into a know-it-all leer. "That's all I said."

"OK, OK, keep your knickers on."

"I did." said Helen, then her bruised face split into a painful grin.

"Well I'm gonna tell that bastard of mine tonight, I've add it up to 'ere with im, boring shit. It's always the same routine - ee goes boozing and spends my money as well as his, the house is a tip, we av'nt got a pot to piss in... and."

Her friend's sudden hesitancy caused Helen to urge Lucy to continue "Go on, don't stop now." Lucy smiled a little embarrassedly. "Well it's the other, you know?"

Helen feigned naiveté and shook her head

"The other, you know, Sex!"

"Ooh!" nodded Helen, trying not to look overly interested, then added, "Wot about it?"

"It's always the same an' I don't like it." Her friend waited for her to elaborate. "Up me arse." Lucy paused to see that the words had had the desired effect, and Helen was looking suitably horrified, before continuing. "It's always the bloody same, ee comes in pissed, strips off, drags the bedclothes off, strips me, turns me over an' shags me up the arse." "Bastard," whispered Helen but in a way designed to encourage her friend to reveal more.

"Look, I'm only telling you this because you're my best friend and I know you won't tell any one."

"Lucy, you know I would never breathe a word."

Suitably reassured Lucy continued. "I sometimes pretend to be asleep but it dun't matter, ee does it anyway an' if I put up a fight I get 'ammered then ee shoves 'is dick in me mouth an' other stuff that I don't want to talk about, so it's easier to let 'im get on with it then at least ee falls asleep."

Helen had her arm round her friend, saying nothing seemed the best thing, so she made soothing clucking sounds and squeezed a little more tightly. "The worst thing about it is the way ee treats me; it's as though I'm shit on his shoe. Well I've 'ad enuff, me mum says I can stay with her until I'm sorted so that's it, I'm off tonight, straight after I tell that fucker wot I think of him, the shit stabbin git."

"Good for you girl, I'm proud of you."

With that Helen headed for the kitchen to make a fresh pot of tea. Mark and Mary arrived back about the same time as the tea and Lucy was more like her bubbly self, although the tell-tale puffy eyes gave away enough for Mary's astuteness to realise she had been crying. The children returned to their place before the fire, and Mark watched his sister carefully glue the brightly coloured scraps into the book while Helen and Lucy talked of lighter subjects now the walls had ears. "Well I'll see you at work tomorrow then."

Lucy was taking her leave. "You bet, wouldn't miss it for the world, you can tell me how you made the bugger squirm," then realising what she had just said looked open mouthed at Lucy, and again they both leant on each other sniggering knowingly.

"What's goin on 'ere then?" Peter had arrived home and was pushing past Lucy. Without looking at either of the women he demanded his tea. Helen shrugged at her friend and Lucy flicked a couple of V signs at Peter's back. This made Helen smile and she hugged her friend whispering, "What on earth would I do without you Lucy?"

Lucy's pretty face flushed and she waved her hand dismissively. "See you tomorrow love," and was gone.

It felt like the closing of a prison cell rather than a back door. Sheepishly, Helen made her way to the kitchen, feeling guilty for her recent conversation, guilty for her recent thoughts and some way towards and somewhat guilty for being alive. "You two Lesbos 'ad better not 'av been talking about me."

Helen ignored the combined insult and threat. Peter was becoming more and more paranoid, a symptom common with alcoholism. "An' you better 'urry up wiv me tea, I'm off t'pub after."

There's a novelty! thought Helen, and again she felt guilty, this time for the jealousy she felt for her best friend and her impending freedom.

Chapter 15

"What the hell was going on?" pondered Helen.

She had arrived at work to find the looms silent and a crowd of people gathered in the canteen. Many of the women were crying, others shook their heads in disbelief. "What's 'appened?"

Helen felt that she was being ignored. Looking about for Lucy but not seeing her, she caught a passing young woman by the arm, "Claire, what's going on?"

"Oh Helen, it's orrible, just too orrible for words, poor Lucy."

Helen's grip became vice-like at the mention of her friend's name. "Tell me, what about Lucy, is she hurt? Has she had an accident? Tell me!"

The whole canteen was hushed; Helen had screamed the last words. An older woman, Pauline, prized Helen's hand off the terrified young girl's arm and led her to a vacant seat, "Get er a cuppa someone."

"Fuck the cuppa, just tell me what's 'append to Lucy."

"Olright, calm down Helen love, we're all on the same side. Lucy's dead."

A heart stopping blackness fell, and then nothing. On waking, it was obvious she had fainted, and slowly as the darkness subsided she realised she was with the mill nurse. "You feeling a bit better dear?" soothed the nurse.

"Not really," answered Helen. "How? What?"

The nurse interrupted, "That bastard Kenny. I don't know much, just what the coppers said when they made some enquiries at the mill this morning."

"Anything please.... I need to know, she is.... was, my best friend!"

Putting her friend into the past tense caused such anguish that it was a few moments before Helen allowed the nurse to continue. "Well like I said, I don't know much, but it seems that Kenny came in drunk last night and there was a row. Don't know what about, but they had a big fight - Kenny picked up a pair of scissors and stabbed her, a lot. She made it to the street but..."

Helen broke down again; when there was not a tear left to shed the narrator looked compassionately at Helen and continued. "There's one other thing love." Helen looked up. "The coppers said that at the end she was calling for you."

Somehow the painfully dry red eyes flooded again.

In a daze, Helen trudged the streets making her way home, unaware of the passers-by staring at her grief stricken face, nor would she have given a damn. The nurse wanted her to see a doctor but Helen had replied, "What could he do? And any way, he would be just another fucking man."

Over the next few weeks the townsfolk could talk of nothing but the murder, rumours abounded. As one of the last people to see Lucy alive, Helen had been questioned at length. She had not given the police a hint of the extent of her friend's unhappiness. She had told them that Lucy was sick of being ill-treated and was going to leave Kenny the evening she was killed. The detectives conducting the case had already deduced this and as Kenny was admitting everything brought investigations to a conclusion.

Lucy's body was released for burial and there was a huge turnout of mourners for her funeral, although only two people suffered in the knowledge that if they had not encouraged Lucy to break free maybe she would still be alive, those people were Lucy's distraught widowed mother and a devastated Helen.

Two days after the funeral the warder at H.M.P. Strangeways opened the cell door of prisoner 6345781 Byrne, on remand for the murder of his wife. "Oh Shit! I better get the governor," the warder said aloud to no one in particular, then relocked the door; pointless really he thought, prisoner 6345781 was no longer an escape threat.

Helen remarked later, that Kenny Byrne had finally managed to do one decent thing in his pathetic life; he had hung himself with his socks.

Chapter 16

November and a bonfire night consisted of a couple of rockets and a twelve-pack of zero bangers that Peter had left with the kids to do with what they wanted. Their dad was in such a hurry to get to the pub that he couldn't care less if they burnt the street down, never once did it cross his mind that the children could be in danger. Besides, looking after kids was a woman's job. Helen, had been missing more often than usual and was a changed person. Everyone put this down to the loss of her friend; even Peter had eased up on his strict regimen and had turned a blind eye to her late homecomings. Helen made sure however that she was always in before her husband. Before going out Helen would spend time with Mary, showing a keen interest in her schoolwork. Mary had earned her place at grammar school and was considered to be one of the brightest prospects they had encountered in the last ten years. They would also talk in hushed whispers of other things that were not open for discussion to any other member of the family. In a few weeks Mary had gone from girl to young woman.

One week after bonfire night Helen approached Peter with a letter, "I've got to go to London, Dad's not so good."
"What's up with the old sod?"
"Mum says it's his heart."
"When you gotta go?"
"Well, soon as possible, I thought tomorrow, Friday."
"I can't take you; I've got a lot on at the garage this weekend."
"I know, I thought I'd get the midnight from Manchester Piccadilly to Euston."
"Olright, but what about the kids? I can't look after em."
As if you ever do, thought Helen. "I thought I'd take Mary and Mark; Terry and Karl can take care of themselves. I'll be back on Sunday night."
"Ok, make sure you leave some food in and don't forget I'll need a couple of clean shirts ironing."
"I won't forget."
Peter shrugged and went out to the back yard to finish some work on the MG. Helen placed the letter in her pocket, thankful that her spouse had not asked to see it, as close scrutiny would have revealed it to be in Helen's handwriting and that this weekend's visit to her

parents would be a total surprise to them.　She knew that there was no way her story could be checked as Nell and Tommy, nan and granddad to the kids, like so many other people had no telephone.

Looking at her two children, Helen decided they looked as smart as any child in their situation; she then took stock of her surroundings. The platforms of the station were dimly lit and November's dampness helped create an impression of Victorian repressiveness. Although the décor had seen better days, the station was spotless and services were very efficient.　Both north and south bound platforms were almost empty, just a few over-coated travellers dotted about, each finding their own piece of territory to stand alone.

At the platforms' ends were the waiting rooms, again spotlessly clean with a coal fire glowing cheerily in the corners.　A few passengers who felt the cold were occupying seats as close to the fire as possible and every so often the porter would pop in and top up the fire with cobs of coal from the large steel bucket situated at the fireside. Then, as the heat was temporarily reduced, he took a long brass poker and vigorously prodded at the black heap until its heart glowed orange, sending red flames to chase small pillars of black smoke; flames licked the sides of the heap then caressing the soot lined fire back danced gracefully up the chimney.

"There, that's better."

If any of the passengers agreed with the porter they made no effort to reply, staring dispassionately at the fireplace.　The porter stood stiffly, straightened his black jacket and waistcoat, and adjusted the flat-peaked cap. "Right, that's that then."

Again he was met with silence, so headed for the platform.

As the door opened then closed, a billowing cloud of smoke filled the room, followed by a chilly breeze.　This at last brought a response from the group with tut tut's and several heads turned to glare menacingly in the direction of the door.

"Here Mark,"　Helen offered a one shilling coin, "get some chocolate for you and Mary an' be quick, the train is due anytime now."

Mary decided the task of choosing from the machine on the station platform and being quick about it was too great a task for her brother. Although Mark put up a good fight his sister wrestled the coin from his hand.　Mary put the coin into the vending machine that had once been a work of art but which was now a colour-faded piece of scrap. What child noticed the mechanical shabbiness when the colourful contents compensated handsomely? Mary chose the Bourneville dark chocolate, pulling the rickety drawer, removing the bar and replacing the carriage, she turned the metal knob on the machine's side. This released a sixpence which was duly put back into the front slot for her brother's selection of milk chocolate, but before Mary could take the bar from the drawer Mark's hand was there. "I wanna get it!"

Mary shrugged "Get it yourself then"

"Olready 'ave."

His sister left him and joined her mother who was staring up the track as if the very act would bring the train in sooner.

Meanwhile her youngest son had climbed onto the convenient bench and was turning the change knob backwards and forwards in an effort to extract any bonuses that the ancient contraption would provide. This failing, he switched his attention to the slack fitting drawers, checking each one in turn and finding one that was looser than the others. Mark slyly checked about for the station porter or any eyes that might be observing him. Satisfied he was safe, he rattled the drawer with all his might and was rewarded with the sight of the chocolate bar being accessible through the part opened dispenser. A few seconds of wriggling fingers released a somewhat battered paper-ripped bar. Mark was just about to try again when his mother called, "Mark get here, now!"

The train for Manchester was arriving. As the Daceys mounted the two steps into the cream and red liveried coach, Helen noticed many more passengers hurling themselves onto the train at the last minute. These were revellers that had been in the nearest pubs until the last dash for the 10p.m. to Victoria. Once in the city, there would be many clubs that were not governed by the 10.30p.m. curfew imposed on local boozers.

Mary was thankful that the noisy throng of men and women chose a carriage two down from theirs and Helen also felt relieved that they had their coach practically to themselves. She had enough personal experience of alcohol-reeking, loud-mouthed drunks to last a lifetime. The sound of heavy coach doors being slammed and the station master's shrill whistle prompted the train driver to glance back to the guard's van where his partner was waving the green flag signalling all clear. With a jolt as the brakes released and a lurch as the wheels bit the iron tracks, away they went - the pungent smoke, which Mark found far from unpleasant billowed about the train and entered the open carriage windows. His sister rose to close the window. "What have you got there?"

Mary had noticed on reseating that Mark was clutching an extra bar of confectionery "Got it for you Mum," interjected a slightly flustered Mark. "Ees gone an nicked it Mum," quipped Mary smugly. "I never did Mum, it giv it me,'onest."

Helen was in no mood to escalate the discussion into a free-for-all debate on the benevolence of a platform vending machine, so took the battered chocolate bar, now slightly melted by her son's sweaty palm. Brushing aside his protestation of innocence, she said, "Mark you know it's wrong to steal."

A wave of her hand convinced Mark that now was the time to go quietly and hang his head in a sulk. His spirits revived greatly when his mother patted his head. "But thank you for thinking of me."

With glee in his eyes, he cast his sister a sideward glance and stuck out his tongue. Mary's initial impulse to punch Mark was dissolved by the thrusting of a third of the ill-gotten-gains into her gloved hand. Removing the woollen glove, she begrudgingly let things go and watched her mother break off another section of the bar and offer it to her brother who surprisingly was shaking his head. "No Mum, it's for you." This time Helen was genuinely affected and leant across to Mark's seat and kissed his face lovingly on the cheek. "Thank you my little man." He flushed crimson but happy as could be, Mark settled back into the heavy fabric covered seat. Mary sighed and finished her chocolate, Helen continued to look at her son with the amazement only parents know when they discover something they were previously unaware of in their offspring.

Once Mark was convinced his mother's attention was absorbed by the conversation with his sister, he looked out of the window the darkness was interspersed with lights from buildings, street lamps and vehicles, he hoped guiltily, that his mother would never discover that his self denial and generosity had related more to the fact that the purloined bar had been of the plain variety which he hated, and less related to affection for his mother. Unwrapping his own bar of Cadbury's milk chocolate, he discovered that even a small boy's guilt can turn milk chocolate bitter.

On arrival at Manchester Victoria, Mark was bustled along by both his female companions so much so that twice his right shoe fell from his trailing feet, and twice Helen sent Mary scurrying back to retrieve it. They had managed to grab a taxi from the rank, situated in front of the drab grey building. The shoe was roughly twisted onto his foot with more force than necessary. It was after all his only pair. "Piccadilly Station please."

With a nod the driver turned away and gunned the engine of the old Austin cab, projecting it smartly into the bustling city traffic. The driver was too tired for the customary cabbies' small talk and left his passengers to marvel at the hustle of a Friday night-time in Manchester. "That's two bob love."

Her reverie broken, Helen handed the driver two and sixpence in the form of a half-crown from the worn brown leather purse adding, "Keep the change."

"Well thank you love, have yourself a nice trip." Helen felt good and knew that tipping in England's North West was not as common as in the wealthier South, and despite the fact she needed all the money she had, decided the feeling derived from a sixpenny tip outweighed the need for an additional tanner in her purse.

After collecting the two small suitcases from the open front of the taxi and waving the driver off, the trio set out for the ticket office at a more leisurely pace. Helen had checked the time on the huge station clock and there were forty-five minutes before the midnight special left.

With a heavy clunking, two children's tickets and one adult's were issued from the brass ticket machine set in the ticket booth desk, and on passing over the five pound note the tickets were pushed towards her through the arched opening, followed by a few coins change. Leaving the window, her place was immediately taken up by a more hurried passenger from a rapidly forming queue. Mary picked up the luggage and struggled behind her mother and brother. Helen realised that the combined weight of both suitcases was too much of a burden for her daughter, and taking both cases off Mary she ordered her to hold on to her brother like glue, which she did all the way through the booths that acted as ticket check-in and platform information. "London Euston, that's platform one madam." said a cheery ticket clipper.

Thanking him, Helen gathered her offspring and herded them in front towards the platform. Finding their way barred by a folding iron gate, they placed their luggage on the stone floor, then sitting Mark on top of the suitcases Helen looked down at her son. "Stay here, don't move, – 'an' don't talk to strangers, me and Mary will go an get a cup of tea and some biscuit's." As if pre empting her son's fearful response to being left alone in this strange place she added "We will only be a minute and you can see us at the café over there." Mark followed her finger and saw the counter with a number of customers milling about, some with cups and saucers and others waiting. He nodded, and bolstered by the promise of biscuit's, he watched his mother and sister every inch of the way there and back.

On their return, he declined the proffered fruit cake to eagerly accept from Mary the Madeira cake with jam, delighted that arrowroot biscuit's had been replaced with cake. His slice was devoured far too quickly, then he took a steaming mug of tea from his mother who, despite the precaution of putting extra milk into the tawny brew, had to take back the mug from her complaining child "It's too hot."

With a little grimace Helen blew vigorously until her whining offspring took the tea back and satisfied there was no chance of burning his mouth again, started to drink. Ignoring the crumbs that dropped into his brew from his cake-covered face, Mark relished the sweet beverage. When they had finished, Mary grabbed the crockery - first from Mark then Helen. Racing back to the café counter to return the plates, cups and saucers, not waiting for an assistant to take the pottery, she left it in a small pile on the counter and hurried back, unnoticed by the staff. The reason for the haste was that the gate to platform one had been opened and a throng of passengers was heading for the awaiting Express.

Mark was hauled along the platform, not unlike an express service. Breathlessly, the three threw themselves into a spotless second-class carriage and on finding a cabin free slid back the heavy glazed door. Inside they settled into the comfortable seats, unlike the harder commonplace bench seats on rural lines. Mark had already decided that it was going to be the most exciting adventure ever, he leapt from one seat to another, trying to get better views of all the other trains that were puffing vast amounts of smoke, he heard shrieks, whistles, tannoy announcements, and shouting that all heightened the experience, culminating in delight at the lurch and jolt which signalled the departure of the London-Euston Midnight Express.

Mark was eventually restrained and for a while he rested his forehead on the cool glass pane staring out while the train picked up speed creating a hotchpotch of diffused colour. Losing interest in the darkness outside, he amused himself a little longer with the reflections of the cabin and occupants, namely the Dacey trio.

Giggling inanely at his own attempts to outdo his reflection in face-pulling and tongue-waggling, he was brought back sharply from this twilight zone by a heavy clout from Helen, who had caught sight of Mark flicking two-fingered salutes at his translucent tormentor. "Just you stop that now Mark Dacey or I'll throw you off the train and you can find your own way home."

Mark rubbed his head and thought long and hard about the possibility of being pushed out into the cold night air through the small gap in the sliding apertures of the cabin windows. After a decent interval between his indiscretions he decided to disturb the two family members who were both reading, Mary a book and Helen a film-goers magazine, "I need a wee Mum."

With an irritated sigh, she was about to put down her magazine when Mary piped up "It's alright Mum, I need to go anyway."

She placed her book face down on her seat to keep her page, and grabbing her brother's arm, brusquely, Mary slid back the door and dragged her charge into the narrow corridor. Luckily their carriage had the toilets at the end so it was not much of a trek. After buffeting down the corridor, bouncing first off the cabins then the carriage walls, in a drunken manner they reached the end. Mark looked at the door, its window down, and for a brief moment was horrified by the thought that it was an outside lavatory. He needn't have worried; his sister spun him around and pushed him through the toilet door she had opened for him. "Be quick!" snapped Mary.

Mark slotted the large brass bolt home and faced the porcelain Victoriana. After the heavy mahogany seat had fallen for the third time, he decided his aim would have to be perfect. He had discovered the quickest way to take a pee; his technique was to lift the leg of his shorts to one side while the leg of his underpants went the other. This left a lot to be desired as his tackle unhindered usually hosed everywhere. This time however, he thought he had done brilliantly as his woollen socks had received hardly a splash. Instinctively he cranked the lever that he recognised said 'flush', then as he rearranged his shorts failed to understand the logic in the information displayed by a large notice forbidding the use of the toilet in station. Sliding the brass bolt once more, he skipped past his impatient sister ignoring her orders to wait outside for her, and continued skipping down the corridor past the cabins, some with their blinds pulled down, until he reached the one with the door invitingly open and occupied by his mother.

He had hardly settled in his plush seat when his irate sister burst into the cabin. Closing the door and pulling down the blinds as if to enforce privacy, she first clouted her brother then sat with a thud into her own seat. "What the hell was that in aid of Mary?" inquired her bewildered mother.

"That little beast pissed all over the seat and everywhere."

"I din't, it wasn't me Mum, look me socks are dry."

Helen let the petty bickering subside as she had the comforting knowledge that in a few hours she would be home, London, her beloved London.

The knock at the door and the call of "Tickets please" roused Helen. Fumbling in her purse she produced the three tickets, opened the door and passed them to the conductor who clipped them. "Thank you madam, the tea trolley will be round shortly." Helen nodded and the collector closed the sliding door. She checked her watch, which lost time regularly, but satisfied its owner that she had slept for only two hours, leaving just over two hours until arrival. In the fifteen minutes it took for the early morning tea to arrive, Helen occupied her time gazing at her sleeping children, pondering on their future and the enormity of the purpose of her trip South. Just as it seemed all her resolve was dissipating into melancholy, the rattle of the tea-cart made a welcome intrusion on her thoughts. After the trolley lady had served Helen, she wheeled her cart further up the corridor, to attend to other travellers.

Helen placed the tray of tea pots, milk jugs, plates and the mound of warm toast covered with a napkin, accompanied by miniature pots of Robertsons' marmalade, strawberry and blackcurrant jams on the vacant seat next to her. Mary was woken easily but it took a more vigorous bout of shaking to bring Mark round. Sleepily, he reconfirmed his surroundings and robotically accepted the plate with buttered toast, then chose blackcurrant from the proffered pots of jam. Mark preferred these miniature glass jars perfect in every way, to the more familiar big jars, except for the missing paper golliwog found on every larger Robertson's jar. When saved could be redeemed for enamelled badges showing golliwogs in various guises of employment.

The three ate the toast and preserves, finished their tea and put the tray of dishes onto the corridor floor to be picked up by the trolley lady on her return trip to the buffet car at the opposite end of the train. Mark had secretively put an unopened strawberry jam jar into his jacket pocket that was hanging on a hook by his side. That would make a great present for his brother Terry. Their breakfast had taken thirty minutes and Mark spent ten minutes on two further visits to the toilet. All three drifted off uneasily and all woke instantly when an announcement came across the train's speakers informing passengers that the train was approaching Euston Station.

Chapter 17

With stiffness, jackets and coats were donned and hats adjusted. Helen spat onto her white cotton handkerchief and removed the last traces of jam and crumbs from Marks face; he in turn grimaced and squirmed at the assault. Although the weather was not inclement, the air that greeted them, on alighting, was bracing and dispelled the last vestiges of drowsiness.   Helen refused an offer of assistance from a Station Porter who, unperturbed, went off to find a more willing and probably more affluent client.   Helen decided they would walk the distance from Euston to Drummond Street, saving taxi fare.   Despite the frequent changing of suitcases from Helen to Mary and back again, the journey passed quickly.   Mary noticed that even at a quarter past five in the morning the capital was fast awakening. They passed Goodge Street and Warren Street tube Stations, a district that was a favoured centre for car dealers. Finally passing Seaton Street, where the market flourished daily, they took the next turning left and arrived at their destination.

Helen stopped at a tenement building which was in need of a deal of repair and made grubby by city grime.   They made their way through a dimly lit corridor, at the end, Mary pushed a brown Bakelite button on the wall causing a light bulb to illuminate the shabby hallway. Helen knocked at the door as quietly as possible, meanwhile Mark was watching with great interest as the light switch button slowly crept out like a snail from its shell.   When it clicked back the light went out, re-illuminating when Mary pushed the button again.   The sound of a guarded voice attracted Mark's attention, "It's me Mum, Helen."   There was a Sound of bolts being drawn and the door was thrown open.   Framed in the doorway, in the amber aura of the gas light, stood Helen's Mother, Nell.

"What's all this then? Is anything wrong?"

"No everything's fine Mum, I'll explain later. I'm just down here till Sunday."   Relieved, Nell affectionately kissed her daughter, then turned to her grandchildren. Mary threw herself into her grandmother's arms to receive a crushing embrace, laced with the heady scent of cologne and hairspray from Nell and homely cooking smells from Nell's patterned apron.   After releasing Mary, Nell scooped up her grandson, making him giggle, by kissing him all over his face and neck "Stop it Nana!" although he didn't mind the jovial Matriarch's attention in the least. "Come on, get yourselves indoors an I'll get the kettle on." Helen pushed the children after their grandmother, then followed. She put the bags down in the doorway, turned, closed and bolted the door and took off her coat, hanging it on one of the hooks on the back of the door. Then taking the childrens' coat and jacket from her Mother she added them to the spare hooks.

The apartment consisted of two rooms, one a bedroom and one which served as a living room and kitchen. There was a cooker in the corner and a small gas fire provided the flat's only heating. There was no electricity in the building, except for the hall lights. All lighting, cooking and heating in the block, was by coal gas. A sink for domestic and personal use was one floor up, on the landing. It was the only source of drinking water for the building.

The four sat at a table that was covered in a blue-check, waxed tablecloth. The flat, although small and old, was as spotless as brush, soap and effort could make it. Adroitly, Nell produced the steaming tea pot, milk jug and a slab of home made cake.

"They've had no breakfast yet Mum" warned Helen.

"Aw just a little piece for now. An' I'll get breakfast on shortly" replied Nell. Helen nodded in consent

"How's Dad?"

"Oh the old bugger is still breathing and moaning." Insults were really a form of affection and banter between Husband and wife, although, when infused with alcohol, the pair were not averse to inebriated bouts of fisticuffs. This had been more serious in the early days of their marriage, but at fifty-nine, Nell was almost twelve years younger than her husband and now gave back more than she got.

"He's asleep in the bedroom."

"Oh No He's Not!" stated a sonorous voice in the adjacent room. "How can anyone sleep with all this racket?"

"Aw shut your face you old git" responded Nell. As Mark listened to the confusing verbal exchanges, he could hear the sounds of movement and coughing that confirmed his grandfather was alive and about to make an appearance. Mark could remember little about his grandfather except that he was called granddad and lived in London. Now that he was about to meet him face to face, he wondered wether it was a good idea, as so far, he did not sound very friendly. In contrast, he felt he knew his Grandmother as well as he knew his Mother. Cake in hand, he sidled closer to the security of his Nan, who sensing her grandson's apprehension, quipped "Don't you worry about that miserable old sod Mark, if he as much as says a word, I'll spark him out" and to reinforce the promise showed Mark her clenched fist that would carry out the deed. Somewhat comforted, he turned to the bedroom door and witnessed the sudden appearance of Tommy.

Compared to his wife, Tommy could not have been more different. Where Nell's robust complexion, ample breasts and heavyset features gave an impression of a typically buxom English matriarch, Tom's slight frame and sharp facial features presented a more refined appearance. There was no doubt that Granddad Tom had been and was, a veritable dapper gentleman. As a husband and wife, Tom and Nell somewhat resembled Laurel and Hardy, and most of the time could match their antics with Cockney humour. But Tom had a past which he had dearly paid for. He had served in the army during the First World War. He enlisted together with his three brothers', one who was younger and the others his senior. In just a few weeks of the terrible battle of the Somme, Tom lost his older brothers' and was within fifty-yards of his younger brother on one sortie over the trenches, when a whiz bang exploded, killing his younger sibling and at least twelve other soldiers outright, covering Tom with mire and gore. For the remainder of his life, Tom hardly ever referred to his family. He had been born in 1887, one of twelve children. He only ever referred to his Father as an evil bastard, who had owned several hansom cabs, the London Taxi of their day. He often beat his wife and children during drunken rages. Like most of his brothers', Tom ran away from home as soon as possible, which in his case was before his thirteenth birthday. Always an unpredictable character, in wartime he received a notable mention for bravery, but not much later he was sentenced to be shot for selling army hoses to the French civilians for food. The sentence was never carried out, as many condemned men were, at that time given the choice either face the firing squad or undertake a suicide attack. Tommy, ever the optimist, opted for the latter. This was a fortunate decision as he became one of only a handful of men to survive a futile attempt to capture a section of German trenches. It all became a topic of conversation over glasses of whisky in later years, but every so often as Tommy regaled the children with tales of his childhood and war years, the pretence of a bluff of indifference to his life's misfortunes would slip, to reveal moroseness and sadness occasioned by the extreme hardship and grief that he had experienced. After leaving the Army, Tom decided he was going to make something of himself. In this he succeeded although he could not have forseen that his path to success would be through a life of crime He became an expert forger, specialising in stolen cheques and money draughts. In leaner times lead half-crowns fabricated by Tom, would be circulated throughout the south of England. He chose the busy centres of trade and commerce where detailed inspection of coins was less likely. One of his more imaginative enterprises involved aquiring an ape, which he trained to lift letters from pillar and mail boxes. These letters would then be carefully steamed open. If they contained nothing of value, they would be resealed and replaced from whence they came. If, on the other hand, they carried cash, postal orders or cheques, Tom would get to work.

As months went by Charlie the ape, named after Charlie Chaplin, received further education in stealing jewellery and handbags etc, from open tenement windows. This profitable partnership ended tragically when, after one particularly successful day's thieving, Tommy and Charlie had a few drinks at the local den of iniquity. Initially the evening passed uneventfully as Tom treated the house to drinks, but later Charlie, now the worse for booze, did the unthinkable. He stole Tommy's wallet. It would not have seemed so funny, but for the crowds increasing ridicule which was directed at Tom, as he tried to coax Charlie down from the chandelier where he was perched. The more agitated Charlie became, the more merriment it provided for the drunken crowd. Tom was now threatening Charlie with dire consequences but if mans' closest relative understood, he seemed to treat the threats with disdain. It was then it happened. Charlie let the wallet slip, Tom caught it but was not ready for the furry onslaught as his partner-in-crime tried to reclaim his prize. The crowd gathered around, as man and ape rolled about the floor fighting like demons, the landlord of the 'Hole in the Wall' pub, who was concerned that the sound of so much laughter, at such a late hour, would attract the unwelcome attention of the police, decided to rescue tom. With the arrival of reinforcements Charlie returned to his perch on the chandelier, without the wallet. A victorious, but battered and bitten Tom, shook the wallet at the ape derisively, "there yah flea bitten bastard, what's mine is mine!" Charlie wanted revenge and decided that it was a good time to take a crap. Catching a steaming turd evacuating he deftly launched it from derriere to target, Tom's face in one fetid move. Dapper Tom was not so dapper now, as the green stinking mess of primate shit dripped down his face onto his immaculate shirt, tie and suit. After cleaning up in the Gents as best as he could, Tommy returned to find Charlie in a calmer mood and they left the pub hand in paw to the guffaws of their drinking companions. Later, in the early hours of the morning, Tommy's darker side emerged and he beat the unfortunate Charlie to death with a hammer. Later, if anyone asked what had happened to the monkey, Tom would reply that it had sadly died from taking one shit too many.

A two year prison spell in Brixton prison for theft did nothing to set Tommy on the straight and narrow. He assumed once more his dapper demeanour and criminal ways, when he first met Nell near Oxford Street. It was 1923 and she was working as a Lyons corner house clippie. These very smart waitresses served at the fashionable coffee houses. To a twenty-four year old woman with two children, her daughter Helen and a son Sidney aged three and one respectively, Tom was a handsome, debonair, older man of the world and my - what a charmer. Not like the bastard who had walked out on her one Friday night, never to return, leaving her with two babies to care for and no money. Compared to this example of manly virtue, Dandy Tom, with his cutting wit, educated ways and easy spending, swept Nell off her feet and they became Mr. and Mrs. T. Ashman later that year. In time, Nell realised that she had married a lying con-man and thief, but she never ceased to love him with passion and loyalty to the end of her life. Tommy returned that love as much as his selfishness would allow and after himself, Nell was the love of his life.

While Mary talked chattily to her Grandfather, Helen was in deep in conversation with her Mother. Every so often, she would turn her face towards the man, who had been the only father she had ever known and who now was listening to the conversation between Nell and herself.

"Always said he was a wrong un." muttered Tom.

"Yeh, but that's not important, it's Helen and the kids that matter now" replied the agitated Nell. As she spoke she was lifting Mark's sleeping form and heading for the one bedroom. Removing his shoes she laid him on the plump mattress and covered him with the heavy blankets and eiderdown, where he settled easily into the still warm spot vacated by Granddad. "Why don't you have a lie down as well Mary love" urged Helen. Mary shrugged her shoulders then realised she was tired, she yawned then nodded in agreement and in a few short minutes was fast asleep on top of the eiderdown next to her brother. Tommy had to get ready for work; he did not normally work Saturdays but had promised his bosses at the Holborn Parks Department that he would put some extra work into the Russell Square Gardens where he was Head Gardener. They were expecting some visiting dignitaries the following week and Tommy's Garden was considered to be one of the finest in London. He had lied about his age to keep the job he had held since 1946. He had started as soon as his ARP job disappeared with the ending of World War Two and although officials had their suspicions Tommy was much older than his claimed sixty, decided to turn a blind eye as he was the most conscientious employee they had ever had. A far cry from this pillar of society was the same Tommy who, in 1926, had been caught with three cronies stealing Royal Mail, a crime at that time that was regarded as serious as murder. Nell and the five year old Helen remembered well that day at the Old Bailey as the dour judge, in his summing up, accused Tommy of being the evil criminal mastermind behind a heinous crime. The fact that the total haul came to less than twenty pounds mattered not, and he sentenced Tommy to eight years hard labour. On the announcement, Nell fainted and it was to a sobbing Helen he shouted his last message as a free man. "Tell ya Mah not to wait for me, an tell er I'm sorry I got caught." The last words tailed off, as the two guard escort dragged him, handcuffed, to the waiting Black Maria and off to Wandsworth Jail. After four months he was removed to HMP Parkhurst on the Isle of Wight. What Tommy did not know on the day of his conviction, was that Nell was two months pregnant with his future son Tommy junior.

In the ensuing years Nell held her family together by undertaking all manner of degrading but legal jobs and regularly visited Tommy in jail. Her husband had shown an aptitude for horticulture and had been put in charge of the Warden's garden, which carried extra perks, easing life on the inside for him but outside his family were not to be so fortunate. Poverty hit hard, but like so many families at that time in the same predicament, they survived. The war had obliterated many class distinctions and a man's past could be easily hidden, especially by a skilled forger. References and character testimonials were of no problem. The green fingers learned in prison, together with the sticky fingers of an old lag and had helped secure his current employment.

Granddad entered the bedroom and looked at the sleeping children, paying Mark little heed but gazing down on his granddaughter. "My Gaw'd, but don't she look like Helen!" With that he took his winter coat and covered the sleeping girl. As he was leaving, he informed the two women that he would be back after one. On his return they would all go down to the pub on the corner, for a few drinks as his treat. "Thanks Dad." Whether her Father heard or not Helen could not tell as the door was already closing behind him. Her Mother's voice regained her attention. Now they were alone, mother and daughter could resume their conversation in earnest. "I'll put the kettle on for another cuppa, then you can tell me how all me grand kids are doing and what the best plan will be from here." As they waited for the kettle to boil, there was a short silence as the two women who had shared so many hardships in their younger lives, now braced themselves for another dose of the same. Helen could have burst into tears, but as she looked into her Mother's well-worn jovial face, she felt her inner strength returning. A feeling that was reinforced when her Mother's face broke into a huge grin,
"Fuck em all, that's what I say's, - Fuck em all." As the kettle started its slow crescendo, mother and daughter fell into one anothers arms with a mixture of laughter and tears, Helen was once more transported to her childhood, comforted and protected by her loving mother's arms. Nell felt once again that immense maternal instinct that had lain dormant for so long, waiting to be needed once more. It seemed that time had arrived and no power on earth would stand in the way of a mother's love for her daughter.

Chapter 18

It was a little after eleven before the children awoke. In the four hours they had slept the two senior females had discussed the welfare of the whole family in the North and the Southern branch consisting of, Nan, granddad and Helen's two brothers'.   The youngest, Tommy junior, was travelling abroad as a merchant seaman and rarely contacted his parents, which broke Nell's heart.   It seemed that Tommy the child that had the most love lavished upon him had returned the least.   It was not surprising really that he should turn out as selfish as his Father.   The older brother, that was younger than Helen by over two years, was Sidney, Siddy as he was called by his Mother and Sister.   Sidney had lived in Richton some months working with Peter but could not stand him or his ways.   While up North, he had met and married a school teacher's daughter, Hilda, a slim intelligent woman.   Soon after, the pair left England for Rhodesia and went on to South Africa in an effort to make a better living and to escape the dreary English weather.   Sid at least sent the odd letter, but these were too infrequent to be of regular comfort to his Mother, or indeed his Sister who loved him greatly.

Nell learned that it would be a year before Jack would be released from prison, Karl was working hard at his decorating firm, although he constantly complained it was messy. He had no intention of working for anyone, this was a temporary job until he had decided what his next step in life would be.   Nell listened intently as she learned how Terry, Mary and Mark had fared.   With a Mother's intuition she read between the lines "Look love, you gotta leave the bastard.   If you don't, your gonna end up maimed or dead like your friend."   Helen flinched at the mention of Lucy, her feelings still raw from the loss. Nell continued "what ever you need just say, I've got a little money put by an'..."

"No, nothing like money Mum, we'll manage. It's just if anything happens to me, what will happen to my kids?   I mean Jack and Karl will be able to take care of themselves but Terry, Mary and Mark - I just don't know what to do."

"Don't you be worrying on that score; they can come an' stay with Dad and me.   No matter what, blood is thicker than water and we'll manage." Helen nodded sadly then a terrible afterthought occurred to Nell.

"Ere, you don't think that the evil git is really gonna do you serious harm, do you?"   As she spoke she stared intently into her daughter's eyes, and something she saw there sent a shiver down her spine.   "Helen love, is there anyone else?"

"What do you mean Mum?" said Helen, but not at all convincingly.

"Oh you silly cow!" at that Helen's head dropped and she sobbed uncontrollably for several minutes before regaining her composure then, as she dabbed at her red eyes with the handkerchief put in her hand by her Mother, tried in vain not to smudge the heavy mascara, "It's not what you think Mum."

"Nah, bloody well never is, is it?"

"No really Mum, nothing has happened, he's just a really nice bloke." then quickly she added, "Nothing has happened serious like, Honest!" "Serious! How serious do you want it to be?   If Peter gets wind of it, God help you! Oh sweet Jesus Helen, if he finds out he'll kill you for sure, you know that don't you? That's why you're here."

 "Not quite Mum. Yes, I may need someone to look after my kids but it's gonna be me what does the killing!"   Nell moved her lips to form words but no sound issued from them and for the best part of a minute she was mute with shock and disbelief. She questioned what had caused her daughter to even contemplate abandoning her children and perhaps to contemplate a lifetime behind bars or worse. When words finally came, Nell croaked painfully "first Tommy then Siddy left me - now you. Oh my Gawd, where did I go wrong?"   It was Nell's turn to drop her head into her arms, to be comforted by Helen.

Although red eyed and subdued, two more pots of tea had worked wonders and when the children joined them, still half-asleep, neither noticed the effects of the morning revelations.   Nan was one of the best cooks in London; all the Dacey brood knew that for a fact. Her roast dinners, pies, puddings and cakes were a sheer delight. She had the the knack of producing the most wholesome of meals from a single shopping basket, for any number of guests, not one of whom would leave the table hungry. Granddad never failed to remind the diners with one of those Victorian pearls of wisdom he was fond of repeating 'Always leave the table feeling you can eat more.'   Sod that, thought Mary and heaped some more mashed potato onto her plate. Mark, fearing there would not be enough for second helpings, grabbed the spoon from his Sister and attempted to find space on his plate which was already piled high. Granddad had returned from work earlier than expected and after putting a fragrant bunch of flowers, purloined from the garden's green house, into a vase - a perk of the job he explained, he sat down to his midday meal with, his unexpected company. Mark found his wrist seized in a vice like grip, "You've got enough on that plate my boy." He was not going to disagree with his fearsome grandfather and relinquished his grasp on the spoon, returning to the job in hand of eating. Nell was still busy producing food for the table from the various old and battered pans and steamers, crammed onto the ancient gas stove. Placing a gravy bowl into the last remaining space on the packed table, she herself sat down. Reaching across the table she took up the spoon still covered in creamed potato, cast a threatening glare at Tommy, then with a flourish scooped a dollop of mash dropping it on to Mark's mound of food. Her grandson looked up and caught the magic smile that was as famous as her cooking. Checking granddad was not about to arm wrestle him for it, he tucked into his meal with gusto.

"Good Gawd!" exclaimed Tommy incredulously "ee's gone an eaten the bloody lot" and held up the empty plate to show all seated. "You was hungry my boy."

"Well since teatime yesterday they've only had a bit of cake and some toast" Helen explained, feeling embarrassed by the confession. Granddad was a different person now as the golden syrup pudding arrived. The knowledge that the meal they were eating was really tomorrow's Sunday lunch mattered not, he spooned generous helpings into waiting bowls then smothered them with the smooth pale- yellow Birds custard, finally placing the steaming bowls in front of his grandchildren.

"Thank you Granddad" offered Mary

"Yeh fank you very much Granddad" added Mark, not to be outdone in the politeness stakes. Tom smiled at the child, patted him on the head and tugged at his ear lobe "Your very welcome my dears."

"That bugger Hitler used to do that" said Nell in between a spoonful of syrup sponge and custard.

"Did what?" asked a puzzled Helen, then continued "gave em pudding and custard?"

"Nah you silly cow" replied her mother "He always patted kids on the head an' pulled their ears, used to see it on the news reels an stuff." Helen nearly choked as she tried to stifle a laugh and Nell trembled in her efforts to stop the giggles. The kids did not appreciate the humour, so they continued to eat. As for Tommy, he raised his eyebrows in mock indignation and admonished his wife.

"This is a fine way to behave in front of the children, what sort of table manners will they have, if we don't set them an example?"

"Your right of course, sorry my dear." Tommy was pacified, 'umph'

"Ere, pass the custard Adolf." Nell had hardly got the words out of her mouth, when she burst into spluttering laughter. Helen laughed also, then, as the children witnessed their mother's involuntary tears, they too were infected by the giggles followed by spasms of Laughter, which caused them to hold their aching sides. Each time they caught sight of Granddad's sombre, disapproving scowl, it served only to enhance the hysteria.

"That's right, laugh, you stupid bunch of hyenas." More bouts of mayhem, in between which, a chuckling Mark asked his sister,

"wots a high enid Mary?" At this, even Tommy allowed himself the luxury of a chortle or two. Why is it that most of us forget that even if life is hard work and a financial struggle, the greatest medicine for depression known comes free?

Chapter 19

The prospect of lunch and amiable banter had dispelled all gloom, and the mood had more of a holiday feeling to it. Helen and Mary helped Nell with the dishes; these had to be taken up the two flights of stairs to a large, white, stoneware sink with a single cold water tap. A battered cream and green gas-geyser provided hot water. The area was poorly lit, so the trio completed the task as quickly as possible and returned, carrying the clean crockery and pans to the friendliness of the apartment. Each article had its assigned place and once everything had been tidied away it was five past four. Tommy had abandoned his attempts to teach Mark the basics of chess and announced that he was off for a kip before getting ready for the big night out. This suited Mark as he only wanted to play battles with the horses and soldiers anyway. Oblivious to the movement about him, he played happily until his Nan hoisted him gently to his feet. "Come on, lets give you the once over." The once over consisted of a quick wash down with soap on a flannel, which had been dampened with tepid water contained in a chipped, white, enamelled bowl. Nan had undone his top three shirt buttons and rolled the collar down on the inside allowing her to reach his neck. After slopping all visible areas, she continued with his legs rolling down his socks and rolling up the baggy legs of his over long shorts, again attacking every bit of exposed flesh. Then she rubbed the same parts with a worn yellow cotton towel, ignoring Marks complaints of "Me pants are wet, an' so is me shirt."

Nell opened one of the two ground floor apartment windows, checking first one way then the other for pedestrians, she picked up the bowl of dirty water which now had scum forming on top, and expertly threw the contents of the bowl towards a nearby grate in the road. A passer by skipped gingerly backwards to avoid the splashes "Oops sorry Timmy, dint see you there."

"That's alright Nell, you missed me any way ducks" and with that her neighbour carried on to the next tenement and disappeared inside. Nell closed the window with a thud, turned and inspected the troops "right" she said putting the bowl away "hats and coats on an let's be off to Maudies." Maud Golding, was Nell's only sister and lived on the top floor of the tenement next door. Years ago Maud had been badly injured falling from a bus. Her husband Arthur had taken her to the University Hospital, but when the doctors announced the impending police visit he had become restless. Large numbers of people had witnessed the accident and the evidence had pointed to negligence by the driver and conductor. Arthur was a very well known criminal and at that moment in time there were a number of issues that the police wished to discuss with him. Seizing a nearby wheelchair and ignoring Maud's agonised groans, he had taken her home. By the time she received any treatment the damage was done. The hip had been severely fractured and had knitted badly; Maud was left with a severe limp and excruciating pain for the rest of her life. Arthur felt no remorse, as he was another of those selfish bastards, archetypal of London's criminal society. Maud would make excuses for him, reminding her sister how she and Arthur had stayed together through a lot of bad times. "Yep, and not so many good ones" added Nell.

Helen was only a baby when in 1922, Arthur Golding got involved in an armed robbery which had gone wrong. The newly formed 'Sweeney' persued the gang by car, in the first flying squad shoot-out through the Capital. They finally cornered Arthur and his gang, forcing them out of the car at gun point. The three men who were found in possession of two revolvers and a shotgun had returned fire on the chasing police vehicles. Arthur, as the ring leader, was sentenced to fifteen years of which he would serve eleven. During all that time Maud remained faithful, then five years into his sentence Arthur received word from the governor that in a terrible accident his only child Larry, a chubby blond haired seven year old who was the apple of Maud and Arthur's eyes, had been killed by a delivery wagon that had mounted the pavement. Arthur went temporarily insane and was housed for months in the prisons hospital wing, leaving poor Maud to cope with the grief and its effects. The inquest considered the fact that the little boy who had only one eye, he had lost the other eye as a result of an infection contracted in early infancy, the court decided that it was unfair to expect the limited insurance policy to pay out, but did order the haulier to make some recompense. This he promised the Coroner he would do, then, as soon as he left the hearing filed bankruptcy. Maud, with no money, was reduced along with her sister Nell to begging from all and any to acquire enough money to bury her young son. Now, she found herself at her lowest ebb, once more, she was in pain and trouble yet still there were no complaints. Arthur came out of prison at the end of his term and soon resumed his old habits. Maud did not even have much to say, when later that year on Christmas Eve, Arthur reluctant to be saddled with a crippled wife, repaid her love and loyalty by dumping her and running off with a younger woman.

Maud was Nell's senior by three years, but at sixty two she looked much older due to her tragic life. She held open the door for her sister's daily visit and uttered a gasp of delight, to find Nell was accompanied by her niece, who was the only person in the world she loved equally to Nell. "Come in, come on in all of you." As she disappeared into the damp soap smelling single room, the group followed obediently. Mary and the two older women dodged the shirts and various other articles of clothing hanging from the ceiling to dry. Maud 'Took in washing.' This was her only form of income except for a meagre state pension. Mark recoiled when some of the drips from a soggy white shirt dripped down his neck, but as he had been forewarned by all three of his female relatives that he was to say nothing that might insult or upset Great aunt Maud, he remained silent.

Auntie had put on the kettle and was pushing things off her bed to make room for the others to sit down. As she hobbled painfully up and down the small room, Helen could not help reflecting that her problems in life were nothing compared to Maud's. "Now, what the hell ave I got to give you?" It was was customary for Maud to give her favoured guests anything of value that she had, and despite genuine protestations, they would always leave with something whether they needed it or not. To Mark she appeared a comical, little, old lady, though in fact she was as tall as his Mother. He noticed she looked very much like his Nan, but nowhere near as stoutly built. He also noticed, as it was his turn to be hugged, that she smelled the same as Nell but with the added scent of bleach and soap. "Ere lovey, you sit there." Maud sat her great nephew on an exposed part of the bed and shuffled across the room, returning with a pink plastic piggy bank. "This ere is for you two kids." Although the heavily laden pig was placed in the young boy's lap, it was his sister who as soon as aunt's back turned, seized the pig from her brother. Taking a blunt knife that had been wiped clean of jam, Mary turned the pig upside down, prodding the slot and shaking the plastic money box until the final coin fell leaving a considerable mountain of pennies and halfpennies on the bed. Nell helped count out the money and shared the fortune of eight shillings and tenpence evenly between the two. 'There goes Maud's Christmas savings' thought Nell. Mark was about to scoop up his share of the windfall when his Mother beat him to it.

"I'll look after that for you love," then to prevent any complaints she shoved one of the rich tea biscuit's that had arrived with the tea, into his open mouth.   Mary however was much quicker and was filling her pockets with handfuls of coins. She was aware that her Mother sometimes forgot to return 'looked after cash'.

To a small boy it had seemed an age before the three women finished their conversation and the group made a move.   "Well we'll see you in the boozer on the corner at seven thirty then, OK aunt?"

"Yes, that will be lovely dear, it'll be ever so nice to have a drink with Helen wont it Nell?"

At the door, Mark was the last one to be fondly kissed and cuddled and it was the very astute Nell that saw Maud let her gnarled hands linger just a little longer than normal on his face, her fingers stroking Mark's cheeks then running through his blond hair.   Nell knew that for a brief moment Maud was seeing her own small son and despite the cheery, "See you all later" caught sight of the tears welling in her sister's rheumy eyes.   The door closed and Nell shepherded her family down the shabby stairs back towards home and although she found herself saying "We are gonna have to get a move on if we are to make it to the pub on time" drawing attention to the fact it was Saturday night and if they were late there would almost certainly be no seating available, her real thoughts were with her sister "Poor, Poor Maudie."

While the adults busily readied themselves, Mary read and Mark played with the chess pieces. At seven twenty Tommy, his wife and daughter were taking their leave of the children.   "Don't forget, we are only over the road at the pub on the corner. If you have any problems we will be in the snug."

"Ok Mum, don't worry, we'll be alright."

"And you Mark, do as your Sister says."   Suspecting that his co-operation would require bribery, Helen added   "If you're a good boy, you can stay up and have fish and chips for supper."

"Yippee!" shouted her young son and he practically shooed his Mother out of the door; after all, the sooner she went the sooner she would be back with fish and chips. Nell squeezed past Helen and handed Mary a bag of sweets. "There you are love, share them with your brother." In the distance they heard an impatient Tommy calling "Come on get a move on, we'll be late." With that, they were gone leaving sister and brother squabbling over the toffees.

Chapter 20

Arriving at the pub on the corner Tommy, Nell and Helen saw aunt
Maud already seated at a corner table. Although the room was only
half full, she had reserved three seats by putting her hat on one, her
coat on another, on the third a heavy walking stick to warn that this
particular seat was not available. Maud always liked to make her
own way to the pub as she preferred not to slow others down with
her ungainly gait, especially as she would often have to stop,
sometimes holding onto a lamp post or wall while the pain in her hip
subsided. auntie Maud waved happily and sported a Cheshire cat
grin, the three latecomers added Maud's hat, coat and stick to their
now discarded garments hanging on an old oak stand in the corner
near to their table. Then they settled into the seats that had been
held for them. On the other side of the room a generously
proportioned lady was shuffling pages of sheet music and positioning
a stool in front of a heavy upright Grand piano. Tommy attracted
the attention of a lanky hook-nosed waiter who made his way to the
table. "What can I get you Tom?"
"Make it a large Scotch for me please Steve, Nell will have a Gin and
tonic and a glass of Stout for Maud," Tom looked across at Helen.
"I'll have a dry martini and lemonade please Dad." Steve was
already on his way to the bar with the order, when he was stopped in
his tracks by a shrill voice.
"Put a bottle of Mackeson on that order Steve my love!" the waiter
looked at Tom and seeing him nod begrudgingly, he continued to the
bar. You could not mistake that high pitched voice as belonging to
anyone but its owner, Gladys Potts the local busybody and gossip.
"You don't mind Tommy do you? Wouldn't begrudge a girl a
drink, specially such a good pal an all." Gladys was also, as Tommy
called her, 'a cadging cow.'
"I'll get yer a drink back later me ducks."
"I won't hold my breath" Tom muttered. Gladys was dragging a
chair behind her and invited herself to the group. "Move up girls'',
make room for a little un." That's a laugh thought Helen as she
studied the human Christmas pudding, now sat opposite dressed in
ill-fitting drab clothes and on whose head sat a ridiculously small
battered felt hat with a grubby feather that resembled a quill - she
was not even a presentable Christmas pudding.

"Well and who's this then Nell?" thrusting her face so violently near that it forced her Helen to move her head back sharply.

"Gladys you know this is my daughter Helen." That was it, no need for introductions, the way was open for attack. "My Gawd, look at you my girl. Haven't you put some weight on and what on earth have you done to your hair?" Nell and her daughter were then subjected to a thorough inquisition and though they side stepped much of the scrounging gossip's interrogation and ignored the many sarcastic insults, auntie Maud had to rescue them several times by changing the subject. They were finding the whole situation increasingly intolerable. They would all have loved to slap her silly, but they knew from others' experiences that this thoroughly unpleasant character was capable of all sorts of dirty tricks and nasty acts of retaliation. For this reason they always tried to avoid the unpleasant moocher, If she did latch on to them they would make an excuse and leave early after providing her with a couple of drinks and suffering her twisted sense of humour. Tom stood, to go to the bar, thinking maybe he could sneak a second round of drinks without being stung again, "Well go on then Tommy, if you're twisting my arm I'll have another with you." Tom bit his lip and went to the bar. Nell thought now we'll never get rid of the nosy bitch. When Tom returned with a tray of drinks his demeanour had improved "There you are girls'." Maud and Helen looked puzzled but Nell looked worried, "What's the old bugger up to now" she mused. "I'm just off over the road to take the kids some crisps and lemonade, and check up on em like." "Kids! What kids are these then?" Shrieked Gladys her piggy eyes sparkling.

Mary and Mark jumped when the knock came at the door. "It's all right kids, it's me, granddad." There was no point in using his key, Mary had been instructed to put the bolts on and these same bolts were now being drawn back. "Here my dears" Tommy said. He passed them the two small bottles of 'R. Whites' lemonade and two packets of 'Smiths' crisps. The children liked the crisps as they had little blue paper twists containing salt; "Thank you Granddad" chirped the two in unison,

"You're welcome" shouted Tom who was searching the top drawer of a tallboy in the bedroom. "Ah, there you are!" he whispered to himself and he grasped the small glass bottle that contained a dark brown liquid. Once he had pocketed the bottle, Tom left the children who settled down to listen to the old bakelite radio as they had been doing when Tommy had knocked on the door.

Nell looked up and saw her breathless husband at the bar. As there were no trays available, Tom made two trips before he could sit down with another round of drinks, including the expected glass of stout for Gladys. "Oh you do spoil me you tinker!" Nell's suspicions were aroused by Tom's wicked little smile, "the pleasure's all mine my dear." Gladys sank the drink in one and placed the glass down, confident that she could scrounge at least another couple of drinks from the old pushover. But if she had paid a little more attention earlier, she would have seen Tommy furtively emptying half of the small bottle's contents into her glass of stout

"Ah here we go"

"Go where Tom?" asked Nell.

"The music love, the music." Her husband nodded towards the piano and sure enough a big lady started to pound out some lively popular tunes.

"Come on Tommy, your slipping - my glass is empty." Nell was just about to tell Gladys that she thought she'd had enough out of them, when Gladys's face contorted. With a lurch she got to her feet, then with a look of sheer horror on her face slumped back down again. "Bloody hell Mum, what's that smell?" gasped Helen. Nell looked disgustedly towards her husband "Don't bloody look at me," then all eyes were on the ashen faced Gladys as she let rip with a burbling rumble,

"Cor, Fakin ell" exclaimed Maud. She snapped her head back then stiffened, holding her breath in an effort to avoid the stench.

"Jeez" whistled Nell, Helen just retched

"I'm not well" whimpered the crumpled scrounger and let rip again, this time even she retched at the stink,

"Fuck me Gladys, I think you've gone an' shit yourself" Tommy said loud enough for all in the room to hear. The piano stopped and the whole room looked on in bewilderment, as Gladys was making an effort to escape, with another enormous fart, felt the hot liquid flood her drawers and start to seep down her legs. Holding her stomach, she fled for the door wailing "I'm not well" Tommy called after her in feigned concern "You wont be wanting another drink then love," the look of triumph on Tom's face brought a response from Nell "What have you done you old sod?" Grinning like a naughty schoolboy, he placed both elbows on the table and gestured, with a nod of his head, that they should all come close to hear his confession. With the four of them in a huddle, Tommy whispered one word "Jollop" - the three women's mouths dropped open, then they broke into guilty grins for they were well aware that Jollop was one of the most powerful herbal purgatives available. Although they thought it was a cruel thing to do, they agreed that in all the years that Gladys' had scrounged and interfered in their social lives, this was the first time they had managed to be rid of her. The music had started up again and their spirits lfted at the thought of Gladys's well-deserved misfortune. Happily, they threw themselves into the choruses of the old cockney favourites and relaxed confident that they could now enjoy the rest of the evening. Just before the chucking out time, the four left for the chip shop two blocks away, there they purchased three pieces of cod, one hake and two rock salmon with five big bags of chips all smothered in salt and vinegar, and wrapped in newspaper. Even before they reached the apartment, they had managed to waken Mary and Mark with their drunken revelry and a sleepy Mary opened the door wide to let them in. The two youngsters had to endure ten minutes of drunken outpourings of pledges of undying love from the two women and even granddad was finding complementary things to say. It took Mary to remind them that their fish supper was going cold, before they unpacked the deep fried feast. Ripping open the various newspaper parcels still warm but soggy, they shared out the golden messes and ate with fingers from the paper, which as every civilised person knew, was the only way to eat fish and chips. Tucking into their supper with relish, they burst into spontaneous bouts of laughter every time they recalled Gladys and her messy exit.

"Well Nell, I think it will be a while before Gladys has the nerve to show her face in that boozer" said aunt Maud.

"Yep, I think that might save Dad a lot of money in the long run." added Helen. Tommy was now in hysterics which prompted Helen to ask, "What did I say?"

"Long run, you said, long run, I bet she is still running." The children did not understand what was so funny but they enjoyed the excitement, the food and the drunken attention that was lavished upon them. No one in the room wanted to think that tomorrow they had to return to Richton. When auntie Maud had left to go home, the table had been pushed to one side of the room, to allow the bed-settee to be opened out. Helen slept on this with her two children, one either side, and was soon asleep. Mary wriggled out from under her Mother's arm and lay awake for a while, listening to the muted voices and sounds that passed by. The voices became louder as they approached the window, only an occasional word having any meaning, then they tailed away to a gentle murmur until they became inaudible. Mary's eye lids grew heavy and as the voices outside mingled with the voices in her head, she surrendered to sleep.

Chapter 21

Breakfast had been a quiet affair with the children tired and the adults hung over. Shortly before ten granddad announced he was off to the bath house in Camden Town. This was one of the many public bathing houses that were so necessary when most of the surrounding tenements were without even basic washing facilities, and when your apartment was as small as the Ashman's, there was not even room for the famous tin bath. "I'll be gone for an hour or so. It's usually busy up there on a Sunday morning."

"Well I guess this is good bye for now Dad! Kids come and kiss granddad, he won't be back in time to say goodbye before we go to catch the train 'home." The word 'home' sounded hollow on her lips. 'Home' she mused. London was her home; this bustling metropolis of museums art galleries and theatres, its cheery dialect and friendly people. This was her home - why in Gods name had she ever left it? The children had bid a fond farewell to Granddad and Tommy was now putting his arms awkwardly around Helen. "Have a good trip darling and take care" he said with an audible tremble in his voice. "Thanks dad for last night and everything" but Tommy was heading out the door, stick in hand, trilby set at a jaunty angle, soap and flannel rolled in a white towel underneath his arm. "You're very welcome dear; give my love to the other children." Tommy felt he could not turn back as the tears were running down his craggy face and before entering the street he paused and wiped his eyes with a linen handkerchief, then in a forced military gait set out for Camden Town. "Don't be mad at Dad for not seeing you off love, it's just at his age he has said so many goodbyes, and these days it seems they are all permanent. Why! he has been to four funerals in as many months"

"I understand Mum, it's ok." The trip to Euston had been a silent one, Nell had insisted they caught a cab so they were at the station within fifteen minutes. After the obligatory cup of tea from the buffet, they found themselves on the platform. Nell had bought a platform ticket to allow her as much time with her family as possible. The children had said goodbye and were seated in the carriage with their luggage, both sobbing. Mary had her arm round Mark and was encouraging him to wave to Nana through the window, while outside Mother and Daughter clashed teeth in a hurried clumsy kiss.

"You take care my darling girl."

"Yeh you too Mum." Then in an afterthought Helen panicked; in all the time she had been here they had not discussed the very thing that had brought her south - her children.

"Listen Mum, the kids an...." Nell put the fingers of her right hand to Helens lips "Shush now, I know what will have to be done, don't you worry on that score." ALL ABOARD! Momentarily Helen panicked she clung tightly to her Mother, aware that so much was still unsaid. Helen did not feel her Mother slip the envelope containing four five pound notes into her coat pocket and she would not know until she was half way home, when she would find the money and note containing the words that both of them so often failed to say aloud to one another, 'I Love You.'

The banging of doors signalled the train would leave in seconds. It was actually moving when Helen and Nell reluctantly released each other. Helen climbed up the steps of the slow moving carriage, closed the door behind her turned and leant out of the window "Bye Mum, Bye Mum" From behind the glass her tearful grandchildren were mouthing their goodbyes, but Nell could not hear them. Nell wafted her handkerchief weakly and Helen waved back erratically. Even after the train gathered speed and rounded the first bend, they continued to wave, reluctant to surrender the bond that they had shared during these last few days. Nell sensed finally that she was alone on the platform, covering her face with the handkerchief that she had just been waving; she remained there, weeping, until she felt able to control herself once more. She left the platform gate to mingle with the throngs in the main hall and was startled by the small figure barring her way to the exit. "Maud what are you doing here?" Auntie Maud had taken her leave of Helen and the kids at supper the night before so was not expected to be at the station. But her sister had been at the station before her family, having made her painful and slow progress much earlier. Once there she patiently waited for them, watching unseen as they made their farewells and wept with them, sharing the heartache of uncertain separation and now she made her appearance for the reason she had made such a titanic effort - her sister, "Me? Oh I was just passing ducks!"

"God bless you Maudie"

"Come on Nell; let's get a cup of tea."

"Bollocks, let's get a bloody proper drink" and with that, the sisters' left Euston arm in arm for the nearest waiting black cab and the 'Sols Arms.'

Helen tried to raise the spirits of her son and daughter but when she felt miserable as they did, it was an impossible task. It was past six and the skies were darkening prematurely when they alighted at Richton station, a chilled drizzle had just started but the sight of an excited Terry waiting for them brightened up the damp walk home. Mark gave Terry the miniature pot of jam he had saved from the trip down south and Terry gave his mother the news that he had cleaned the house from top to bottom as a surprise for her, and also that his Dad had been on the booze non-stop since she left, returning only to sleep, wash and grab a sandwich. They arrived back at Castaires with Mark skipping in front and Helen with her arms over Terry and Mary's shoulders, one either side of her. Karl opened the door

"Hiya Mum, you ok?" Helen kissed him on the forehead and nodded. The house seemed even more repressive than when she had left it. Helen had to force herself to perform the familiar routines of supper, baths and bedtimes. With the kids in bed, she settled into the parlour chair waiting in dread for Peter's return and hoping that the tea which she was keeping warm on a saucepan, would be some sort of peace-offering for audatiously removing herself from his company.

Helen was fortunate, when Peter returned, he ate his tea and passed out.

Chapter 22

The next morning Helen left for work early, leaving Terry to make breakfast thereby avoiding her husband for another day. The following two weeks passed in an uneasy truce; Peter was busy at work but spending all the money at the pub and Helen was busy regretting that she had promised Mark that he could have a party for his fifth birthday on December the fifth. When the big day came some of Mark's friends were conspicuous by their absence, not that he had many friends anyway. The group was bolstered by family including his cousins Stanley and Cathy, Auntie Jenny was helping Helen cater for the kids' needs while for some strange reason Peter felt the need to celebrate his youngest child's fifth birthday with his brother Larry and other cronies at the Red Rose on Barnham Road. Karl had presented his brother with a boy's annual with a picture of a big yellow digger on the front, then, grabbing a couple of triangular sandwiches, he informed his Mother that he was off, out to meet friends. They saw very little of Karl those days.

The party was in full swing. The children were playing 'pass the parcel,' happily ripping off sheets of newspaper in a search for the prize, whether the music stopped or not. The game lost some of its appeal with the arrival of Peter and Larry.

"Ave you got anyfink for me Dad?" asked an excited youngster. He had received a couple of matchbox cars earlier from his Mother but his Father had promised him a surprise.

"Yep I have" slurred his father. He staggered over to the sideboard under the window and opened the cupboard door, he removed a box of fireworks that had been saved from November the 5th and passed a handful of tubes to Larry. With the remainder of the box contents in one hand he produced his lighter in the other,

"For Christ's sake Peter, not inside near the kids!" Cathy tried to grab the fireworks from Larry but in a childish gesture he held them above her head, just out of her reach. His antics distracted both women long enough for Peter to light a jumping jack and throw it under the children's chairs. In a second the room was in pandemonium. The firework seemed to chase its victims around the room and by the time Helen and Cathy had wrestled the fireworks off Peter and Larry, the children were in a state of shock. No amount of comforting could prevent them blurting details of the outrage to their parents when it was time for them to be as collected. Peter thought the whole thing was hilarious and was stunned when, as the last blubbering child left, he found he was facing a furious Helen, "It was only a bloody joke you miserable cow, the kids liked it didn't you son?" Mark backed away from Peter, still traumatised from his Father's 'Joke'. Smack! Helen's fist struck Peter in the face, not with full force, as she had had to leap up to allow for the difference in height. Smack! This time she caught him in the eye. "Why you fucking bitch, I'll kill you!" Larry, Cathy, Mary and Terry leapt on to Peter before he could make good his threat, Smack another right hander landed while Peter's arms were pinned. Her husband was now screaming with rage and with the strength of a mad-man, Peter threw his assailants from him and raised a huge fist. "Go on, try it you pathetic bullying bastard." Peter was drunk but not so drunk that he failed to see the large carving knife that Helen was holding. He weighed up the situation for a moment, but the look on his wife's face convinced him that now was not the time to seek revenge. He screamed at her "I should have you committed, you fucking stupid nutter," then reeled towards Larry. "Come on lets get out of here." Larry looked guiltily at Cathy, who nodded, anything to get Peter out of the house she thought. They were long gone before Helen put the knife down,

"Bloody ell Helen, you better get yourself out of here for a few days till things settle down" gasped Cathy.

"Nah, no chance. I'm done with putting up with his shit" replied her sister in law. Nevertheless, in the early hours of the morning Peter returned for revenge. When he realised that Helen was safely double-locked in their bedroom, he stomped off to smash up the house. Helen listened to the racket and when it had been quiet for some time she crept downstairs. With carving knife in hand she eventually found Peter amongst the debris that had once been her home. By his side was a large hatchet with which Helen assumed he had intended to chop down the bedroom door. Fortunately he had passed out in a drunken stupor, before he could commence the task. Warily Helen stooped and picked up the axe, her heart leaping into her throat when he stirred and rolled onto his side. Looking down at him, no longer afraid for herself, she felt nothing but hate and disdain. After she could not present a single saving grace in his defence decided that it was time to put an end to this villain For all their sakes, in a state of emotional detachment, she lifted the hatchet high above her head and tensed, checking her aim for the exposed neck and its vital arteries.   Helen knew it would take several blows to do the job and she would have to be prepared for a struggle after the first blow, after all Peter was a very strong man.   Taking a deep breath she lifted herself on tip toes

"Don't do it Mum please, he's not worth it."   Helen let her arm fall but still held onto the axe.   It was Karl.   When he heard what had happened after he had left, he decided he would wait up and do his best to ensure his mother came to no harm.   He had secretly watched while Peter smashed up the place and had heard his muttered threats of murder.   When his Father had passed out, it was Karl who had taken the axe from the cellar, where it was used to chop firewood and it was he who had dropped the axe, when his Mother's footsteps had disturbed him.   Then, from his hiding place behind the long drapes, he had watched his father and had witnessed his Mother contemplating the same murderous intentions. "Let me do it Mum, the kids need you.   I'd rather spend ten years in nick than see you suffer a minute more."   Helen now became terrified at the prospect of losing any of her children and put her arm around Karl.

"No, you are right son. He isn't worth it, we'll find another way."

Karl stayed in his Mother's room that night, guarding the door, axe in hand.   Studying his mother's sleeping face, he smiled, it had been a long time since he had spent the night in his Mum's room.

Chapter 23

Surprisingly, things seemed calmer.   Peter, unaware of his close shave, kept out of the way. He didn't have the stomach to face his family and endure their silences when all the while he guessed their feelings, after all what could be expected when he had destroyed nearly everything of value in the house, not even sparing the children's playthings.   Except for Mary's doll and scrapbook collection which had luckily missed her Father's attentions, all the other toys were an assembly of scrap, that held increased significance for the children. They did their best to nail, glue and 'Sellotape' their prized possessions into the objects for which they now held renewed and reinforced affections.

Helen was absent more than ever and her offspring were missing her. Christmas 1958 was one week away and the alien feeling that pervaded the house, was becoming infectious to its inhabitants. Terry tried his best to recreate previous pre-Yuletide excitement for his younger brother, but was fighting a losing battle. With his Mother never there, his brothers' and sister too consumed in their own unhappiness to be of any comfort and a Father whose presence sent shivers down his spine causing his little legs to tremble, Mark had to come to terms with the sad fact that festive spirit was a commodity in short supply for any of the children. It was during this period that the trauma produced regular and terrible nightmares, always ending with Mark wetting the bed. This necessitated his sleeping separately from Terry, at the foot of the double bed, on a canvas army cot. A thick, red, rubber sheet was placed under the cotton cover and during the night it would slowly work its way to the bottom of the bed, leaving the rubber protector to stick uncomfortably to the infant's skin, contributing to an even more restless sleep. On the mornings that followed a nightmare, Mark felt great shame in informing some member of his family that 'He had done it again'. Eventually he developed a regular routine. He stripped his bed, removed his sodden pyjamas and with the saturated and stained sheet gathered to his bare chest, he trundled off, cold and naked to the bathroom. Washing was piled in a heap on the floor as there was no washbasket. The little boy stood on tip toes to turn on the cold water tap. Taking a tatty piece of cloth that he had been told was his alone to use, he wiped it across a large bar of green soap. The bar was one of a pair taken from a cardboard packet which was adorned with a picture of a naked cherub dragging a fluffy towel. 'Fairy household'. After washing, he turned the freezing flannel and used the side that was devoid of soap to wipe as many suds from his skinny body as he could. After taking a towel from the peg and half-drying himself, he toddled back to his room to put on the vest and underpants that Helen had left out for him the previous night.

At breakfast, on the rare occasion that Helen was present, she would give Mark a sniff or two, which at first he thought was the prelude to a kiss and some affection, as usual there was neither kiss nor affection. Helen was solely concerned that she gave no cause to neighbours to think that she was a negligent mother by sending her small son out into the world smelling of piss.

Chapter 24

A few days before Christmas, the school holidays commenced. As Peter had acquired a television set to replace the one he had smashed, evenings in the living room became a more entertaining prospect. Later, the children would come to think of this holiday as the Christmas they could hardly remember. It was also this festive season that Mark would realise that Santa did not like little boys' that wet the bed, a proof of this would be on revealed on Christmas morning when his usual small pile of presents would be severely diminished. The small boy would fail notice that, the packages for his siblings would be considerably less than his.

On 22nd December, Mark had been bathed and dressed in his best. It was early evening; Peter had gone to the pub straight from work and not come home. Helen was buttoning up Marks coat somewhat hastily and a little roughly. She wanted to be out of the house before her inebriated spouse returned. With a sigh, Helen had noticed a small stain on his collar. Licking her thumb, she rubbed and scraped her long nail at the blotch until it was practically invisible. When she was satisfied she scraped the residue from under her nail with the tip of a key. Seizing her son's arm and closing the door behind them, Helen made brisk progress. Mark's legs were definitely moving faster than they were safely able and Helen had to regularly slow down giving Mark time to untie his skinny legs. Feeling that his inability to keep pace with his Mother would incur her wrath, he decided to say something that might put him in the good books, "You don't half smell nice Mum." Helen looked at Mark but instead of the expected smile and gratitude there was only a stern gaze. "Come on Mark, hurry up will you. We've got a bus to catch."

There would be no tea waiting for Peter Dacey that evening, just a note telling him that Helen was staying with a friend from work until the next day and that she had taken Mark with her. Peter no longer demanded to know Helen's whereabouts and actions, as he had come to relise he would receive no answer. As he read the note he thought fuck her, lousy fuckin' bitch then readied himself for his evening's usual alcoholic sojourn.

Mark had enjoyed the bus ride as the other passengers had seemed not to be afflicted with the Dacey's lack of seasonal goodwill. Everywhere happy faces smiled at him. On disembarking, the light shower had dried up and the street lighting reflected off the small puddles that had gathered in the worn hollows of the huge stone paving slabs. Helen's pace had not eased and her impatience had not abated. Her only conversation with the small boy who was in tow was the occasional "Mark, for fucks sake keep up" or "I am late" and "you're pulling me arm out of me socket." Eventually they turned down a narrow side street that Mark did not recognise, his Mother knocked at the only house that was not boarded up. The battered and ill-fitting door was opened by a young woman.

"Hello Helen."

"Sorry I'm late Amy, but getting this little sod ready and away is a task in itself." Mark felt uncomfortable and was reluctant to accept the blame. His mother had spent so much time getting ready, constantly smoothing her nylons and checking her appearance in the long mirror on the wardrobe door, cursing loudly as she decided her make up was not up to scratch.

"Don't worry, warn't specting you any particular time." Mark was pushed through the open door. "You coming in Helen? Wanna cuppa?" "No thanks love, I've gotta get off, I'm a bit late see." Amy shrugged then beamed as Helen pressed the two half-crowns into her hand. "Thanks Helen."

"That's OK, thank you for looking after him. I'll be back tomorrow about tea time, is that OK?"

"Course it is, you get off an enjoy yourself." The young girl tipped the departing woman a knowing nod and wink. Amy was an unmarried nineteen-year-old workmate, she lived with her three-year-old son in a one up, one down cottage slum. She had been Helen's only means of escape. The five shillings it cost for her co-operation and alibi in the event of Peter's suspicions, was money well spent.

"Eat up your jam butties you two, then it's off to bed." Mark's young baby sitter was in a hurry to get him and the grubby little urchin seated opposite out of the way as soon as possible. She was expecting another visitor shortly, one who would not appreciate the two boys' presence. The little cot had no sides and when the boys' were tucked up too tightly for comfort Amy pointed to a tin bucket in the corner. "If you need the toilet, it's there." She spoke slowly as though he was an imbecile, Mark thought, but just nodded his head. The little boy at his side said nothing, in fact he had not uttered a word since Mark had arrived, despite various attempts to start a conversation. "Whatever appens, I don't want a peep from either of you two and don't come down the stairs, understand?" Amy moved closer to the cot and if her manner had now become menacing to Mark it had caused the tot whose bed he was sharing to cower, pulling the worn rags that acted as bedclothes about him, prompting Mark to say a sincere "I won't." Satisfied she had made her position clear, the young girl went back downstairs, closing the badly painted, simple door. She ensured that the metal latch clicked into its hasp, happy that her small charges were suitably locked up She checked her make up in a small mirror that hung in a faded yellow plastic frame from a nail above a small badly chipped stone sink. Contented with what she saw, Amy pulled up the pleated ankle length skirt and took off her knickers. She checked them for stains then sniffed, displeased with the odour she opened the drawer of a tatty chest and rummaged around until she found a pair that passed the inspection and sniff test, she put one leg then the other into the 'Baggies' that she had bought as 'French knickers'. Amy gave a final check in the mirror, then a sudden thought occurred. Reaching to a shelf that hung lopsidedly above the chest, she took a bottle of cheap cologne. Splashing liberally into a cupped hand she lifted her skirt with one hand and pushed the cologne filled hand down the top of her pants, rubbing the tops of her legs and outer private parts with the diluted scent, but obviously not diluted enough as she did a little dance hissing "Fuckin' 'ell, that burns." In the room above she heard the distinct sound of someone urinating into a bucket. "Urry up an get back into bed" shouted Amy. Mark did not answer but continued to chase the small, floating torpedo shaped turd that was none of his doing around the bucket until he ran out of ammunition. Giving his little cannon a last shake, it was put away and Mark climbed back into bed. Not long after there was a knock at the door and a male voice coupled with Amy's chirping. The talking soon stopped and Mark found the animalistic grunts and groans interspersed with giggling disturbing and as quietly as possible turned over. In the glow from a solitary table lamp its the light subdued by a heavy fabric shade, he found he was looking into the sad, saucer eyes of his bedmate. He was surprised when the child put his arm round his neck and felt a warmth, so he reciprocated and without a word the youngsters drifted off, arms round each other's necks, one feeling the comfort of a kindred spirit for the first time in several weeks and the younger experiencing the feeling for the first time in his life.

"Don't make so much of a row Vince; I've got kids upstairs" adding "I'm looking after one for a mate." Vince ignored Amy's request and forced her onto the rickety sofa that was so threadbare it was covered with a colourful but grubby throw-over. At first her hands grasped his in an effort to slow down his advances then the task became too energetic and Vince was using more force. The more stimulated he became the more force he used. He felt his partner relax and surrender. He shifted his position and lay on top of her, pinning her down with the weight of his body then with one free hand he hoisted up Amy's skirt slipping it up the leg of her knickers. Running his fingers over the mound of soft curls he then pushed his open hand in a spear like thrust between the tops of her legs. At first there was a token resistance so he twisted more violently, thrusting his middle finger up and inside the wet vagina. Amy gave a loud gasp as the last of her defences were breeched. Vince turned onto his side, his left leg covered her right and his left arm restrained both her arms above her head, then unhindered pushed her legs apart. With his right hand fingering the wetness bringing more gasps and kitten like mewing that were synchronised to each thrust he made, then with heavy laboured breathing he released his grip on her arms knelt in-between her open legs and in a deft movement slid her underwear off her legs and cast them to one side. With the skirt up above her waist he inspected her nakedness holding her legs wider and caressing the parted plump pink lips with the tips of his fingers and thumbs occasionally thrusting one or more digit's into the lubricated void, then turned his attention to the woollen jumper. Using both hands, he lifted bra and jumper upwards and off the arms that Amy had outstretched to speed the process. When he had removed her skirt Amy's nakedness was complete. Vince was also naked now and he grabbed Amy's hair at the back of her head turning the face that was looking away to the fully formed erection. He straddled her small firm breasts, his forcefulness was so violent now that the girl realised she had no power over anything that was about to happen, "open" he commanded menacingly and opening her mouth she took his firmness between her lips. This was not enough for her partner who forced so much of his eight inches into her mouth that she nearly choked causing him to withdraw a little. "Suck it, suck it ard" he commanded. At first she went through the motions, then as he tugged viciously at her hair she sucked and licked hard

enough to bring moans from the man on top of her. He withdrew and this time Amy looked excitedly at the erection. She wheezed with the roughness as he seized her legs, lifted up her backside with one hand causing her to arch her spine, while the other grasped his penis and rubbed it against the vagina that the now thoroughly willing Amy was writhing and thrusting upwards desperately seeking penetration. "I'm gonna shag the arse off yer" he hissed
"Yeh?

Oh yeh!

Come on then" whispered Amy.

"Ask me" pleaded Vince.

"Ask you what" gasped the girl, eyes wide open.

"Ask me to shag you."

"Shag me, come on shag me, fuck me stiff, come on." Vince could tease no longer and thrust as violently as he could into her. Amy shrieked with pain and pleasure. She wanted to say things, rude disgusting things, but Vince's pelvic thrusts and gyrations were so physical that she could not speak. Every so often he would change positions and angles until he placed her legs over his shoulders. In this position his thrusts became erratic prompting a desperate plea "Don't cum in me Vince; I can't afford to get pregnant." But Vince was starting his climax and in no mood to care. It was only when Amy, sensing the impending rush of his ejaculation issued a further panicked warning, "If I get pregnant your wife will find out...." That did the trick; with one last brutal thrust he withdrew the length of his manhood spurting his cum over her tight lower belly and breasts, when the spasms had ceased he lay exhausted on Amy's still gyrating and unfulfilled form. Desperately she fumbled for his fingers and tried to force him to finish the job he had started but which he had only half-completed. With sharp finger nails of one hand digging into his buttocks and the others grabbing his limp member, she persisted until she felt him going hard again, but instead of his fingers bringing her climax as she had intended, it was his engorged penis that re-entered her, again thrusting rhythmically but this time with less urgency. Amy arched up leaning on her elbows taking as much of him into her as she could. Then she came noisily - and so did Vince. They held each other for a few minutes then Vince rose. As his spent member slid from her it raised an involuntary gasp. She watched dispassionately as he dressed and then she replaced her knickers and other clothes with the exception of her

Playtex, thinking 'that was a waste of money, he didn't even notice my fancy bra'. At the door they kissed and Vince fingered her a last time as if to say 'I've been there'. When he had left, he began to worry wether his wife would be waiting up. Would she be astute or suspicious enough to recognise the yeasty smell of spent sex?

Standing before the chest and lopsided shelf, Amy picked up the thirty shillings Vince had left, a one pound and a ten shilling note, putting them into a can that would have been a coffee tin if she could have afforded coffee to put in it. "Not bad" she said aloud "Thirty bob for a shag." Moving the short distance to the sink she filled the carbon encrusted kettle and was about to strike a match from the yellow box of swan vestas to light the gas, on one of the two rings of the small stove, when she felt the sudden sliding sensation caused by sperm filled mucus. Startled, she did a sharp intake of breath and expelled a surprised "ooh!" as it ran from her most intimate parts on to her inner thigh. She did not envisage that in just over nine months time Mark's little bedfellow would have a brother of his own to share his miserable existence and the one pound ten for sexual intercourse would not be the bargain it had seemed.

Chapter 25

Helen picked up Mark just before tea time and if she seemed nervous Amy could not see it. "He's been a proper good un he as, no trouble at all." That was true to a certain extent, there had been a feeling of despair in that house and Mark had decided to say as little as possible, waiting patiently for his Mother's return and giving rise to no complaint from his minder. On the bus ride home he thought of the sad-eyed youngster, who at his young mother insistence had waved goodbye. Something seemed strange to him, then he realised what it was, in all the time that he had been there the child had scarcely spoken a word and Mark did not even know his name.

"So you know what to say if Daddy asks you, ok?" Mark understood enough of what his Mother had told him. Mummy had gone for a Christmas drink with lots of ladies and a big girl had looked after him until Mummy got back later and he and his Mum had slept on the couch. Oh yes, and he could not remember any names or where the house was. That will have to do thought Helen. As they neared home her heart was pounding. "What on earth have you done? You silly woman" she scolded herself. "What's that mum?" asked her son.

"Nothing" then picking him up she looked deeply into his blue eyes. "Don't forget to say what mummy told you if anybody asks, otherwise daddy will hurt mummy." Helen felt it was a cheap shot but it worked. As he was lowered to the ground, her son was as determined as a five year old could be, that he would make sure no wrong word of his would cause harm to his mum. In the event there was no need to worry. Peter had been arrested for being drunk and disorderly and upon being released without charge at ten that morning, he had promptly entered the 'Crawley Arms' through the back door, for an out of hours drink, and there he remained still.

Helen was somewhat relieved by this unexpected Christmas gift, but she remained fearful of discovery. She had met Barry as arranged. They had seen a lot of one another lately and that was the reason for the neglect of her family. But last night was different. For the first time in her life she had found and made love to a truly gentle man. She still trembled when she contemplated how marvellous it had been, compared to the drunken rutting and animalistic purpose of procreation which until last night she believed was normal. Barry was an attentive lover and had come to genuinely love Helen for herself, admiring the qualities that her husband feared and despised.

That evening, while preparing the grocery lists for the following day's Christmas Eve shopping expedition, Helen found her concentration slipping continuously; it was hard to think of the Season of Goodwill when you wanted to be elsewhere and with someone else.   During an involuntary lapse of concentration she made a momentous decision. She would spend the rest of her life with Barry. Nothing would be allowed to get in the way of her intense feelings of love for this man and that, she admitted to herself guiltily, included her children.

Chapter 26

A Non-event, Christmas had been and gone and to all intents and purposes life had returned to its usual monotony, the children's moods matched the sleet and gloom that was January and February. March had brought winds that were so severe that they had caused damage to many roofs and buildings in the area. It was during a light April shower that one evening, T erry whispered to Mark.

"Look, I gotta tell you sumfin important." Sat on the big bed face to face he had his brother's full attention. "Mum has left us." The room disintegrated as Mark floated in a sea of disbelief, what on earth was Terry saying? Mother leaving him, why? Where? Never.

"Dad's downstairs crying." That also seemed impossible. Dads did not cry. "Mum left im a note, telling im she was leaving an' never coming back." As the room started to reassemble the floating sensation still persisted, but it was the words Terry blurted next that were to make this a particularly clear memorable event in his young life.

"An she as gone an' took our Mary wiv er as well."

Mark's despair, once the words had taken effect, was not due to the additional loss of his sister, but to the selfish deduction that it was Mary and not himself who commanded Helen's love. Throughout that night he sobbed intermittently feeling rejected and dejected. Terry showed understanding way beyond his years, placing his arm around his younger brother and vowed he would take care of him.

"Don't you go an' leave me Tell will you?" It was more of a desperate plea than a tearful appeal and prompted a most sincere response.

"Never, it's you and me now Mark, I will take care of you an I'll never leave you, I promise"

"Cross yer 'art an' 'ope to die, Tell?"

"Yeh cross me 'art an' 'ope to die Mark" and to validate the claim he made the sign across his chest. Comforted thus, the two brothers' started to drift away. The youngest boy had no idea how his brother Terry had been devastated by the note's revelations. These last weeks he had cooked, cleaned, looked after Mark, shopped and struggled in an effort to help ease the burden on his Mum. He had not taken it badly when he did not always receive fair recognition from any for his hardships. But now his Mother had left them and she had not even found time to say goodbye. Stifling back the tears he told himself that he was a man now and had to be strong for Mark's sake, and then he wondered if his sister, who was only just over a year older than him, already missed him as much as he missed her now. That note, with its few hastily scribbled lines, had destroyed his family, his brothers' and sister separated in uncertainty for the first time since birth.   Squeezing Mark's sleeping form to his chest, this little man not much bigger than the child he held so protectively, made one last statement before sleep finally carried him off.

"It's just us now Mark, jus me an you."

Downstairs, unaware of his sons' dramatic pact, Peter red-eyed and deflated slumped at the kitchen table reading in disbelief the words of the note yet again.

Chapter 27

Peter kept Terry off school to let him take care of Mark. For a few long weeks, life and Peter continued, waiting for a penitent Helen to return at any moment, once she had realised that Peter had learned his lesson.

Helen finally consented to meet on neutral ground to discuss the situation; their meeting place was Redmans cafeteria.

Peter was soon in no doubt as to Helens objections in the discussions firstly, she wished to know what she could expect in the way of recompense, namely household possessions or cash in lieu, and secondly to decide what arrangements were to be made for the children she had abandoned.

Once Peter had tried pleading, he went on to blackmail, using the fragile state of the two younger boys' as a lever for a conditional return.

Karl had not been shocked and in some ways was relieved that his mother was well out of harm's way. Helen knew this as she had met and spoken to him shortly after leaving, while Jack was more occupied with his impending release to care one way or another about his parent's problems. The welfare of the boys' however was a problem that required a speedy solution, but she would not allow her husband to blackmail her. Peter had considered Terry and Mark as his trump card. But now finding it useless, he resorted to threats of violence. This only brought a haughty mocking in response, Helen's sarcastic laughter, was forced and false.

"You are never gonna hurt me again you lanky streak of piss."

She glared with defiance, safe in the knowledge that the seething rage building up in her estranged husband would be constrained. The presence of Saturday morning customers and staff in the cafeteria ensured Peter's reasonable conduct. They parted as enemies, one vowing his wife would gain custody neither of money nor possessions, and the other realising this but desperately hoping that she would eventually.

She felt bitter remorse that even if she were to succeed in their rescue, she could provide no home for her sons.

That week Terry had missed school several times, much to Mark's delight. They were constant companions, so life actually seemed to be on the up and up. It was Friday and Peter had hardly visited the pub this last month, working when he felt he could and spending time round the house when he didn't go to the garage.

The first of the lodgers had already arrived, there were several somewhat strange paying guests at Castaires, mostly foreign, and they spoke poor English.

That evening Mark and Terry were sent to knock at each lodger's door, when the doors were opened Terry made the sullen request, "Rent Please."

The cash was deposited into a bag that Peter had provided, and on completion of their duties as rent collectors, they handed the cash bag to their father who had been sprucing himself up and who now had the resources for an enjoyable evening. "You off out Dad?"

"Nah, just thought I'd clean up a bit," Peter lied.

"Look, you've been a great help son, I want you to take this and get off to the pictures."

Terry looked at the two large silver coins in his hand. "B.. b.. but Dad, that's five bob!"

"Yeh an' you deserve every penny."

Terry had not been out for weeks and with this wealth he could join his mates for a Friday night at the Regal Cinema. Assured that Mark would be fine watching TV with his dad, he set off to catch the bus into town.

Terry had been gone fifteen minutes when Peter turned off the television. Mark looked up and saw his dad was holding his coat, "Come on lad, let's go see your mum."

Peter felt no remorse at lying to his second youngest child, as he had done so to get him out of the way. With Mark sat at his side, he drove for five miles arriving at a row of old brick built main road terraces. He brought the car to a stop outside number six, his sister Ethel's rented two up two down and Helen's refuge.

Helen, although having left, was not yet prepared to set up house with Barry, she still had sufficient moral fibre to wait a decent interval, secure in the knowledge that there would be accommodation for at least for her daughter if not for the boys'. Ethel had always been a good friend and was the first to offer support when the split came. Having Helen as a house guest had its advantages. As long as Peter thought he could keep an eye on his estranged wife, the less likely he was to resort to more direct efforts of revenge. More importantly, he still had no proof of any other correspondent's involvement, despite his growing suspicions.

Luckily, Barry was not going to be calling this weekend as he was finalising the split from his own marriage and trying to explain to a son and daughter that even though he was leaving, he loved them very much. His had been as a teenage wedding to a Dutch woman, whom he had met had met during wartime. When he was demobbed, Barry found himself teenage husband to a pregnant war bride. On returning to England, their relationship deteriorated to the point, where he was no more than a paying lodger, so much so, that even before meeting Helen he had asked for a divorce. This had been vehemently refused as his wife was a staunch Catholic who fully believed that marriage was for life, regardless of the extent of marital misery that had to be endured. This was the last time he would see either of his children for more than an odd fleeting glimpse as they were indoctrinated to believe he was the evil anti-Christ and although he often thought of them, was not heard to as much as mention their names again.

Mary stood paralysed with shock at seeing her father for the first time in over one month.

"Hello love." Peter spoke in a feigned act of sadness,

"Is your mum in?"

"Who is it Mary?"

Helen had joined her daughter and standing behind her suffered a similar reaction at the sight of Peter. Her first impulse was to slam the door before he could attack her, but at the sight of her youngest son now dragged confused and dishevelled from behind his father's back, she froze.

"We have to talk," hissed Peter. For a few seconds her gaze went from door to Mark, then to Mary, who thinking her mother was asking for advice, nodded slowly. The pair moved away from the door and let Mark through, Peter followed. Ethel was in the tiny kitchen and had heard all that had passed. Not particularly liking her brother and well aware of his foul temper, she came from behind the curtain that separated the main room from the tiny kitchen area at the bottom of a set of creaking wooden stairs. The stairs led to two small bedrooms, one which Ethel and her two children Frank and Sandra shared, the other which was only half the size was now temporarily occupied by Helen and Mary.

"Hello Peter, ow are you love, all right?"

As his sister had already answered her own question, he just
nodded "Well I've got to rush, sorry to leave you, but I suppose you
want to be alone anyway."

Grabbing her coat that hung at the back of the door, Ethel
disappeared in a show of cowardice.

"Well you better come in," said Helen, in a voice that quivered with
emotion, "and you better behave."

Peter shrugged, closed the door behind him and sat at the small
wooden table.   As he rested his arms on its top, the whole table
rocked on the uneven floor. Mark was looking at his mother, who
wanted to hold him so badly that she ached, but she could only rest
her hand on his head and ask his sister to remove his coat, "see if you
can find a biscuit in the kitchen."

Mary hustled Mark behind the curtain and found a part-full packet of
morning coffee; she passed several biscuit's to her brother, popping
one into her own mouth. She then sat at the bottom of the stairs and
pulled Mark down beside her.

On the other side of the curtain negotiations had begun, and soon
voices were raised and hostilities commenced. In an effort to shut out
the rowing Mark tried to draw Mary into conversation. "Hiya Mary!"
but he became silent again when he was given a heavy nudge
followed by "Shush."   It was obvious that Mary was far more
interested in the row than in what her little Brother had to say.   But it
was not nosiness and indifference to her sibling that had caused Mary
to act so. Sitting with the heavy rolling pin in hand she was readying
herself to rush to her Mother's defence, should temper's flare.

"Look. I'm telling you, there is no way I can cope with work and the
two boys'."

"What are you talking about? Terry's no trouble at all; I bet ees bin
doin all the bloody work round the house, while you've been sat on
your fat arse."

Peter ignored this tirade, although the only untruth was the reference
to his fat arse.

"The boy needs his mother," he repeated.

Peter's plan was to saddle Helen with as much in the way of
problems as he could, mainly in the shape of her youngest son. With
no room in this dump for him and the extra care his age demanded
there would be no way Helen could continue her own work, she
would be forced to return home to him with her tail between her legs

and wouldn't he make her pay then, the bitch.   This plan, however, was unravelling. Helen was not budging and shouted "An' I've told you I cannot possibly look after the little bleeder, it's impossible."

Peter rose, resting both fists clenched on the table and yelled back in her face. "You 'ave got no say in the matter, I've brought the little bastard 'ere and 'ere ee stays."

"I DON'T WANT HIM!" screamed the demented woman.

"AND NEITHER DO I!" yelled the man in reply. With only seven feet and a flimsy curtain as an obstruction, Mark had understood ninety percent of the conversation. Suddenly the discussions beyond the curtain were brought to a dramatic conclusion, Peter triumphantly storming out to his car and driving off at some speed while Helen stood in the street screaming.

"Come and take the little git home with you." But to no avail, the car and Peter had gone. Dejected, she turned to go indoors, as she did so she noticed her next door neighbour, a skinny hawk-faced beanpole of a woman, arms folded on a non-existent bosom, she had enjoyed the evening's unscheduled entertainment. "And what the ell are you looking at you poxy faced cow? ... Fuck off."

The neighbour, sensing Helen's rage, needed no further direction and vanished, the knocker on the door giving an involuntary bang as the door slammed behind her.

Mark did not cry easily, the whole situation was one of unreal melodrama - but sufficiently real enough to cause him to experience a strange emptiness, and an apathy bordering on the morose.   He was aware his father had just abandoned him and that for the second time a parent had either forgotten, or had shown no inclination, to say goodbye. The little boy did not understand that he was experiencing the mental anguish that all have to endure, when they lose a loved one.

He felt hungry and tired; hunger was a problem as he was frightened of being thrown out into the street by an angry mother, currently raving about the impossible situation she and Mary were in, because of his presence. He remained, his need to sleep was satisfied almost immediately. Mary was ordered to put him to bed; tonight there would be three of them sharing. Mary was horrified. "But Mum, he bloody well pisses the bed."

"Just get him off to sleep, I need to think. Get him to wee in the bucket before he gets in."

Mark was nudged up the stairs with a firm push in the back; he looked over his right shoulder at the half-packet of biscuit's wanting to ask for more. But another forceful shove sent him sprawling.

"Move it," Mary hissed threateningly, and another push forced him to comply.

The bedroom, although the smallest of the two, benefited from a small sash window. Floor space was practically non existent as it was lost to one large bed, a single wardrobe that leant at a crazy angle because a stubby corner leg was missing and replaced by an unequally sized house brick, and a small pale blue, hand-painted chest of drawers. Mark noticed that the top of this chest was his sister's territory, evident from the few possessions she had been permitted to take with her on the flight from Castaires.

Disrobed with a roughness borne from Mary's impatience, the boy was stripped to his grey baggy Y-fronts that had once been white, then grabbed by the shoulders and guided to the bucket in the far corner. Mark obeyed the command. "Hurry up," only when his sister conformed to his own request. "Don't look." Mary tut tutted mockingly, then averted her eyes, while he carried out his task.

The lavatory was outside at the rear of the the back-to-back terrace. It would have entailed a considerable walk to the courtyard that housed a red-brick privvy that was shared by the whole block. Most of the neighbours and the residents of number six found it more convenient to use a bucket at night, this would be emptied early in the morning. There was a strict ban on number two's. The turd embargo was a necessity, because the last thing that one wanted at five or six am was to cross paths with a neighbour when you were carrying a slopping pail of piss which contained several floating bankers. This practice caused a permanent odour of ammonia to permeate the houses making them particularly unpleasant, especially in summer.

The small boy lay in the dampness of the near slum, surrounded by peeling paint and ripped and faded wallpaper, he listened fearfully to the voices, clear and distinct below. This was entirely his fault, no wonder he was unwanted – well, with the exception of Terry. But his hero was not there and Mark wondered if he would find this terrible place and rescue him. Then a surreal horror conjured in his confusion gripped him; maybe Terry did not want him either. He shook his head violently from side to side on the thin pillow in an effort to dispel such a dreadful notion.

Hearing his Mother and sister coldly discussing him as a problem, he cried pitifully but almost silently. There would be no good night kiss, no comforting tuck up in bed, because whatever it was he had done, it had made him despicable and consequently alone.

Something changed in him that night, though he did not know what. Tears dried up and he turned onto his side. Pulling the coarse woollen blankets about his neck, his eyes became accustomed to the gloom. Illumination from an outside street-light mingled with the evenings fading light cast a smoky amber hue through dingy net curtains that in turn animated demonic shadows in a corner of the room.

The boy's first impulse was to cover his head with the blankets to escape, but instead he found solace and distraction in releasing one arm from the bedclothes to pick at a corner of the heavily embossed paper on the wall only inches from his face. Finger nails gathered plaster, as he dug deeply to release the next strip and before he became bored, he had removed a considerable patch. Screwing up the bit's of paper and plaster as tightly as he could, Mark thrust them behind the mattress where the head board should have been, until the debris fell on to the bare floor boards.

Flinging himself over and away from his vandalism he recognised the smell of hairspray and 'Chanel No. 5' that immediately identified Helen. Burying his head into the pillow he snuffled like an over enthusiastic puppy until he found the nucleus of the semi-stale scent and for a few brief seconds he held on to that heady perfume, it reminded him of what had been, then as if wanting to break free from its cruel spell threw himself back to face the wall, fighting the covers angrily with hands and feet.

Downstairs and on their third cup of tea, the apologetic landlady and sister in law, auntie Ethel, had just rejoined Helen and Mary. The women made contingency plans and their problems seemed less insurmountable. So that they even allowed themselves the luxury of laughter.

On the other side of town, another small boy felt betrayed and abandoned; his little brother, whom he had sworn to protect with his life, had gone to live with his mother. Terry imagining the open-armed welcome that Mark would have received, while he himself was deserted and forgotten.

Peter smiled a knowing smile, with the inconvenience of the extra burden and too little money, he told himself. "She'll be back." That night Mark ceased to be anyone's baby. Infused with his parents' venom and lack of concern, he pondered before falling asleep which one of them hated him the most.

Chapter 28

Summer had arrived; the heat of the sun was relentless at midday but more forgiving by early evening. Outside, under the window of number six, his back resting against the wall, Mark sat in the dust and grime of the busy A58 thoroughfare. The stone flags adjoining the walls of the house received shade so were cool, but filthy.

It was in this dirt that the small boy was contentedly playing, first drawing aimless patterns with his finger, then on discovering a pathetic grime-encrusted dandelion fighting for survival in its polluted refuge betwixt wall and pavement, he used a flat wooden lollipop stick that he had found in the gutter, to play Mark the gardener, but he only succeeded in snapping off the weed where it protruded from brick, dirt and stone. Mark had a transitory notion of ingratiating himself with his mother, but decided, he did not want to give her, 'his' flower.

Laying his prize bloom aside, he excavated the dirt from the gaps between the pavement slabs, penetrating the dust to reach the damp soil beneath. Soon he had enough muck to make a small pile. For the next thirty minutes this heap became a castle, a garage, a mountain to be conquered. He reached the summit of Everest and claimed it for Mark Dacey and Richton by placing a flagpole that resembled a spent matchstick, atop the peak, and he did all without the aid of Sherpa Tensing. He was heedless of the passers-by and most passers-by were unmindful of him.

An old man in voluminous grey flannel trousers, spotless white shirt, with the optional collar removed and sleeves rolled to his elbows, was enjoying a promenade along the main road. He wore dark green braces and the obligatory working man's, flat cap. At seventy-five years of age it was ten years since he had been amongst the ranks of the employed and he still hated his enforced idleness. He beamed down at the grubby urchin at his feet. "Ee ta be young again eh? If only, 'ad be den theer wi' thi." He made a series of shuffling side-steps to avoid the prostrate form of the oblivious mountaineer. Returning to his evening constitutional, he smiled in recollection of his own distant but 'not so long ago' childhood. As he shuffled away, Mark from his horizontal location noticed that the old gentleman was wearing worn plaid carpet slippers.

Mary alighted from the blue and cream double deck bus. The sign on the front informed passengers that its final destination, before returning to Richton Town Centre was Ludbarrow via Worthing Lake.

Ludbarrow was a village four miles further down the road, at the side of which Mark was sitting. Worthing Lake was a local beauty spot with a manmade body of water. It had been formed to provide a back up supply for the nearby Richton-Leeds canal. In its hey day before the motor car became an achievable dream for the working family, it had been very popular with thousands of mill workers who found it within easy reach of the little train station close by. The rare halcyon holiday's enjoyed by the cotton workers were still fondly remembered by many, and Worthing Lake was referred to as, 'The weighvers seaport.'

These days the only time this tiny lake saw large crowds was on Bank Holidays, or during the annual fun fair, but it still saw its fair share of weekend picnickers and children, who found relief from stifling summer heat by paddling from a small shingled beach.

This particular bus made a circular detour down a fairly steep hill called 'Halliday Lane.' The delights of Worthing Lake were a far cry from Mark's main road playground, but the boy was more content today than at any other time during his occupation of number six.

Brother studied sister as she waved up to some school chums on the top deck. Mary was immaculate as she always was, in a brilliantly starched white blouse and sharply pleated grey gymslip. The mid-green school blazer was folded neatly over her left arm, while a worn tan, leather satchel, heavy with books, hung from her right shoulder, its thin strap biting into her flesh. As she walked towards him from the bus stop, the weight of the satchel imposed a slightly lopsided gait. "What the bloody ell do you think your doing?"

"Playin'."

"Just get up now you dirty little sod, get inside. What must the neighbours think?"

Mark, in an effort to curb his sister's admonishment, produced the wretched dandelion, "Ere Mary, it's for you, I picked it meself." His big sister looked curiously at the limp wild flower in her brother's grasp.

"Throw that dirty thing away and get inside now." I'm going to get changed out of my uniform then I'll have to clean you up before Helen gets home."

So saying, Mary disappeared to the bedroom to change; Mark stripped off his shirt and tried to turn on the one cold water tap. Hot water in the house had to be produced by boiling a kettle, and that was a luxury this small boy would have to forgo. "Ere I'll elp yer." The offer came from Frank, Mark's cousin.

"Fanks Frank."

Gratitude for Frank's assistance was a little premature, as the boy who was same age as Mark's sister proceeded to grasp the blue rubber spout wedged over the running tap and directed the stream of water all over the younger boy.

"Don't do that Frank, please." Laughing, the bigger boy let go of the nozzle and the water splashed into the stone sink. The laughter became more enthusiastic when he observed water cascading onto the flagged floor from Mark's drenched head and face.

Mark started to cry. The bully, for that's what Frank was, had done everything in his power since Mark's arrival, to make the young boy as miserable as possible. It always ended in his tears and always ended with the bully punching Mark in the stomach, where it would leave no tell-tale evidence of assault, so that the victim would be accused of being a cry baby. Doubled over, the little boy stifled his sobs into sporadic gasps; he was educated to the familiar drill of having to gain control of his emotions fast or a second blow would be on its way. Derisively, Frank prodded the child then sneeringly demanded his sister's whereabouts.

"Sh..sh..she's upstairs getting changed," replied the bedraggled wretch with a sobbing stammer.

"Is she now?"

Frank gave a lecherous smirk. Grabbing the boy by the throat, he hissed into his terrified face, spraying drops of spittle with every word. "I'm going upstairs an looking through the keyhole, you better keep look out an tell me if anyone is coming."

By anyone he meant Helen or his mother Ethel. Cat like, taking two steps at a time, he made his way as silently as he could, trying to avoid the loose floorboards that creaked alarm when stood on. Kneeling, he put his eye to the keyhole having to make a conscious effort to halt his heavy breathing. "Fuck!" he whispered with disappointment. The Peeping Tom had been foiled; the large iron key was in the lock and prevented any sight into the room beyond the door. Creeping back down the stairs he told himself he would have better luck next time.

Finding the cowering Mark where he had left him, Frank for some reason felt he had to humiliate his young cousin. "I've just seen your Mary's tits," lied the bully. Mark was horrified; he knew what tits were. There were always the smutty conversations of the school playground that helped fill in a child's educational blanks.

But until that moment he had not even wondered if his sister possessed them. Any further discourse on the subject was stymied with the appearance of a casually dressed Mary. "What are you two at?" Mark looked on innocently while Frank leered "oh not much."

Turning a searching, suspicious gaze on her Brother brought a swift response.

"Frank hit me."

"So what!" replied Mary, offering neither sympathy nor support. Consequently deflated, the boy avoided Frank's hate-filled countenance,

"Tell -Tale –Tit," Frank snapped.

The first line of an insulting rhyme, used at other children that dared to tell tales, went. 'Tell -Tale -Tit, your mother can't knit, your father can't walk with a walking stick.' However, in this instance it only served to prompt the dejected youngster to an afterthought,

"Oh yeh," he weakly offered his only other fragment of information, "an' ee went up stairs an' peeped through the keyhole an ee said ee saw your tit's."

Mary at first could not believe her ears, but one look at the blustering crimson-faced yob, told her there was something in her sibling's words. "You did what?"

"Nah I was only kiddin 'im." Frank grinned nervously, then feeling a shade cowardly told himself, well what if I did, what can she do about it?

"You did what? You filthy little pervert."

Once more Frank flushed beetroot red and once more he felt belittled by this girl, half his size, and him the hardest lad on the block. All the lads ran away from him. "Ah big deal, I couldn't see owt anyway the keyhole was blocked."

If the confession helped assuage his feelings of macho inadequacy, he found the benefits very short-term. 'SMASH! Mary's clenched fist struck Frank in the eye, his legs gave way and he immediately felt nauseous. SMACK! This time the same fist struck the side of his nose and top lip. He had never been hit so hard in his life and, almost fainting, wilted onto his knee, grabbing Mary in a pathetic bear-hug and attempting to limit the effectiveness of the attack by pinning his aggressor's arms.

It was to no avail. Mary easily released his grip with an elbow, flattening the other side of his nose. Once unencumbered, one hand grabbed his mid-length greasy black hair and the other made a clenched fist, SMACK! "You" SMACK! "dirty" THUD! "Bastard" SMASH!

With every blow, the infuriated female added yet another expletive, until she became too exhausted to continue the beating. Wheezing loudly, she leant back on the unstable table and surveyed the damage. Although Frank's punishment started in the tiny kitchen, he had ended up in the front room, a quivering, blubbering coward begging for mercy, his face bloodied and bruised. The victor's knuckles were heavily grazed but she was oblivious to the pain. She realised the extent of the bully's injuries and thought on how she would explain the situation to his mother, and her's.

Mark had watched the whole thing in hypnotic trepidation, delighting in his tormentor's downfall but fearful of possible retribution.

"Come here Mark love."

Mary had calmed down and in soothing tones she explained to Mark how they must tell their mother and aunt how Frank had tried to break into the bedroom, and how when Mary had warned him she would tell his mother, he had attacked her. With her alibi secure, she no longer felt she needed to be as pleasant. "Don't get it wrong, or else!" She nodded towards the snivelling heap.

Mark understood clearly. "Mary"

"What?" asked his sister irritably.

"Do you think Frank will die?"

"Dunno, doubt it. I mean no, course he won't."

"Aw, I wish he would."

Mary never heard the last remarks, as she was busy at the sink cleaning up. The wet semi-dressed five year old knelt by the side of the heap and whispered into his ear, "If you touch me again, my sister will batter you." Then he lied. "She told me."

Lie or not, it was a threat that stood him in good stead, and Frank was never a problem again.

Mary glibly recounted her story to Helen and Ethel, backed up by Mark's enthusiastic nods. Helen decided her nephew had learned his lesson, but a disgusted Ethel took up a wide leather strap and beat the nether end of her obnoxious offspring, until she was drained and he was sent to bed, a thoroughly whipped cur.

Eating supper that night, Mark pensively mulled over the evening's events and decided there and then, that he was never going to look at his sister's tits.

Chapter 29

Barry called most evenings to take Helen out and occasionally Mary would be invited to accompany them. Mark was always left behind with auntie Ethel, who, as soon as the lodgers had disappeared, took the money given to her for baby-sitting and leaving the young boy in the company of her daughter Sandra, she departed for her favourite pub.

The Wagon and Horses was just a few doors away, next to a grocery shop. On rare occasions Mark and his sister, armed with the few spare coppers that their Mother had managed to wrest from the austere weekly budget, would climb the grocery store's two stone steps and make their all important choices from the jars of sweets on the shelves behind the counter or from the chocolate tray in front. Sometimes there was a queue and they would shuffle in an orderly line until it was their turn to be served. At other times a breathless woman would push in front saying, "You don't mind do you love? but I'm late getting th' usbands tea on." The loaf of unsliced bread, bottle of sterilised milk and pot of jam were already being put into a string bag by the shop assistant, even before permission had been given. So there was not much that could be done in the face of such effrontery.

Mary made the observation that on any visit made to 'Two Steps,' one could always find at least two women hanging back to chat with the shop-keeper and in the quieter periods of business drinking tea and gossiping, about current affairs, and generally putting the world to rights.

The Harridan's resembled the cartoons on seaside post cards, with heads full of lurid spiky curlers covered with brightly coloured scarves. They wore starched checked cotton aprons, and cigarettes hung precariously from the sides of their mouths. The cigarettes were not removed to chat. Faces contorted from the smoke and ash finding its way into their eyes, the smokers would talk from the sides of their mouths.

They habitually accosted other regular customers who because they had more pressing engagements were unable to stop and chat. When they had left the shop with cheery farewells, they would be the subject of whispered character assassinations. The tea drinkers never failed to have something detrimental to say about their home life, appearance or morals. Mary was amused by the way the group of gossipers changed at regular shifts, and each one in turn would have their personal lives scrutinised by the resident corner shop magistrates. Invariably one of them would say on leaving, "Well I can't stand here talking all day," never dreaming for a moment that her so called friends were only smiling and waving until she was out of sight, before spinning their heads to face each other like chickens pecking corn.

"Well I know I shouldn't say, but if you promise not to breath a word."

Conditions had deteriorated at number six to the point that Helen realised they could not impose on Ethel much longer and although her sister-in-law needed the extra rent money, the woman found sharing her bedroom with two teenage children uncomfortable and socially restrictive.   Towards the end of July on a lovely Saturday morning, brother and sister returned from the weekly shop and found Barry sitting at the wobbly table opposite Helen. They had the house to themselves as all the others had caught the bus into town. One look at their mother's beaming face told them something had enlivened her flagging spirits.

"We've got a surprise for you two."   The kids put the heavy baskets down and waited in anticipation. "We are moving."

Over the next hour the children were told how Barry had found a cottage nearby that had two bedrooms, a kitchen, living room and as the cottage was on a hill it had an extra floor at the front. The ground floor basement would be decorated and used as a study bedroom for Mary. Mark was pleasantly surprised to find the black mood into which they had all desended, could be so easily expelled. He settled at the table, chin on arms, listening in excitement as plans were made.

Their few possessions could be transported from number six with one car trip. As the time was already 10am they would have to go immediately to the 'Sally' and other second hand furniture shops to buy as much furniture as possible with their meagre savings.

Several minutes later the four spilled out of the front door and there Helen and Mary stopped.   Slightly stunned, Helen enquired, "Where's your car Barry?"

Barry had been very proud of his immaculate dove grey Standard so it came as a shock to see its replacement - a tatty black Austin that had at one time in its life served as a private hire vehicle. "I had to sell it, we need the money."

Moments later they were on their way to town and their first port of call- the Salvation Army. The 'Sally,' undertook house clearances, mostly on behalf of grieving relatives in cases of bereavement. They also recieved donations of household goods, from generous sponsors, who had had the good fortune to move on to better things. The goods would be put into the sally army's salerooms. The prices always compared very favourably with the other second hand shops, so much so that one morning a week traders were allowed to buy there at slightly reduced rates. It was a very agreeable state for all: Salvation in heaven for the generous, charity for the poor from the proceeds of the sales, and affordable furniture for eager bargain-basement home builders, and sly deals on the side put a few quid in certain less virtuous back pockets.

Arriving at their first port of call was a relief. The Austin missed, backfired and stalled throughout their journey to the acute embarrassment of the driver and his passengers, with each bang and involuntary stop they felt more keenly the inquisitive, sometimes amused attentions of nearby pedestrians. "Don't worry, I'll sort it out later," said Barry as he was trying to close the driver's door for the third time.

Finally he succeeded, and passed through the dark blue double doors of the saleroom to catch up to Helen and the two children. They had escaped from that jalopy as fast as they could, not wanting to be associated with that particular vehicle.

For the best part of an hour the two adults haggled and bargained, and sometimes Mary would participate. The result was, that as they suffered the ignominy of continuing their quest in the black banger, they had paid for and had been promised delivery in two days time of, a well worn, heavy, fabric settee and matching arm chair, an assortment of four odd dining chairs, two rickety bentwood bedroom chairs, a glazed cabinet, a decent blue and cream kitchenette unit and two single bed frames. They had declined the lumpy, black, striped mattresses as they were heavily stained and looked as if they already had long term occupants. A particular acquisition, an upright, walnut inlaid, iron frame piano, put Mary into such a good mood; she was even being nice to her brother.

By 5p.m. the small group had visited almost every second-hand establishment in the district. Completing the checklist of wanted and must haves, now tired but contented in a job well done, the quartet arrived to an empty house and sat down to eggs, bacon and beans prepared by a much happier Helen.

"I don't know when we are going but it's soon, an' it's a big house 'an am getting me own room."

Mark was explaining in every thrilling detail the events of yesterday to the next-door-but-one's kids he had made friends with over his time at number six. Colin was a big boy of nine; his sister Marion was a pretty, seven-year-old with long dark hair. Steven was their three-year-old baby brother.

"My mum told me that it is only at the bottom of Buckley Road, so it's only five minutes walk, we will still be able to see each other and play," said Marion.

Mark had reservations. To move only five minutes down the road seemed to misrepresent some of the importance of the adventure, but Marion had only meant to allay the younger boy's fears of separation, she could not have known that in all the excitement her little friend had not entertained any fear of separation from those he was leaving behind.

Marion's mother called her children in for Sunday lunch, from pavement where they had been sitting. They disappeared inside promising to come out to play later, Mark could not help feeling that he was missing something. Then the delicious smell of the roast-beef dinner and the rumbling in his stomach reminded him that the something he was missing was dinner.

Inside number six Ethel had already left for the Wagon and Horses and Sandra and Frank had gone off with friends to occupy their day. Mary had put the two plates onto the rickety table each containing beans on toast.

"Where's me mum?"

"I've told you already, they've gone to the house to paint it an' clean up and stuff."

Satisfied with the brusque reply Mark finished his meal in silence. Mary and her brother spent the afternoon, one studying at the table the other playing alone in the back courtyard. For reasons unknown his playmates were not allowed out, so in a world of childish fantasy he remained alone, fighting dragons and various foes with a stick until the arrival of Barry and Helen.

"We are going to take you and show you the house," declared an exultant Helen.

'The Black Banger' was behaving much better now that Barry had changed the spark plugs, contact breaker points and condenser. They arrived at number 2 Saxon Place, Buckley Road with no unscheduled stops and without provoking slack-jawed gawping from passers-by. Barry had stopped the car outside a row of three-storey cottages on a steep incline. He placed a house brick behind the rear tyre as an added precaution, to the banger's dodgy hand-brake. "Usually it's ok if you leave it in first, but it's started jumping out of gear now," explained Barry with an acquiescent shrug.

Helen led the way followed Indian file by Mary then Mark, while Barry was rear guard. Ignoring the front door they filed up the side of the cottages on a narrow uneven dirt track turning almost immediately to gain access to the back of the cottages. A black lettered sign on grubby white background was fastened to a crumbling wall announcing to all that this was 'Saxon Place.'

Passing a mushroom-coloured door on their left, they found in front of them a blue door, next to which was a small window. On the pavement below the door's one step was a warning in white chalk, 'WET PAINT.' Turning the mortise-lock key, Helen opened the door by pushing the unpainted letterbox. "Don't touch anything, everything is still wet."

As his mother raised her voice to accentuate the threat, Mark was well aware all that eyes were on him. Inside they stood in a small kitchen that even empty had trouble accommodating four people. This part of the house was a single storey extension, with blue slate roof. On the wall with the window was an old green and black gas cooker, which thanks to elbow grease and scouring powder, was now spotless. It had been left by the previous tenants, considered too good to throw out. The papered walls had been painted in an off-white distemper and the skirting-boards and woodwork a battleship grey.

Through an aperture, where at one time there had hung a door, was the living room. This was about sixteen feet long by a little over fifteen feet wide. Through a large bay window the paleness of the failing evening's light illuminated the almost square parlour. The white net curtains had been gathered up and tucked into their supporting wires, to prevent them from touching the freshly-painted sills and frame. Reflections sparkled from panes that had been cleaned with vinegar and newspaper. The light played on the beige and orange embossed circular patterns of the newly- papered room. Barry had worked throughout the night to create the transformation.

On the left, as they looked at the window, was a brown and cream open tiled fireplace and where they stood was a door that hid the stairs to the two bedrooms.

The first was a very small room with a sash window that looked out over the kitchen annex offering only slate roof and brick wall as a vista. Once a small bed and a tea chest, painted china blue and resplendent with jolly pictures. that would act as a toy chest took their place, the room would be at capacity. A landing of six by three feet led to the master bedroom which, being above the living room, was of a similar size.

Mary also noticed that the previous occupant of Mark's bedroom had also been a little boy and the wallpaper had pictures of trains all over it. This made the room seem even smaller but Mark loved it immediately. 'All well and good' thought his sister, 'but what about her accommodation?' For that they had to return down to the bottom of the stairs back to the living room.

The door to the ground floor was in the corner opposite to the bay window and adjacent to the doorway from the kitchen. As the adults led the way they had to duck to avoid the underside of the stairs leading to the bedrooms, the two youngest having no problem. The room was identical in proportion to the living room. It had a large sash window that lay under the bay and an old Lancashire range that had not been used for year's, was built into the chimmney breast. Next to the window was the door which led out onto the paved main road where they had parked the car. The room smelled damp and the stone flag floor made it seem more Spartan, but Mary was already chatting animatedly about what could and would be done to turn this into her very own palace. "MUM look!"

The whoop brought everyone's attention to the object that now held Mark in its hypnotic sway. A rusted heap of tin plate that had at one time been a child's pride and joy. "It's an army jeep!" gasped the incredulous boy, and no matter if his sister did say it was a pile of crap, to him it was a thing of beauty.

It took a lot of false promises of renovation and fixing up to prise Mark away from his find, and over the next days it seemed Christmas had come early; he found the waiting for the following weekend's big move unendurable. Mysteriously the Jeep disappeared.

Friday night saw Mary baby-sitting Mark, while Helen and Barry arranged the furniture that had arrived midweek. Helen had a couple of days off work feigning illness, an excuse to receive delivery of the furniture and complete preparations for the imminent move, but she was 'sick, of decorating and cleaning,' as she mentioned on more than one occasion. Alone, she had moved all but the heaviest items, and with Barry's help, by late Friday evening, they had completed the tasks. Looking about and satisfied with a job well done, they called it a day.

Barry dropped Helen off at number six then went back to Saxon Place. He had moved his scant belongings from his digs earlier.

Mary was still waiting up but her brother had surrendered to sleep an hour before, despite his insistence that he was so excited that he would never get to sleep. Mary questioned Helen as to the readiness of her room and fidgeted elatedly as she listened to a detailed summary of the day's work schedule. Her mother assured her all was well.

Once his eyes opened, it took all of thirty seconds for Mark to realise that he was on his own in the bed and noisy voices downstairs told him that the rest had started the final move without him. The truth was, Barry had turned up at 7a.m. and knocked gently on the door. Helen had been up since six, as had her industrious daughter. After they ghosted around the house picking up and packing the last bit's and pieces, Barry had taken their belongings and Helen back to Saxon Place. By the time Mark was dressed and ready it was 8a.m.

Mary was waiting in the front room taking her leave of auntie Ethel, who had risen to say goodbye and good luck to Helen. Brother and sister were to set off hand in hand for the ten-minute walk to their new home. It seemed to auntie Ethel, as she hugged the two children, that they were emigrating rather than moving less than one mile down the road. Ethel waved one more time and went inside. Closing the door behind her, she tightened the belt on her skimpy towelling housecoat. She then went into the kitchen to make a cup of tea. As she sat at the wobbly table sipping her strong sweet brew Ethel felt her usual optimism somewhat deflated. With her lodgers gone, the interest and excitement that she had come to enjoy left with them. Even the thought that after nearly three months she would have a bedroom to herself again failed to raise her spirits and as her own children started to stir upstairs, oblivious to the earlier farewells,

Auntie Ethel looked about her partially abandoned slum and spoke aloud with an air of inescapability, "My God, what a shit hole."

Skipping down the main road holding hands with Mary, a small boy was in a state of contentment greater than he could recall in his five-and-a-half years. His ritual request for sweets was refused as they passed *Two Steps*. "It's too early for sweets, you haven't had your breakfast yet." Unperturbed, his bliss remained undiminished. He came second to his longer-legged sister, in a one-sided race up the steep approach to their new abode. Extra impetus was added when the girl shouted back at her adversary with glee, "last one there is a smelly pig."

Mary had also decided the location of the finish line, which happened to be the point where she was, as she put it, *knackered*. Panting uncontrollably, they pushed open the back door of 2 Saxon Place, becoming momentarily wedged as they both tried to get through the opening at the same time. The boy lost out in this struggle as well, with a wriggle of her hips and a firm push from her elbow, Mary sent the lad back down the steps he had just climbed.

"Oi, that's enough mucking about you two." Helen was bustling happily in the kitchen. The appearance of her breathless but energetic children, rather than exasperate, enhanced her domestic joy. Barry was putting some finishing touches to downstairs and the smell of a full English breakfast, intermingled with fresh paint and wallpaper paste, welcomed them to a celebratory morning repast; the first in their new home.

Chapter 30

"But why do I ave to go to school?" It had been left to Mary to take Mark to St. James for the first day at his new primary school. Helen had told her that she had wanted to take him, but she could not afford any more time off work. So his sister it was that had dragged his unenthusiastic body from his slumbers, giving a silent prayer of thanks to the powers that may be for smiling on her and for seeing fit to spare the inconvenience of a wet bed.

Adroitly, she produced a soft-boiled egg accompanied with buttered and de-crusted soldiers of sliced white bread. On his insistence his tea was poured into 'his cup', a small white beaker adorned with the picture of a yellow duckling. It had originally held a chocolate egg, one of two he had been given on the most recent Easter Sunday. Two-and-a-half spoonfuls of sugar and enough milk turned the brew into the tepid beverage he relished, the dregs of which he had just spit back into the cup. "Tea leaves, you went an put tea leaves in."

In her haste, the girl had forgotten to use the red plastic tea strainer, instead pouring directly from the large white and blue-striped teapot. "You know I don't like tea leaves," whined her brother, convinced it had been a deliberate act. "Ptah blah phtt," the boy spit out several times in an effort to expel the uninvited, bitter fragments.

Ignored by his sister, he finally cleared the last remnants by wiping his tongue vigorously on a red-checked cotton tea towel that lay across the back of his chair.

The school was conveniently located not more than three hundred yards from home, but it entailed one major drawback, Leeds Road. This very busy main thoroughfare over the Pennines and on to Yorkshire separated home and school, St. James was set back from the road's dangers by the width of the paved footpath. A heavy steel tubular frame ran half the length of the school frontage, its purpose was to protect the pupils from traffic. The frame was twisted in places at crazy angles where vehicles had collided with the barrier. This barrier had a second function, to channel the pupils to a small gap in the fence, where for forty minutes in the morning, and forty five minutes in the afternoon, they would encounter the 'Lollipop lady.' Regardless of climate, she was always resplendent in a long white plastic McIntosh, shiny black Wellingtons and flat, black peaked cap. She carried the all important symbol of power a black and white lollipop sign, with the single word of command emblazoned across the disc, 'STOP.' She traipsed back and forth in all weathers, guiding her charges to the safety of the educational establishment in the morning, escorting the more excited throng of children escaping from a prison of learning in the afternoon. At the crossing an impatient and agitated Mary held her dejected brother by the arm and waited for the signal from the 'lollipop Lady' to cross. As the crowd of noisy children, and in some cases mothers' and guardians (although most children seven and over were unaccompanied) passed their officer of the highway, many of them hailing her with a "Good morning." Others would say "Thank you Mrs. Green." The sixty-two-year-old ex-office clerk would beam and reply aptly to each well-wisher, amazingly seeming to know the name of the entire mob.

Mary's chagrin was due to the impending arrival of her school bus to Farley where the grammar school was situated. Mary was never late, although on this and every future morning she would insist that she was positive she would be, the blame always resting with Mark, and to be fair if she had been late on this morning the blame would have rested in the correct place. "It's coming!" she cried and on reaching the wide open double doors of the school pushed Mark through, shouting as she departed that he must take care to cross with the 'Lollipop Lady', to return by himself that afternoon and reminding him he knew where the back door key was hidden.

Why anyone went to the bother of concealment however was hard to understand as everybody used the same trio of hiding places: A, under the matt, B, under a bucket or plant pot, or C, under a loose house brick forming part of the outside toilet wall. Until the time it was deemed safe for Mark to take himself to school, this morning ritual would start and finish in the same way. Mary was concluding this first such ritual by running for the bus stop thirty yards away, heavy satchel swinging, beret slipping, arriving at the end of the queue just in time to board. Mark concluded his part in the proceedings by waving forlornly at the bus carrying his protector away. As always Mary, her duty done, overlooked his existence until they met again.

"Hiya Mark. Is this your first day?"

Confused, the boy turned to discover who knew his name, his confusion changing to joy born from relief. Long dark hair cascaded over white-bloused shoulders, Marion France wore a plain navy dress, white knee- length socks, her feet shod with a pair of well-worn but well-polished shoes. Mark had not seen Marion or her brothers' since that last day of play before he had left auntie Ethel's. "Hiya Marion. I din't know you came ere."

"Oh yes, I started here in the tweenies class when I was five."

St. James was a typical Victorian village school, built from red brick, with a profusion of square, iron-framed windows, a large wooden-framed glazed section in the centre of the building provided ample light for most of the second and third floors. "Come on, I'll show you where to go." Her companion learned that although they were in the main reception area of the school, they had to bypass the large stairway leading to the main hall on the second floor, pass several classrooms and go through a door behind the stairs into a corridor that led out into the 'big playground'. The 'small playground' was on the other side of the school and primarily under the jurisdiction of the classes containing the school's youngest members. The 'big playground' was crammed with laughing, playing children, some stood in twos or threes comparing trinkets or small toys smuggled into the school in their deep pockets. Larger groups had leaders who controlled and marshalled them into order for some popular playground game. Isolated individuals, who had neither the courage nor the opportunity to join in, milled around the perimeters longing for some friendly arm to drag them into the happy melee.

A privileged student, one who had either done excellent work or who had arse-kissed his way into the job, was at a doorway ringing the large, brass, school bell with its polished mahogany handle. As if transformed by magic, the noisy horde quietened to a murmur and in seconds as if entranced, they formed orderly lines.

"Come on now!" roared a teacher. "Straighten those lines, boys' go left, girls' to my right." "Stop that talking; I will not tolerate this infernal row."

All chatter ceased and the duty teacher addressed the two lines again in a more sedate tone, "Now, that's better, Girls', you were the best behaved so you may enter first."

One boy unintentionally whispered, "Aw it's not fair!" too loudly and was heard by the teacher.

"Who said that?" screamed the adult. Dozens of hands now pointed unanimously to a scruffy urchin, condemning him in unity. "Bamber. I might have known. See me at playtime and we will discuss the meaning of what is fair and what is not fair." The urchin looked sullenly at the floor. "Did you hear what I just said boy?" ranted the official.

"Me Sir? What Sir? I mean yes Sir," blurted the flustered individual. "See that you also remember to come to see me at morning break." This time his manner oozed menace.

"Yes sir," answered the unfortunate wretch.

The last of the girls' had entered through the doorway above which the word 'Girls' was carved into a stone lintel. "Lead on" urged the teacher, "smartly now!" and the boys'' line passed through the doorway which announced 'Boys.' Up the main stairway the boys' tagged on to the end of the girls' line to enter the main hall and filed into rows of wooden school chairs; girls' sat on the left and boys' on the right. Facing the seated pupils was a staged area on which were assembled the staff, smart, clean and dour. Mark looked about in wonder. The silence was transformed into a cacophony which was distorted by the height of the vaulted ceiling.

"Silence!" roared another teacher, this time an older, tweed-suited female wearing heavy make-up and highly polished brown brogues.

Once again a hush descended. The silence had endured for almost a minute when the Headmaster, Mr. Conrad, appeared dressed, in a dull, dark-green, three-piece suit over which he wore a gown, and at an angle on his balding head sat a mortar. His approach prompted the staff, followed by the children, to stand. The noise of wooden chairs being pushed back caused a deafening banging and scraping, before silence was once again restored.

Mr. Conrad was a pompous, wheezing, tall overweight gentleman his chubby, round face, made all the more dish-like by large round, metal- rimmed spectacles, which gave the impression of a grandiose fat owl.

"We will sing hymn number forty seven from the blue books."

The pupils bent in unison and chose one of two books that had been placed on the floor in front of every two chairs. Mark's neighbour on his right absent-mindedly turned to the correct page, then held the book in such a position as to allow them to share the old version of the Church of England book of Prayer and Hymns. Mark looked up from the small print, to see one of the teachers tapping a wooden ruler on the back of a chair. Galvanised by this cue, the music teacher who, was the only person in the room to remain seated, began to strike the keys of a highly polished, upright piano with great passion, leading the congregation into 'Onward Christian Soldiers.'

Most of the boys' liked this hymn because it was about soldiers.
If it was about armies and stuff, it had to be good.

Mark blah-blah-blahed his way through two hymns, hardly looking
at the book, while the boy who was holding it confidently sang the
wrong words for most of the time, pretending he could read the
complicated script.   The boys' knelt in prayer in response to Mr.
Conrad's sonorous tone. "Let us pray."   Mark noticed that the staff
did not kneel, but simply bowed their heads in pious acquiescence.

After praying, the boys' were told "Arise," then, "Be seated,"
followed by another infernal racket as once again chairs were
dragged, this time back to their original positions.

Here and there mischievous faces made merry of the legitimate
commotion they were making, then, as always there was calm. The
Head spoke for fifteen minutes, offering a brief welcome to all,
especially to those students for whom this new term was the first at
St. James Church of England Primary School. He also enlightened
them with a description of the establishment's draconian rules of
conduct, drawing special attention to the punishments that rewarded
disobedience.

Mr. Conrad made several more announcements, extolling the virtues
of the school's extra curricular activities. Then he called "All stand"
and "Lead out."   Teachers descended from the stage and flanked the
children swiftly shepherding the re-forming lines out of the main hall
in the direction of their relevant classrooms.

Mark hung back in uncertainty and fear until others in his line
overtook him as though he did not exist. He had ended up at the
entrance to the Hall, alone until a deep voice assured him that his
was a temporary isolation.   Spinning, wide eyed, and mouth agape,
the boy stammered when faced by the daunting figure of the
omnipotent Headmaster. "I… I....Im.. L..Lo…Los…" stammered the
child.

"What's that? Speak up boy! What's that you say?"

Mr. Conrad spoke as if he himself was hard of hearing and as it
transpired, this was the truth of the matter. "I think he is trying to tell
you that he is lost sir."

For the second time that morning Marion had been there to rescue
him, which was no coincidence as she had looked for him on leaving
assembly. "Lost? Balderdash!" insisted The Head.

"He's new Sir and has only just moved to the area.   I was going to
take him to his class when you found him Sir."

"Humph. Humm, very well, but do it quickly before registration ends," and with a swish of his cape he turned and marched away.

It took Marion three attempts before she found Mark's allocated classroom and teacher; taking him by the hand she led him to Miss Fowler's desk. Being the youngest and most recent member of staff, she had not yet succumbed to the soured opinions expressed in the staff room at break times by her older colleagues, that all children were the devil's spawn and if you spared the rod you spoiled the child. In fact her rationale was to educate with reason and to build an affinity with her pupils, fostering a desire in the children to learn, motivated by interest. There were other like-minded teachers at St. James, but most were either planning to retire imminently or to find alternative, more lucrative employment, it could be deduced that this was a time where a good, modern thinking, caring, educator shone out as an example. From day one Miss. Fowler was a diamond in Mark's eyes.

"And who have we here?"

"This is Mark Dacey Miss; he's new and needed to find his class."

"Well thank you, Marion."

"Miss, before I go to my class, could you write a note explaining…."

"Of course Marion," the teacher had stopped her mid-sentence pre-empting her request and quickly started to scribble a brief note on a small scrap of paper taken from her desk. "Whose class are you in this term?" "Miss. Vickers."

Miss. Fowler smiled as she completed the letter that asked the girl's teacher to please forgive her lateness for registration as she had been seconded for an important school task. Marion took the note, thanked its author and turned to leave, giving Mark a cheeky grin, she winked, "See you at playtime Mark."

Once in the cream and green corridor, she walked sedately over the red painted stone floor, knowing that the note backed together with the headmaster's endorsement protected her from late class arrival punishment. Suddenly, deciding dawdling could be seen as a separate offence, the girl increased her tempo; after all she did not want to end up on the wrong side of Miss, 'No Knickers Vickers'.

Marion was only a year older than Mark but she was far more mature.

At a vacant wooden desk, Mark sat on a small wooden chair. Inspecting his bureau, he found it to have seen better days. The top was decorated with illegible graffiti here and there were innocent doodles and designs in ink. These had been scrubbed by the caretaker, who had only succeeded in giving the pictures and text a faded appearance. No work was done that morning; it was spent taking names for the register and collecting dinner money, two shillings each child for a week's school dinners. Some children who had no money, hung their heads and informed Miss. Fowler that they received 'free dinners,' they whispered in the hope that no-one would hear as it could lead to taunts from insensitive bullies. If only they had known that over one third of their classmates received free meals and that the vast majority of the school's company of children were poor, they would have been spared this shame. Mark was just glad his mum had remembered to wrap two shillings into a piece of paper and put it into the pocket of his baggy black shorts. Before leaving him, Mary had reminded Mark to pay for his dinners with the coin in his pocket. That task completed, each child was given several lined school exercise books and one larger, plain-sheeted arts book, of an inferior quality. They wrote their names on each cover with a yellow and black striped pencil that had also been presented to them.

"Children put away your books." Desk lids lifted, books and pencils were deposited then the lids were slammed shut, bang, bang, bang resembling a lazy firecracker. "When the bell goes for playtime, take your milk from the crate on the way out to the playground."

Miss. Fowler finished speaking and looked at her class. Each pupil sat at their desk, straight-backed, hands clasped in front, silent but expectant. Ding, ding ding, somewhere in the distance the arse-kissing student was ringing the school bell announcing the morning break. "Orderly fashion, calm down, do not push." The teacher had lost them to a frenzied stampede, each child making it a source of pride to be first through the door. Mark allowed himself to be jostled to the door, following the example of other children he picked up the small glass bottle of milk, ensuring that the silver-foiled cap was not too battered. He took a single plastic straw from the grey cardboard box, he would learn that if any child had the audacity to take two, another child would cry out "Aw I'm gonna tell you've got two, you aint allowed two.... Miss!" but already the culprit would have replaced the incriminating straw and fled.

Invariably some of the most envied drinkers in the playground had two straws in their bottle.

Slurping the last dregs of slightly warm milk, Mark returned the empty bottle to the latticed metal crate situated at the boys' playground door, then he started to look round for Marion. "Hiya. Have you had your milk?"

The boy nodded, "Do you know that if you go back and find some left you can have a second?"

Shaking his head incredulously, Mark indicated he had not known.

"Well I've 'ad three already an' I might 'ave another." The boy now telling lies to Marion and Mark in an effort to impress, was none other than the urchin who had fallen into the duty teacher's bad books that morning.

"Oh, you fibber Bamber," said the girl.

"Am not, I'll show yer."

He grabbed Mark's arm and led him to the milk crate.   Marion followed. "See that one, an' that one, an' that one?"

The two nodded. "Well them's the ones I just drunk."

Fred folded his arms across his chest and smirked his triumph. "They could be anyone's" dismissed Marion.

"I bet you 'undred quid."

"You aint got 'undred quid."

As every child in the playground knew, no-one in the whole world was rich enough to have a hundred pounds, except the Queen. "Well me uncle is in the navy an 'ees got more than 'undred quid."

"Well my dad was a sailor in the war an' mum said he's never seen 'undred quid."

Marion's truthful reply prompted Fred to think for a moment then his face lit up, "Yeh, but my uncle is a captain."

"Bloody liar!"

The urchin thought of defending the lie but realised with Marion he was out-gunned, he always was, so he countered with his best defence - he changed the subject. "Who is he anyway?"

"He," said the girl in tones that were meant to convey her superior intellect to this annoying oaf, "He," she repeated, "is Mark Dacey and he is my friend."

The two boys' weighed each other up, then Fred thrust out a grubby hand. "Wanna be friends?" Mark took the proffered hand while nodding. "Good," smiled Fred, then added, "Course you can't be me best friend coz I've already got three best friends an' one bestest friend."

Feeling she was in danger of being sidelined, Marion interrupted "Anyway Bamber, I thought you 'ad to go see the beanpole."

A look of fear appeared on Fred's face at the mention of the duty teacher's nickname. "I.. I forgot" stammered the wretch and with a cry, away he flew leaving Mark to turn round and face the grinning Marion.

"Any way, you're my best friend Marion."

Marion's embarrassed look made Mark aware that something he had just said was unacceptable. Marion looked around to ensure no one had heard or would hear any part of their subsequent conversation. "Look don't you know that boys' can't have girl best friends and girls' can't have boy best friends. They can be friends but not best friends."

"No I didn't" said the boy sheepishly, wanting to ask why not, but he found himself apologising instead.

Placated, the pretty little girl sighed, and checking that the coast was clear, went on to explain that the only time a boy and girl are best friends is when they are 'Going out together.' "And you know what that means." Again Mark shook his head. "They kiss and stuff, then they 'ave to get married."

The boy's mouth fell open, "And then do you know what happens?" More negative head shaking. "The other kids all make fun of them." Staring intently at Mark she then said, "Now do you understand?"

This time Mark nodded vigorously. "Good," sighed the little girl, then rewarded Mark's attention with a pleasant smile.

Ding, ding, ding. 'Arse-kisser' was at it again, this time causing the hoard to stampede towards their classrooms.

"See yer later."

"Yeh see yer later," echoed Mark and they passed through their respective portals.

For the rest of the morning 'Miss' drew letters on the blackboard, then the children copied them onto small framed slates with chalk which Miss. Fowler had snapped into two equal smooth tapered white sticks. Rationing the chalk in this way was an attempt to stop waste, by ensuring the child had thoroughly practiced their numbers and letters before writing them into the more expensive paper books.

Mark allowed his tongue to loll between his teeth as he concentrated on the curves and lines of the capitals and smaller letters, often rubbing out a mistake with his finger and then wiping the living eraser onto his short pants, leaving white dusty prints. Sometimes he licked his finger, fascinated by the way in which the shiny wet trail left by his spittle corrections slowly disappeared. By the time Apple, Ball, Cat and Dog had been correctly entered uppercase and lowercase into his best writing book, the bell was ringing for lunch.

Mark found himself sat next to his new friend Fred and opposite Marion, who in turn sat next to one of her girl friends, Pat. Although students at St. James were still separated according to gender when entering or leaving the building and in assembly, the practice of segregation in the playground and at lunch times had now been abandoned.

"Great, I love meat pie, mash an' carrots."

Actually Fred loved any of the school dinners, as it was usually the only guaranteed nourishing meal of the day for him. Mark agreed that it was also one of his favourite meals and Marion took it upon herself to fill the chunky glass tumblers in front of each of them with water from the aluminium jug.

There were four jugs on each table for the twenty four diners, at one end of each table sat two teachers whose turn it was to supervise. The meals were brought out on trolleys by dinner ladies dressed in blue smocks; the plates were passed down from the top of the table, enabling the adults to be served first. When the entire school had been served, the headmaster who was seated at a separate table accompanied by the school hierarchy boomed out: "Let us be thankful."

The room full of diners bowed heads and clasped hands; The Head intoned a brief often repeated grace. Fred kicked Mark under the table to attract his attention and pulled a monstrous face, crossing his eyes and sticking out his tongue. This made the two boys' and both girls' giggle into their clasped hands, careful not to arouse the attentions of the adults who sat at the table. "May the Lord make us truly thankful, Amen. You may begin."

The permission was greeted with the tumult of eating and conversation. After the main course, providing they had eaten all on their plates, the children were delivered their sweet course in the same manner as the first. A collective sigh went up "Tapioca, awwh."

"What's tapioca Marion?"

"Milk pudding with lumps in it."

"Made from frog spawn," added Fred, knowingly.

Mark moved back from his dish in disgust then prodded the tadpole-like blobs with his large spoon; it did not look or smell like any of the frog spawn he had seen. "Take no notice, he's lying again," but Fred just grinned and pretended to grab Mark's plate.

"Well if you don't wannit."

Mark seized hold of his pudding. "I do wannit!" and to emphasise the fact, stuffed a spoonful into his mouth.

Unperturbed, Fred was asking the adults on the table, "Can I go for second's sir, miss?"

"That is 'may I go' Fred, and yes you may," the male teacher corrected condescendingly, but that did not bother Fred who was already at the hatch to the school kitchen.

"Any seconds Mrs. Jones?"

A very thin, white-smocked head cook gave Fred a feigned expression of annoyance, "You again Fred?"

The waif grinned as Mrs. Jones doled out a slice of meat pie, potatoes and carrots. She ladled a generous helping of thick brown gravy over everything, as she knew her little regular was rather partial to gravy. "Thank you Mrs. Jones."

He slurped the last word of her name as he was already salivating at the prospect of his second lunch. As Mark watched his friend tuck in, more children, emboldened by the example of others also asked for seconds, eagerly enquiring if there was any more until there was nothing left and Mrs. Jones closed the hatch. Mark had wanted to follow Fred but Marion whispered to him "He's a greedy pig."

Not wanting to be classed similarly, he decided to forego extra helpings. Instead he replenished their glasses from the water jugs, the dinner ladies had deposited these on the tables before disappearing into the kitchen. Mark was pleasantly surprised to discover that the jugs no later contained water. At first he thought it was drinking chocolate but as he sipped the hot, sweet, milky concoction from the same glass that had held his water, he did not need to enquire of his friends as to its nature because Marion's friend Pat asked, "Do you like coffee?"

It was the first time that he had tasted coffee and nodding his head, said, "Yes I do, it's great."

The rest of the afternoon passed with a long art lesson, interrupted by afternoon break. During the lesson the classmates gathered in separate groups around three large square tables that were covered with bright plastic, there was a blue table, a red table and the table at which Mark was seated, the green table. Mark had not succeeded in the mad scramble for the coveted red table; he had not bothered to compete for the second most popular choice, the blue table. Sat at the green table he found one advantage, it had fewer pupils permitting more elbow room and there was less time to wait to use the shared paints and crayons.

Mark's very first entry into his art book consisted of three brown blobs, a thick line of darker brown wash with two blue splashes above. He assured Miss. Fowler that it was, as she could obviously see, a camel in the desert and she of course, once the work of art had been explained, obviously saw that to be the case, although she also reconciled herself to the fact that at least in Mark's case she would not be responsible for nurturing a budding Rembrandt.

After the art class had cleaned up, the group sat down to listen to a story, the story-telling was delayed because some children were talking, so the whole class had to sit with hands, fingers interlocked, on heads until Miss decided they were sufficiently well behaved to commence. These afternoon story times were the best part of Mark's early school years and stimulated his desire to read more complicated publications for himself. Five minutes before the end of school time, Miss. Fowler stopped reading. "We will find out what happened next, tomorrow," leaving Mark a little frustrated.

The class spent the remaining minutes with their right forefinger on their lips to show what good quiet children they were. Ding, ding, ding, 'arse-kisser' was on time yet again and despite their teachers' pleading the children stampeded, after all each one wanted to be the first to get their coat from the cloakroom and reach the 'lollipop lady.'

Mark was not in that first rush of his classmates because he was hanging about the corridor waiting to see either Marion or Fred emerge from their classrooms. When they did so the three childred raced for the exit and freedom.

It had seemed an eon to Mark since that morning when his sister had hauled him down Buckley Road, having crossed the road with his friends, here they were standing outside Scars' Butchers. "See yer tomorrer Mark."

"See yer Fred."

Fred had become superman by fastening his coat round his neck like a cape, and in this guise he disappeared up Leeds Road. To others he might have looked like a demented urchin leaping up and down, his skinny legs lost in the massive, hand-me-down short pants, his ill-fitting shoes flinging themselves from his baggy, socked feet at every opportunity. Marion waited until Super Fred became a dot then decided it was safe to take the same route home without the embarrassing prospect of catching him up. "Mark?"

"Yes Marion?"

"I'm going to ask me mum an' dad if you can come to tea on Friday," then slightly embarrassed said "That's if you want to."

"Oh yes please!" said Mark, adding a very sincere, "Thank you Marion."

"Well they haven't said yes yet, but you better ask your mum and dad if it would be alright, just in case."

Having said their goodbyes Mark, elated at the prospect of spending more time with his friend, slapped his backside and became the Lone Ranger, tying his jacket about his waist, then galloping into the sunset, across the wide open plains of Leeds Road past Jimmy Duckworth's, past the Red Lion. Here he reigned in his steed until an adult accompanied by children came to cross the road, which he himself had to cross to reach home. The mother of the children realised that the boy had been advised by an absent parent to, "Wait until a grown-up helps you to cross the road."

"Alright come on now, quickly, let's cross, look right, look left..."

Her attempts to instil the Highway Code were lost on the Lone Ranger who with a fading, "Thank you ma'm" on his lips, he charged onwards.

Finding himself outside the Bull's Head, which was opposite its competitor the Red Lion, he turned his trust nag, Silver, west, or was it up the hill? He raced for home past the chip shop, past the sweet shop and the cobblers' that lined his route. From his saddle he glanced at the Conservative Club with its bowling green and the low stone wall hiding the hill that lead to the brook, which ran opposite and in front of his house, the brook was definitely out of bounds. He rounded the corner onto the little dirt track and entered the small square, outside his door the shattered little hero dismounted and stabled Silver until the next time he would be called upon by the masked avenger. Finding the key in the outside toilet which was the hiding place of third choice, Mark stood on tiptoe to fit the key into the lock. Two turns and a pull of the levered handle allowed access. The kitchen was cool and dark and provided a welcome relief for the tired cavalier. Throwing his jacket onto the kitchen chair, he looked for a glass then turned on the cold water tap, leaving it to run to allow the sediment from the lead pipes to flush away, before rinsing out his glass twice. When he filled the glass he checked to make sure that the water was crystal clear and satisfied, he turned off the tap and slumped at the table with his drink, spilling a little onto the floor. It was while he was congratulating himself on his perceved importance in Marion's affections, she had invited him to tea, he recalled something she had said and it dampened his zeal. "Ask yer mum and dad if it's alright?" His head drooped and he slumped back into the chair spilling more of his drink. "I don't even know where me dad is."

Chapter 31

Late autumn 1959, Mark's sixth birthday was imminent. He had been a regular visitor to the France household and on a couple of occasions his friend was allowed to visit Saxon Place for Sunday tea. Marion had helped with Mark's integration into the neighbourhood by introducing him to children in the vicinity whom she knew well, in this way several local children joined Mark's circle of friends though, after Marion, Fred was his main companion.

Barry, as a skilled motor mechanic, was responsible for a fleet of vans owned by, 'Sunshine Dry Cleaners' in Blackley, Manchester. He also kept the boiler room running and maintained the machines. This made him a valuable asset to his Jewish employers, who thought very highly of his easy-going nature and absolute integrity.

On most Saturday mornings, Barry went into work to carry out the maintenance he was unable to do during business hours, as machines and vehicles were constantly in use. The Jewish Sabbath was an ideal time for the task, as that day he was sure to be the only person in the factory. Barry always left at 5am so he could be back before lunchtime. Sometimes Mark was allowed to accompany him, he was undeterred by the early start on what seemed an adventure. At the factory the boy was impressed by the way Barry possessed the keys to the building. He watched him disappear through the small door of the large tatty brick factory that was shared with other businesses. When Barry entered the building an alarm bell rang for a few seconds, then the large roller doors lifted, slowly exposing first Barry's feet then the rest of him, pulling at a heavy chain that operated the door. Once fully opened, Barry drove the car into the concrete bay, closed the door behind him and set about his tasks.

Mark was left pretty much to his own devices, being forewarned to touch nothing. After wandering the factory floor inhaling the odour of soap and bleach, he came back to the garage bay where he was allowed to sit in the different delivery vans. His favourite was a brand new Austin, with its rounded front and internal engine that resided between driver and passenger, as a huge hump. It was in these various vehicles that Mark and his imagination would drive to London. Sometimes they were spitfires or army tanks. He would play happily in this way, until his reverie was interrupted when Barry called him to come for a cup of tea. They drank the tea from chipped white pint-pots, which made the small boy feel somewhat manly, and

Barry opened the waxed bread wrapper which contained either corned beef or ham sandwiches. Mark washed the food down with noisy slurps Barry warned, "Watch out for the tea leaves."

Mark left a quarter of the brew to avoid any contact with the dreaded vegetation, regretting that he had to leave so much of an enjoyable drink.

In the twenty minutes during which they shared breakfast, Barry asked Mark what he liked and disliked in an effort to get to know him. As the actual time they spent together was minimal, Mark liked these talks, feeling happy that someone was interested in him, and chattered eagerly in response.

On one occasion he asked Barry what part he had played in the war. The man, silent for a time, his face sad recalled how he had loved being in a snow-covered meadow in Germany, near the war's end, as it made everything appear clean and serene. "Yeh, but we won. We did them Jerry's real good din't we?"

"Well, actually lad, there are no winners in wars, you see, all those people dead and all the cost of war, I think you could say that in a way we lost."

Lost! Lost! Mark could not believe his ears. He had never heard any grown man talk in this way, it was usually 'we gave the Jerry a dam good beating' or 'we taught the Hun a lesson he'll never forget'.

The journey home following this particular conversation was subdued and it was not until they were were only ten minutes from Buckley Road, that Mark realised the unthinkable and shuffled uncomfortably in his seat. What was it Barry had said? He had been in Germany and had liked it, he had said that we had lost the war, and he had also said that he worked for Jewish people. Now he recalled something about the war and Jews. 'Oh no,' thought Mark, arriving at what seemed the obvious conclusion to him....... 'Barry is a German.'

That Sunday morning Helen was in the main bedroom changing the bed sheets, the bottom of the sash window was open and a bracing breeze filled the room. She finished smoothing the cotton covers that she had folded neatly over the top of the coarse brown blankets and gathered the dirty laundry into her arms. Mark had been watching her perform her domestic tasks when suddenly Helen put down the sheets and pulled her son towards her as she sat on the newly made bed. "Look Mark, there is something I want to ask you." The boy looked at his mother who, to his puzzled inquisitiveness, seemed a

little apprehensive. "You do like Barry don't you?" her son nodded slowly, "and you know he really likes you." "Yeh."
"I thought, well I mean, if you…. Erm." Helen was struggling, then with a sharp intake of breath blurted, "Well if you like you can call him Dad."
The boy's face hid nothing. The shock was obvious from his expression. His mother, thinking she had upset the boy, quickly reassured him. "Of course Peter is still your real dad and if you don't want to call Barry Dad, you can carry on calling him by his first name. It's not important."
But it was important to his mother. They were trying to start a new life as a family and Mark was complicating things by referring to her new partner in public as Uncle Barry or Barry. "I don't care about me dad" snapped the boy, after all he did not want him nor had he been to see him. Helen seemed pleased by the outburst and smiled. Before she could speak, Mark continued… "But I don't know if I want him to be my Dad, because.. be…." Helen sensed that he was struggling and tried to help. "Because what love?" She cooed in her most appealing voice to relax the boy and after a moments hesitation Mark divulged the terrible truth. "Barry is a German!"
At first he was annoyed by his mother's hysterical laughter then, greatly relieved with the assurance that Barry was a true-blue Englishman and who had actually been decorated for valorous acts against the enemy.
Later that evening, when Mark was in the basement room with Mary, listening to her piano practice, the pair were disturbed by raucous laughter from the living room above. Helen had just informed Barry of her son's misconception. Mary tutted and resumed practice, banging the keys harder in a concerted effort to drown out the sounds of joviality. Her brother however had decided to investigate the reason for such mirth. Seeing Barry and his mother so happy together made Mark simultaneously glad and embarrassed, but a little jealous too that Helen never paid him as much attention.
Barry was the first to speak "Mark, I want to show you something."
Intrigued, Mark waited while Barry, still grinning, came back down from the bedroom with a khaki beret and small tin box. He let Mark inspect the beret with its bright badge and Barry explained the words, 'Royal Engineers' and then he placed the cap at an angle on the astounded boy's head and opened the tin box. Inside were four service medals; taking them out one at a time, he allowed the

youngster to thoroughly inspect them. Completing his proof of nationality, he produced a sepia photograph showing a younger Barry with some army buddies standing at the side of a destroyed German Tiger tank.

"Did you kill any Germans?" Barry's face turned pale and austere. Taking the boy firmly by the shoulders, he looked piercingly into eyes that were now wide with fear. "To take a person's life is one of the most terrible things to do and I never want you to ask me that ever again, understand?"

Mark nodded emphatically. Barry, realising he had scared the youngster, tried to remedy the situation with a forced smile. And a sudden announcement, "Who's coming to the sweet shop?" This served a dual purpose in cheering up the boy and relieving Helen.

Barry and Mark departed for the sweet shop hand in hand.

Over the years Mark learned in snippets of conversation, usually when watching old war films on TV, that Barry had been seconded with a digger to the Americans on clean-up duty in one of the most notorious concentration camps, Belsen.

Mark found addressing Barry as 'Dad' very difficult and often found himself saying "Barry, I mean Dad." When Mary continued addressing Barry by his name Mark felt a bit of a traitor.

Chapter 32

The most memorable thing about Mark's sixth birthday was being taken to see Terry. Helen had arranged to meet her older son in Richton at the Orchard Café in The Walk, next to the small open market with its busy stalls.

An aroma of fresh coffee assailed their nostrils. Many shoppers were also stopped by the tempting fragrance and like Helen and Mark; they entered the glass door, which was always fastened open to allow the seductive powers of the espresso machine to permeate the café's vicinity.

The long narrow counter appeared to stretch forever with towering bar stools which, although fixed in position, swivelled, giving extra entertainment to children agile enough to master them. The counter-front was padded black vinyl and on the ceiling a huge fan whirred noisily in the summer. At the back of the counter the mirrored wall had shelves stacked with cigarettes and various bottles of cordial, a heated pie machine contained amongst the delicious savouries one burnt offering hidden unappetisingly in a corner, the proprieter was hopeful that once covered with gravy the unwary consumer would not think it worthwhile to return the unsatisfactory snack as unfit for human consumption, usually customers ate the centre leaving the rock hard shell before leaving the establishment vowing never to frequent it again. Two large cooling bubbles, one of which contained milk and the other fresh orange, sat side by side. The latter had a paddle that constantly stirred the liquid. Next to the entrance was a hatch on to the busy thoroughfare from which almost every flavour of ice cream could be purchased by passers by. The centre of the counter housed the most important machine in the building, a shining monstrosity of chrome contrasted with contrasting black handles. The monster whooshed and hissed sending up columns of steam, the operator expertly twiddled knobs and pulled levers to produce the Italian style beverages.

Mark felt unfamiliar when he saw his brother, who now sported a crew- cut hairstyle which made him appear much older than his thirteen years. "Hiya Mark"

"Hiya Tell."

After a few minutes they conversed in their old familiar ways, Terry told his mother and brother what was happening to Castaires. Its cleaning had become his responsibility and more paying guests had moved in.   Peter went to the pub every weekday evening and every weekend, Jack had been released from prison three weeks ago. Helen knew of Jacks release but was disappointed that he had not visited her.   Terry tried to comfort her by explaining that Peter had made Jack feel that visiting his mother while she was with her 'Fancy man' would constitute a betrayal. His Father had hinted that in the face of such a betrayal his hospitality might have to be withdrawn.   The last thing that Jack needed at this time in his life was to find himself without a roof over his head.   Helen reluctantly agreed the best strategy, for the present at least, was to wait until a better opportunity to meet her eldest son presented itself.

Terry continued, to relate how Karl had been ever-distant and busy, and then with a sudden sadness changed role from intelligence reporter to intelligence gatherer. "How was Mary? How was she doing at school?"

When Helen left the brothers' alone to go to the market, Terry asked Mark about the house, how he was finding school life, wether he had any friends and then in a more serious tone how he was being treated, especially by 'That bloke.' "What bloke Tell?" asked the youngster, slurping the last dregs of strawberry milk shake from his tall glass.

"That bloke that lives with you," said an exasperated bigger brother.

"Oh Dad, I mean Barry?"

Terry looked at Mark, revulsion clearly registered on his face. "Ee is not your dad. Our mum left our dad, and if you ever call im Dad to me again, then we aint brothers' any more."

Tears welled in the six year old's eyes, he had no idea what he had done to upset Terry. All the small boy could find to say was, "It's me birfday today Tell." Why the youngster, tears now freely flowing, had said the words he had he couldn't explain to himself, but the effect on his brother was astounding.   Oblivious to the stares of the other customers he grabbed his little brother and hugged him tightly, the two of them balancing precariously on their high stools. "I'm so sorry Mark I din't mean it, it's jus I miss you an' Mum an' our Mary so much" tears now filling his eyes, "An' I'm so lonely," he whispered, "an' that's gotta be our secret, alright?" Mark agreed. Becoming aware of the interest they were arousing, Terry sat up stiffly, gently pushing the clinging youngster from him. Swallowing hard and clearing his throat, he reached into his pocket and brought out a half-crown. Looking shamefacedly towards the white coated young woman behind the counter, he held out the coin. "Two more milk shakes please." This time they had chocolate.

Terry excited the birthday boy with tales of his exploit's as a member of the school rugby team. Mark listened in amazement as his sibling explained how his performance had earned him a place on the county team that was to compete in France the following March. Peter had promised to find the money for the trip.

Helen unaware of the earlier emotional scenes, returned just in time to be a party to Terry's great news. "I'm so proud of you son."

"Well," said a subdued Terry, "I suppose I had better get back to Castaires, I've got work to do."

"Terry love, are you getting enough to eat? Are you..."

"I'm fine Mum don't you worry bout me."

Mark intuitively recognised in Terry's glance that their earlier tête-à-tête was a secret. Without a word, he returned his brother a look that conveyed concurrence.

With Terry's departure from the coffee shop, Helen tried to dispel the gloom that was settling on the pair who remained. "Come on then, let's go to the toy shop and get you a present."

The toyshop was around the corner from the Orchard in the little open market it was one of the few permanent buildings, not a market stall. Mother and child stood gazing at the crowded shop-window display and after a few moments the small boy made a decision. "Soldiers please." In amongst the birthday cards he had received that morning was a five shilling postal order from his nan and granddad, a half-crown postal order from aunty Maud and five shillings from Mum, Barry and Mary. With the shilling that Terry had given him from his change from the milk shakes, this amounted to the princely sum of thirteen shillings and sixpence.

Helen allowed her son to spend ten shillings on two boxes of plastic medieval knights, six to a box. The ones with red plumes he designated 'Goodies' and the ones with black plumes became the 'Baddies.' After some serious begging, his mother finally gave in to his pleas for her to release a further three shillings to acquire four similar figures but mounted on horseback, that left him with sixpence. All the way home on the bus he impatiently waited for the stop that would allow him to run pell-mell for Saxon Place, which he did, pressing eagerly against the door, prompting Helen's response "Bloody slow down, let me get through the bloody door."

As the handle turned, Mark's pressure burst the door open. Mary, who heard the pair's approach from her ground floor window, came to greet them and was almost bowled over by her eager young brother's haste to get to his room. "You pratt."

Mary's admonishment went unheeded as Mark stomped noisily up the wooden staircase, arriving breathless at his bedroom. Tearing open the box lids and opening the brown paper bags that contained his cavalry, he removed the soldiers one by one, giving each of them a name and rank. Arranging the empty boxes at the pillow end of his bed, they became an impregnable-fortress, well almost.

As the goodies laid siege to the baddies' stronghold across the battlefield of blankets, some questionable manoeuvres ensued including aerial assaults in which goodies were hurled over the ramparts by imaginary catapults. For almost two hours the battles raged and it was only with the arrival of his new dad that the new-six-year-old was forced to put away his armies and go down to the little tea party that Helen and Mary had prepared.

By mid-December the first snow had arrived, it was sparse but sufficient to accelerate the children's excitement to new heights. During school break-times the entire pupil complement would organise themselves into opposing armies and would each defend their part of the playground with fervour. During the lunchtime the armies would rush out to try and gain the advantage of stockpiling snowballs and pelted the late arrivals as soon as they appeared. This always included some of their own troops, some of whom would yell, "I'm on your side" while the more aggrieved would take up arms for the opposing side.

On the odd occasion the battle became one-sided a few, renegades had to flee through the school gate across a small courtyard to an old farmhouse where, sheltered behind a low stone wall and with abundant ammunition in the shape of fresh drifts of snow, the valiant few would hold out until the bell rang and all hostilities ceased. Of course, leaving the playground was strictly forbidden and although a blind eye was turned on occasions, if the farmer or his wife complained, or a child was injured, then retribution was swift. The ring leaders were sent in a crestfallen line to the headmaster's office where corporal punishment not reason was the order of the day, and the prescribed sentence was always six of the best across the weeping transgressors posteriors.

On one particular farmyard sortie, Fred and Mark had heroically beaten off all attacks and were rightfully flushed with pride when the elderly farmer's wife appeared, yelling at them to be off. Surprisingly it was Mark who instigated what followed next. Squeezing the soft snow in his hand, he formed the spherical missile then took aim and fired. The snowball struck the woman directly on her wrinkled forehead and she bellowed in rage, "Bastards!"

Any further invective from the woman was cut short when Fred's missile hit almost the same spot, leaving the farmer's spouse spitting snow from her wet face. Further missiles sent the woman scurrying back to the safety of the house, then the hysterical duo ran back to school, as the school bell signalled a return to class. They were in no doubt that they had just achieved a great victory.

The warm glow that Mark felt disappeared when, a little later, the classroom door burst open and there, to his consternation, stood the outraged farmer's wife, the furious farmer and the livid Head. Mr. Conrad was holding a squirming Fred cruelly by the ear. "That's the little animal, I can tell that blond mop anywhere," shouted the woman.

The septuagenarian farmer made a lunge for the terrified boy whom all eyes were upon, but Mr. Conrad held him back with his free arm. "Leave this to me Mr. Fields."

The disgruntled farmer stepped back, allowing the headmaster to grab Mark's ear. "Come with me my lad and we'll see if I can beat the meaning of civilised behaviour into you pair of savages."

Mark and Fred were hauled off and the classroom exploded into an excited furore as, classmates discussed with malevolent glee the probability of death for the hapless couple. The farmer and his wife disappeared, leaving justice to be served.

Holding each boy by the left ears, The Head pushed one and dragged the other to his study at a pace the pair could scarcely match. They sat momentarily while Mr. Conrad went to the other side of the room to take his thin cane from a shelf. "I never told on you Mark," whispered the ashen-faced Fred.

"I know," was his similarly pale-faced conspirator's reply.

Mark had guessed that the woman and her husband had come to Conrad berating him for his ineptitude in matters of student control. The discomfited headmaster had immediately escorted them on a tour of the classrooms, until they had first found Fred then himself. As Conrad seized Fred by the scruff of his neck, Mark stood up shaking but defiant, "Sir it wern't Fred wot dunnit, it were me," then seeing the puzzled look on The Head's face he felt encouraged to continue. "Ee jus watched sir, ee never did nuffin, it was me." Mark's defence of his friend, although admirable in Conrad's eyes, did not afford any reprieve for Fred who recieved six of the best and Mark earned an extra two strokes for his exaggerated honesty.

Punishment complete, they were thrown out of the study with the dire warning that they were never to transgress again. The boys', despite being told to return to their classrooms immediately, stopped off at the cloakrooms and finally managed to stop their tears and frantic rubbing of backsides. Splashing their faces and putting on brave smiles, the boys' declared themselves heroes, and after a vigorous hand shake swaggered off to class, where their exploit's ensured their status as school idols for the remainder of December until the Christmas break. Needless to say, neither of the lads mentioned a thing of this escapade to their parents, as a confession would have brought more retribution.

Chapter 33

The last day at school before the holidays always consisted of taking a favourite toy to play with, as schoolwork was not usually on the afternoon's agenda and the day would be filled with festive spirit. School lunch was a wondrous excess of party fare, the cost of this extravagance eased by parents' donations of biscuit's, jellies and other goodies. Paper hats were worn and even the teachers donned celebratory crowns as the season of goodwill spread a welcome infection.

At morning assembly the school choir sang familiar carols prompting enthusiastic choruses of Jingle Bells and Rudolph the Red-Nosed-Reindeer, as well as traditional favourites. Mr.Conrad brought the morning worship to a close in a more sombre tone with the Lord's Prayer; Fred then lightened the proceedings again with his own rendition. "Our Father who Farts in Heaven" sending his friends into fit's of giggles. Fortunately for them the impious frivolity was overlooked, as the staff were already imbued with seasonal gratification, knowing that at the end of the school day they would not have to see this unkempt bunch of reprobates for two weeks.

"Merry Christmas Miss," "Merry Christmas Sir," "Ave a nice time Miss. Fowler." Mark was on a joyful roll. Under his arm was the stack of paintings and home made Christmas cards, while hanging out of his bulging overcoat pockets were streams of brightly coloured paper-chains. For the last few weeks these had decorated classrooms, but now redundant they had been shared amongst the children who were allowed to take them home. Some mothers', unimpressed by the home made decorations would slyly throw them into the bin, other more sensitive parents would heap praise on their offspring for artistic excellence, vowing the work was of such a standard that it would be kept forever. Nevertheless when January 6th arrived these masterpieces could be found decorating the interior's of dustbins.

Miss. Fowler gave Mark an affectionate pat on the head and wished him all the happiness in the world. "Thank you Mrs. Green, Merry Christmas!" yelled Mark, Fred and Marion in unison, hurtling past the tinsel-bedecked lollipop lady; the sparkling strands were a present from some thoughtful scamp.

"And a Merry Christmas to you scallywags," grinned the cheerful woman.

The trio set foot on the pavement outside the butchers, their usual spot for leave taking; they looked at each other for the last time that year, parting with wide smiles and cheery waves, each skipping off towards home.

Mr. Conrad looked down from the lofty vantage point of his study window, his pale wrinkled hands resting on the sill. He was observing the children scurrying back and forth like euphoric ants, and pondering on the kind of Christmas the good Lord would see fit to bestow. He decided to wait a little longer until all the staff and pupils had left before making his way to the bus stop and home, a detached bungalow in the nearby village of Winton, his Yuletide celebrations had been poor affairs since his wife passed away six years earlier. She had never recovered from the death of their only son in the last year of the Second World War. He had been a brave boy and an officer. With his passing, the light of life went out for his parents who found each other's company a poignant reminder of what was and what could have been; so they avoided each other as much as possible, thus compounding their loss into a double tragedy. He had not wept when he lost his wife, the despair at being left alone manifested itself as a void, relieved only by the enforced concentration of his work. But always, when the working day was over, the tormented spectre of his own vulnerability would take the seat beside him on the bus, his only companion until he could return to the asylum of his study.

Now, as he looked down at the six-year-old boy on the opposite side of the road, he studied the way he galloped up and down, his coat tied about his neck, recognising the child as that bloody urchin Fred Bamber. He felt a sudden rage, at first directed towards the boy for having the audacity to enjoy the precious gift of life when his beloved son had had his life brutally snatched away. Unabated, rage then found the most popular target for his grief, 'God, the Creator.' 'Christmas be damned' he thought, why should I celebrate the birth of his child, when he took mine?

Glancing miserably to the street he saw young Bamber still playing outside the Red Lion waiting excitedly for his father who had been in the bar since lunch time. At that moment Mr. Bamber staggered out of the pub and far from being full of Christmas spirit at the sight of his excited son braving the freezing cold just to walk home with his dad, he set about Fred slapping his head for no other reason than that he was there. The boy fearfully but expertly dodged the worst of the blows and walked behind the staggering oaf keeping at a safe distance. He too, like his unseen observer, had lost the spirit of the season.

Up in his sanctuary, not wanting to witness anymore of this Dickensian melodrama, Mr. Conrad sat as his desk and realised he would have to wait a little longer before leaving to catch a later bus. It just would not do for anyone to see the headmaster of Saint James weeping like a child.

Chapter 34

On the morning of Christmas Eve Mary and Mark went shopping at 'Jimmy Duckworth's,' one of the first chains of shops to try to rival the Co-op. Their local store was situated between the Red Lion and Jack Scar's, the butcher's.

Helen was not at work as fortunately it was her shift day off. She had awoken the children at seven with a cheery promise that, if they were not up and about in five minutes, she would be back with a pan of cold water and their early morning shower. In response, neither of them had made a move to leave the warmth of their beds, when Mary had popped her head from under the blanket, she had seen her breath form icy clouds and promptly dived under the covers again. Uncannily, brother and sister had simultaneously heard the rattle of saucepans and the sound of running water coming from the kitchen and it had galvanised the pair into action.

Helen had heard the commotion and panic and had smiled, congratulating herself that the ruse of banging a few pans and turning the water tap on fully for a few seconds had worked to perfection. Mary, with Mark's Assistance had lit a coal fire in the front room, and then both had eaten breakfast. While they drank their, tea Helen had explained to Mary the various notes - each one a shopping list for a specific store. With 'don't forgets' and 'if they haven't got' coupled with, 'get the cheapest' or 'ask for the best' and the odd 'don't let that skinny sod with the specs give you short measure' ringing in there ears the two intrepid shoppers had sallied forth, well-wrapped against the cold in worn but clean apparel.

"Mum says she doesn't want them cheap foreign biscuit's Mr. Grant."

"Well what about a nice box of tea time assortment?" asked the Manager of Duckworth's,

"Yes please, and could we have a pound of mixed, plain biscuit's from the tins?"

The tins had glass tops so that you could see the contents, and each one had a different variety of unwrapped sweet biscuit's, digestives, arrowroot, ginger nut, morning coffee and nice fingers, which Mark always pronounced 'nice' meaning pleasant, whereas Mary had just asked for 'Nice' biscuits as in the French resort. There were several boxes and a hand-written sign which proclaimed that they contained

'Broken Biscuit's' which were for sale at less than half-price. Helen would never stoop to purchase such 'battered and soft crumbs.'

Mary continued to read from the list, she did not follow the general practice of handing the list over to the assistant to complete. "Half-a-pound of Black and Green's tea, four ounces of dark roast coffee beans, fresh ground please."

Mark and his sister shared a common appreciation for the rich aroma, produced by the big red coffee grinder as it crushed selected beans to a course powder.

"1lb of Adams best butter, a jar of Dundee marmalade thick cut." Eventually when the list was complete and had been checked twice, Mr.Grant touching each hand-rapped package as it was named Mary was satisfied. She ignored her brother who was pestering for sweets, and took out a five-pound note and some silver and coppers to make the requested total of five-pounds, three and eleven-pence-Halfpenny.

Mr. Grant took the money to the till, paid an assistant and packed the two shopping baskets. "Mind your eggs love, they're on the top."

When the children had entered it had not been busy, but was now becoming crowded and it was with some relief that they squeezed past the throng.

Their next stop was the butcher's, not Jack Scar's as he was thought too expensive. Further along towards Richton between Post Office and Coates' Dental Surgery stood Whites' Quality Meats. Once they had reached the front of the large queue, their task was easy as Helen had already placed their order the week previous. They bundled the brown, paper-wrapped parcels into the empty string bags that Mark had been carrying, while the assistant added up the total. "That's four pounds seventeen please."

Mary opened Helen's worn, brown purse and handed over the card which showed that their mother was a member of the shops Christmas club and had been saving small amounts each week since July. "You've got four bob left on the card love, do you want that as change?" asked the spotty-faced assistant butcher who was serving them,

"No thank you, my mum said can you make up the difference with roast ham?"

Happily the youth obliged, telling Mary with a wink, "There's a bit extra in weight there love, you being such a pretty girl an all."

Mary really wanted to say "piss off spotty," but instead thanked him and gave all the staff and customers the season's best wishes, to which they responded in a like manner.

However, Mark was not going to let Spotty's unwelcome advances to his sister go unchallenged. On the way out he turned and checking that the only person paying them any attention was the love-struck *spotty*, letching after Mary. He pulled his most grotesque face and silently mouthed the profanity, "Fuck off!" adding "spotty" as an afterthought. Then this self appointed guardian of his sister's virtue obderving the glare of the vexed butcher's boy, legged it to rejoin his innocent sister who was well on her way to the greengrocers.

All their allotted tasks completed, the weary shopper's laden down like two-legged pack animals, hauled their Christmas fare up Buckley Road and home, where a pensive Helen checked then double checked that nothing had been missed or forgotten. Finding no fault, a relieved mother heated a small saucepan of milk on the old stove. Pouring the hot milk into three mugs, she added to each a huge spoonful of Cadbury's drinking chocolate, the powder scooped from its brown/red tin and stirred vigorously.

While the ladies sipped their drinks, Mark insisted he needed at least two sugars to make it perfect. Without a thought, Mary dumped the Tate and Lyle granules into her brother's mug, giving it a token stir. "Mmm it's luverly!" declared the youngster and smacked his lips to clear the milky froth that had formed a moustache.

Chapter 35

In the early afternoon Barry arrived barely containing his excitement, he insisted Helen and the children sat on the sofa in the front room while he brought in a surprise.

"A telly!" whooped Mark. Even Mary's typically cool acceptance of most events was pleasantly disturbed by the significance of the occasion; it was the first time they would be able to watch TV since leaving Castaires.

The next two hours saw Barry climbing onto the roof to fix the aerial to the chimney stack and fiddling with the big knobs of the second-hand set, until he was happy with the resulting quality of the two channels, BBC and ITV. "It's not new, but it's got a great picture" declared a proud Barry.

The other's agreed, then with a wink to Helen he said, "Don't suppose there will be any complaints about your mum and me going out tonight then?"

If silence was an answer Barry had it. Far from being upset at the prospect of being left alone with the TV, the children were impatient to be rid of the adults and when eventually two very smart revellers departed that evening they left brother and sister sharing sweets and chocolates, totally enthralled by whatever flickering black-and-white visual delights television offered. That night the programme was an 'Old Mother Riley' slapstick comedy starring Arthur Lucas and Kitty McShane. Although not as high brow as Mary would have liked, it was nevertheless enjoyed immensely.

Despite arguments about who should turn the big knob in an effort to find a more exciting programme, or whose turn it was to fetch more coal for the fire or which variety of fizzy pop would be opened next, the evening was a most amiable affair. They had been under strict instructions not to eat everything in sight and to leave some pop for the next few days, but at that point in time the dilemma was which to choose, Jusoda, Tizer, or Dandelion and Burdock. Mark got to choose as his weary sister relented and handed him the half-filled, heavy, fluted, glass bottle, which contained the orange Jusoda drink he loved. Unscrewing the black Bakelite stopper with its bright orange rubber washer, Mark was just about to take a swig from the bottle when Mary cuffed his ear. "Put it in a glass, you dirty sod."

The blow had not hurt, so the boy obeyed without a whining protest, pouring the orange drink into a small glass decorated with transfers of jolly snowmen. "Want some Mary?"

His sister took the bottle from the two hands he needed to hold the weight. "Thanks," then looking around her feet she realised she had put her glass in the kitchen sink.

Rather than stir from her position of comfort in front of the fire, she put the bottle to her lips and took a long gulp. "Oi you said that was dirty!" complained the incensed boy.

"Yeh you are dirty, but my mouth's clean," and she laughed at the insulted expression on her brother's sticky, sweet and chocolate-covered face. Mary fastened the stopper back into the bottle and reached over the back of the sofa, placing the bottle onto the dining table, then with a loud scream she leapt at Mark and they became embroiled in a savage play-fight that ended with Mark being allowed to claim victory. Breathless, they sat back on the sofa and listened to the carols being sung on TV.

Out of the blue Mary turned to her brother and asked, "Would you like me to tell you a story?"

The boy replied as he had recieved the greatest invitation ever. "Yes please,"

The girl had already reached the mahogany glazed cabinet and had removed a volume from a green leather-backed set of books. She closed the doors of the cabinet and turned the small key that was always left in the door. Passing the table, she grabbed two tangerines, one in pale pink tissue and the other in shiny red and silver foil, casually holding them out for her brother to choose one. He took the gaudier of the two as he believed that it would taste better.

Mary sat next to a table lamp and pulled the small chrome chain that illuminated the corner of the room with its one hundred watt bulb. Mark winced as the sudden brightness stung his eyes and he rubbed them with the back of his hands, he settled himself at Mary's feet and with his head on her lap, looked up at Mary's facial features lit up by the electric glow. She opened the book and spoke aloud. "A Christmas Carol, by 'Charles Dickens'."

With the TV carols being sung softly in the background, Mary started to read to the mesmerised little boy, who was entranced with the joy he felt this Christmas Eve, enthralled by Mary's clear, honeyed voice and captivated by her exceptional beauty.

At one o'clock in the morning very jolly parents returned making a fair old racket. They tumbled through the door that Mary had sleepily opened for them. "Hello love," slurred her semi-inebriated mother, "Had a nice time?"

The first thought that came into her head was "no," but as she reflected she revised her opinion, remembering her brother's wondrous attention and how, when he could remain awake no longer and had fallen asleep with his head on her lap she had put down the book and had struggled to pick him up. Despite her most careful administrations when she had carried him upstairs to bed she had bumped his head on the banister and on the wall. This had not aroused the boy from his almost comatose slumber, but had made him grunt. Mary had pulled back the covers and placed his unconscious form in the cold bed, so cold that she had decided to leave his little flannel housecoat on. Removing his slippers, she had drawn the covers over him. As she was leaving the room she glanced back and watched him curl instinctively into a foetal ball she had felt a wash of deep contentment and had wished she had said a few more nice things to the sleeping child. But it was not their way to openly display affectionate. In fact, Peter always inferred it was a weakness. Whether that was true, her little brother would not contest it as he had no recollection of anybody telling him that they loved him.

After wishing Helen and Barry goodnight, Mary went to bed she pondered the direction her life would take, she could hear the adult's tipsy merriment as they wrapped presents for the morning, putting them under the little tree in the bay window. When the sounds abated, she realised that they had completed their tasks and gone to bed.

Mary lay on her back with the blankets pulled tight about her neck and stared at the shadows on the ceiling made by the glow of road lamps through gaps in the ill-fitting floral curtains. It was then that the girl made a decision, speaking out loud. "No matter what, I'm leaving here and Richton as soon as I can."

Chapter 36

Mark was first to rise at 7a.m. he rushed downstairs and seeing a small stack of brightly coloured packages under the tree, he ran back upstairs to ask permission to open his presents from Santa. Barging into the main bedroom, he shook his mother by the shoulder until he got a response. "What bloody time is it?" Helen was hung-over.

"I don't know, I can't tell the time can I?" jibed the youngster, jigging impatiently from one foot to the other.

"Oh Mark! Go and wake Mary an I'll be down in a minute," lied his mother.

It was enough for the youngster; hurtling down the two sets of stairs he leapt onto his sister, who had heard him clomping about earlier, so his attack was not unexpected. "Yeehaa, ees been and we've got presents Mary!"

"Go upstairs and I'll get dressed," she said, and then to mollify him. "See if you can read the names Santa has put on the presents and sort them into piles."

"Tadada!" yelled the boy and he charged back up the stairs to impatiently inspect the parcels. When his big sister joined him, she had to break the news that his reading abilities had deteriorated to such an extent that half the presents in his pile were meant for the other members of the household. Seeing his disappointment, she managed to soften the blow and restore his enthusiasm by observing that his presents were the biggest.

Mary carefully opened her three gifts, folding the paper so that it could be used again, and discovering Father Christmas's bounty. A tin of toffees with a reproduction of an old master on the lid was a present from Mark via his mother, two second-hand books and a pen and pencil set from Helen and Barry and an envelope contained money from her relatives in London.

Mark had ripped open his presents rendering the paper useless, much to the annoyance of his thrifty sister. Opening the smallest parcel first he found it contained a large book entitled, 'Modern Wonder's of the World.' On the cover was a picture of smartly-uniformed gun crew loading huge shells into the latest cannon, on the most advanced Warship of the day. What the small boy did not understand was why it had "Merry Christmas 1959 from Mary," written on the inside cover, when the book was a present from Santa. Mary tried unsuccessfully to divert his attention to the educational pictures in the book and, to be fair, she had her brother's attention focussed on her thoughtful gift for all of ten seconds before he impatiently tore open a second parcel, a selection box. This was discarded and he ripped into the next one.

"Soldiers!" He waved the box at his sister, then, a rapid inspection revealed that it was in fact a set of four plastic Red Indians, a totem pole and a tepee The problem of having no cowboys to engage in battle with the indians was solved when Mark fashioned cowboy hats from a small ball of plasticine, he found covered in fluff beneath his bed, which he used to temporarily transform his Knights.

At last, with trembling fingers he opened a huge parcel, checking with Mary that there had been no mistake and it really was meant for him. On seeing the large box appear from the shredded seasonal wrapper, he delighted in the picture of Popeye, Olive Oil and Bluto emblazoned across the lid and the large white words that Mary read aloud. "The Popeye Colouring Set," the lid was removed to expose six crayons and four large pieces of paper on which were black lined pictures for colouring, Mark's dismay and disappointment was almost palpable. Mary whispered, "Wow, isn't that great Mark?"

The boy swallowed hard and nodded weakly. His hopes rose a little when his sister lifted up the packing to see if there was anything to be found underneath the excess cardboard, but no. The girl put her arm round her little brother, sensing his immense disappointment. "Father Christmas has not had much money this year Mark," she said with sadness that was motivated by an understanding of six-year-old's feelings. She silently cursed the unscrupulous bastards who profited from Christmas rip-offs such as this. She gave him a little squeeze and said, "I bet you get loads of better presents next year." Sensing that his mother would be upset if he complained, he simply nodded his head and tried to hide his disappointment. Through tear-blurred eyes he closed the the lid on this devastating misrepresentation and slid it back under the tree, then he opened the box containing his Red Indian encampment.

Satisfied, Barry looked at the gaudy red and silver electric clock he had just affixed to the wall above the doorway that led to the stairs and Mary's basement room. It was his present to Helen together with a bottle of cologne. From Mary she received a brush and comb set and from Mark – well it was a joint gift to Barry and his mother, a papier-mâché thingamajig that he had made at school. After some deliberation, Helen announced that it was too fine an object to be left on open display, so it took pride of place in the glazed cabinet - at the back.

In addition to Mark's masterpiece, Barry received slippers and aftershave from Helen and Mary's offering was a thick pair of grey woollen socks. "Ahh it's after eleven!" cried Barry, as he hurriedly dropped onto all fours and plugged in the television's large *Wylex* plug, twisting it slightly at the skirting board socket to enable the round centre and offset side-bars to locate. To make sure it was in, he gave it a firm thump with his clenched fist. In his excitement to rise, his right hand gave way and he did a sort of sideward roll, banging his head on the television table and floundering into Mark and his Indian village.

Thinking that this act of undeserved aggression warranted retaliatory measures, the youngster leapt on to the laughing Barry. "Yahoo!" yelled 'Geronimo' and as they wrestled he attempted to scalp Barry with the sawing motions of an open hand that had just become his hunting knife.

"Here, don't go cutting my hair off!" joked Barry, "I 'aven't got that much I can afford to lose any."

The 'any' referred to a longish bunch of brown strands that he combed over his pate in an effort to cover his premature balding, a style that later would become known, as the 'Bobby Charlton.' However at that moment in time the Manchester United footballer, who had survived the previous year's February 6th tragic Munich disaster, possessed a reasonable head of hair.

Suddenly, Barry realised why he was on the floor. He picked Mark up and held the squirming brave under one strong arm and turned on the TV. Geronimo became Mark once more. As he was released, he gave Barry's leg a final punch before throwing himself with a little backwards jump onto the old sofa. Barry had not even registered the punch but he did hear the springs of the worn settee behind him boing in complaint. "Stop jumping on the furniture."

"Sorry," said an unrepentant Mark, preoccupied with the images on the screen in front of him. Barry tried impatiently to fine tune the ITV channel. Contented he could do no better he joined the excited boy and together they watched the Western Christmas Day film silently, until Helen and Mary, who had been in the kitchen for most of that morning preparing the Yuletide feast, announced, at five minutes to twelve that dinner was ready. The four sat around the table, Mark looking the odd one out as even his party hat could not disguise his sulks, caused by Helen switching channels from the exciting Cowboy film to the boring BBC alternative. Their first Christmas together was a contrast from all others that they had known. As they tucked into roast chicken, boiled and roast potatoes, green beans with buttered carrots covered in delicious thick gravy, Mary laughed "Ah Bisto!"

It was the first Christmas dinner at which all three could relax without the fear of violence. Thoughts of financial worries, the hard grind of everyday labours, exams and unpleasant teachers, were replaced by a sense of well being and for the next few days, a time of plenty. Barry turned off the TV and they all proceeded to do justice to the meal. After lunch, which was always referred to as 'dinner,' Mark, disappointed at the TV remaining off, went to his room to play, while Barry stretched out on the sofa, legs hanging over the side and snatched forty winks.

The two women were once more in the kitchen, scrubbing, cleaning and preparing for the more casual affair of their evening meal. Mary was sipping a dark sweet liquid from a small glass, as was her mother. "Decent drop of sherry this 'Harvey's'."

Her daughter, being no expert on the relative merits of fortified wines agreed with several nods of her head. When Helen went into the front room to ask Barry if he would like a drop of sherry, Mary took the opportunity to empty the rest of her sherry into the sink. When her Mother returned she would see the empty glass, proof that it was indeed a fine sherry and obviously had been an appreciated treat. In Mary's other hand however was the lemonade that was her preferred beverage, useful for swilling the aftertaste of the alcoholic treat from her taste buds.

In the front room Helen looked at Barry and with a resigned sigh said quietly, "Some of us have the life of Riley" then, with a little smile she returned to the kitchen. Seeing the empty sherry glass in her fifteen year old daughter's hand she asked "like another love?"

Mary's emphatic 'no' followed by the announcement that she would like to go to her room and read for a while, convinced Helen that sherry was not to the girl's taste, a deduction supported by the sight of dark brown syrup running slowly down the side of the white Belfast sink. She allowed herself a little knowing smile and as the teenager left, continued the evening preparations, pausing now and then to look out of the small kitchen window at the fading light and un-festive brick outbuildings, wondering what her absent children were doing at that moment and whether enjoying their Christmas day. However, her imagination conjured pictures of Peter in the pub with Jack, Karl at some friend's house and fourteen-year-old Terry at home alone, the table set as merry as he could make it. Finally realising his lonely state would not be relieved until the early hours of the following morning, taking off his paper hat and eating his dinner.

Mary did not go to her room, but went upstairs to her little brother. There she showed him the green leather-bound book and helping him to throw his toys off the bed and onto the floor, she lay alongside him and read out to him in soft tones, the remainder of the story during which he had fallen asleep on the previous evening. Charles Dickens 'A Christmas Carol.'

At evening tea and supper everyone was subdued but spirits lifted when they watched Laurel and Hardy on television. When 'The National Anthem' finished, a faceless voice reminded them, "You won't forget to switch off your sets, will you? Good night." followed by the high pitched tone that signalled the end of transmission and Christmas Day 1959.

Chapter 37

Boxing Day came and went and Barry and Helen returned to work. Mary, when she was not studying in her room, would visit friends leaving her brother alone. He did not mind the solitude but his parent's insistence that he could only watch the box if his sister were there to supervise irked the child. Fortunately however he soon discovered a compromise. During his sister's absences, he would simply disobey their orders and after plugging in, would revel in the afternoon.s 'Watch With Mother' programmes of 'Rag Tag and Bobtail', 'Bill and Ben', 'Andy Pandy' and the 'Woodentops'. He had even worked out a clever little ruse to avoid his sister discovering his disobedient pastime in front of the flickering set. The boy would wait until his sister left the house, then run to the bay window to watch her walk down to the bus stop, waiting until the bus passed by the bottom of the road confirming his sister had boarded and was gone, then he would run into the kitchen and bolt the door. In that way, even were he was so engrossed in his entertainment that he did not hear the key in the door on Mary's return, he would hear her rattling and cursing when she found access barred. This minor fracas would give him time to switch off and unplug. When he calmly unbolted the door to his sister he would answer her chastisement by reminding her that he was only six years old and had been frightened that someone might break in and get him, Because 'Someone' had left him all alone. This usually made the girl feel guilty and served the boy well for almost a week. Eventually her suspicions were aroused by the fact that the TV always came on instantly when normally it took a long time to operate from cold.

Mary returned one day and stealthily entered by her own front door, creeping up the stairs she leapt into the front room, startling her brother so badly that he could not stop screaming for thirty seconds, after which, he continued to cry for a further two minutes. It was only by telling the victim that she would not inform their parents of his naughtiness and that she had only meant her surprise as a jest, that she eventually succeeded in calming the youngster. It was not the shock of sudden and unexpected discovery that put an end to Mark's solitary viewing, but the red, finger stripes left on his legs by the ferocious slaps of his mother's hand when Mary reneged on her promise of secrecy, on the first occasion that the boy annoyed her.

There was no thought of punishment a day later where an air of imminent celebration reigned over the household, once again. It was 'New Year's Eve' and it would be another night in front of the TV for Mary and Mark and another alcoholic outing for the adults. This time, however, Mark managed to stay awake and with his family he enjoyed counting down the seconds to the brand new exciting 1960.

As they whooped and shouted "Happy New Year!" hugging and dancing about the room, the drunken adults were in constant danger of falling over, but as they all felt the warmth of hope in better days to come, each in their own way intended this new decade to be the start of a better life, all that is except for Mark. He was only interested in avoiding being crushed and stepped on by the others' irrational antics.

Chapter 38

The younger children had been back at school for over three weeks and at the end of January, Christmas seemed so long past that Mark was already wondering if it could be around the corner once more. It had taken the first week for his depression, occasioned by his return to mundane routine's to dissipate sufficiently to allow him to believe there could be life after December the 25th.

Throughout February and into March, there were regular snowfalls and temperatures were very often below freezing both day and nightime. The unremitting cold and bitter winds caused many hardships. The outside toilet, continuously froze-up, sometimes they would find the lead pipes had burst in the night and the water that escaped had frozen into static icy waterfalls. When Barry had the time he would get the blow-torch from his tool kit and with a large bar of lead solder, small tin of flux and a moleskin cloth, would, repair the burst. Unfortunately he rarely had time during the week, so if the burst happened on a weekday, it could be weekend before the repair could be carried out. When this was the case, they would have to take a bucket of water with them and after completing their business they would tip the bucket of clean water down the toilet pan simulating the cistern's flush.

Mary hated this task because the water bucket was too heavy for her brother to carry and she had to carry it for him. Standing outside the toilet door in the freezing cold she had to wait furiously for the little brat to finish. When he had, she would tell him to lift the seat then she would drag him outside. To avoid involuntary inspection of her brother's handiwork, she would hurl the water at the toilet from a distance, a practice she was soon told to discontinue as the water that landed on the stone floor formed an icy carpet to complement the frozen waterfall.

Barry tried to limit the damage and likelyhood of burst pipes by placing a paraffin lamp under the rising main at floor level and using strips of blanket to lag the higher sections of pipes. This seemed to work as the last few weeks of the freeze produced no more plumbing mishaps. To light the coal fire on such cold mornings was another tedious and arduous chore. The coal would have frozen into big lumps where water had penetrated the roof from melting snow during the daytime, only to re-freeze at night. To fill the bucket whoever's turn it was to 'bring in the coal' would first have to break the frozen lumps into manageable sizes with a hammer, then fill the pail, ensuring that they put in sufficient 'Slack'- a kind of lumpy coal dust that would damp down the fire, causing it to burn more slowly, thus saving fuel. This slack was shovelled from the stone flagged floor with an old tin-plate shovel that was kept in the bunker with the hammer. Getting through the two doorways to the front room with a heavy bucket or, in Mark's case a not-so-full and not-so-heavy bucket, was made more difficult by the blankets that Helen had fixed task from the doorway of the sitting room, in effort to keep out the bone-chilling draughts.

The fire-lighting ritual was the same each morning; the fire would be raked out vigorously until all the ash had dropped through the slotted cast grate into a tin-plate pan. This would be wriggled back and forth until the ash pile was sufficiently flattened to allow the pan to be withdrawn. If the ash and clinker were cold they would be deposited into, several sheet's thickness of newspaper, when the hearth had been swept clean and the little brass shovel had been used to top up the pile on the newspaper, the brush and shovel would be returned to the 'Companion Set,' a little carousel stand that held a matching brass handled poker. The newspaper holding the ashes would be folded into a parcel, taken outside to an open bunker next to the coal store and deposited in the steel dustbin. Sometimes, when the ash contained glowing embers left from the previous night's fire, it was impossible to put into newspaper and it was carefully taken in the pan directly to the dustbin, the last glowing coals extinguishing en route. But that was not always the case. Often there would be frantic running back and forth to the kitchen for water to put out the fire that had started as a result of embers igniting paper and cardboard that was already in the dustbin. Sometimes the hot pan handle would burn the carrier's fingers, causing them to fail to negotiate the doorway and to catch the corner of the pan on the woodwork, scattering hot ash. Close inspection would reveal black burn marks in rugs and linoleum, proof of regular carelessness. These mishaps were often accompanied by foul mouthed obscenities, except when Barry was within earshot. Barry never, used bad language and hated to hear anyone else curse, so one swore with caution.

When the fireplace had been cleaned and the hearth-grate reassembled, it would be laid with twisted brands of newspaper onto which sticks of wood were criss crossed. Coal cobs were piled around, but placed in such a way as to allow air to pass through.

The loose paper would be lit by match in several places then, before the small flames died, a sheet of metal with a large handle, 'the blower.' Was placed over the front of the fireplace sealing the opening and forcing air up the chimney, making the flames dance higher and burn more fiercely in the oxygen enriched up-draught. Sometimes sheets of newspaper were placed over the blower making an even better seal and soon the fire was roaring, first the wood catching, then slowly, lazy tongues of flame embraced the smoking coals.

The trick was to remove the paper as it was just turning a crisp toasted brown. At this stage it was only seconds from bursting into flames. When this happened the fire lighter had to juggle the burning newspaper. Shouting "look out!" and screwing the flaming mass into a ball had to dash for the kitchen sink, leaving floating black tissue fragments in their wake.

Experts could manage the task with no blower, using only a sheet of newspaper and a long poker or tin-plate shovel for a centre support to draw the flames. They could time their hurried removal of the paper, from the greedy blaze with deft precision. Less expert individuals who mis-timed their careful operations found themselves performing the fireball shuffle. Sometimes the paper would disintegrate into burning fragments, disappearing mockingly up the chimney. Occasionally it would set fire to the soot-lined flue, resulting in pandemonium and filth, when the fire brigade arrived to douse the smouldering stack. The soot, smoke and dust always managed to escape from the protective canvas sheet fastened over the fireplace, while the firemen on the roof turned on the hose that had been fed down the pot to reach the minor inferno. When the job was completed, the firemen would leave the unfortunate householder with a terrible mess and a few words of advice. "If I was you I'd get a blower."

"Here, said Mary, take that outside."

Mark took the hot blower by the huge handle. As he placed it outside the back door, he noticed that holes were appearing where heat had been conducted at its fiercest. He knew that the bigger the holes became the more likely someone would soon be doing the incendiary juggle. When he returned, Mary had swept the hearth clean and the fire, although smoking heavily, had started to take hold and before long the front room would be cosy.

Mary went into the kitchen and took the pink bar of Lux, from a metal dish screwed to the wall above the sink. She washed her hands, not bothering to use hot water from the old cream-painted geyser but scrubbing at the grime with the scented soap, a stiff, bristled brush and freezing cold water. When she was happy that the bright pink and slightly sore hands were spotless, she rubbed them brutally on a limp cotton towel trying to warm some life back in to them. She poked the towel into the rubber-cupped receptacle that held it in place with its star shaped grasp, then returned to the fire to hold her hands as close as the increasingly ferocious flames would allow, every so often rubbing them together briskly.

Her hands now glowing, she pushed her brother, who was emulating her hand-warming, out of her way and turned her back to the fire. In seconds her backside and her scalp were tingling, making her feel warm and contented. When she could stand no more and Mark said that the back of her legs looked like corned beef, she relinquished her position to her brother and continued with her mornings, chores.

Chapter 39

It was a mild April morning and Mark's incessant chatter revolved around how big brother Terry had been to France and won a medal and a trophy for playing rugby. It never crossed the youngster's mind that it had been a team performance. No, his older brother was the one and only reason for victory over the feared enemy the French, who, as everybody knew, were the worst people on earth except for the Germans. It would be some years and the acquisition of improved reading skills before the astounded boy would learn that the French, with whom England had been at war for nigh on nine hundred years, had actually been allies in the Crimean and in the last two great wars.

Terry had seen his mother twice since his triumphant return. On the first occasion he had presented her with the carved head of a grotesque monk whose tongue lolled to one side in a drunken leer. At both meetings he had brought her up to date with happenings in his part of the world, but was disappointed that at each get-together his little brother had been left at home. Helen had twice failed to mention to Mark that she was going to see Terry until after the event, considering him too young to care anyway. She could not have been more wrong and it was a wonder that she failed to read the hurt in her youngest son's disappointed expressions.

March had seen Mary reach her sixteenth birthday and in the same month Jack became twenty-two. Karl would not be twenty-one until the end of July, while Terry and Mark were still fourteen and six respectively.

"Well I bet you aint even got a brother."

Mark's second best friend had heard enough of this brotherly bragging and was pleased to see the shock on his chum's face. "I 'ave, you know I 'ave Fred."

Noticing that he now had the attention of several onlookers, Fred took further delight in launching an accusative tirade against the boy who moments before had been the only real friend he had. "I've never seen em an' no one else has Dacey, I think you're a big fibber." Fred squared up to Mark, waiting for the inevitable confrontation that must follow such a derogative attack, but none came. Mark retreated past the several jeering onlookers, struggling to hold back the tears that threatened to expose him to the ridicule of the playground. "Yeh see, ee is a fibber, an' a chicken!" Fred yelled after Mark. Now confident that the thoroughly deflated boy posed no physical threat, Fred puffed out his chest and soaked up the admiration of the enlarged band of onlookers. "Yeh an' if you come near me telling your fibs again, I'll.. I'll 'ammer you."

Humiliation complete, Mark slunk off to the cloakroom to hide until the bell rang signalling the end of break. At lunchtime Marion, who had witnessed the earlier events but had stayed out of what she saw as 'boys' only business', tried to cheer up her forlorn friend. "Well I believe you, after all I've seen your sister Mary loads of times, an even if I 'av never seen yer brothers', I still believe you."

Although she had not meant to, Marion also had cast doubt on Mark's claims of family ties. The remainder of the day was spent trying to avoid Fred who seemed to have gained a bunch of new admirers who'm he regaled at the afternoon playtime session with an exaggerated version of Fred's dealings with that liar Mark Dacey. Several times a child passed Mark and made a sly comment. The boy found that instead of subjection a new feeling was beginning to rise from within - rage. Fred was recounting his embellished story when he felt a blow to his stomach and the air was forced out of his skinny body with a whoosh. "Right Bamber, 'am gonna 'ave you a fight."

The boy who had once been a friend now standing over him both fists clenched, had a similar effect of being plunged into freezing water and he was taken aback by Mark's intention to forego custom and start the fight there and then. "You can't fight 'ere Mark you'll get dun."

Marion had stepped between the two boys', much to the disappointment of the fast growing crowd, "E'll see you after school Bamber."

Alerted by the sneaky arse-kisser who had run immediately to report and was now innocently ringing his bell, the the duty teacher arrived at the scene of the conflict. Finding only the remnants of the group making their silent way back to class, he glared suspiciously and with a shrug of his shoulders, the beanpole bellowed for all students to "Get a move on."

Throughout that afternoon Mark's feelings fluctuated from frightened misery to enraged fury and the constant fluttering of stomach butterflies made him feel queasy. When it was time to go home, he tried to bolster his courage with thoughts of how he had been wronged, humiliated and ridiculed. A small, excited army flocked over the crossing place taking Mrs. Green by surprise. The two combatants found themselves swept side by side to the front of the small mob. The nearest available venue was - between the butcher's and Jimmy Duckworth's on a small patch of waste ground, just off the pavement and far enough away from prying adult eyes.

"Right Dacey, I'll give you one last chance to give up," Fred's words became a high pitched scream as Mark, not observing protocol, steamed into his foe, fists flailing. "You twat" yelled Mark, and if Fred had wanted to, he could not have answered the insult as he was busy spitting blood from his burst lips, his arms flailing wildly trying to avoid the onslaught. In a moment of respite, Fred staggered past Mark and the group and made a run for it, realising he was no match for the boy he had baited all day. Fred's luck was out as demon Dacey found a second wind, goaded on by the fickle mob who changing allegiance to the strongest combatant, bayed for blood. Finding his first route of escape blocked by a section of the crowd, he darted through a more thinly congregated group, only to find he was running in the opposite direction to his preferred line of escape. In the confusion, he realised the falling sensation experienced, was due to standing on an untied shoelace, his landing was painful and final. Looking up, he saw he had reached the doorway of the Red Lion.

Rolling over slowly, he sat up and inspected the grazes and cuts caused by his fall. Mark reached him and seeing the damage felt his anger fade and like most of the others in the crowd, felt sympathy for the vanquished. "Av you 'ad enuff Bamber?" Fred nodded his head, then as tradition demanded announced, with tears streaming down his face and loud enough for all to hear, "Yeh I give in, you win."

"NO EE BLOODY WELL DUN'T GIVE IN!" boomed the voice of a man who had come out of the pub to satisfy his curiosity as to the commotion. Fred felt himself hoisted to his feet by the collar of his shirt, two of the top buttons pinging into the gutter. "Now lad, get this blond- haired softy 'ammered," commanded Donald Bamber. Fred protested first his reluctance then his injuries, but his brutish father was having none of it. "Go on lad, get stuck in, look 'ees shittin' imself."

Mark, felt he was now fighting father as well as son and was fast losing his appetite for the battle he felt was about to be renewed, but in an effort of bravado shouted at the drunken adult and the wretch that used to be his friend. "I aint afraid of you Bamber, nor yer stupid dad!"

Mark ducked just in time to avoid a punch, from the enraged father, "Stupid am I yer little bastard?"

The crowd of watching children was subdued and one or two adult onlookers, tried to intervene, but soon backed down when the bully they knew as 'Mad Don' threatened them with a pasting if they interfered again. "I WOULDN'T TOUCH THAT LAD IF I WERE YOU,"... Don spun about to face the interfering do-gooder.

Seeing a dark-haired six-foot-two young man, slim in stature and handsome of feature, Don spat out and spoke menacingly. "And who the fuckin' 'ell 'ave we got 'ere? Fuckin' Zorro without 'is mask."

"No, I'm Jack Dacey and that's my kid brother you just took a swing at." The crowd gave a collective sigh, the children because here in the flesh was one of the mythical Dacey brothers', while similar gasps were emitted from a large crowd of adults, most of them had heard of Jack Dacey.

"I, I din't know you were out Jack an', an', I din't know ee were out to do wi' you."

Mad Don's stuttering excuses brought a huge smile to the eldest Dacey son, his pearly white teeth glistening. In a swift motion Jack pushed through the two young boys' and seized Bamber senior by the throat. Although a bully, Don was no coward and swung a right hook at Jack's head. Unfortunately for Don the head was no longer there, as the perfectly placed head-butt revealed. With a sickening crunch mad Don's nose flattened and a searing pain stabbed into his head as his nerve endings relayed the broken nose and cheekbone to his brain. It had taken less than ten seconds from Jack grabbing him by the throat to the pathetic sight of his attempted crawl towards the pub door, all the while whimpering incoherently. Dropping to one knee, Jack grabbed Bamber's jacket collar, registering further pain to his bewildered reasoning. Bamber was jolted upwards until his left ear was touching Jack's lips. "What you feel now will be nothing compared to what I'll do to you if you finger me to the coppers."

Don gave another yelp as Jack threw him to the ground. As he stood up, running his fingers through his hair, Jack looked about the muted gathering and seeing his dishevelled younger brother, grasped him gently by the shoulder and said "Come on, show me where you live now." Mark sensed the fear and respect that the men in the crowd held for his brother and the excited adulation from the bloodthirsty little monsters who, overcoming the initial shock by recent event's, were beginning to chatter noisily.

The last face Mark noticed as he left was young Fred's, - pale, blank and miserable. Thankful to be leaving the scene, Mark instinctively reached for his eldest brother's hand. As they touched, Jack recoiled and looked down at the six-year-old he hardly knew, due to the law enforced absences from his young life, then with another big grin, hoisted him effortlessly onto his shoulders. If the delighted youngster had only looked back, his delight would have been doubled by the envious gazes from many of his young schoolmates. With great strides Jack turned the corner and on Mark's directions he made his way up the hill for Saxon Place.

In the distance a bell was ringing announcing an approaching police car, but the pair could not have cared less. At the small kitchen table Jack studied the small boy who was busily making cups of tea for them both. He gritted his teeth with resolve, as he realised that he had come here to do a job. Being at the right place at the right time to save his brother from a beating was a bonus presented by fate. The real reason for his visit was not going to be so rewarding.

The brothers' sipped their tea silently and waited for Helen, Mary and Barry to return.

The ambulance arrived at the Red Lion just after the black police car. The now pitiful, but more alert Don, was telling the police that he had fallen on leaving the pub. Most of the adults disappeared at the arrival of the coppers and the landlord had shooed off the kids. With no witnesses and the fact that Mad Don was intensly disliked by the police due to his tendency to take drunken swings at them on their frequent calls to incidents of domestic violence, they saw no point in reporting anything but a drunken accident and left the injured party to the ambulance men's administrations. Breathing a sigh of relief, the landlord watched the departing ambulance, glad that his warnings of retribution from the Dacey family for any police informers had had the desired effect, and at least he and his pub would be safe from similar revenge-motivated attacks from that lunatic Dacey.

Chapter 40

Although delighted to see her eldest son, Helen felt uneasy. Something about his demeanour worried her. As she and Mary bustled about the kitchen making tea, she popped in and out of the front room, maintaining conversation with Jack who returned her questions while staring with little interest at the TV.

Helen and her three offspring had finished their evening meal a good hour before Barry arrived home and she announced cheerily that Jack had come to visit. The awkward glance as she removed his food from the saucepan where it was keeping warm, told Barry something was not quite right. Bracing himself, he went into the front room and, draping his jacket over the back of the settee, turned to face Jack who had started to rise from his seat.

Barry threw out a right hand to the visitor and said, "Ello lad, it's nice to meet you at last," then before a slightly embarrassed Jack could reply, added, "Yer mum has told me a lot about you." Again, before Jack could compose himself to reply, he carried on, "You don't mind if I get me tea do you?"

"No, no course not" replied Jack and found himself relieved as Barry disappeared into the small kitchen.

Their first meeting had not gone the way it was supposed to.

After Barry finished his meal, he came into the front room and sitting in the worn armchair, moved it around slightly to face Jack. Taking a cigarette from a packet, he offered Jack one, which was accepted. Replacing the packet onto the small side-table, he took up the heavy lighter and lit Jack's cigarette first then his own. For the next thirty minutes, Barry showed a great sympathetic interest in all that had happened to Helen's eldest son since leaving prison, and then both Barry and Helen inquired in a positively friendly fashion as to his future plans. At the end of the amiable discussion Jack felt more at ease and a little flattered by the interest shown in him. "Well do you fancy a pint Jack?" The request caught the young man off his guard once more and he meekly nodded. It took ten minutes for Jack to convince Helen that he would return and say goodbye after leaving the pub and it took a further two minutes and a promise of a trip to the cinema to prise his younger brother's arms from round his neck.

While Jack was enduring this unfamiliar family camaraderie, Barry washed his hands and face at the kitchen sink and donned the clean shirt Mary had brought him. With a final brush of his hair and a last check in the small mirror, Barry joined Jack on the door step. "I tell you what, after the pub why don't I bring us some fish and chips back for supper?" Jack was about to protest but Helen, Mary and Mark's enthusiasm decided the issue and with a forced smile he agreed.

"Say good night to Jack, Mark. You'll be in bed when he returns."

Tears immediately sprang to the youngster's eyes when he learned that he was to be excused from the late evening feast, but were just as quickly stemmed when Barry said, "No, let him stay up this once. After all, he needs to spend time with his brother."

"Oh alright, just this once," replied Helen.

The door closed and the two men walked side by side down the hill. Reaching the bottom Jack quickly said his preference was the Black Bull rather than the Red Lion. The last thing Jack wanted was to walk into conversations regarding his earlier exploit's. Although the 'Bull' was only twenty yards across the road, it was frequented by a different set of locals, who hopefully would keep his name out of the frame while he was with his mother's new partner.

Barry returned from the bar with two pints of bitter and placed one glass before Jack then, sitting next to him on the high-backed bench, spoke. "Jack lad, I think I know why you have come." Jack was not surprised this time but again, before he could reply, Barry continued "And I understand that you feel bad that your mother and I are together."

Jack's thoughts raced, this was not how he had planned things. Far from being the evil home-wrecker that his father had constantly described until Jack had felt compelled, during a drunken state the previous evening, to promise he would sort this Barry bloke out. Jack found himself liking the amiable man. Ashamedly, he thought of the wicked flick knife in his pocket and what he had intended to do.

"All I can say is, that if you still feel you want to sort this out with fists, then so be it. I've never backed down from trouble in my life and providing you are doing this for your own reasons and not someone else's, then after it's over there will be no grudges held by me and I hope none by you."

Jack eyed Barry and thought, this bloke's all right; he was no mug and decided a swift victory over this resolute man was out of the question. "No, there's no need for grudges. Me mum and brother an' sister are happier than I can remember them being."

Barry grinned and grabbed Jack by the shoulder. "I'm really glad. I din't fancy rolling about the pavement in a good shirt."

Jack laughed and the rest of the evening was spent in genuine amiable conversation as the two men got to know each other a little better.

For several days after these events, Mark basked in the glory that victory, and finding oneself the centre of attention, brings. During this euphoric period Mark could have claimed to have a hundred hidden siblings and no one would have argued the point.

On the third day the heady joy took a downturn when his former friend- turned-foe, Fred, appeared at school. Mark had anticipated this moment, daydreaming of how the miserable, beaten and humiliated wretch would squirm before the whole school. But on facing Fred at that morning's break, the victor found little to gloat about as he was shocked by his former tormentor's appearance. "I din't think I 'urt yer that much," stammered Mark.

"Yer dint" replied the subdued Fred.

The black eyes and livid bruises, causing the small boy's enforced absence from school, were due to a father's revenge on a son he blamed for his own sorry state.

"I'm sorry I called yer a liar Mark."

"An' I'm sorry I hit yer Fred."

"Oh that wernt nuffin," replied Fred and as if to accentuate the fact made an attempt to grin through the still puffed lips. "Wanna be friends again?" Mark looked into the swollen eyes and thrust out his hand, "Yeh."

The small crowd that had gathered hoping for a resumption of hostilities between the two drifted away, disappointed at the rekindled friendship.

Over the coming weeks, as July and the eagerly awaited 'Big Holiday,' five weeks end-of-term break approached the two boys' and Marion were constant companions. If not obvious to the boys', the redistribution of power from Fred to Mark was not lost on the girl. Seeing her friend suddenly becoming the undisputed leader of not only the trio but a variety of new found playmates both pleased and yet at the same time disturbed her. She did not know why, but she felt that not all the changes were for the better, however with the 'Big Holiday' only days away, it was easy to brush aside her concerns.

Chapter 41

During the first week of freedom there was an added bonus of watching one's sister disappear down the hill on her way to school. Mary had to attend school during the first weeks of holiday to sit exams, which allowed her acerbic brother's taunts to ring after her. "Ave a nice time at school Mary."
Even from the distance of the opened bay window to the bottom of the hill, the juvenile tormentor could make out his sister's scowl and on receiving a two-fingered salute scampered inside, slamming the sash down in triumph.
Wrestling his way through the net curtains he proceeded to plan the day. The morning was spent at first attempting to find something to watch on television; that failing, out came the soldiers, and by the time hunger stopped play it was almost noon. Mark studied the saucepan, the egg and the bread and butter. He was fully aware that the specific instructions on preparation of boiled egg, handed down from his mother via his sister, were not open to interpretation. However after deliberating for a few moments, he decided that the four minutes needed to cook the egg was a waste of precious time. After quickly dressing, the small boy grabbed the egg from the willow-patterned saucer, leaving two slices of bread. Departing from the house by the back door, he hurried across the cobbles and turned left up the dirt track. As the nearby allotments came into view, he cast a few furtive glances around, satisfied that the coast was clear, he hurled the raw egg at the furthest building's gable end, delighted at the way it splattered its contents over the dull red bricks, almost like a work of art. Fear of discovery lent speed to his retreat and he found himself breathless but safe behind the locked back door, stung with remorse at the wanton waste of food he recalled a well-worn phrase of, "Someone, somewhere in the world, would be glad of that there food." Shaking his head to dispel the guilt, Mark continued to butter the two slices of bread then, taking the bag of 'Tate & Lyle' granulated sugar from the kitchenette, he sprinkled a thin layer onto the buttered surface. After all, thought Mark as he munched his way through the second sugar butty, this is better than a borin ole egg any day.

Mark found his friends at the 'Rec,' His annoyance and disappointment over the last forty minutes when he had failed to find any of his pals were forgotten as they yelled out greetings from the cast iron frame of the swings. "We waited ages for you at the common then thought you wern't coming," stated Fred who was lying on his stomach, face down on the wooden swing, scuffing the toe sections of his worn shoes on the concrete, making the mouth-shaped holes even larger.

If his friend had any intention of answering, it was curtailed by Marion's sudden exclamation, "Oh shit, 'ere comes that Ronnie Grey."

The boys' looked up to see the imminent arrival of a schoolmate who, although being of a similar age to the trio, was twice their size. "Hiya Ronnie, do you want my swing"? Volunteered Fred.

The bigger boy took the chain of the offered swing and hoisted himself into place. Mark could not help feeling that even without Fred's unselfish offer, the bigger boy would have been sitting in that exact same spot notwithstanding. "So what you up to Dacey?"

Mark feigned apathy sensing that his friends expected him to stand up against the unwelcome intrusion, "Mind your own business Grey" "Or else?" retorted Ronnie, flabbergasted at the effrontery of this skinny nonentity swinging at his side. Mark carried on with his charade of indifference, "I said or else what Dacey?" shouted an enraged Ronnie.

"Or else I'll kick yer 'ead in."

The bigger boy, flummoxed by the smaller boy's impudence, stuttered in an attempt to reply. Seizing the initiative, Mark leapt from his wooden platform and with heart beating wildly, stood on the grassed area just off the concrete base, purposefully making an exaggerated show of rolling up his shirt sleeves. "Cum on then, yer fat fucker."

Ronnie's poise was further undermined as he became tangled in the twisting chains of the swing. Finally, struggling free, he faced his opponent. "I can't fight yer."

"Why not?" asked a slightly confused and slightly relieved Mark.

"Coz 'ave got me best clothes on, 'ant I?"

It was a fact that one did not get into fights when wearing Sunday best clothing, as the battering dished out by exasperated mothers' for the ruination of good apparel far outweighed the physical injuries of scrapping.

"Well if yer not gonna fight, give me mate 'is swing back an' fuck off."

"Yeh piss off you fat fuck," added the emboldened Fred.

Ronnie looked at the small group of friends whose confidence had grown with belief in Mark's ability to defeat him. Seeing the only alternative to fighting the whole gang was to retreat, this he proceeded to do. As Fred leaped triumphantly into the vacated swing seat, Mark watched the purposefully slow departure of Ronnie. The bigger boy turned with a sudden thought of rushing Mark, but he found the smaller boy facing him in a prepared stance. Without the element of surprise, deeds turned to words. "I'll see yer later Dacey when 'ave got me playin-out clothes on." Mark gave a shrug of his shoulders, then Ronnie glared at him malevolently, "When you aint got yer gang with yer."

"I don't need me gang for you shit 'ed," the smaller boy returned the glare. Something told him that this bigger boy was more than a match for his bravado, much more!

With the interloper's departure Marion pushed the buoyant Fred off the swing and joined Mark's side. Only half-grumbling, he left the pair on their own and headed unperturbed for the nearby slide. They swung aimlessly, passing each other in lazy reverie; several minutes passed in silence, then as the hypnotic pendulum motions faded, the girl grabbed hold of the almost static chains, locking her chain and Mark's with two hands. "Mark, you be careful of that Ronnie, he's too big for you an e's a tuff un."

The boy had no inclination to argue the point and pensively nodded. A shout from Fred put an end to their conversation. "Let's go up 't' paddlin pool."

The gang, for with some new arrivals that's what they had become, gathered and headed up the steep hill to the concrete pool at the grassy incline's summit. At 3p.m. the sun was still fierce and the group were perspiring heavily by the time they reached the pool. Compared to the relatively few people on the playground, the crowd and the cheerful noise around the water came as a surprise to the group. After exploring the perimeter of the throng, they managed to wriggle their way to the pond's edge. Although at its deepest it was only a few feet, it could just as well have been an ocean to the gang. Everyone except Fred removed their shoes and socks to dip their feet into the warm water. They all laughed when Fred joined them, still wearing his footwear, only Marion guessed that this silliness avoided the embarrassment Fred's filthy feet would cause and the subsequential ridicule.

Mark's mood darkened abruptly as he caught sight of Ronnie opposite, watching him. Ronnie turned to a boy at his side and after a few words he gestured towards Mark with a jerking thumb. The boy looked first at Ronnie then at Mark. Seeing the friends accompanying Mark he shook his head. Leaving Mark in no doubt that Ronnie had attempted to persuade the lad to assist in an attack on the gang.

Ronnie decided that now was probably not a good time for revenge and so satisfied himself with sneering knowingly at Mark, slowly raising a clenched fist and slamming it several times into his open hand. Mark understood that Ronnie would have his revenge and now regretted his show of heroics and realised there would be no forgiveness or quarter given. Only Marion, ever vigilant, had noticed this mute exchange and sensing her friend's unease nudged him gently "Come on lets go." Putting on shoes and socks the pair started to leave, Fred and some of the others scrambled to their feet and with squelching sodden steps they followed.

Mark stopped and headed back to the pool. Without a word of explanation to the others, he made his way intently towards the large boy who was crouching by the waters edge, floating lollipop sticks and unaware of the stealthy approach of his recently acquired enemy. Ronnie noticed a shadow over the pond, the distorted silhouette of Mark. Although he had come to terms with the presence of Dacey and his purpose, it was all too late to prevent the forceful push that sent him, best clothes and all, into the crowded pool.

Disbelieving and desperately gasping air, Ronnie tried to find his footing but his frantic efforts only caused him to slip again and again. Any thought of violence was second to survival, as Ronnie was sure he was about to drown. His thoughts of self-preservation increased as his attacker leapt at him and they both went under water.

Mark, with more luck than judgment, had landed on top of the winded Ronnie, and had gulped only a little water, while his swimming partner behaved as if he had swallowed most of the pool. Parental hands hauled the boys' from the water. Mark who was the first to shake off his rescuers, shouted in rage at his sodden nemesis, demanding a continuation of the fight. Satisfied that both combatants were in no imminent danger, the adults decided not to intervene. There was little need for concern as the deflated Ronnie was fully occupied imagining the punishment his mother then father would dish out later for his current state. "I'm gonna get fuckin' murdered!" moaned the bigger boy, "An' it's your fault Dacey, you fuckin' nutter."

"You started it, you big twat."

An outraged mother screamed at the pair for their abuse of the English language and meted out a flurry of back-handed blows, "We should have let the little buggers drown!" The boys' followed by the gang, made a soggy retreat.

Breathless, they reached the stone-gated entrance and made their way to the adjacent main road that led to Mark's home. Compared to the laughing throng that arrived at Saxon Place, Ronnie cut a crestfallen figure. Ignoring the gang's taunts, he headed for home and his mother who would be waiting to take him to his aunts.

The friends arranged to meet up the next day and dispersed for their own homes and evening meals. Finding he was alone, Mark surprised himself as he chased after the now invisible Ronnie. He caught sight of the lad crossing the main road and followed him down the lane at the side of St. James school. Forty yards further down the lane he stopped at the open doorway of a small back-to-back cottage, third in a terrace of four. He could hear the bellowing of the matriarch, "wait till your father sees you." Mark saw Ronnie, head bowed, soaked and crumpled, he was waiting for the first of the many expected blows to land.

"Excuse me Mrs. Grey."

Mark's interruption brought a look of bewilderment from the stout woman and a look of sheer terror from Ronnie.

"I'm very sorry to be a bother, but I have to tell you that it's my fault that Ronnie got wet. You see I fell into the paddling pool and I can't swim an' Ronnie jumped in an saved me."

Mrs. Grey perused the small boy. "Did he now?" she asked.

Mark nodded enthusiastically. Thankfully, the woman was so confused regarding the procedure for punishing a hero, that Mark was able to make his excuses of having to return home as soon as possible to face punishment for his own stupidity. Ronnie, finding himself raised to the status of saint, escorted Mark to the door. Grabbing his saviour's arm he looked into the blue eyes, puzzled at the actions of the boy. "Thanks" Mark grinned and shrugged his shoulders "Solright."

Reaching the pavement he was again pulled back to face the bigger lad. " Yer still fuckin' barmy Dacey."

"I know," he said with a chuckle.

Fortunately, when she heard the truth of that afternoon's events, Mary decided Mark deserved her support. She made him change and hung out his partially dried clothing and by the time the last rays of the summer day bled away, the clothes were dry enough to put at the side of his bed ready for the morning. That night in bed, Mark was not only amazed at his actions regarding Ronnie but also at the assistance given by his older sister.

Chapter 42

In August the hot weather became oppressive, tempers were exceptionally short. Mary had completed her school exams and like thousands of others across the country, she was impatiently awaiting the results. Today, during his Sister's abscence, Mark had found a ball of string and had tied two long lengths to a large polythene, toy aeroplane, the aeroplane was almost half-his-size and the boy was swinging the craft from the open bay window. Sometimes he narrowly missed passers-by who shot him threatening glances, causing him to rapidly hoist in the toy and disappear temporarily behind the voluminous net curtains, only to return to his aerobatic display once the offended parties were out of sight.

As it was Friday, Mark had to keep his eyes open for the double-decker-bus that would bring his Mother home from the early shift. Just in time he hoisted his aircraft and closed the large sash window, when Helen was midway up the hill.

The youngster ran happily to greet his Mother. He threw open the back door for her, fatigued, she allowed Mark to swing from her neck with his arms clasped in a genuine embrace. "Let me put the shopping down Mark." Helen said, "An' don't think I didn't see you 'angin out the bloody window you little sod."

Mark was busy looking in the net shopping bag for his customary treat. Sure enough, there was the bar of chocolate. "Canna 'ave it Mum? Please!" Helen nodded and allowed herself a little smile, after all she did not see that much of her son these days and moments like this were rare. Mark had not noticed that his mother was looking more tired than usual recently and Mary, seemed to be forever exhorting him to behave and not make his mother angry nor cause her any extra work. So he thought nothing of it when Helen asked him to go out to play while she made herself a cup of tea and relaxed for a short time.

The boy knew what that meant. Helen would be going in to the front room and putting her feet up while lying on the old settee. Not wanting to have to tiptoe about the house, Mark found himself at the front of the building on Buckley Road where he sat on the low stone wall underneath the only window that allowed natural light through the ubiquitous nets into Mary's room. Chocolate finished, he was engaged in digging out the perished mortar between the stones of the wall when he heard a shout "Hiya Mark" he recognised the voice instantly, but because his older brother Terry had arrived unsteadily astride an old pushbike, the younger boy had been taken by surprise, not for long though as he yelled out in happiness and practically dragged his bigger brother off the rickety machine. "Watch it Mark yer daft bugger, you'll ave me flat on me arse." Mark, saw that Terry was sporting a grin, so knew he was not in anyway annoyed and together they pushed the bike the remainder of the way to the back door. Mark skipped as they went. He sensed a change in his brother's demeanour, they propped the bike against the wall and were about to enter the house when, as if on impulse, Terry faced his brother and purposefully thrust a hand into his pants pocket producing two pennies. "Here, go t' shop an' get some sweets."

Mark guessed that his presence wasn't wanted but decided that if he ran very fast he would be back in no time. After all, Terry was here now and they would play later. So off he sped down the hill to the small sweet shop.

Helen was startled, not so much by the unannounced appearance of her older boy as Mark's shouts had warned of a visitor, but by the conversation that ensued. "Have you thought about everything seriously?"

The boy nodded, "and yer dad agrees?"

"It were his idea," confirmed Terry.

It all seemed like a bad dream to Helen and before she fully comprehended the situation, she had kissed and hugged the son who would be fourteen years old in two-weeks-time and with salt laden tears burning her eyes she had waved goodbye to his departing back. Terry could not bear to see his mother upset, so left as quickly as he could, so quickly he almost ran his little brother over. "Tell! Where are yer goin?" asked the little lad.

"Ave gotta go Mark, sorry."

"Yer comin back arn't yer Tell?"

Panic swept over the child as his older brother shook his head.

"But where are yer goin Tell?"

With one word the elder boy struck fear in the heart of the youngster. "London." For a moment Mark stopped breathing. "I'm goin to live with nan an' granddad in London, blurted Terry.

Without words and in slow motion, Mark's hand reached despondently for his friend, confidant and big brother. For the briefest of moments his fingers brushed against his jacket, the youngsters panic increased as the bicycle picked up speed. "Don't leave me, don't leave me again. Take me wiv yer Tell, I'll be good."

Terry did not hear the last desperate pleas as he had his head down to hide his own tears and misery. All the sad events that Mark had experienced were as nothing compared to what he now found himself experiencing. In a daze, he half-ran, half-stumbled after the bicycle, then realising Terry was gone, he turned and ran to his mother who, could offer him no support. Mark sat huddled on the back doorstep and started to cry. He allowed the few sticky wrapped sweets to fall from his hand, contemplating that he had been choosing those same pieces of confectionary when he could have been persuading Terry to stay. Furiously stamping and grinding the sweets into the dirt, he sobbed angrily, feeling he had betrayed his brother for a few sweets.

Helen was weeping too, but in the knowledge that she had just given her blessing for her son's new life. The stark realisation hit her that she had just lost her fourth born child, the family, that until recently had been her prime objective to keep together, was falling apart. Expecting no forgiveness, she joined her youngest son on the step but neither of them finding any comfort in the other's company, each commenced lamentations though sitting side by side.

Later Mary returned, and busied herself making tea. As the trio sat around the little table playing with the food on their plates, Mary let loose with a torrent of abuse at the absent Terry. "Typical, why should he be the one to get out of this bloody hole, and not me?"

Helen stared at her in disbelief but could not find the energy to admonish or discuss the outburst. Mark took himself off to bed early and was missed by neither mother nor sister. Lying on the bed, the six-year-old watched the sun's rays fade through the thin curtains. He had tried to draw them himself, but had failed to make them meet. He lost track of time and he heard muted voices downstairs when Barry came home from work and then the louder sounds of the television.

No one came to wish him good night nor to tuck him. Worn down with intermittent crying and the miserable prospect of having to face life without his precious Terry, Mark pulled back the covers, kicked off his shoes and crawled into bed fully-clothed. Exhaustion quickly claimed him but in the early hours of the morning the little lad was woken from his nightmare and his misery was complete - he had wet the bed again.

Chapter 43

Terry had been in London for almost a month and his granddad had got him into a rough, but local, school, the 'Sir Robert Peel'. As promised, he had written every week and although he had tried to keep his letters upbeat, reading between the lines revealed an unhappy state of affairs caused by a status as a, 'Foreigner,' at the big city school and the unfriendliness of the locals.

The year 1960, saw many changes. Britain's first motorway service station opened, at Newport Pagnell on the M1. On the silver screen Billy Wilder directed the 'Oscar' winning Apartment, Burt Lancaster was awarded best actor for his performance in Elmer Gantry and Elizabeth Taylor took best actress for Butterfield 8. Exodus, Never on a Sunday, Spartacus, Alamo and the Time Machine were also big box office hits. May 6th Princess Margaret married Mr. Anthony Armstrong-Jones at Westminster Abbey, in June Congo gained independence from France. In the same year the Crown unsuccessfully prosecuted Penguin Books for publishing Lady Chatterley's Lover. In November the USA elected a new president, John F. Kennedy, who had narrowly defeated Richard Nixon in a bitter election campaign. American scientists invented the laser, Barbie dolls were 'born', Russia shot down a U2 spy plane piloted by Gary Powers and December 31st was the last day for call-up for National Service in the United Kingdom.

The golden age of vinyl arrived with record sales jumping 60% in just over a year. A pop group formed as the 'Beatals,' had changed their name first to the 'Silver Beetles,' then to the 'Silver Beatles' and by the years end the band had been joined by Pete Best and had made their final name change to the 'The Beatles' and made their first trip to Hamburg.

On the football pitch, Scotland drew 1-1 with England at Hamden Park in the Home Championships; England then managed a 3-3 draw with Yugoslavia in a friendly match. Other friendlies saw England lose to Spain 3-0 and again to Hungary 2-0 but a 5-2 win over Northern Ireland (Home Counties) set the national team up for a 9-0 victory in the World Cup Qualifier against Luxembourg. They gained revenge in the friendly against Spain at Wembley winning 4-2 and in the last International match that year, played in the Home

Counties, England thrashed Wales 5-1. In the 'F.A. cup,' Wolverhampton Wanderers beat Blackburn Rovers 3-0.

On TV Bootsie & Snudge was a spin off from the 'Army Game,' starring Alfie Bass & Bill Fraser. On Friday 9th December at 7p.m. a fortunate few turned on their sets to catch the first episode of Coronation Street, the rest of the nation would have to wait until the following spring when the episodes were shown on Mondays and Wednesdays. Few could have forseen that the thirteen episode series created by Tony Warren and originally conceived as, 'Florizel Street,' would go on to become such a massive hit.

By the year's end, Jack Dacey would meet his future wife Katy Harvey. Helen's second born, Karl, would leave Richton and join Terry in London and Barry would attempt and fail to teach Mary to ride a 'BSA Bantam,' motorcycle. Demolishing sections of the nearby allotment fencing, she would pick herself up for the umpteenth time. Much to her little brother's amusement, the furious girl would storm off screaming "Fuck It," thereby ending her foray into the realms of two-wheeled freedom.

It would be Mary's turn to laugh at Mark when she observed his shocked expression on his return home from play, to discover that he had a new sister. At first his disbelief would turn to envy as he became even more of nonentity around the house, but as he became used to the idea, he would find the thought of having a younger sibling appealing and besides, baby Corinne, could be seen as compensation for his not being allowed to have a dog.

From July to December the rain fell nearly every day and much of the country was flooded at some time or another. Christmas was a disappointment as, with the new baby money was tighter than ever.

Mary, however, seemed a little happier in the knowledge that 1961 was the year that she too would escape the constraints of the northern town the highlight of December 1960 for Mark, would be becoming the age of seven.

The year started with the kind of speed that always prompts someone to say "Where have the past few months gone?"   Helen had been forced to find a minder for her new daughter Corinne a happy baby who was growing fast and because Mary was fully occupied with school work, her responsibilities for Mark were also taken over by the child minder. To finance this child care Helen had to find two-pounds-ten-shillings per week. It was the economics of survival that had forced her back to work early, as it did for every working class mother in those days. At first Mark was delighted with the arrangement as the woman engaged to look after Corinne and himself was none other than the mother of his friend Marion. Spring was slow in arriving and miserable dark cold mornings heralded the 5.30a.m. start to the day which was necessary for Barry to drop off the children and arrive in Manchester for 7a.m.   Helen's, early shift started at 5a.m. and she usually worked any overtime available. Life settled into a routine.

Marion's mother did not provide breakfast but Mark was given a drink of tea while her own children ate. Corinne was given the milk that had been prepared by Helen. At 8.50a.m. Mark and Marion left for school which was only five minutes walk away. Marion's older brother Colin left earlier to get to the more distant secondary school. Steven the 4 year old stayed at home.   After school, Mark waited with Corinne for their big sister to collect them, usually at 4.50p.m. Then, as Mary pushed the small pram towards home, Mark was ordered to walk someway in front and not to indicate in any way that a scruffy 'Oik!' like him could possibly be related to the superior being, who was pram pushing behind.

Arriving back home before his sisters', Mark dragged his feet over the cobbles and dirt patches that made up the side street leading to Saxon Place.   Leaning against the back door he looked down disinterestedly and noticed his scuffed shoes, his only shoes. Spitting fairly accurately, he rubbed the spittle into the abrasions and for good measure added a little dirt until the unsightly scuff marks had disappeared under a layer of grime. Any delusions that he would escape punishment for mistreating his only pair of shoes were dispelled when his sisters arrived. "What are you doing you dirty little sod?" demanded Mary.

"Nuffin," replied the sullen boy.

"Well we'll see if Mum thinks kicking holes in your shoes is nothing." Mark looked up and saw that even little Corrine's eyes seemed to stare at him accusingly, so he did not offer any protestations and knew that he would be in trouble when his mother returned. "Ouch!" shouted the surprised boy. "What you do that for?"

"Accident," said Mary. Mark rubbed his shins where his older sister had just rammed him with the pushchair. "Get out of the way stupid."

Mark obeyed and Mary roughly half-lifted, half-dragged the pram and its bouncing occupant backwards through the doorway. Mark's pleas to be allowed to go out to play were immediately silenced as Mary ordered him to light the fire and as if to reinforce the necessity of the command added, "It's bloody freezing in here!" then continued, "I'll see to the baby then get the tea on, so get a move on with that fire." The boy set about the task while grumbling about the unfairness of life, although in truth he was not that bothered. He did not mind lighting the fire in evening's as much as he did the morning's, though even that was not often as the expense of a fire were seldom justified by the amount of time the house was occupied.

Usually the dreaded morning fire-making chore was restricted to weekends and Mark had developed the technique of offering to do the Saturday morning shopping. This ensured that his eldest sister got the job as she would not get out of bed until her mother's threats became sufficiently convincing. On Sunday morning's Mark rose early slipped quietly out of the back door on a quest to find playmates who had escaped similar chores. Many times he found the world as deserted as only Sunday mornings could make it seem, On these occasions the youngster would amuse himself with imaginary role-playing games. In his assumed superhero persona he imagined saving individuals, then whole families from dangers that ranged from house fires to alien invasions.

One particular Sunday morning, however, more important events caused him to race home to his sleeping family. If the bang of the back door being flung open did not wake them, then the excited, shrill voice of the panting Mark did so as for the whole households edification, he announced several times each time with increasing volume. "IT'S SNOWIN"!

Barry's voice boomed down the stairs to the excited boy who was waiting for an enthusiastic response. "Well light the fire then!"

It was not the response anticipated but it was a reasonable request and the task did not seem so onerous, knowing that the thick, heavy flakes would have covered more of the land by the time the fire was roaring. Excitement changed to disappointment when, at the insistence of his mother, Mark rushed out suitably garbed Eskimo fashion only to find that the snow had turned to rain.

His mood would not have been improved had he known that the snow, now turning to a rapidly disappearing slushy mess, would be the last he and his friends would see that year.

Chapter 45

One Saturday afternoon the rain gave way to a watery sunshine and although the weather was cold, the general demeanour of Mark and his friends was cheerful as they prowled the neighbourhood looking for something to brighten their day. After playing 'hide-and-seek followed by some stone-throwing on the 'common', the group realised that the darkening skies and a drop in temperature signalled the probability of a downpour. With the change in the weather came a sympathetic shift in the gang's mood. As if by telepathy, first one then another said a hasty, "See yer later," before rushing for home. Mark was the last to leave the common, he gazed anxiously skywards telling himself that it must be time for tea anyway.

On that particular day Mary was in charge until his Mother returned from town. Barry would not be home until late that evening as he was working overtime. The last thing that Mark needed was a problem with his big sister for being late for tea. Five minutes from home, the boy met up with a group of slightly older boys' and girls' who were strolling down one of the narrow dirt lanes that led from the allotments. "Where you lot goin then?"

Despite repeating the question several times, the older children ignored Mark, impatiently pushing him aside. The boy in the tail end of the group was a lad called Stephen and Mark knew him vaguely as he was only a little older than himself.

"Come on Dacey."

"Where we goin?"

Although he had asked the question Mark was already scampering after Stephen and the disappearing mob to get an answer. Reaching the older boy's side, he was rewarded with a conspiratorial grin, "We're all goin to watch Meeksy shag Freda Connor!"

The only intelligence that Mark had on Meeksy was his full name. Kevin Meeks was one of the big boys' who Mark and his friends tried to avoid. After all, to a seven-and-a-half-year-old a thirteen-year-old is almost an adult. Mark knew that Freda, a twelve-year-old, came from a large family that lived on the other side of the 'common'.

The Connors were a rough and nasty family by most peoples standards and several times Mark had been warned by his mother to stay away from them. That was the sum of his knowledge of the individuals they were going to see, which was little enough but much more than he knew about the subject of 'shagging'. Rather than reveal his ignorance and risk being the butt of ridicule he allowed himself to become part of the excited group.

The journey ended at a derelict cottage that was awaiting demolition the throng, laughing and chattering, jostled one another over piles of bricks and debris and through a doorway that leaned at a crazy angle. It never occurred to them that the barricades that they had removed to gain access were there to save lives from the imminent danger of the building's collapse.

Soon the tiny, dank, semi-dark room was full to capacity. Stephen abandoned his travelling companion and on all fours he pushed his way through the legs of the crowd. As Mark's eyes became accustomed to the gloom caused by boarded windows and fading daylight, he saw in a corner of the room the remains of a staircase and an available perch on a partially rotten step. With serious pushing which invited much swearing and objection, the lad finally made it to this prime viewpoint. As he heaved himself up, the timber gave an ominous groan and shifted. He was afraid he would fall until the step settled into a reluctant stability. Keeping as still as possible, he looked out from his precarious vantage point over the heads of the crowd and saw as clearly as the gloom allowed, Meeksy and Freda facing one another.

Rays of light pierced the gaps in the timber causing the dust to sparkle, creating a theatrical atmosphere. He watched as, egged on by the crowd, Meeksy put his hands up the girl's flimsy dress and pulled down her knickers. Some of the spectators surged forward and at the request of one of them he hoisted the dress higher and for a few moments the girl's private parts were displayed for public inspection. Although she did not complain, she turned her head away from the audience and hissed for Meeksy to hurry up. The noise subsided as the boy undid the belt then the fly buttons of his long flannel shorts. In one swift movement he put his thumbs down the top of his underpants and dropped them to his ankles. The sight and size of his erect penis brought gasps of admiration from the boys' and embarrassed giggles from the few girls' who were present.

At first he tried to enter the girl from a standing position, but after a few, brief, abortive thrusts he dragged the girl to the floor where he removed her knickers completely. He forced her legs apart as she was now trying to keep them together then, wriggling between her skinny thighs, he clumsily gyrated then thrust a few more times, until a sharp yelp from Freda, confirmed that she had been penetrated.

More gyrations and violent thrusts of Meeksy's buttocks followed. Shrill, intermittent protests from Freda that it hurt and that she wanted him to stop, in fact seemed to stimulate the boy to make greater efforts. Meeksy's gyrations became faster and more frantic, then his thrusting became eratic, losing timing and rhythm, finally they slowed down and stopped.

Slowly the boy became aware of the hooting, jeering crowd and pulled up his pants as fast as he could. Embarrassment replaced the swaggering bravado as he fled through the crowd of children, most of whom followed him. Only a few observers remained to watch Freda slowly get to her feet and shaking the dust from her previously discarded underwear, she stepped first into one leg then into the other and pulled up the grubby pants. With her head bowed, looking at no one but the floor, she made her way out of the house and seeing that the others were following the disappearing Meeksy, she departed for home in the opposite direction. She pulled the worn, woollen cardigan around herself against the damp chill and as the rain that had threatened all afternoon finally made good its promise, she started to run shakily, with one hand she gripped her cardigan where the buttons were missing and in the other she held the two shilling coin that had been handed over by Meeksy. Mark was not a spectator to these scenes as he was already home and in the process of being scolded for his late arrival.

As he ate, Mary asked

"Well where have you been anyway?"

In a matter-of-fact tone, he announced, "I went an' watched Meeksy and Freda Connor shagging in an old house."

Mary almost choked on a mouthful of tea, but recovered sufficiently to calmly ask what he meant by that. Mark felt at once worldly and knowledgeable as he explained the whole escapade in detail, proudly repeating the new words he had overheard and memorised during the performance. "Yeh, an' then ee shoved his nob in her fanny and shagged her."

Mary didn't know whether to be amused or to be outraged. The decision was rendered unnecessary as the door opened and Helen entered, soaked, flustered and weighed down by several shopping bags. Assisted by her eldest daughter Helen took off the wet coat. "How's the baby?" "She's been great, no trouble, been asleep for about two hours now so she is due to wake soon."

Not entirely reassured, Helen checked the sleeping infant then sat at the kitchen table, accepting the cup of steaming tea proferred by Mary with grateful thanks. She had only taken a couple of sips when Mary put her hand on her little brother's shoulder. He looked up from rummaging in one of the shopping bags. "What?"
"Why don't you tell Mum what you have been doing today."
Cheerfully, the boy obliged, recounting in full the tale he had just told his Sister in the self same newly acquired colourful dialogue.

Bruised, battered and alone in bed, Mark wondered why his mother had seemed so angry with his tale and why she had attacked him with such ferocity. What had she called him? 'Filthy little beast', that was the expression that had remained in his mind. He also remembered while he was being slapped silly his big sister was roaring with laughter at every stinging blow. So as he lay painfully awake, not exactly sure which part of his tale had so infuriated his mother, he resolved that the next time he went to see someone 'shagging', he would remember not to tell his sister nor his mother.

Chapter 46

During term time Mark's evenings were spent watching 'Wagon Train', 'Rawhide', 'Emergency Ward 10' and any other television programme that could hold a small boy's attention. The days progressed in a seemingly endless routine, child minder, followed by school, followed by child minder, followed by TV then off to bed. At last summer arrived. Mary's departure from Richton seemed To Mark to be sudden and unannounced, although the event had been his eldest sister's sole topic of conversation since the start of the year. The farewell tea seemed a happy enough affair to the small boy, but a more astute child would have noticed the sad glances that Helen regularly cast at Mary and the manner in which she quickly hid her pain behind a smile whenever Mary's eyes were on her.

During the following weeks the daily routine changed Barry continued as usual to drop Mark and Corinne off at the minders early in the morning. Helen, or sometimes Barry, picked the pair up at various times but much later than when Mary had been on hand. Mark missed his big sister more than he had thought possible, especially now that he was spending much more time than before at the child minders. In these hours of enforced captivity, the young boy discovered a darker side to his carers. Marion's mother Doreen was a small, skinny, sharp featured woman with a manner that was just as austere as her appearance. In contrast, her husband George, although of a similar height, was fairly stocky, his round face and balding pate usually sported a friendly grin that gave the impression of a likeable rogue - an impression that Mark learned was mostly false. The family had recently gone up in the world when they had successfully applied for tenancy of a house on the new Council estate. Their new home was situated at the rear of the main road slums where, in a time that seemed long ago they had lived next door to Mark's aunt Ethel and cousins Frank and Sandra. The house had 3 bedrooms, an inside bathroom and separate inside toilet, it also had a small front garden and a larger rear garden making it one of the more desireable residences in the area. With their increased social standing came a feeling of superiority that the whole family, with the exception of Marion, readily displayed. Aunt Ethel and her son and daughter had moved to the other side of Richton, on an estate where the houses had been erected as temporary accommodation during wartime, but which had since been renovated to reflect their

permanent status.   Mark had not even noticed that the slum
dwellings that had been vacated had been demolished.

At the beginning of summer Doreen aquired a new charge, a three-
year-old girl called Elizabeth, whom they all referred to as Beth. The
child was shy and hardly ever spoke or played. The only occasions
on which she showed any signs of emotion were when her exhausted,
single mother called at 5.20p.m. each evening to reclaim her.

 Mark observed that the child usually ignored and neglected by the
minders, was showered with attention when her mother appeared.
Doreen and George would make a fuss of the child, praising her
behaviour and tousling her hair in a friendly manner that Beth would
shrink from, forcing herself against her mother's legs and deep into
her long coat for protection.

 It was during the summer holidays that Mark found the reason for
the little girl's terror at the prospect of any contact with her paid
protectors. It was raining heavily and the children's presence had to
be tolerated in the new house, although they were confined to the
kitchen. All that day, while drawing and playing with Marion at the
plastic-covered table, Mark found himself studying the treatment of
his infant sister Corinne and the other girl Beth. He found little
cause to worry about the treatment of his baby sister. However, he
witnessed Doreen shouting irratibly and pushing the three-year-old
without reason and regularly exclaiming that the child was an idiot
and backwards.   The vulnerable and abject child suffered in
unnatural silence, but suffering was clearly displayed in her doe
brown eyes. The maltreatment culminated with Doreen directing a fit
of screaming at Beth for wetting herself. As the miserable creature
stood in the puddle, head bowed, George returned from work. In a
few seconds he was made aware of the heinous crime and instantly
devised a fitting punishment. As if that poor creature had not endured
enough, she was then made to stand in the hallway next to the back
door with her wet pants forcibly stuffed into her mouth. Rigid with
fear at the command that she was not to move, Beth's heart-
wrenching sobbing, as she gagged on the ammonia-soaked knickers,
was too much for Mark to bear. "Please let her sit down. Please."

Any further pleadings by the boy were cut short as George rose from
his chair, grabbed the boy by his jumper and shook him violently.
This George bore no resemblance to the likeable rogue he liked to

portray. "How dare you speak when not spoken to!" fumed the man. "What the hell is it to do with a snot-nosed brat like you anyway?"

Then a more sobering thought occurred to George. If the boy knew enough to have an opinion, then he also knew enough to tell some other adult about his barbaric treatment of the girl. His attitude changed and he sat the boy down in an armchair. Firmly, but with less menace he said "Look lad, it's for her own good." Then he added "We are only trying to teach her some manners."

George noticed that although nodding frantically he was staring at a large bottle on the sideboard. A sly grin came over George's face, "Do you like snakes then?"

Mark was now shaking his head. In a swift move George seized the glass specimen jar holding several species of pickled snakes. He had acquired this item in his working capacity as a council refuse collector. Holding the terrified boy in one hand, he thrust the jar onto his lap. Mark let out a scream and with strength that belied his size tore the jar from George's grasp and launched it as far away as possible. There were three more screams, the first came from Mark as the glass bottle shattered on the nearest wall, the lifeless stinking reptiles spilling over the floor terrifying the boy. The second scream came from George as he saw his prized possession destroyed a third, more urgent, scream came from the kitchen where Doreen France was being battered by Beth's mother who had returned unexpectedly early to discover her distraught child's predicament.

Mark and the snakes were forgotten as George attempted to release his wife from the grip and rage of the manic mother. It was only after many more blows had landed and George himself had received a thrashing that the exhausted woman breathlessly ceased the attack. Pausing for a few moments to recover, the woman glared with intense hatred at the villainous twosome. Finally, she grabbed her child, swung her into her arms and left with a parting declaration that was shouted for all the neighbourhood to hear. "And don't think you'll be getting one penny more out of me, we won't be coming back here, you evil pair of bastards."

Perhaps it was wishful thinking on Mark's part that, as he looked on little Beth's face for the last time, she gave him a smile - the first he had witnessed. Tears were streaming down Marion's face. "I'm sorry yer mum got bashed Marion," soothed the still shaking boy.

"I'm not sorry, I'm glad," said Marion through tears but with absolute honesty.

Chapter 47

Helen made her young son recount the previous day's events, several times over and word for word. When she was finally satisfied of all the relevant facts and had sifted out her youngest son's embellishments and exaggerations, she pushed him into the front room where the boy sat on the old settee, almost immediately becoming transfixed to the TV screen. Helen returned from the kitchen with sausage, egg and chips and a slice of thin white bread with 'Adams' best butter. Mark took the plate that was thrust at him and without removing his gaze from the screen fed himself, blindly missing his mouth on several occasions. He was unaware of the spectacle he made, and as his little sister was asleep and Barry and his mother were talking in the kitchen, no one else was privy to the scene either.

In the kitchen Helen was furiously describing the treatment that had been handed out by George and Doreen France to a defenceless little girl.

"I don't care Barry, the kids' arnt going back to that bitch."

"Ang on love, am on your side you know and I agree, but we have to have somewhere for the young uns to go and neither of us can afford time off work."

Helen calmed down a little. "I'll have a day off sick tomorrow and get things sorted."

Barry was aware that the matter was not open for further discussion.

The next day Mark had the luxury of not having to get up early and it was novel experience to have his Mother walk him to school. Even more unusual was the pleasure he experienced and pride he felt in pushing little Corinne in her pram as far as the school gates, His pleasure increased as many of his school friends crowded around the pram and made a fuss of the swaddled infant, breaking into fit's of laughter when Corinne beamed and excitedly acknowledged their attentions. The show came to an abrupt end when the school bell sounded. Mark lingered as long as he dared and found himself waving to his departing mother, who was unaware of the lad as she was now on a mission.

That evening witnessed a happier reunion of mother and son. While they were eating their evening meal, Helen explained. "Listen Mark love, I want to ask you something important." She now had the lad's full attention. "I need to know if I can trust you to be a big boy and look after yourself a bit more." Ignoring Mark's premature nodding she continued, "Do you think you could get up, ready and off to school by yourself?" Mark was nodding more excitedly. "It means making your breakfast after you have had a proper wash and making sure you lock the door properly when you leave. It also means you will have to let yourself in after school when you can have a biscuit or some bread and jam to put you on until I get home and make something proper."

The reason for this trust was because the best arrangement Helen could make was with an ex-workmate who was willing to take care of Corinne but who wanted more money than Helen could afford and more than she had been paying Doreen France to look after both her children. The solution was simple. Mark would have to grow up a little more quickly and this would also save a few shillings. And so it was, that the following day Mark joined the thousands of British 'Latch-Key Kids'.

Chapter 48

The journey had taken over six hours, with a single stop to eat the prepared picnic and drink tea from a metal flask. Mark had only been informed the previous evening of the decision to visit his grandparents and his excitement had made sleep almost impossible. They had left at 6a.m. that Friday; he had fitfully dozed on the way down. In the late afternoon Barry, Helen, Mark and Corinne arrived safely at nan and granddads. Barry parked the big, black, 'Vauxhall Wyvern' that he had bought two days before. Nan met them at the door to the apartment block, after hugging each one in turn she led them to the rooms that were her home and where she served them tea and cakes, it was Corinnes first audience with nan and she found herself perched on her grandmother's knee, chortling in-between bounces.

The visitors were informed that granddad was not due home from work for a couple of hours and that Terry would be home an hour after that.   The reason Nell explained, was that he had got a part-time job at Vic's the butchers in nearby Seaton Street. Friday was the busiest day of the week as the shop prepared for the Saturday market, orders for meat had to be made up, cuts prepared, displays planned. Mark's heart leapt at the thought of meeting his brother for the first time since Terry had sped away on a bicycle.

With all attention focused on baby Corinne, Mark felt left out and a little jealous. While the adults caught up with current events and nan enjoyed playing with her new granddaughter, the young boy took himself into a corner of the room and pulling several plastic toy soldiers from his pocket, lost himself in a make-believe-world, apparently for the time being, unmissed.

Granddad came home from work and the family ate together. The adults resumed their conversation once a sleeping Corinne had been settled in the bedroom. Mark still feeling neglected returned to his soldiers. His daydreaming was dispelled when the door opened and Terry bounced in. Terry seemed changed, older, more grown up, but what was obvious was that even though he had been grabbed and hugged, first by Helen and then by nan as she made a place for him at the table, he was genuinely happy to see his young brother and the others. "Hiya Mark, you alright?" Mark nodded, grinning ear to ear. They did not hug or even touch, but as Terry ate the food Nan put in front of him, the younger boy drank in every moment. Although

Terry's light banter and conversation was directed at the adults, frequent looks and smiles cast his way assured the younger boy that he was fully included in any and all topics. Corinne, her nap curtailed was crying irritibly when Helen collected her from the bedroom to introduce her to Terry. He remarked what a lovely baby she was. After a while, Terry obtained permission to take Mark to the 'Bon Fini' café on Marylebone Road, a fifteen minute walk away, to meet some of his friends. Nan made him promise to be back early as he needed his rest, for the following day would entail a 5a.m. start.

The brothers'' washed their hands and faces in a bowl that had been filled with water, from a large white, enamel jug and Terry changed. Helen took a last look at Mark to make sure he was sufficiently presentable to go out and meet people. Wishing the pair goodbye she returned to the adult's conversation.

Immediately they reached the street a wave of balmy, evening air washed over the boy's. Terry grabbed Mark and hoisted him onto his shoulders as he had done so many times before in what seemed like a different life. Then the pair strode along Hampstead Road past the almost deserted Seaton Street. Where Terry pointed out the red-and-white painted butcher's shop where he worked, they continued past Euston Station until they came to a busy road. Terry put his brother down to traverse the broad highway, clasping his hand until they were safely across, not minding at all when Mark retained the grip even after they had safely arrived on the opposite side of the thoroughfare. A few minutes later they entered a busy, brightly lit café, the large letters on the frontage announcing to the nation's capital that this was the 'Bon Fini'.

It reminded Mark of the Orchard Café back in Richton, but this was bigger and livelier. It was full of young people in bright smart clothes, shouting and bantering in that peculiar accent that his nan, granddad and mother shared. The pair jostled through the crowd at the counter until they reached a long table where Terry was greeted by half a dozen friends who had been awaiting his arrival. "Were all goin down West to the pictures later Tell, you cumin?"

"Nah, can't tonight. I got my family down from the North and I'm looking after my little brother ere." With that, Terry pushed a slightly shy Mark forward. "Say hello Mark."

If Mark had felt shy, he now flushed with embarrassment as the four young men seized hold of him. Sitting the boy amongst them, they bombarded him with friendly questions, taking great delight in getting him to repeat various words that his broad northern accent made sound particularly funny to the London set. By the time Terry returned with the two bottles of '7-up', each with a straw, he found that his little brother's accent and antics had drawn a larger crowd, and finding himself the centre of attention, Mark was starting to enjoy himself, to such an extent that he was showing off a little.

Seeing everyone behaving very kindly to his brother, Terry smiled and sat opposite the boy. For a time he watched in amusement as his sibling not only entertained his friends by translating Cockney into English, but also as he managed to invent some words that he swore to his new friends were bona fide. Whether they believed him or not, his audience genuinely appreciated his performance.

All good things come to an end and eventually tiring of the welcome deviation from their usual evening's entertainment, the audience drifted away until only Terry, Mark and the original four friends remained. Mark sipped at his fizzy drink and quietly listened to the lads' conversation which ranged from music to girls', cars, back to girls', fighting and back to girls'. Mark briefly contemplated telling the gang about his 'shagging' watching escapade but thought better of it. He noticed that every time one of the boys' swore his brother winced, but it was pointless to object as every second word from the quartet was a 'fackin ell' or a 'you cant.' Mark was aware that nearly everyone he knew swore but that if he joined in or was caught by Barry, who never swore, or by his mother who always swore, then he was in serious trouble.

Time passed and Terry was preparing to take leave of his friends when there was a noticeable hush in the crowd. Several mean-looking men had just entered and one of the friends whispered, "Fackin ell it's the MANK!"

The 'Mank', the youngest boy had learned during the initial banter with Terry's friends earlier, was a native of Manchester. Terry's chums referred to them collectively as 'Manky's'. This particular 'Mank' was fast making a name for himself as one of the hardest, most vicious young men in London. "Fack me" added another, "he's camin' over ere." Mark was in the process of turning when he found himself being man handled into the air, wide-eyed and somewhat shocked; the bewildered lad looked to Terry for help, only to see a calm indifference, while the others at the table exchanged anxious glances. The strong grip threw him up, spinning him at the same time to face the 'Mank Monster.'

"Hello shit face," said the monster.

"Hiya Karl!" gasped the surprised youngster, recognising his second eldest sibling. Then, as his breathing returned almost to normal, he quipped. "Are you that Fackin' Norvern Manky then?"

Karl put the youngster back down and looked at each member of the group in turn. One by one as their eyes met Karl's gaze, they realised their dilemma and that the smiling little boy who was seated opposite, was the reason for the predicament. Terry was the last to make eye contact and his countenance reflected the agitation and concern he felt, not for himself but for his friends. "It's just a joke Karl."

Karl grinned and forced his way in-between the four lads who by now were looking at the table top. "Oh good, I like a good joke, don't I Paddy?"

Everyone at the table and most of the Bon Fini regulars who had not made good their escape looked as one at the slim dapper figure to whom Karl had directed his question. "You do that Karl, but I'm finkin that these mugs is takin' the piss."

A cacophony of protested of innocence was stilled by Karl's third companion, a huge man with a head to match. A badly broken nose and livid scar on his right cheek added to the menace he exuded. That cold menace and the presence of Paddy who had squeezed down at the table, over-crowding the bench seats, "You cant's wouldn't be takin' the piss out of me mate now would you?"

The whole room knew 'Harry the Axe'. He was a slightly older man and a well-known 'face' about the manor. This 'face' was recognised as a notorious villain in the local gang hierarchy. By now the café quartet had decided to keep their mouths shut in an attempt at damage limitations. Karl let out a roar of laughter, joined by Paddy then Harry, whose massive form trembled with cruel mirth that increased as he closely scrutinised the petrified 'straights', or non villain's.

Karl turned to Paddy and thrust a five pound note into his hand. "Get these gents a drink."

It never crossed the minds of the visibly relieved lads to refuse the offer of a soft drink as it might have been construed as an insult. The lads' disposition slowly returned to normal as Karl talked to his youngest brother, playfully pinching his cheeks, maybe a little harder than necessary but without complaint from Mark. "So Shitty Drawers, who you callin a Monkey"?

"I din't call you a monkey, I said Manky."

The group around the table laughed, some more nervously than others. "Well what do you think you are then? You are a little Norvern shit." Mark felt a little hurt and embarrassed but tried not to show it, although a reddening of cheeks betrayed him. Cruelly, Karl laughed again at the boy's discomfort and then added, "Well, if all Norveners ave a nickname, what name do you think they give the suvveners?"

There was a noticeable hush as Karl looked across at the boys'. his humour somewhat diminished. One of the boys' nervously volunteered "I've got a cousin from Birmingham an' he calls me a 'Cockney Wanker'" "Cockney Wanker', what's one of them then?" asked the puzzled lad. Karl grinned and ignored the boy then after a moment's pause he looked at Mark. "You choose. What do you call people you don't like back in Richton?"

The lad frowned, "Fairies, that's what we call 'em, fairies."

The young men sported more nervous grins and shifted uncomfortably in their seats. Karl stuck out his chin, it was a habit and he gave he gave a thin smile, "That's it then, it's official. You lot are 'Suvvern Fairies." The boys' again laughed nervously, two of them nodding in sham merriment when Karl's cold stare met theirs. "Don't you lads worry too much about bein 'Suvverners', coz you see I was born in fakin' London, wasn't I Tell?"

While Karl had been occupied with Mark, Terry had been engaged in friendly conversation with Paddy and Harry. Both knew and genuinely liked their leader's younger brother and had noticed with mild amusement how he had been cautiously monitoring the situation since Karl's mood change. Terry knew better than anyone that his older brother's manner could, and very often did, change from saint to sinner in an instant. "That's right" nodded Terry.

"So you see boys' that must make me a Suvvern Fairy too!" then to spare his victims any further embarrassment he added, "But you won't tell anyone, will you?"

Laughing and shaking their heads, the boys' fully aware that they were involved in a game of cat and mouse, were in no doubt they were playing the part of timid rodents.

"Tell you what, since we are now all best mates, why don't we ave anuvver drink." The quartet nodded enthusiastically, "An' why don't one of you boys' go get em?"

At Karl's 'request', three of the boys' leapt to their feet and comically collided and tussled to be the first to please their powerful new friend. Terry refused the offer of another 7-up and seeing Mark's green bottle half-full said "Ees ok as well."

Mark quickly dragged out the straw and putting the bottle neck into his mouth he tipped his head back and gulped down the fizzy pop.

"Am not olright, av finished. Can a 'av another please?"

His request was unnecessary, as one of the lads had already returned with a bottle for him and another for Terry. The other two returned, one handed Karl his tea, then handed Paddy his coffee while his friend passed another coffee to Harry. As the young men sat down, the difficulties of restarting a meaningless conversation was eased when Mark let out an enormous belch. "Oops, sorry, I mean excuse me!" said the abashed boy. Karl's look of contempt changed to one of amusement. "You know what you are Mark? You are a peasant from the sticks."

The shame-faced younger brother had no idea that 'sticks' meant the countryside and no inkling as to what a peasant was either, but he joined in the groups' laughter anyway.

After what seemed a reasonable amount of time, Terry's pals made their excuses and farewells. Once outside each of them breathed deeply, relieved to have escaped unscathed.

Marylebone Road's multitude of brightly-coloured lights, noisy traffic and crowds of cheerful people out to enjoy their weekend respite from work, re-ignited the youngest boy's excitement.

Terry and Mark parted company with Karl and his companions at around 9p.m. "Are You cumin to see Mum?" asked Terry.

"Nah, got some business down West tonight, aint we boys'?"

Paddy and Harry, with big grins on their faces, nodded knowingly at Karl. "Tell er I'll try to cum over tomorrow."

It was Terry's turn to nod.

"See yer tomorrer Karl!" Mark waved at his brother and his friends, who waved back "See yer tomorrow you Norvern Monkey."

Terry grabbed his younger sibling's hand and hauled him away, but not before Mark had reduced the trio of villains to hysterics when he answered Karl's friendly insult with an equally friendly two-fingered salute.

"I really like your friends Tell."

Terry said nothing in reply but wondered wether come the morning, he would still have any mates after that evening's farce. Mark skipped along happily holding his brother's hand. Here he was in London, he had been the centre of attention in a café, had enjoyed the company of his big brothers', had drank more pop than ever before in his life and was out after 9p.m. at night. Life was great!

Chapter 49

Helen rested her left arm on the big black car's open front passenger window, while she held Corinne on her lap with her right arm. As the car started to move she lifted the tot and grasping the tiny hand she forced it into waving motions directed at the child's grand parents and brother. Tommy was the first to leave, crossing the quiet road, humming aloud to cover the sadness he felt at the departure of the car and its passengers', which heralded a return to normality. Without a backwards glance, Tom disappeared inside the doorway of the apartment. Nell remained on the pavement her arm round their Grandson Terry, both waved until the moment the car found a space in the Sunday evening's traffic to turn left on the direction of the A1 and the North. The car paused at the junction for only a moment before it lurched forward and away. But in that moment Terry was transfixed by the tear-streaked face that was pressed against the rear window. It would be late when the travellers reached Saxon Place that night. They were all depressed at the prospect of work and school already, with the exception of Corinne who was soon asleep.

Nell and Terry linked arms and after looking both ways crossed Drummond Street to join Tommy. "Come on son; let's go an ave a cuppa." Nell busied herself making tea for three, which became tea for four when Terry's aunt Maud arrived. "Ello ducks, alright are we"? enquired Nell's beloved friend, confidante and sister.
"Yeh we are fine Maudie, aint we son?"
Terry nodded but could not fail to notice that his aunt had also been crying. Maud had done her weeping earlier when the family had come up to her room in the adjacent building. They had spent an hour or so chatting before saying their goodbyes. Maud did not like farewells or outpourings of emotion so she had saved her tears until the family had departed before succumbing. After waiting until she was sure that Helen, Barry and the children would be on their way, she splashed her face with cold water and called in on Nell, hopeful that they would find solace in each other's company. "Why don't you go out and find your friends for a bit Terry?" asked Nell,
"Yeh I think I will"
Terry did not feel like making the trek to the Bon Fini but the alternative was to stay in alone listening to the old Bakelite radio, because he was certain, that come opening time his grandparents and

aunt would be making their customary trip across the street to the 'Sol's Arms' where they would remain until closing time. Then all three would return arm in arm, unsteadily supporting one another.

On his way to the café the thought that he might no longer have any friends occupied Terry's mind, but he realised that his worries were unfounded when Ginger, Billy, Howard and John looked up from their usual seats, their faces instantly lighting up. "Whey hey, 'ere ee is then," shouted Ginger causing the café's clientele to turn to see what famous or infamous character was deserving of such a greeting. Curiosty satisfied that it was only Terry, they returned to their conversations. John handed Terry a 7-up and shepherded him to a vacant seat. He soon learned that far from blaming him for his older brother's behaviour, his friends revelled in the fact they could brag to other teenagers that they were not only on speaking terms with the well known 'faces' but were friends of these 'tasty geezers'. "Ere Tell, why don't you let on to your bruvver about that bastard bubble Phil?"

Bastard Phil was a Bubble, Terry mentally translated his recently aquired knowledge of Cockney rhyming slang. 'Bubble and squeak'- Greek. This particular 'Bubble' was considered the hardest lad at the friends' school, also known as, 'Phil the Greek', he was making their lives a misery and had being paying special attention to Terry who, unlike his friends had not been subjected to any physical attacks, but he had suffered continuous threats and mental bullying since his arrival in London.

"Yeh why don't you?" Ginger added.

"Nah I don't need anyone to fight my battles."

Terry replied with all the confidence he could muster but nobody at that table, not even he believed it. Try as they might to steer the conversation to calmer waters, the gang found it inevitable that all topics converged on the morrow and school.

In the little bed in the front room, Terry tried to get to sleep with little success. His meditations revolved around the speed with which situations change. Earlier that day, surrounded by family he had felt contented for the first time in months. and When his grandparents had arrived noisly from the pub, he had pretended to be asleep to avoid drunken conversation. Nell and Tom had fallen asleep in the next room the instant their heads had touched the pillows. It would be a little longer, before Terry reached the land of nod. For he was busily formulating a plan, that concerned himself, the Bubble and the rest of his life.

Sir Robert Peel was deemed by Terry and his schoolmates to be a 'shit House'. The difference in the attitudes of both teachers' and pupils' was just one thing that Terry had problems coming to terms with, Many of the teachers seemed to have little or no interest in the youngsters who were on the threshold of adulthood, unless the students in question were academically gifted or especially compliant. The students were not much better, with many having bad manners and total disrespect for their supposed betters. This situation was a far cry from the near military- regimens of his old school back in Richton.

As a newcomer, Terry had been prepared for a difficult period of time until he settled in, but it had been a total nightmare from the very first day. He had immediately fallen foul of the school bully. Philip Andropopolis, son of orthodox Greek's who had moved to Britain and London shortly before his birth. At home in the kebab house, his father was strict and brooked no backchat while in contrast, he was overly spoiled by his mother. Philip had developed into a sadistic psychotic who liked to torture animals and people with no allowance for age or gender. At a little under six feet tall and with broad shoulders, Philip could have been mistaken for an athlete, although he was not one for physical exercise. He was extremely vain and would spend an abnormal amount of time in front of the mirror arranging the tight oily black curls that, contrary to the contemporary fashion for men to wear their hair short, was fairly long and almost girlish. He would look beyond the large Romanesque nose staring into his deep blue eyes and would usually finish his self admiration by checking his large pearly-white teeth, carefully scraping with a finger nail any spot where his earlier vigorous brushing had failed to remove the velvet plaque coating. Without a doubt Philip Andropopolis saw in the mirror the love of his life.

Monday morning's were important to Philip as they determined the pattern for the whole week. Perched on a low brick wall at the top of the stone steps leading to the schools main entrance, he would check out the girls' and if any took his fancy, he would use chat up lines which were always the same. The macho lewd comments served to enhance his reputation amongst the girls' as a slime ball.

He would also mentally arrange the order of his victims for that week and the level of abuse to be meted out. Expertly he studied each pupil, looking for any opportunity to add to the growing number of unfortunates who paid him to leave them alone. This enterprise was becoming extremely lucrative and was bringing in over a tenner a week, more than some adults made with honest work.

Terry's appearance caused the young thug's pulse to increase. 'Ah' he thought, 'it's about time I put that fucker straight'.

Terry tried not to look at the Bubble and had almost skirted around him when the much bigger youth jumped off the wall and blocked his way. "Oi, I wanna word you Norvern Cant."

Terry looked up at him, staring unflinchingly into his eyes.

"Fuck off you fat greasy Bubble."

"What you say?" bristled Philip, looking around to see who else had heard the belittling insult.

"You heard, you golliwog-headed piece of shit."

Philip could not comprehend the extent of the insults as he was totally non-plussed. By the time his Neanderthal brain had grasped the specifics, Terry had disappeared into the school and temporary safety.

All morning Terry received messages from the Bubble through different channels and all the messages were the same - explaining in detail the different ways he would die before another day had passed and that if he were a man he would meet his adversary and settle their differences after school had finished. Ginger delivered the last communication at morning break. The message was all the more menacing as the Bubble had punched Terry's friend several times in the face to emphasise his resolve in the matter.

"Fuckin' 'ell Ginger, you look a mess."

"I wish I could say you should see the uvver geezer but I don't fink I even 'urt is and." Ginger did his best to smile, "Listen Tell' you gotta fak off before end of school coz that bastard will be waitin."

"Ginger, I gotta favour to ask. I want you to go to the Bubble an' tell im I'll see im on the playing fields after school."

Terry looked at his friend and saw that, although he had not nodded in agreement, neither had he shook his head. "Are you fakin mad?"

It would have been a wide-eyed exclamation had not one eye been nearly closed. "Will you do it?"

Something in Terry's calm request seemed to convince Ginger that reasoning was useless, so he nodded despairingly then disappeared to do his friend's insane bidding. Later, Ginger caught up with Terry at a prearranged rendezvous. Terry was taking great care not to bump into the Bubble and listened attentively as his friend relayed the Greek's answer. "Ee asked me to find out what flowers you want for your funeral."

Terry smiled. At least now the Bubble would be content to wait until that evening for revenge, leaving him a free hand to make his own arrangements.

At lunchtime Philip was doing the rounds. He was in the process of taking the money out of a much younger kid's pocket when another first year student shouted from a distance, "Oi Bubble, you poxy fakin' poof." When the boy was sure he had the Bubble's full attention, he flicked him several 'v' signs and ran like hell when he realised that Philip was charging at him in a murderous rage. By the time he reached the place where his tormentor had been standing, the boy had disappeared, "where did that cant go?" he screamed.

Ginger was on hand and pointed the direction. Off raced Philip through the busy area of the playground, scattering any individual in his path. He reached the almost deserted far end of the yard at the side of the school's furthest corner where Terry and Ginger's friend John shouted, "Ee ran down there!"

'Ah' thought Philip, 'so that's where he's gone hiding,'

His pace now slowed and his erratic breathing became more regular. Descending the steps to the boiler house, he knew there was no rush as there was no way out of the little below-ground courtyard. He had only just cleared the last step when the first punch hit him, a perfectly placed blow that broke Philip's nose and split both lips. A second punch sent red flashes through his brain as a fist made contact with his left eye and bridge of the already twisted nose. "You Fakin' bastard!" screamed the Bubble "I'll kill yer."

An uppercut caught him a glancing blow but did enough to slam both jaws together, splintering two of his teeth. Philip found himself morbidly looking at his own blood and fragments of pearly whites now pooled in the centre of his cupped hands. He looked up, and though he realised that it was not the youngster he had given chase to who had inflicted the damage, he could hardly believe that his attacker was that evenings intended victim.

"I just couldn't wait" said Terry calmly.

"You cant!" growled the Bubble.

Terry raised his arms and adopted the boxing stance he had been tought to use when sparring with Karl. The catalyst that had made his mind up the previous day, was the thought of the beatings he had received at the hands of his brother, the knowledge that he had sometimes held his own and the belief that this Bubble bastard was far less dangerous than Karl who, even when sparring with his younger brother, could get carried away. So, Terry had thought, 'what the hell have I got to be frightened of?'

Side-stepping, the smaller boy neatly avoided the larger youth's manic lunge. Thwack! A right cross struck the side of Philip's face, stopping his charge dead. Smack! Terry punched with his left so hard he thought he had broken his hand, the blow caused a huge gash to appear under the Bubble's right eye and Philip was beginning to resemble a traffic accident. The Bubble moved faster than Terry expected, not towards him, but towards the corner of the courtyard. Philip stooped and in a swift motion stood up to face his enemy.

'Shit! Where did he get that from?' thought Terry. The Bubble looked a lot bigger now that he had the heavy, long-handled, steel shovel in his hands. Philip said nothing, he knew that he was badly marked and this northern bastard was now going to be made to pay. The smaller boy's agility saved him from the first scything attack, which passed only inches from his neck and chest in a crosswise cut. Terry was caught off balance and could not attempt a counter. The Bubble recovered from the swing which had missed its mark and he was now striking down at his opponents head. With no where to go, Terry threw himself back against the clammy yellowish bricks of the wall and waited for the unavoidable blow to land.

There was an almighty clang and several sparks as the shovel hit the wall just above Terry's head. The force of the weapon's impact sent a shock up the steel handle, making Philip yelp in pain and drop the weapon from his grasp allowing it to ricochet off the wall, nearly shaving the side of Terry's head. The pain in his joints made the Greek clasp his arms across his body, throbbing wrists gripped tightly under his armpits. He groaned loudly and emitted a soprano's scream as Terry's right knee made contact with his groin. Collapsing into a ball he tried to ease the pains in his wrists and the even greater pain in his testicles.

Terry was shaking and unsure of the extent of his own injuries. He leaned against the wall to recover and take stock, all the time watching the writhing bundle on the floor. Unable to continue the fight, Philip could only shout at Terry.

"You fakin bastard, I'll 'av yer for this. You better 'av eyes in the back of your 'ead coz I'll pay you back, I swear to God."

Terry believed him and realised the next time the Bubble would be calling the shots and he would never allow himself to be drawn into such an ambush again. Terry had planned everything down to the last detail for this confrontation, he had known that the three friends and the accomplices of the Bubble who had assisted in terrorising the school, were in a different class and got out for lunch ten minutes later than their leader. In the interviening time with the Greek alone the plan kicked in. John's younger brother performed the insult routine, Ginger sent the Bubble the opposite way to the youngster and John had completed the misdirections, sending the Bubble out of everybody's sight to his unexpected assault. Billy and Howard had joined Ginger and John and between them they had managed to keep every nosy onlooker away as Terry had instructed. While they had carried out their tasks, each had cast frequent anxious glances in the direction of the hostilities and had expected the victorious Bubble to surface from the pit at any moment.

"Yeh, I guess you will come after me," agreed Terry.

"You better believe me," coughed the beaten but defiant yob.

He raised himself on one elbow, still unable to stand. He squinted through his closing eyes and spat out the jelly-like blood collecting in his mouth. The crimson spittle became an accelerating projectile with the first blow of the shovel received so hard on his head that instant unconsciousness, caused by his skull fracturing, spared Bubble any further pain. The next came from the edge of the weapon striking his collar bone, snapping it like a twig while a third blow broke an arm and several ribs.

Calmly Terry took out his handkerchief and wiping the handle of the shovel clean of fingerprints he threw it wearily onto the prostrate form. Then he climbed the steps to rejoin his amazed pals.

The friends watched the Bubble's three partners cross the asphalt and stroll towards them. Terry walked to meet them, the sub-lieutenant of the gang was a coloured boy about Terry's build and just the right size to recieve the head butt that dropped him in an instant. "Now fuck off or you are gonna get what I've just given to that fucking poof Bubble."

The other two had no stomach for this confrontation as their leader was missing and their second-in-command was out for the count. Observing the grim and determined looking boy's joining Terry, they picked up their friend and dragged him away, to explain when he came round that there had just been a coup d'état and they were now out of government.

"Fak me Tell, you gotta get away from 'ere, I just slipped down to see how you done an' I fink that if that cant aint already dead ee soon will be."

Terry nodded. When he picked up the shovel he had decided to make an end of it there and then. If the bastard were to die and he were to get life, he had not cared. However now his mind raced, he had to get away and find Karl; he would know what to do. With injuries causing his limbs to stiffen Terry slipped away. His four friends promised they would try to make sure that no one grassed him up. The task was not as difficult as it should have been, since nearly every pupil hated the Bubble. Only the gang and John's younger brother had, actually witnessed what Terry had done and they were prepared to do time before grassing their mate.

Terry was long gone when an ambulance and then the police arrived to find teachers and student's milling around the crime scene, the rest of the day's classes abandoned. All the kids involved were well versed and by the time the coppers had set up an interview room in one of the classrooms, most of the kids including the Bubble's fickle gang had lost all memory of the day's events and had gone home early.

This was not going to be a simple case for the 'Old Bill' and that gave Terry a slim chance of avoiding arrest, providing the Bubble lived, If he died, then all bets were off. The coppers would put all their resources into solving a murder at a school, but a fight, no matter how bad, did not warrant the same manpower nor the same effort to bring the guilty to task, especially as there was so much serous crime to occupy them.

Terry could not believe it but he found himself silently praying for Phil the Greek's recovery. He was on his way to clean up at aunty Maud's room, not daring to risk being caught at home. His aunt did not ask any questions. None of that mattered, he was family and the rest, including the 'Old Bill,' could go fuck themselves.

Cleaned up and in a starched shirt belonging to a customer, who had left his laundry with aunt Maud. Terry set out to find Karl where he knew he would be at this time of the day. Maud promised to let his nan know everything that Terry had told her and also to tell Vic he couldn't make work for a few days as he was sick or something. Kissing her nephew on the forehead, she shooed him out of the door telling him to get away from the area as quickly as possible in case someone directed the coppers to his home address.

Chapter 50

Terry appeared through the door of the 'Green Man' pub, interrupting his brother's business of planning a robbery with his small gang. Business was put on hold as Karl listened to the story, every so often interrupting Terry's flow to ask a question or to clarify a point. Although the other gang members were captivated by the violent tale, none of them had the same excited sparkle in their eyes as Karl. He was in his element as he plotted his brother's escape from the long arm of the 'filth'.

Less than nine hours after the brothers' meeting and shortly before midnight, Karl and Harry knocked on the door of Paddy's apartment in the large Edwardian house in Camden Town. A sequence of knocks, soft and hard, proved to Paddy that the visitors outside the heavily reinforced door were friendly. The pair marched in Paddy closed and bolted the door behind them. "Just avin a piss," said Harry to no one in particular and he made his way to the sink in the corner of the room.

"Ang on Arry" shouted Karl, "Paddy, fill the fuckin' kettle before that big fucker pisses in it."

Harry and Paddy laughed. As the only toilet was on the ground floor and communal; the sink was the first choice for all of them, except Terry, who could never bring himself to use the place where you washed yourself, eating implements and cooking ingredients as a toilet.

Harry allowed Paddy to fill the kettle before relieving himself. Then he turned on the tap to act as a flush, Paddy lit the single burner of the grease-encrusted, cast-iron, table-top-gas-ring and balanced the battered aluminium kettle on the burner. All Karl's friends and closest associates drank copious amounts of tea. While they waited for the kettle Karl sat on a rickety bedroom chair and Terry sat on the only other seating in the room, an old, heavy, three-seat settee that like the room smelled of bachelor occupation.

Seeing how worried and vulnerable his young brother looked somehow urged Karl to relay the information that he had more rapidly than he normally would.

"You done a great job on that Bubble wog and lucky for you ee as an 'ard 'ed, but 'ees not out of danger yet."

"The geezer at the 'ospital said ee 'ad seen worse an' expected 'im to recover ok" added Harry,

Karl nodded then continued.

"We met up wiv them pals of yours and they are sweet, I versed 'em well and me an' Arry 'av been busy sortin' a few witnesses. A couple of geezers who owe me favours 'av kids at the school an' they will say you was wiv them all afternoon an' could not have been involved in anyway. Their dads are villains, so they know how to 'andle the filth. I checked wiv a bent C.I.D. sergeant and they ave got nuffin' concrete, no prints nuffin'."

Terry slowly realised that his sibling was telling him he might not be going to jail for years. "But what about my face and injuries, won't the coppers ask when they interview me? You can bet they will check out every kid in the school, alibi or not."

"Yeh I'm really sorry about that son," said Harry scowling in mock apology, "but you were such a cheeky fucker when you came in the Green Man earlier tonight that I 'ad to give you a couple of slaps."

Terry and the rest of the men laughed. "We ave plenty of witnesses who saw that you were perfectly pretty when you walked in and that you were a little bit lippy with Arry ere. Well, boys' will be boys', but you are too young to drink anyway, so it must ave gone to your head." said Karl happily, then he slapped his brother on the shoulder, making him yelp and causing the others to laugh again.

"But what about is mum an' dad?" asked Terry, still anxious.

"Oh don't worry on that score son," said Karl grinning evilly, "It seems they hate their fucker of a son more than you cos they just want things to get back to normal as soon as possible and 'ave no intention of talking to the filth."

Terry, who felt like a condemned man who had just been reprieved, would not be told that an earlier visit to the take-away the Andropopolis family owned found it shut, as both parents had been visiting their son in hospital. Karl and Harry had sat in the Ford Consul and their patience had been rewarded when the couple returned. No sooner had they opened the Kebab-house door than they had been bundled into the shop. Karl closing the door and pulling down the blinds with gloved hands. Fifteen minutes later Karl, had returned to the ford followed by Harry, They had checked about for witnesses and seeing none they had driven away to dump the stolen motor car. There would be nothing to connect them with what had happened in the 'kebab-shop. Nothing that could be proved.

Bubble Senior had at first sworn at Karl's suggestion that talking to the police would be a bad idea, but when Karl had dragged the struggling, portly man over to the kebab oven then forcefully slammed his hand onto the upturned spike that awaited a hunk of processed meat, he had revised his opinion. Karl covered the shocked Bubble Senior's mouth until the pain had subsided sufficiently to allow a silent scream to give way to blubbering. When Harry took the razor sharp carving knife in his gloved hand and put it to Mrs. Bubble's throat, even the whimpering stopped as fear for his wife overcame his own pain. When it had been explained to husband and wife, that failure to see reason would entail another visit, which would be for Bubble Junior's benefit and that he would not be recovering from their attentions, the pair made an instant decision. The only talking they would be doing once their son was out of hospital was to an estate agent, as they would be moving out of London as soon as possible.

When Terry returned to school the next morning the other kids eerily avoided all mention of the previous day's events, but in hushed voices they exchanged whispered false or half factual accounts between themselves.

It was Friday by the time the police got round to interviewing Terry. Almost miraculously, hardly a sign of injury was visible on his face, but it was sufficient to arouse the interest of the copper who was asking the questions.

"Let me guess, rugby eh?" The smiling officer was pointing his pencil at the fading bruises to his face.

"Ow did you know?" gasped Terry, relieved that more complicated alibis were unnecessary, then he gave the policeman a look of amazement that would have challenged most thespians.

"It's my job to know these things, so you keep your nose clean my lad, there is no escaping the law and you remember that."

Then he flashed the still suitably amazed boy a wink, after all, the papers and statements in front of him showed that this nice, polite kid was in no way involved, he had been nowhere near the scene. As a matter of form all the students had to be interviewed and at the end of the day he would be wrapping up this one. The investigation was a no-goer so would be shelved. "Go on lad, off you go and enjoy your weekend, keep up the rugby it's a great game"

"Oh I will officer."

Outside Terry allowed himself a smile, he had not played rugby since he left Richton and he was not even a member of the school team. That evening working in Vic's, he thought of how at that same time in the previous week he had been excitedly anticipating the arrival of his family and all that had happened since then. One thing of which he was sure, his life had taken a turn for the better and as he scrubbed at the wooden butcher's blocks looked forward to a weekend out with his mates with a lightness of heart that he had almost forgotten was possible.

Chapter 51

Karl sat in the little café that was situated amidst a terrace of grubby shops in Somers Town, a stone's throw from the Sir Thomas pub, a known haunt of villains. He sipped at his hot brew and looked out of the dirty half-curtained window, observing every activity that was taking place in the busy streets.

He had been in the café since breakfast at 7a.m. and a glance at the 'Timex' on his wrist showed that it was now 11a.m.. Staring at the dial he lifted the time piece to his ear and though he heard its reassuring tick he gave it a vigorous shake then looked at the time again and as nothing had changed he decided that it was indeed the time. He was not due to meet the other two members of the gang until noon, but wanted to spend some time on his own to think. The job was going ahead that night and if all went well it would make him a great deal of money. If it went wrong, it would make him a guest of Her Majesty, for seven to ten years. Shaking his head to dispel the thought of incarceration, Karl allowed his thoughts to drift to events that had overtaken him since his arrival to 'The Smoke'.

One day approximately six weeks after Terry had left home. Karl had finally had enough of Richton and Peter. During his last months in Richton he had worked all the hours he could at the decorating firm that employed him and he had saved about forty-six pounds. Deciding this was going to have to be enough, he and two pals, Jimmy Carter and Roy Lumb, who had likewise decided that their town was too small and restricted their prospects, were catching the train that evening.

Earlier, Karl had taken leave of Peter who had accepted the news calmly, shaking his son's hand, wishing him all the best and offering him a couple of crumpled pound notes to help. Karl thanked his father but had refused the notes saying that he had plenty, a lie but he had no wish to take his father's only money from him. Peter left for the pub shaking his son's hand once again and urging him to write when he was settled in. On the walk to the pub Peter had hoped that he had enough money to drink himself senseless. He did not want to dwell on the fact that now Jack was living with his girlfriend Katy and all his lodgers had moved on, for the first time in almost twenty four years he would be returning to a large empty house. Although Peter was a survivor, the rest of his life would be a mixture of denial, regret and resigned acceptance.

In London the three friends spent several weeks aimlessly wandering around until most of their money had gone. Several times they visited Karl's nan and granddad. Tommy would complain grumpily that they were a bunch of moochers but Nell was always ready, with an infectious grin and the frying pan, to feed the ravenous trio. If on those occasions the Dacey brothers' met, then all the Richton ex-pats swapped updates of the latest news from up North and when Terry was absent Karl would discuss the latest villainy with Tommy, while his two mates ate greedily. Tommy proved to be a mine of information, using his own criminal background and experience to advise and guide Karl through many potential pitfalls, helping with introductions to several old boys' whose age rarely diminished their influence as they all had relatives of some standing in the city's underworld. Without these introductions access to the centre of the criminal fraternity would have been impossible. But Tommy was a respected 'face' and character; his recommendation was as good as years of aquired trust. Tommy's circle of friends and associates were amongst the top old lags in the various firms. Their friendships had been born from long years spent together in various prisons up and down the country. Karl knew that without his Grandfather's help he would have been just another hard lad on the fringe.

Karl and his mates were picking up odd jobs of manual labour at the fish and meat markets or as temporary porters at Covent Garden market. All these jobs came courtesy of the organised criminal 'Firms' who controlled access to work in those places. Sometimes these jobs were given as a favour to Tommy. But they came at a price, which was a percentage of their earnings. These dues were paid every Friday evening to the villain concerned at the particular pub or club that the 'face' frequented, or in many cases owned.

When times were particularly lean, the friends would push the famous street-market fruit barrows. Karl hated this job, as he could never get the hang of shouting the wares nor the special banter between seller and customer that was required to achieve high sales. In fact, as the firms running the markets learned of the trio's lack of expertise, offers of employment as 'Barrow Boys'' dried up. Nevertheless all three agreed on was that it was a doddle to earn money compared to 'up north'.

Twice a week they travelled to 'Camden' where a budding entrepreneur had leased a run-down theatre and turned it into a dance-hall come-club. Rock and Roll music was changing with the times, influenced by skiffle, trad jazz and a new type of funky music introduced by an influx of commonwealth citizens, mainly Afro-Caribbean's, who brought with them the 'Reggae' which was played in seedy smoke filled dives.

These meetings were often drug-fuelled affairs. Marijuana was the popular choice, although the Caucasian bright young things, who were drawn from London's affluent educated classes preferred pill popping. They had formed into a highbrow clique and found slumming in Brixton night life the coolest or 'neatest' thing to do with one's weekends. At the exotically renamed Alhambra, which regular's referred to as 'The Palace', a name it had been given during its day's when it had been a theatre, music was restricted to the whites-only popular style. The coloured R&B and soul bands and solo stars from America were accepted as part of the entertainment revolution, but the tycoon behind The Palace had given strict instructions to his new manager that there was to be no 'nigger music' in his establishment.

It was Saturday evening and the trio's money had run out early. They were on the point of leaving when Karl was galvanised by a sudden thought. He marched to the group of young men who were sitting along the side of the wall which faced the dance floor and from where they could weigh up the talent. They were also far enough from the stage to shout some form of conversation to each other.

"Who's the Guvnor?" demanded Karl. The group looked up and seeing the geezer's small stature, laughed thinking it some kind of joke.

A swift uppercut launched with a catapulting hip technique shot from Karl's waist to the exact height of the nearest laughing Cockney's temple rendering him unconscious so quickly that only those that were immediately next to the victim noticed the attack. It transpired that the unconscious southerner was the most respected fighter in the group, so the others were reluctant to respond aggressively to Karl's challenge. They watched sheepishly as Karl strutted to the centre of the dance floor, barging his way through the puzzled, offended and embarrassed dancers. The movements and rhythms of the dancers were disrupted and became a shuffle, eventually brought to a bewildered standstill, as they tried to make sense of the situation in the low lights of the dance hall. The local band, who were used to fights and rows breaking out would usually stop playing and wait until the bouncers showed up and order was restored before recommencing, with more gusto causing the dancers to become even more animated, revitalised by the rush of adrenaline that violence always seemed to produce. The lead guitarist realised that something was different this time. There was no melee and the man in the centre of the crowd was so short that he could hardly be seen, even from the raised stage. There was still too much noise for Karl to hear himself speak. Shouting at the top of his voice, his words only reached those closest to the centre of the room. Not that it mattered, as they in turn relayed the jist of what he had said. Brashly, Karl announced that he was the hardest man on the manor and that he wished to know if anyone disagreed with him. Several of the young bloods felt they had to do something, as all the girls' were now watching and expected one of their admirers to answer this big-mouthed under-sized foreign shit.

"Out, Now!" the huge bouncer yelled at Karl whose arms were seized by a hulking doorman.

Between them they half-carried, half-dragged Karl to the accompaniment of jeers, threats and insults from the crowd of onlookers, man-handling him to the foyer and onto the street. The largest brute, the one who had done the shouting decided to give this little nuisance a parting slap. He swung a fist at Karl's face, only for it to hit fresh air.

Jimmy and Roy were handy young men themselves and had smacked a couple of the mocking lads in the mouths hard enough to cause a lot of blood spattering and to discourage any further derogatory comments at their pal's expense. However, they were embarrassed by Karl's antics and made for the exit to join their pal who had been ejected. In the foyer they stopped staring wide-mouthed as Karl bounced back into the club. He had left the two bruisers unconscious on the pavement and was now heading back to the still congregated dancers and spectators who were chattering excitedly waiting for the band to start up. In an instant Karl stood once again in the centre of the room, his legs splayed, his chin jutting as he hissed through clenched teeth, "You fuckin' mugs had better learn some manners and who's the new guv'nor?, I'll be back next week so get the best you got, and we'll sort it out on Friday." With that, he swaggered from the room.

After the band had restarted their performance it took the revellers some time to get back into the swing. The dance floor watchers remained in their seats, but with more than girls' on their minds.

As the Richton trio left The Palace they stepped around the club's remaining three doormen who were helping their colleagues to rise from the pavement to a sitting position. Karl grabbed the nearest man, who happened to be the manager, by his immaculate dinner-jacket, pulling him up from his kneeling position where he had been attending to the hulk who had previously tried to teach Karl a lesson. "Listen, they started it and I finished it right?" One of the other kneeling bouncers attempted to rise but Jimmy stepped over him and growled, "Stay put."

The man sank back down again and Karl continued, "I'll be back next week and if you refuse me entry or grass me to the filth....." Here Karl paused to make sure they understood him and to add effect he gave each an evil look, "I'll make it my life's ambition to make you all cripples, you got it?" Again he stared menacingly into their faces, but none dared to respond with aggression. The Manager realised that anyone who could so easily dispatch his toughest employees, was extremely dangerous and he nodded meekly.

Karl released the manager gently, then straightened his collar and jacket and helped him to his feet, without taking his eyes from the man, his manner changed to one of exaggerated reason. "Listen lads, it really wasn't my fault, they tried to give me a kicking when I was leaving with no bother. If you are fair wiv us I promise you'll get no trouble from me or the lads." Roy and Jimmy sucked in their breath and drew themselves up to their full height when they heard their names mentioned. The two doormen who were conscious, said that was reasonable and that they held no grudges and the manager shrugged his shoulders in resignation.

Later, in a late night drinking den, Roy asked Karl where he had got the money that they were now spending, when earlier they had been skint "Well, those bouncers I chinned dint seem to want it, so I 'elped out, took it off their 'ands sort of" and as the trio laughed he shared out the notes he had taken from the pockets of the unconscious bouncers.

"Right, we gotta be up early in the morning an' ask a few questions about the manor."

"Why and what about?" asked Jimmy.

"We gotta find out where those twats live an' work."

"What fer?" interrupted Roy.

"Use your fuckin' 'ead, as soon as they came round those geezers started thinking of revenge, so we are gonna give it to 'em first."

"Fair enuff. Ready for another beer?"

Karl answered with a nod and a request for a bottle of light ale. Tomorrow would be the start of his new life and if he were going to use his fists, then he would earn money with them.

Over the next few days and nights the trio haunted the area using guile and charm and where necessary menace, to glean information. It was relatively easy to find the whereabouts of their quarry as the pair had been bragging loudly about the manor of their intentions to exact terrible retribution, should Karl be stupid enough to show up at The Palace again. By the middle of the following week they had not only discovered the whereabouts and habits of their prey, but they had also scheduled some surprises for them. The surprises involved the use of an iron bar and the outcome would be that neither men would ever return to their previous occupation.

Separate ambushes were carried out late on the same night in different but similarly dark, secluded, back streets. These were the mens normal routes home and as usual one of them had left early to please his girlfriend on his only night off. While his drinking companion who had the same evening off and who was unattached, remained at the pub until chucking out time. This allowed the attacks to take place within two hours of one another, so that each victim was totally oblivious to the fate of the other until many days later, when during the months of convalescence they compared what little recollections they had of that night's events.

In hospital they were both visited by that lunatic northerner who had done them over at The Palace. He brought flowers and fruit at a time of day when they had no other visitors and he spent a little time chatting and amazing them with his knowledge of their personal lives and family members. He sincerely wished that they made a speedy recovery and that they would henceforth remain in good health. He enquired if the police were any closer to catching the beast that had done that terrible thing to them. Both patients swore to him that they would never help the filth and that they considered the matter closed. When he was leaving he smiled at them "By the way I'm Karl the Mancunian, people call me 'Karl the Mank'. I don't suppose we'll be seeing much of one another from now on."

Both men concurred that they were positive that there was not a chance of them meeting again, not as long as they and their families lived.

It was not so much the brutal beatings they had witnessed, as the enjoyment Karl experienced in the delivery that worried Jimmy and Roy. For the first time they began to think that 'The Smoke' was losing its appeal. For Karl, however, there were no such thoughts, as he knew this was the way of life and the home he wanted, except that he now needed money - and lots of it.

In the ensuing months, not only was Karl accepted as the guv'nor of The Palace, he actually came to an arrangement with the manager who paid him a fair pension to help with any trouble his new doormen could not handle. Karl became the perfect gentleman, so much so, that petty villains would approach him at the club with offers of involvement in jobs they were pulling. Most lucrative of all, he controlled the sale of knocked-off gear in the manor, making him a small fortune. This alienating his compatriots from Richton, and by the end of the year Jimmy and Roy had returned home.

Karl missed them for the first few weeks but he was making new friends and business associates who, once they learned that Karl had been born in London, accepted him unconditionally in a way that would not have been possible were he just a foreign monkey from the North.

Early in 1961 Karl forged some interesting friendships. Harry Rivers or 'Harry the Axe' as he was better known due to his personal choice of weapon, was a well-respected freelance enforcer. Paddy Marne, an exceptional thief and con-artist who had been in a tight spot one night when the Mank had come to his aid. He had been Karl's man ever since. Karl, Harry and Paddy developed an unbreakable bond. The small gang's meteoric rise in the lower echelons of the underworld made it inevitable that they would come to the attention of the top Firms. Karl, as their leader, would eventually have to do business with the upper echelons of the firms and their ruthless ganglords and like-minded psychopaths. He knew one wrong move or mistake could make him a statistic on the missing persons' list at Scotland Yard.

In the small café, Paddy collected three steaming mugs of tea. His first two fingers which linked the mug handles were burning and the discomfort made him rapidly cover the ground from counter to table. As he slammed down the mugs of scalding tea, he spilled a small quantity onto the bare, wooden table, jolting Karl from his reverie.

"Fakin' 'ell that's hot!"

"Course it is you silly cant." Over the months Karl's accent changed to a Cockney twang that was beginning to become indistinguishable from his accomplices. "It's just come out of the fakin kettle aint it?"

The café owner Sol, at the request of Paddy, threw him a chequered cloth and caught the same when Paddy had mopped up the spillage and thrown it back. "Where's 'arry?"

Paddy pointed at the lonely coffee mug.

"On 'is way to get some 'Wrigleys'."

"Whats ee want chewing gum for?"

"Well ee stopped smoking cos you don't like it, so now when ee's a bit nervous ee uses Wrigleys."

"A bit fakin' nervous, what you on about?"

Paddy pushed his cup forward and came closer to Karl, resting on his elbows and whispered, "It's the job innit, it's a fakin' big un an' that's for sure."

"You two fakker's aint getting cold feet are ya?"

"Nah, leave it out will ya, course we ain't. It's just a few butterflies, that's alright innit? Don't you get 'em then?"

Karl contemplated lying, then grinned at Paddy. "Nah, I shit bricks."

The two were laughing loudly when they were joined by Harry. He sat down, picked up the spare mug and asked "What the fak's so funny?" "Naffink, just giv us a fakin' stick of gum," said Paddy grinning, his hand outstretched.

"Stay on the fakkin' floor, one move an' I'll blow your fakkin' 'ead off!" The terrified owner of the small jewellery shop obeyed the screaming, balaclava-masked robber a little too slowly and received a blow from the stock of the sawn-off shotgun for his sloth. The young female assistant behind the counter screamed when her father was struck, the second robber, who was nearest to her, slapped her hard with the back of his hand. "Shut the fak up you fakkin' yid bitch or we'll kill 'im."

Father and daughter, as the thieves well knew, usually arrived a good forty minutes before their two employees. So far, everything had gone like clockwork for the gang, at 6.30a.m. Hatton Garden was not very busy but in thirty minutes it would be a hive of activity as the mostly Jewish community commenced their daily business.

The villains had pulled on masks and two of the gang had bundled through the door before the girl could lock it. In seconds the blinds were down, the door was locked and they had about ten minutes to get the job done. The girl's father and owner of the store had already placed the key in the ancient metal alarm control box that would ring a bell on the exterior of the building, alerting the neighbours and the public. When he was thrown to the ground, his assailant had an easy job to turn the key in the box with his gloved hand, he removed and held the keys, inspecting the small bunch in his search for the larger safe key.

"Where's the fakkin' key, you fakkin' fat Kkike?"

"Fuck you, you shit cunt shmuck!" retorted the owner, who by now was recovering from the initial shock at the speed and violence which had accompanied the men when they had burst through the door. "I give you nothing you fuckers."

Another blow on his back from the stock of the shotgun persuaded him to keep quiet, but for the thieves the clock was ticking. They knew that outside in the stolen getaway car their driver and lookout was waiting, engine running, ready to sound the horn if there were any problems. But inside the store they needed the keys fast, time was running out.

The thug with the shotgun calmly turned to the thug who was holding the girl, "Shag the arse off the Jewish bitch."

Without a moment's hesitation the big brute forced the girl face down onto the low counter and hoisted up her long skirt. Before either father or daughter had fully realised what was happening, the girl's baggy drawers had been ripped off and the big thief used one hand to hold the girl cruelly by the hair, the pain just enough to stop her screams whilst his other hand was fumbling with his trousers. The sight of his plump sixteen year old daughter's pasty buttocks shocked the Jeweller and his opposition dissolved. Minutes later, as he was trying to console his daughter who had been thrown forcefully to join him on the ground, he barely noticed that the robbers had left as swiftly as they had arrived, taking with them most of his best stock of watches and jewellery along with a large amount of cash.

Two pedestrians had just turned onto the street and from a distance of seventy-yards they were the only witnesses of the crime. There were by that time several more people around, but they were not looking in the right direction to see the masked bandits flee, carrying several bags. As the doors closed on the black Ford Pilot V8, the two witnesses were busy memorising the number plate details, plainly visible on the boot of the getaway vehicle. They repeated to one another the descriptions of the desperados, so that they could, like the good citizens they were, help the police as much as possible.

When they were at a safe distance, the two thugs removed their masks and Paddy accelerated away quickly, but not so quickly that they would attract attention. The three men were not worried about being seen nor by anybody recording the vehicle's number, as they would change motors in a few more minutes. They all wore thin ladies gloves and there would be no fingerprints or personal effects to aid the authorities.

In the front passenger seat Karl, out of breath, turned to the back and spoke to Harry busy stuffing cash and jewellery into the waiting white canvas bags. Large black lettering on the bags stated boldly: 'LAUNDRY.' "I saw you limpin' on the way out, you ok?"

"I wer'nt limpin' pal, I just couldn't run proper wiv a fakin' 'ard on." Paddy turned into the side street, having checked continuously for hangers-on in the rear-view mirror. There were none so he took the next turning right onto a deserted narrow back street. Twenty yards along, parked innocently at the side of the road half-on the pavement was a cream coloured Ford Thames van, which bore the same letters as the canvas bags. 'Collins & Co. Laundry Services.' Paddy parked behind the van leaving sufficient space to open the double back doors. Harry and Paddy threw the bags into the back and Harry climbed in after them.

Karl was giving the motor a last once over, making sure that Paddy had left the keys in the ignition, hoping some other thief would take advantage of the gift, further hindering the police he also checked for witnesses. The coast was clear. A sprightly Karl jumped into the passenger's seat and closing the door he gave the order for Paddy to get clear of the getaway vehicle and then to take it easy through the now busy, Friday, city traffic.

They were fairly confident that the laundry van would pass unnoticed through the city as it had been stolen a couple of weeks before from out of town. They had added lettering to the plain van to associate it with a well-known laundry firm whose headquarters were located in an outlying district. The area in which they were travelling was not an area in which the laundry firm did any business, so the van was unlikely to attract unwanted attention. For good measure a false number-plate made traceability very unlikely.

Paddy dropped Karl and Harry at his home or 'gaff' and left them to dispose of the van in a busy part of King's Cross. It would be some time before the police were alerted to the abandoned vehicle. Possibly they would not connect it with the robbery provided that no-one remembered the laundry van parked on the side street where they had left the getaway vehicle.

The job was as perfect as any job could be, when Paddy returned to his gaff he gave the secret knock and was admitted by Harry. Paddy locked the door behind him, then joined the other two on the floor to help sort out the swag. One look at Harry's face told him that the haul was better than expected. A look at Karl confirmed his assumption. Although sporting a little smile he seemed much calmer than either Paddy or Harry. Well, that's why he's the guv'nor he thought.

"Where's my cup of fakin' tea then?"

"On its way guv" grinned Paddy.

The local newspapers carried the story and two nationals found space on their inside pages to describe a violent robbery of the most heinous kind. Karl had been relieved that there was no mention of the sexual threat to the young Jewish girl, as somewhat surprisingly he had had this on his conscience since the raid. He had had no intention of allowing Harry to carry out the threatened rape, but neither had he intended to leave that place empty-handed. As well as risking their liberty for nothing, the gang would have been a laughing stock amongst other villains on the Manor. Any pangs of guilt dissipated when he read that the jeweller had reported a theft three times the value of the actual loss. "Well fak me! The fakers made more money than us!" laughed Karl aloud to the other gang members.

"That yid bastard is gonna screw the shit out of the insurance company," added Paddy.

"Yeh, you fink we could put 'im under the cosh wiv a bit of black mail?" joked Harry. In fact the total monetary value of the stolen jewellery to the gang once the 'Tom' (Tom-Foolery – Jewellery) had been fenced came to a little over two grand, which was roughly a quarter of its actual worth. When that total was added to the cash taken, they had netted just over four grand. There had been no arguments when Karl doled out a grand each and some change, saying that the remaining thousand would be put on one side to fund their next venture. All agreed that this made good business sense.

Karl's last words on the matter of that particular raid were the same words that he would in future reiterate after every successful venture. "Be wary how you spend the money, don't draw attention to yourselves and don't go gabby or lairy when you get pissed."

There was very little chance of the men over-spending, talking out of turn or being flash as they were seldom out of sight of Karl or one another and Karl made very few mistakes.

Chapter 52

Arriving at Saxon Place, Jack Dacey found only his youngest brother at home. It would be another couple of hours before Helen returned from work after collecting Corinne from the child-minder.

While they waited, Mark told Jack about the previous week's trip to London and Jack listened politely, although the only reason for his visit was to try and borrow some money. Jack never repaid the loans that his family made to him, nor any loan for that matter. He was taking Katy out that night and was skint, having lost what little cash he had at the bookies that afternoon. He had already approached Peter, calling at his place of employment, an engineering firm, but Peter was as hard up as his eldest son. Jack had given no thought to his father's changed circumstances, from self-employed money-making dynamo to down-trodden employee, interested only in having enough money to survive and to frequent 'The Red Rose' after work from opening time to closing time. The landlord of the little pub would put Peter's drinks on the slate as he was a good customer and without fail or excuse he would settle his debts come Friday evenings. Jack had declined Peter's offer to add his son's drinks to his slate if he met him after work. He was already forming a plan to use the four bob in his pocket to amass a tidy sum on the horses. That scheme had failed, hence he found himself sitting with Mark, already thinking that this attempt to raise money was doomed to failure. He could already imagine his mother's response as she reminded him, despite his promises, he had not repaid the quid that he had borrowed from her a couple of weeks ago.

Jack's ears picked up. "What was that?" he said, now really looking at his brother and urging him to repeat his last words.

"I said I 'ave got nearly eight shillings in my money box."

The money had been given to him in London and he was saving it towards a fort. He had been visiting at the toy store weekly for the last three months and the fort was the subject of his current day dreams. Day dreams they would remain until he managed to save the other five pounds that were needed to liberate the wood and cardboard castle from the toy shop window. "You 'ad better be careful and hide that money away Mark."

"Why?" asked the boy innocently.

"Coz a policeman told me that there has been a burglar about these parts."

"Oh ee won't get my money box cos it's already hid, in the bottom of that cupboard there, behind some books."

"Clever lad, don't tell anyone where your hiding place is." Mark promised he would not and beamed importantly as Jack enquired if he was also clever enough to make a cup of tea. "Course I am, I've made you a brew before, don't you remember? And I make my own breakfast and my tea sometimes," and to prove he was telling the truth he went into the kitchen to make the tea with milk and two sugars as requested by his eldest brother.

Mark was just adding the sugar when Jack came into the kitchen. "Listen, av just remembered, I gotta go meet this mate of mine who knows about a job that's goin."

Surprised and disappointed, the little boy watched his brother disappearing through the back door. He called at Jack's departing back that he would tell his mum he had been, but there was no reply as Jack had turned the corner. Mark sadly added another sugar and some more milk to the brew, making it more to his own taste and took the steaming chipped mug into the front room. Since his promotion to a 'Latch-Key-Kid' he had been given permission to watch TV. After lighting the fire and making his own tea, he had no inclination to do so and sat on the old settee, caressing the now lukewarm brew in both hands. After the welcome surprise of Jack's visit, the house became a lonely place again and Mark reflected for him it had never and most probably never would be a jolly place of abode, even when his parents and sister were around. Mark had been engrossed in an old comic that he had read many times previously but which he still found interesting, even though he knew the stories by heart. When he heard the kitchen door opening, Helen struggled through the living room door with Corinne under one arm. When she had put Corinne down, Mark unbuttoned the simulated fur coat and the hood fell back, to reveal the chubby round face and fair hair of his baby sister. Once Corinne's coat, mittens and wellington boots had been removed, he placed the waiting slippers on her feet and his face-pulling and funny sound-making were rewarded with her smile and her customary greeting to him, "Mark, Mark."

This never failed to amuse the others as she sounded like a puppy with a speech impediment. Corinne turned her attentions to a small box of toys that lived under the TV table and crawling as quickly as the large terry nappy would allow, she happily grabbed her favourite toys.

Helen returned once she had folded the push-chair and stored it downstairs in Mary's former room, then she closed the door and noticing the fire was low, she added coal from the scuttle that Mark had filled earlier when he had lit the fire. There was a hiss from the damp fossil fuel accompanied by an immediate drop in temperature in the room and as flames gingerly flicked through gaps in the small pile of black coals trying to set light to them, Helen cursed the damp northern climate. "Jack came."

"Did he?" said Helen, taken aback.

"Yeh, he said ee wanted a cuppa tea an' then ee dint drink it, said ee 'ad to go."

His Mother took Corinne away from the television where she had hauled herself into an unsteady standing position and was happily bashing the blank screen with the dismembered head of a doll, making unintelligible conversation with her obscured reflection. "Did he say what he wanted?" "No, ee just told me to watch out for my money cos there is a burglar about."

Helen froze. "You didn't tell him where you keep your money did you?" The boy nodded, perplexed by his mother's concern. He was further puzzled when she went to the display cabinet and frantically pulled away the books. Finding the money box gone she looked at her small son's blank face. Then with a sudden, renewed flurry she reached to the back of the top shelf, finding the old, china, miniature teapot, she removed the lid, peered inside and dejectedly slumped from her kneeling to a sitting position.

As Mark realised that his dreams of owning his prized fort were now further away than ever, he started to cry. Helen resigned herself to the fact that her eldest son was, and always had been since his first steps, a thief. She put her arm around the heart-broken child and muttered to no-one in particular, "The bastard 'as also nicked the milk man's money." Discovering that Jack had also stolen the four saved shillings in the teapot moved Mark to more tears which caused Corinne to leave her play and join her mother and brother. Then, Corinne joined her brother in simple lamentations.

Jack had felt no remorse at stealing from his family, they, like the rest of the world, were fair game. He had been in The Spread Eagle for about an hour when Katy joined him. She had just finished work as a hairdresser, with a tired smile she hung her coat on the stand, then sat next to her handsome rogue.

Her family had not been pleased when they found out who was responsible for their daughter's pregnancy, but Jack was a charmer and had played to perfection the part of a penitent resolved to do the right thing. The lad had been so convincing that Katy's dad, Gordon, had taken Jack to the local pub near his home for a celebratory drink. It was agreed that Jack would be marrying his daughter, but it was also agreed that when they informed Gordon's drinking pals of the momentus occasion, they would forget to mention that Katy was already in the family way. The 'Almighty' could be relied upon to provide an unusually short pregnancy.

A bonus for Katy's family was that Jack, although lapsed, was a Catholic boy. The priest did not have the same bias as he would have had if Katy had done something unforgivable as getting knocked-up by a heathen bloody Protestant. For the sake of their immortal souls they had suffered his hell-fire sermon on the evils of pre-marital sex, after which the engagement was official.

The wedding was arranged at lightning speed for that September, only a month away.

The father-to-be and erstwhile piggy-bank robber returned from the bar with half a mild for his future wife and another pint for himself. Jack's mood further improved when Katy informed him that she was only having the one drink as her mother had invited relatives, who would help with the wedding, round to the house that night, she wanted to get home on the next bus in order to bathe and look her best for when the visitors arrived. She was quite excited by the prospect of coming face-to-face with her jealous female cousins who were having trouble finding a man, never mind marrying one.

Jack waved Katy off from the bus stop at the top of John Street and then walked back into town along Lancashire Street, stopping at The Black Swan. It was while he was sitting at the bar in the snug that he spotted Jerry Barker who was in the other room. Jerry was the local bookie.

He had been blessed with such a good day that although he had not been in the Tap Room long, he was ordering drinks all round for his cronies. They in turn crowded round, slapping him on the back and shaking his hand for being such an exemplary mate. Jack noticed with an imperceptible sideward glance the large wad of banknotes that Jerry had deliberately pulled from his pocket in order to amaze the gathering sycophants. He was slyly enjoying the effects that the wad of notes had had and was pretending not to notice the nudges and wide-eyed looks the others gave one another when they saw the bundle of money, which represented a year's wages for any one of them.

Jack was alone in the snug and invisible, even to the new barmaid who had served him. She did not know him from Adam and was likewise ignorant of his reputation. She was far too busy with the important Mr. Barker to pay attention to the only customer in the best room; regulars preferred the camaraderie of the games room. Jack decided the show was getting too much for him, so, unnoticed, he slipped off the bar stool and left the pub and sound of raucous laughter and the shouts "get 'em in again".

At 10p.m. Jerry left the lads and the party which was in full swing, having bought them all a farewell drink. He staggered down the steep, cobbled, side street to his Jaguar saloon. It was where he always parked it, out of the way in case some angry punter blamed him for their misfortune and took it out on his motor.

The August night was mild and there was still a fair amount of illumination in the sky, but the car was in a deep shadow caused by the surrounding buildings. Overweight, Jerry wheezed as he unsteadily stooped to retrieve the keys he had just dropped and it was from that position that he saw a black form appear from the shadow of the buildings. Before he could straighten up and focus on the stranger, his head exploded twice in quick succession and his last recollections were of the pain in his arm, which he had instinctively thrown up to ward off the blows. He lay unconscious for twenty minutes before a passer-by alerted the police and an ambulance was called. In the attempts to find a witness the police were at an immediate disadvantage, the drunken barmaid was useless as a witness to the events which had taken place prior to the attack, she was twice as useless the next day when she had sobered up. As for Jerry's drinking cronies, all any of them could remember plainly was that wad of cash. Eached wished they could have been the one now in possession of the money.

Fortunately for Jerry, he had a hard head and got off fairly lightly with a broken arm. There had been no fingerprints on his car nor the piece of timber used in the attack to provide clues as to the identity of the culprit. His aching head had already deduced that it could have been any of a number of people including one of his so-called friends, so not only had his cash disappeared that night but so too had any inclination towards future acts of generosity.

Jack caught the bus to Castaires and waited until his father returned from the Red Rose. Once they had established an alibi, should one be needed, that Jack had been with his father and no doubt his friends at the time of the opportunistic attack, Jack pulled out a large wad of cash, peeled off a fiver and handed it to Peter. "Don't go flashing that about son, it will bring unwanted attention." Jack grinned wickedly. "Aint that the truth."

Now Jack was unexpectedly wealthy, he had a good opportunity to make amends to his mother and youngest brother for his earlier petty theft, however he gave them no more thought than he gave to the unfortunate Jerry, which is to say, no thought at all.

That weekend saw Jack and Katy travel by train to London, where they called briefly at Nan and granddad's to invite them both and Terry to the wedding. Although they accepted, Nan already knew that the notice was too short for them to take time off work or buy new clothes etc. that weddings necessitated.

Terry had left school and had accepted an offer of full time employment with Vic the butcher. He had been put in charge of two junior part-timers and took his job very seriously. He would not take time off work for a wedding so soon after being given such an important position.

The future newly-weds left Nell and Tom and met up later that night with Karl who showed them round 'Soho.' The next morning they caught a bus to the West End then they walked to Trafalgar Square, through St. James' Park, Buckingham Palace and to all the popular nearby tourist attractions. Jack was barely interested as he had seen them many times before, but Katy was overwhelmed. They ate in a restaurant, a first for Katy, and later they hailed a taxi to Euston where they caught the six o clock train back north.

By the time the wedding day arrived, Jack had spent most of his ill-gotten gains; this did not worry him as there was always more to be had. Katy was nervous and shook whenever marriage was mentioned, but Jack could not care less. He preferred to push the imminent occasion to the back of his mind and his forthcoming fatherhood even further to the back of his mind.

Mark could not understand why his brother had not chinned the priest who had just slung water all over him and Katy with that baby's rattle thing he was swinging about. He had been dragged to the wedding under protest as he had still not forgiven the thief.

He could not justify being scrubbed up and polished and losing a Saturday morning's playtime just to please the person who had destroyed his dream and he sat in the church, bored stiff.

The reception held at the bride's parents' house was a strained affair. Helen and her family made their goodbyes as soon as decency allowed, blaming Corinne's and Mark's fatigue for the regrettable need to leave such a wonderful occasion so early.

The newly weds had rented a one-up-one-down, brick-built, terraced cottage which was situated behind a large factory within five minutes' walking distance of Katy's parents' house. Jack played the part of dutiful husband and landed a job courtesy of his new father-in-law's contacts at the new dam that was being built on the Pennines above the village of Ludbarrow. To be fair, apart from the few bouts of violence that he had inflicted on workmates and weekend drinking partners when he had been either drunk or sober, Jack had managed to surprise everyone and himself. In the weeks since his marriage he had changed for the better and gone straight. The newly weds had been regular visitors at Saxon Place and Mark had eventually forgiven Jack for the theft of his piggy bank and looked forward to his visits once again.

Chapter 53

One day after school, Mark who was nearly eight years old came home to the unexpected sight of his mother and sister-in-law sat in the kitchen drinking tea and discussing Corinne's first birthday in October, which was only two weeks away. Mark sat down at the table and the two women endured his presence but continued their conversation.

Katy was a handsome, bleach-blonde haired woman and standing a little under six feet she was almost as tall as her husband. Her build was slight and perfect white teeth provided a ready smile to accompany her broad northern accent. On that day however she did not smile as she apologised again for going to Helen's workplace and causing her to leave the factory early. Helen reassured her that it was not a problem and that as she was family now, nothing was too much trouble, especially in her delicate condition. Helen was looking forward to the birth of her eldest son's child but secretly hated the thought of becoming a young grandmother.

"It's just that he's never been missing long, well not as long as this anyway."

"So how long exactly is that again?" Helen knew full well that Katy had said tearfully several times before, "three days", but Helen had been studying Katy's face and the remnants of a black eye and some bruising. "Is our Jack hitting you?"

Katy lowered her eyes to the table, partly to hide the shame that was not hers but which she felt a party to and partly to avoid Helen's piercing gaze. Her daughter-in-law gave an almost imperceptible nod. "The bastard is turning out just like his father," spat Helen, prompting her daughter-in-law to collapse into floods of tears.

Mark did not need to be told that this was the cue for any male presence, no matter how small, to disappear. Mark sat in the front room before the muted TV, not that he wanted to eavesdrop on the conversation in the next room, rather that he did not want to incur his mother's wrath for having the sound of the television too loud.

It had only been a couple of days before that he had confided in his friend Fred his curiosity about his real father. He had hastily added that Barry was a great dad - though in truth, he had little time for Mark when his small daughter was around. Mark did not resent Corinne, he loved her dearly and her growing affection for him made up in some way for the lack of interest he felt from the adults. Fred

Bamber, as usual, had all the answers. "Go an' see 'im then," Mark looked at Fred, the thought of visiting Peter was not novel, but the thought had not yet developed into an intention as he was constantly reminded by his mother that his real father was an evil bastard. To please his mother, he agreed, untruthfully recalling with her the times he had been locked in cupboards by the drunken beast. In truth, Mark's memories of the dark prison were vague and fading, he recalled believing that if he were to make a sound the 'bogey-man' would get him, but he also recalled that he had known that by waiting patiently, one family member or another would release him as soon as daddy passed out.

"I don't know 'ow to get to is 'ouse."

"Do you know what the street is called?"

"Castaires" was the nearest Mark could provide as an address.

"Don't know where that is," remarked Fred.

"I think I remember the way from town," said Mark.

"Well then, that's easy. On Saturday we'll go into town and then see if you remember the way."

"But what about me mum?"

Fred laughed, and gave his chum the answer to that problem. "Don't tell er."

"Yeh I'm sure it's this way." Mark was pointing up the incline of Mallard Street and unsure as he was, something at the back of his mind, pictures of past shopping forays with his brothers' and sister guided his steps. Ever since they had alighted from the bus, his nerves had been frayed with guilt at deceiving his mother and with fear of discovery. But these feelings diminished the farther he travelled up the shopping thoroughfare and the more confident he became, as shops and landmarks confirmed that he was on the right path.

Passing a butcher's shop he noticed the chickens hanging unplucked in the window and the black puddings piled on a large white tray brought a distant memory closer and a mischievous grin to his face.

"Hey Fred, do you know how they make black puddings?"

Mark embellished the story of black-people puddings and was so convincing that the gullible Fred swore that he not only believed Mark but he had a friend who had seen it happen. They found themselves outside some urinals which were puzzlingly recognizable to Mark.

The black and white sign on the wall next to the toilets acknowledged the area: "Penny Bridge'.' Mark experienced an eerie feeling of déjà vu, as side by side, at the slate, the two boys' playfully threatened to direct a cascade towards one another, jumping backwards and swearing until they ran out of ammunition.

They then continued their journey until they came to the Red Rose. This did not provide any clues as Mark had no recollections of the small pub, but the stone humped-bridge that spanned the canal stirred memories. Pausing to peer over the parapet, they looked into the filthy water and Fred jibed "Bet there's some dead dogs in there, and cats."

Fred, like Mark, saw only debris and polluted water but they resumed their journey, having convinced one another that they had witnessed swarms of giant rats devouring the corpses of at least two missing pets. Fifty-yards on Fred followed Mark along a cobbled road, forty feet more and he suddenly bumped into Mark who had stopped. "Sorry" mumbled Fred, but his friend was unaware of the collision and of the apology, he was too busy staring at the school on the corner and the sign on its wall. 'Surrey Street.'

As they turned right, Mark felt a giddiness that caused his feet to slow down, memories came flooding back until his legs seemed to realise that there was no need to carry him much further. On Mark's left was his former home, Castaires.

"It's a fuckin' manshun!" gasped Fred.

Mark was pleased that his companion had been suitably impressed, and now felt that the bragging he had subjected Fred to over the past week had been justified.

"Well go on then!"

Mark hesitated before approaching the back door. Fred was beginning to think that this could be one of the biggest hoaxes of all time and that his friend might be the biggest liar of all time. Not that he would say as much as he was well aware of the consequences of calling Mark Dacey a liar. Sheepishly, Mark told himself that it was his dad's house, that he had every right to be there and that his father had a duty, if not to welcome him with open arms then at least to say, "Hello, what are you doing here?" Knocking loudly, he had an awful thought, what if his dad did not recognise him? He had not seen Peter since he had abandoned him at his paternal aunt's one-up-one-down hovel and that had been over two years ago. That there was no answer to his rapping brought a separate fear, what if there was no one home?

A short time before at the canal bridge, Fred had inquired of a passing man, "Ave yer got the time please mister?" The elderly flat-capped gent had consulted a pocket watch which he had been brought out with a well-practised flourish, "Aff past ten lad" and both boys' had replied "Ta mister."

"Try again, knock 'arder this time," ordered Fred.

Still no one came and the discouraged youngster turned to his companion and without any emotion in his voice said, "Cum on Fred, there's no one 'ome, lets go."

"Curtain juss moved," replied an excited Fred.

Mark too had noticed the movements of the nets and an unrecognisable figure behind them.   Another thought occurred to Mark, what if his father, like himself, no longer lived here. His instinct was to run away as fast as he could, but as he heard bolts being drawn he found his feet frozen to the stone step.

Peter looked much older than Mark had pictured him and for a few moments the tall man looked down in bewilderment at the small boy. He was about to ask "What do you want?" but was forstalled by Mark. "Ello Dad." "Bloody 'ell…… 'Ello son."

Peter opened the door wide enough to allow access.   Observing his father's suspicious perusal of his companion Mark said, "Ive brought me friend cos ee knew the way."

Peter poked his uncombed head out of the doorway to check for any other unexpected visitors. "Ave you walked all the way here?" asked Peter incredulously.   Both boys' nodded, deliberately omitting to mention that they had caught the bus for the first part of their trip. Peter gave a huge grin and hurried the two boys' inside. "I bet yer mum don't know yer 'ere does she?" He bolted the door again and led the lads into the dining room.   While Peter made a cup of tea in the galley kitchen the two boys' looked around, Fred searched for signs of wealth but was disappointed.   Mark experienced surreal pangs, as unchanged furniture, décor and smells reunited him with long forgotten birthdays, Christmases, white rabbits and violence. "Here, I found some biscuits as well."

The three sat at the table sipping scalding, sweet tea, whitened to the shade of caramel by sterilised milk poured from a tall bottle with a long neck.   The boys' grabbed greedily at the sugar-covered, pale biscuits that were stamped with the word 'Nice' so of course they must be, and they were. While they drank, Peter studied Mark who hadhis eyes on the last biscuit, but it was Fred's grubby paw that claimed it. "So what you bin up to?"

During the next half hour Mark recounted every relevant happening that had taken place since they had parted company. He also noticed with great satisfaction that Fred was unsuccessfully trying to recover most of the last biscuit from his tea, he had allowed the heavy soggy snack to collapse into the mug before he could transfer it to his open mouth. It was now lying at the bottom of his mug amongst the tea leaves.

Soon the conversation dried up and Peter said, "Well I guess you two 'ad better be getting 'ome, I'll get me coat and see yer to tha bus stop." On reaching the coat pegs Peter paused, looking at his son amazed at the changes in the boy since they had last met, then he came to an impulsive decision. He went into the kitchen and returning with several more biscuits, dropped them in front of Fred saying, "We'll only be a minute lad, you wait ere."

Fred cared not a jot that Mark had just left the room hand-in-hand with his dad, as he was busily ensuring that when he returned to the room that he would find all the biscuits had found a 'Nice' new home.

"Mark, before we go in 'ere you muss promise me not to tell what you see."

With Peter stooping and staring him fully in the face Mark nodded, apprehensively wondering what mystery lay behind the solid door.

"Jack!" exclaimed the boy in disbelieving repulsion. His handsome, eldest brother's face was covered on both sides with thick wads of lint dressings, closer inspection revealed dark brown stains and the lighter red of uncongealed fresh blood.

"Hiya Mark."

The boy could not understand why his brother was so cheerful when there was something so terribly wrong. In a state of shock, the boy was made to realise that he was to deliver the note written by Jack as they talked, to Helen and no-one else. He was to tell no-one of their meeting and most of all he was to tell no living soul where his eldest brother was.

From behind the net curtains, Jack watched his father and the two boys' as they set off for the bus stop. He wondered if the false explanation of his injuries, an accident, had been believed, more importantly would his little brother keep his mouth shut?

Sinking back onto a large leather settee that had been serving as a bed, he took a bottle from a side table, painfully tilted his head backwards and threw several bitter white tablets into his mouth. He took two large swallows of 'Johnny Walkers' to swill them down. Then he waited for the whiskey and painkillers to take effect. He pondered on the events that had placed him in his agonisingly painful situation.

He had been very drunk and had failed to notice the big Samoan professional rugby player who had swaggered to the bar, forcefully pushing other drinkers out of his way with the bulk of his huge frame. The Samoan had used his elbow to clear a space on his right for two smaller companions. "Who the fuck do you think you're shoving? You big black cunt."

Jack Dacey's response to being almost knocked off his bar stool was not the one that Roy Maluluha, a famous new acquisition of a professional rugby team had anticipated from anyone, never mind from this lanky streak of piss.

"Duz yah know whoo a am boy?"

Roy spoke with a heavy, island accent. He snarled the words imperiously, while glaring malevolently at Jack, but also intended for the pub's patrons to witness. "Don't give a fuck," came the reply. "Rupert the fuckin' bear!" Jack added. This reference was not lost on the regulars of the Working Men's Club where Jack was finishing off his payday's solitary drinking binge. The beige checked pants and bright red jumper were reminiscent of the childrens' annual character 'Rupert'.

Such an insult called for immediate retribution and huge arms encircled Jack, instantly crushing the breath from his body. The hulk reared back as Jack used all the force he could leverage from the stool's footrest to head-butt the behemoth that was restricting his movement and breathing. In an instant the slimmer man used the respite from the powerful embrace to deliver a second, far more lethal, head-butt to Roy's face.

Staggering, the huge Samoan managed to save himself from falling backwards by holding onto the bar rail, recovering just in time to see Jack smash the heavy, barrel, pint glass on the bar. Roy panicked as the broken glass in the other man's hand caught him a light blow. It was then that Roy's accomplices had leapt on Jack. The combined force of inebriation and their bodies took Jack to the floor. The stool he had been sitting on and the men landing on top of him. His brain told him that he must somehow get to his feet or he would be lost. His chance came as the stool had deflected one of his opponents away to the side, freeing his arm and allowing him to jam his thumb into the other's left eye, bringing a terrible howl of pain and instant cessation of hostilities. Jack hauled himself up and leaning on the bar for support, tried to regain his breath and balance. The Samoan was already heading for the door, not that he was in anyway afraid of the skinny bastard that he had underestimated and allowed to surprise him, but he knew well that the last thing his budding professional career needed was the ministrations of the law and the interest of the press. Jack was just about to launch a stream of insulting rhetoric when, unnoticed, the Samoan's uninjured friend struck from the side. The attack lacked power or ferocity and was over very quickly. As Jack watched his assailants escape, they shouted, "It's not over yet, wa'll be back for yez Dacey yer bastard." The thick Belfast brogue was temporarily lost on Jack, as was the threat. He was too busy trying to come to terms with the horrifically deep slashes on either side of his face. There was now so much blood he was trying to stem the flow, desperately using both hands to try to hold his face together.

Irish Mick, a regular and silent witness, had staunched the bleeding as much as he could with bar towels, had got Jack quickly into his car and had taken him to the only place that Jack thought he could go to for treatment. The Infirmary was out of the question as that would involve the police and Jack was under no illusions that due to his hostile ongoing relationship with Richton Constabulary, they would find that he was in some way to blame.

Peter listened to Irish Mick recall events as accurately as he could, while in the other room an elderly, retired doctor and drinking pal sewed his son's wounds with small neat stitches.

Jack groaned but held on bravely until finally the doctor announced that, he had sewn the last stitch. After suffering the agony of the iodine, Jack had his wounds dressed with gauze pads and sticking plasters. Shortly afterwards shock, loss of blood and alcohol helped him to pass out. The retired medical man made little protest as Peter pressed his last five pound note into his newly-washed hands. "See yer at 't' pub later then lad."

It went without saying that as far as the man was concerned, he had seen nothing.

Before Irish Mick left, Peter gleaned as much information on the man who had so expertly used a cut-throat razor on his eldest boy. "Is name is Doherty, ees a Scouse tinker an' a mad dangerous bastard, everyone that knows 'im calls 'im 'Razors' on account of that's the tool ee uses." Peter nodded his thanks. At the door Mick said "One more thing, ee must know Jack cos as Razors was leaving ee used his name; yeh Dacey ee said, an ee also said it wernt finished, believe me if ee said it, ee meant it. Best tell your lad that lunatic is out of his league. It would be best if he got out of town for a while, cos that bastard is one of the most dangerous cunts in Liverpool and he will be back."

Peter sat watching his eldest boy fitfully sleeping, every so often the throbbing pain causing him to groan. "Liverpool," said Peter softly, and he silently watched over his once-handsome boy who would be permanently disfigured.

That had been five days ago and Jack, had apparently come to terms with his spoiled looks, he knew that he had come up against the first division of violence and had lost. He found that he had a morbid fascination for the ease with which he had been disabled by that fearsome, cut-throat razor. Far from being reformed by the violence, he had decided that in future, weapons would definitately be an addition to his arsenal.

Mark departed Castaires half-a-crown richer, despite Fred's suggestion that his dad might have meant them to share the money he had put into his youngest son's hand, along with enough coppers to pay bus fare home for both the boy's. The first bus reached Richton and Fred asked for his fare for the second stage from Richton to Burnbridge. Mark handed over the pennies and Fred announced cheerfully "Am walking 'ome an' then a can spend t' money at 'Two Steps'."

Mark did not care that Fred was leaving him to continue homeward alone, as he was preoccupied with the reception he would receive when he walked through the door of Saxon Place. He silently prayed that the secret note he carried and the terrible news of Jack's accident would prove a sufficient talisman to ward off punishment. As the double-decker bus rumbled away from its town centre stop, Mark asked the conductor as he took his two pennies fare, "This bus duz stop at Buckley Road dunnit mister?"

The conductor nodded and turned the chromed handle of machine, which noisily churned out the white paper ticket.

The bus passed the municipal swimming baths on its way along Birtwisle Road and as it trundled past the little figure of Fred Bamber, comically slapping his backside urging on the imaginary steed, Mark waved from the rear side window. Fred waved back cheerfully as he raced on until the bus was out of sight. He then slowed down to a walk, relieved that his pal had finally gone, saving him the necessity for the gleeful charade he carried out every time he saw a bus coming. Every now and then he would look at the two large, dirty brown coins in his sweaty palm to comfort himself on the long walk home, happy that he would eventually come to the sweet shop 'Two Steps' and spend the only pennies that in the past three weeks, he could call his own.

Chapter 54

Mark's luck was in. Helen read the note and listened to her remorseful, youngest son's account which omitted all mention of Peter.

She made an empty threat to kill Mark if ever he went anywhere without informing his mother again, the boy gave the threat little credence as he was often required to babysit. That night Barry drove Helen to Katy's to tell her why her husband had been missing.

When Helen and Katy telephoned Castaires, Peters had silently passed the receiver to Jack who, holding the phone away from his injured face, reassured the distressed women that he was fine and a visit was unnecessary.

A week later Jack came home. Corinne had her first birthday party and at the end of October Karl and two friends arrived at Saxon Place. Mark was sent to bed early that Friday while all the adults talked late into the night. Helen handed out spare blankets and pillows and they were coerced into sleeping wherever they could.

The next morning Helen rose early to make breakfast. Barry had eaten and had left for work, although he had promised to return before noon. Mark got up and dressed as soon as he was awoken by the strange sound of so many male voices downstairs, then he remembered they had guests. Mark enjoyed immensely the way his brother and his old friends from the 'Bon Fini' playfully teased him. They erupted into laughter when he greeted them. "Ello you suvvern fairies!" and they replied, "Allo you norvern monkey!"

After breakfast Mark was excited to see the motor that had brought his brother home from 'The Smoke'. In the little lane at the back of Saxon Place the parked car, a huge black, shiny beast with a very long bonnet was a unique sight. The boy could not believe that his brother possessed the most impressive vehicle he had ever seen. He ran back to the house as fast as he could. "Karl is that YOUR Humber?"

Karl looked at the boy and nodded. "Canna sit innit?" Again, without smiling, Karl nodded then said "Won't be for long though, we 'ave to go soon."

By the time he had reached the vehicle it was surrounded by local children who were convinced that the beautiful machine was owned by a famous person or filmstar. Feeling very important Mark pushed his way through the small crowd to the vehicle. The small boy's confidence stunned them into silence. "You lot 'ad better not be touching our kid's car."

They were about to say that Dacey was a liar. However, when Mark opened the driver's door and climbed onto the huge leather armchair of a seat, they were visibly impressed and envious. He closed the door behind him, almost decapitating one small urchin who had tried to poke his head into the car for a closer inspection.

Imperiously, the lord of the 'Humber Super Snipe' lowered the driver's window. Revelling in his newfound importance, his bragging knew no limits. "Yeh our kid lets me drive it sometimes."

"Oh you big liar Dacey!" said a girl at the back of the crowd.

"Am not! I'll show you all 'ow to drive if you like."

He explained with copious bull shit and feigned knowledge the intricate workings of the automobile. One of the older boys' peered through the windows and asked whether the knob he had just described as the super, go-faster button was not in fact the volume control of the valve radio. The 'Fangio of Burnbridge' rolled his eyes back and tutted at the idiot's ignorance. "So make it go then, if yer so clever!" said another voice. "Can't, ant got a key," said Mark, "but if I 'ad a key all I 'av to do is do this," he turned a heater knob on the dash, "an' then this," sliding a lever that operated the de-misters, "and then if I 'ad a key, this, an' we wud be off."

Karl had not used the hand-brake, but had relied on reverse gear to hold the vehicle stationery on the incline. When Mark depressed the clutch, the vehicle crept forward, slowly at first but then picking up speed and causing the urchins to scatter. The surprise registering to the faces of his audience was as nothing compared to the shock on the driver's face. Just in time, Mark removed his foot from the clutch pedal and the car's gearbox complained noisily as the big Humber jolted to a stop. Relieved, Mark wound up the window, shakily got out of the car and slammed the door with a bang. Karl, Harry, and Paddy arrived and most of the children dispersed, others ran up to the three men. "That yer car mister?" then added "coz if it is, Mark Dacey juss drived it."

Mark looked at his big brother who had noticed that the Humber was not as far up the hill as it had been when he parked it. With a reddening face 'Fangio' waited. Karl, fully aware of Mark's desire to save his dignity, climbed into the driver's seat then he called his little brother over and for all to see, he handed him a ten shilling note. "Thanks for getting the motor ready for us Mark."

As the car sped away, all three men waved back at Mark who, in the eyes of the local children, was now the important rich boy in the neighbourhood. He ran back to his mother to tell her of his good fortune and was desolate when Helen relieved him of his riches, telling him that she would look after his money. He had a feeling that that would be the last time he would see that particular ten bob note!

Karl turned to Paddy, "Next time you nick a motor make it one less fuckin' flashy, this thing draws more attention than a whore in a monastery."

The car picked up one more passenger, Karl's brother, Jack. The two nodded to one another. "Fuckin' 'ell Jack, you are an ugly cunt now."

Jack laughed, "Yeh, over thirty stitches an' I'm still better looking than you, you ginger 'eaded fucker."

Karl laughed as did the others but not loudly enough for Karl to hear. They journeyed without stopping and arrived in Liverpool as dusk was settling. All the men were now fully conversant with events and the plan for the evening. 'Razors' whereabouts had been discovered by Peter's discreet enquiries and assistance from his brother Larry who had dealings with some dodgy business associates on Merseyside, the gypsy, easily traced was a well-known 'face' around Scotty Road and Dockland. Peter had wanted to go with them but all had agreed that four was enough, any more would look like an army and this would have alerted anyone with reason to be curious or any undercover copper.

With time to waste before the meeting with one of uncle Larry's associates, the men decided to combine a little business with pleasure. At 'The Palace' a scouse punter called Chas Varney who was a doorman as the 'Top Ten Club' had told Karl about the music revolution in Liverpool and the money it was bringing in. He had mentioned a local band who had returned from a second visit to Hamberg where they had gone down a storm and how, on their return, they had been booked for ninety-two nights at the club. The same band performed at another Liverpool hotspot, 'The Cavern Club'. On that night the band were appearing at 'The Top Ten' and since Karl had treated the scouse doorman so well on his visit to 'The Smoke' Chas was eager to reciprocate - especially as he had heard disquietening rumours about this London 'face'.

Sat in the corner of 'The Top Ten' in a spot chosen by Karl and cleared of other occupants by Chas, the visitors studied the gaff. It was a club for youngsters and not the kind of place that 'faces' preferred. Usually important villains tended to be older and more serious individuals who looked on this new wave of popular musicians as screaming louts with no musical ability.

Karl showed most interest as he watched the punters at the bar and calculated how much they were spending, mostly on soft drinks. Not enough he thought, but more than he had expected from these northern kids. A census of opinion confirmed that they were impressed by the support the band had amongst the dancing crowd and the excitement they created, particularly in the girls', but to their minds it was probably a localised fad.

During the interval, the baby-faced band were brought over to Karl's table by Chas. After meaningless small talk, the band had to return to the small stage. The young man who seemed to be the leader offered his hand to Karl who took it and shook it warmly. "If you make it to London, come to 'The Palace' down Camden Way and ask for 'The Mank'."

"I will," smiled the young man, calling back above the crowd. "By the way I'm John Lennon, and we're 'The Beatles'."

Harry and Paddy jostled each other out of the narrow doorway. "Beatles, they looked like fuckin' black-jacks in them poncy leather get-ups." Paddy had not enjoyed the performance. "I dunno, it was Rock an' Roll but different somehow," replied Harry.

Soon after 'The Beatles' had finished their last number, Karl had said his goodbyes to Chas. "Listen pal, if you get fed up of the 'Pool' come down 'The Smoke' and I'll look after you."

The doorman nodded and shook hands, first with Karl and then with Jack. The quiet man with the livid scars that marred his good looks caused Chas to feel uneasy. There was something in his blue eyes and in his smile that sent shivers down the doorman's spine. Chas resumed his duties and the visitors turned into the side-street where they had left the big, black, stolen Humber. They passed a side door to 'The Top Ten' where they saw the band once again. One of the musicians who looked younger than the rest was complaining bitterly about something to the one who, earlier in the evening had introduced himself as John Lennon. They were loading some equipment and themselves into a light-greyish van, Karl noticed, as they skirted the motor quickly, not wanting any further conversation, that the first numbers on its registration plate were three, three, seven. Thirteen, he thought. "Well maybe it's their lucky number." The big saloon pulled past the van and it was obvious from the way John Lennon was kicking the slatted front that it would not start. "Well maybe not," said Karl under his breath.

On December 9th that year, John Lennon, Paul McCartney, George Harrison and Pete Best performed for the first time in the south of England at Aldershot's Palais Ballroom. It was not a great success, as there were only eighteen customers that night. However, on December 10th the band appointed a Liverpool businessman, Brian Epstein, the owner of a prominent music and record store, to be their new manager.

A Decca Records representative saw 'The Beatles' perform at 'The Cavern Club' three days later, he liked what he saw and arranged an audition with Decca chiefs for January 1st 1962.

The gang had been waiting in the shadows outside a gloomy, run-down warehouse in Liverpool's dockland for over an hour. The windows of the car had misted up from the four men's breath, so that Karl and Jack had to regularly wipe the windscreen with the backs of gloved hands. Uncle Larry's friend, 'Johnny Fingers,' a well known pick-pocket, was more than pleased to set up 'Razors Doherty' as the didicoy was leaning on him and he was paying protection to 'Razors' to avoid ending up like so many others, scarred like Jack.

After leading them in his Armstrong Sapphire to the warehouse, he performed look-out duties. 'Razors' visited at this time every Saturday evening to collect money from the old soak who owned the premises. Mack, was a short, fat, red-faced drunk who, before prison and booze had taken their toll was a respected 'face' in the city. Now he made a living by allowing his warehouse to be used by the dockers to stash pallets of stolen gear that were robbed on a daily basis from the many ships that called from all corners of the world. An arrangement with the dock police was lucrative for all involved.

Mack hated the gypsy bastard but feared him, and the possibility of turning up one day to find his premises burned to the ground.

Handing over the bank notes, he looked at the floor saying nothing. "I'll see yer next week," said 'Razors', and with no other exchange, he and his accomplice, Shaun, left for their next pick up.

Shaun followed 'Razors' out into the dank atmosphere of the docks. As usual at this time of year, a stinking mist from the water cast a weird gloom over this particular area. The damaged left eye was a legacy of the fracas in Richton several weeks previous.

An Irish tinker cousin, who lived in a cotton town fifty miles away, had contacted 'Razors' with a view to blackmailing a professional sportsman. 'Razors' unsavoury relative had discovered by accident that the rising star had a fancy for young girls' and one young girl in particular; a fourteen- year-old who lived in Tarnton, another nearby cotton town. The two of them had been spotted at a well-known nightspot and dance hall in Alton, 'The Savoy'.

The gypsy weasel had been drinking at 'The Savoy' when the flash Samoan had made his entrance. When he had seen the way the Samoan threw his money about, he had thought that there had to be a way to relieve him of some of it. So he called his cousin. That day they had arranged to bump into Roy as he left the club after the training session. They had told him that they were great fans and that they had come all the way from Liverpool to see him. He had been so impressed that after he had given them his autograph he had invited them for a drink. He was OK to have a beer or two as a slight injury would keep him out of the game for another week.

And that, thought Shaun, was when they had encountered that nutter in that working mens club. 'Razors' had picked up on him straight away, asking his cousin, who was about to leave the club, "Who's that there?" "Ee's one to watch that one indeed, can go a bit ee can, Jack Dacey, that's him."

'Razors' had watched him and when the opportunity had presented itself he had slyly done the deadly and striped the lad. Since then he had repeatedly told Shaun that he was going to go back and finish the job as the young bastard had robbed him of his prize, the money he had expected to extort from the big, stupid Samoan.

Roy had gone to ground; the debacle in the club had left him worried and wary. He dumped his child girlfriend and threw himself into training, keeping well away from possible trouble spots and unsavoury individuals. Earlier, 'Razors' had said, "Shaun my boyo, it's time we sorted that Richton lad Dacey, maybe next week."

"Why bother Razors?"

"Why? I'll tell yez why, coz ee cost me that's why."

Shaun thought that there was another reason and that reason was fear. 'Razors' feared any man who was capable of beating him, Shaun had seen that fear in 'Razors' face, that day in Richton. "That," thought Shaun, rubbing his damaged eye that Jack Dacey had so nearly gouged out, "is why 'Razors' will do the deadly on the bastard, because what he fears, he takes care of."

Still rubbing the itching ache that he experienced together with the permanently blurred vision, Shaun thought out loud, "Good, the sooner the better, let's see 'ow 'ard the bastard is when we blind 'im."

"What you sayin?" asked 'Razors' as they crossed the small distance to the side-road which led away from the warehouse in the direction of their parked car.

"I was just sayin, you were right earlier, we need to think about finding that bastard Dacey."

"Well," laughed Doherty, "it won't be difficult for sure, a left my callin' card all over his face."

Shaun and 'Razor's merriment was cut short when they came to the big Humber, which was empty and seemingly abandoned. Shaun cautiously tried the two nearside doors - they were locked. Doherty looked about and then walked around to the driver's door. It gave a click and sprang open. He looked up to grin at Shaun, just in time to see Harry bury a meat-cleaver into his friend's shoulder, bringing instantaneous screams that were silenced when Harry and another attacker dragged the injured man away from the car and into the shadows, where they threw him against the wall. The other man was Karl who struck so savagely with the broad machete, that he almost severed Shaun's head. 'Razors' did not stay to witness the end of his only friend, as instinct told him that this was a situation that his cut-throat could not handle. Too many of them, he thought.

Sensing other presences, he ran, all the time fearing that restraining arms or blows would follow. There were none, and he was almost back at Mack's warehouse and safety. He felt a mixture of terror and elation at his close escape. Then he realised it had been too easy. His ambushers had ensured that his only alternative route of escape was to flee back the way he had come.

Something moved in the darkness, he did not turn or he would have seen Paddy who was pursuing him with a hooked iron bar, all 'Razors' wanted to do was to reach the door. For a split second he almost whimpered in terror, what if the door was locked. He frantically reached out, his fingers closed around the handle. Suddenly the door flew open and the handle was torn from his grasp. The tall slim figure had been waiting expectantly behind the door that 'Razors' had been so desperate to reach.

'Razors' Doherty knew he should be doing something to defend himself, but the pain in his chest and the way his legs buckled told him, long before his brain registered, the deep stab wound piercing his right lung and sending blood into his mouth, that his destiny was no longer his own. His destiny would be determined by the hands and stiletto of a man who bore a freshly livid scar on his face, a 'face' he recognised as Jack Dacey. Jack was grinning from ear to ear; he had imagined this moment over and over again. He ignored the now childlike pleading and excuses, that tend to accompany this kind of mortal terror and reached into 'Razors' inside pocket. His fumbling, gloved fingers found the cut-throat, he looked at it almost reverently as if respecting the damage it had inflicted on him so easily. Then with a one-handed flick of his wrist, the wicked blade flew open and Jack again grinned grotesquely at the disabled blood-spitting gangster. The tall man stooped and snapped back to a standing position so smartly that 'Razors' wondered what had happened. Great gushes of his life blood spouted through his fingers, he instinctively clutched at the wound that his own weapon had inflicted to the soft tissue of his throat. It was a useless exercise trying to stem the flow, as the vicious stroke had sliced so deeply cutting sinew, muscle and arteries with ease.

'Razors' felt dizzy and his eyes became unfocused. He was much calmer now, accepting that his term on this earth was over. His last thoughts were an attempt to make sense of the words of his killer. "Hey Doherty you fuckin' wanka, I think this game is now over, cos you are a dead cunt."

The reference to the last words they had shared at that fateful meeting in Richton, never registered with the tinker as he had slipped into the shock and brief unconsciousness that precedes death.

"What a fuckin' mess," gasped Mack.

He had witnessed the murderous scenes from a distance, in the doorway where Jack had hidden.

"Well come on let's get to work then," said Karl.

Mack was also one of uncle Larry's long term associates and the brother of 'Johnny Fingers', who was still keeping lookout at the deserted junction that provided the only way into the secluded cul-de-sac. Paddy and Harry silently wrapped Shaun's lifeless form, in one of the tarpaulins from the Humber's boot and the two of them placed the swaddled body into the large wheeled cotton bobbin hamper that had been readied by Mack and Johnny much earlier. Razors body was also wrapped in a canvas shroud. "I din't think it was gonna be that messy," said Mack.

"Get the buckets of water an' bleach that I told you to have ready," ordered Karl and in a short time all obvious traces of bloody had been swilled down the drains where the big saloon had been deliberately parked.

When Karl was satisfied that the car was also cleaned of tell-tale crimson splatters, they turned their attention to the spot where Razors had fallen. This proved more complicated as most of the blood had to be mopped up with rags and then swilled with seemingly endless amounts of water and bleach until all visible evidence disappeared through the muddy gaps between the stone cobbles.

Attention was then directed to the wrapped bodies. Mack and his brother Johnny, who had returned from look-out, pushed the hamper to the water's edge and up the gangplank to the small cabin cruiser and the brothers' pride and joy. The others helped to lift the trolley onto the low back of the boat and then assisted the brothers' as they covered the hamper with tarpaulins and ropes, hiding it from view.

Returning to the warehouse, Paddy stood lookout sentry as the others stood in front of the furnace stark naked. They had stripped off after taking it in turns to hose each other down in an icy shower from the hosepipe. The water and gory evidence disappeared down the grate in the centre of the tiled area of the windowless room that at one time had served as storage for livestock prior to shipping. They rubbed themselves dry on the clean rags Mack provided and then these too followed all their clothes and shoes into the fierce flames of the furnace.

Once they were all dressed, in the spare outfit's that each of them had brought, Shaun relieved Paddy as lookout and he too cleaned up with as much attention to detail as the others. When all were assembled and they had checked and checked again for the slightest evidence of that night's deadly work, they could find none. Karl shared out the paper money that Paddy had taken from the bodies. He carefully inspected each banknote for visible signs of blood which might attract attention, and threw any stained notes into the flames. It was still a tidy sum and a bonus for that evening's venture.

Paddy filled the huge petrol tank of the Humber from the jerry cans that Johnny had brought, as per Karl's instructions. He had arranged this so that they would not have to stop at a petrol station or risk running out of fuel late at night in a stolen car. Karl had worked out accurately what was needed then allowed extra.

While the car was being readied, he handed a small paper bag to Mack. "Dump them separately, I've cleaned em." Mack took the few items of jewellery, which had been taken from 'Razors' and Shaun's corpses, so that in the unfortunate eventuality that their bodies ever reappeared it would be virtually impossible to identify them. Neither had ever seen a dentist during their lives so in death those limited records would not be available to the authorities. Karl had been adamant that the jewelery could be recognisable to someone, and that it had to go. Mack for one was not going to argue with him. "It's cheap shit anyway," sneered Johnny.

"Well that's that then," sighed Karl wearily, "we'll be off."

"Yeh, so are we," said Mack and after they had concluded the gruesome affair by sharing firm, knowing handshakes, they parted company in a calm and casual a manner.

At roughly the same time that Jack had been dropped off in Richton and the Humber was heading south, Mack and Johnny were waving to their mate in the port authorities building as they headed out on one of their regular weekend fishing trips. By late morning there was a parting of companies between the heavily weighted dead and the living, the jewellery and the hamper were dumped at different spots in the middle of the Irish Sea.

The southerners were watching from the window of the café at Birmingham Station's New Street with great amusement as two young rogues stole the beautifully cleaned black Humber, unaware that their every move was observed by the grateful gang.

"Told you not to leave the keys in the motor" joked Harry.

"Yeh shame; was a luverly motor."

"Never mind, we'll just have to use these train tickets I've got, to get back to London."

"Just remember what I said Paddy."

"What was that again Karl?" he asked.

"Don't ever nick a motor that flash again, it draws too much attention."

In the first week of November the front page of the local papers reported the story. Brutal attack on a local rugby star, the big Samoan, Roy Maluluha. He had been stabbed on Mellor Road in the early hours of the morning, after he had left friends at a small quiet pub. He was out of danger but although he would live his injuries were so serious that he would never play games of any kind again. Jack had not bothered about the outcome, when he impaled Roy with the Second World War bayonet. The force of the blow had pinned the giant to the wooden fence that he had his back to, when Jack in disguise had ambushed him. Jack had only stabbed once, as he could not remove the blade and this most probably saved Roy's life.

After the ambush Jack had climbed calmly into Peter's car, which had been waiting on the deserted cobbled street and together in silence Peter and Jack had driven to uncle Larry's late night party at his large detached residence in Farley. Jack had left no prints for as always he was gloved. The gloves, the flat cap and the boiler suit he had worn had been burnt. If anyone were to ask where Jack had been on the night in question, then many witnesses could be called to swear that he had been at Larry's party. 'The neighbours had complained of the noise to the police'.

Nan and Granddad came to stay that Christmas but Terry stayed in London as he was working until very late on Christmas Eve. Mary arrived back at Saxon Place for the festive period and the year ended on a high that December 1961.

Chapter 55

In early February 1962 the chief executives of Decca disagreed with their representative Mike Smith and refused to sign up 'The Beatles', on the grounds that they sounded too much like The Shadows, In their expert opinions all guitar bands were on the way out.

A few weeks later Brian Epstein secured an audition for 'The Beatles' at the BBC and a month or so later they were recording songs with George Martin and were poised to set the music business on its head. They never did give 'Karl the Mank' a call when they reached London, as they were too busy and would remain busy for the rest of their lives.

Barry frequently allowed Mark to accompany him to the small fish and chip shop at the back of the Flying Scotsman pub in Richton, where Barry's sister Joy and her husband Robert lived. They had taken over a chip shop the couple of years previously and seemed to be making a success of it. In the small, back room Mark would eat the chips in a bag fashioned from newspaper. Impatience burning his greedy fingers, he would wolf down the red-hot chunks of fried potato. When he had finished, he would lick his fingers and throw the paper into a bin in the corner of the room. Once Barry had completed his family business they would leave.

"Little gold mine that business." Barry said to the disinterested boy, on one visit. "An absolute gold mine."

His sister and brother in law exchanged that fish shop, and took on a larger one in Ludbarrow.

It was also early in the year that Karl and his gang got caught blagging a fashion house. As no violence or weapons were involved they got off fairly lightly, bearing in mind that the lads were now well known to the 'Old Bill'. The 'beak' sentenced Karl and Harry to two years in prison and Paddy, as wheelman, got eighteen months. Karl and Harry would get out in eighteen months and Paddy would serve a little over a year.

Mark sometimes walked the mile to Katy and Jack's house, at the back of the factory to spend time with his new nephew Jack junior. Katy's conversation was limited she would use the brief respite from her baby minding and household chores to nip out to the shops or call at her mother's for a cup of tea, without her child. On a rare occasion she would call in at the pub, which was on the main road at the end of the dirt track that led to the row of terraced cottages where Jack and Katy had made their home. Mark soon tired of this arrangement, as the time which he was left alone with the baby became longer with each successive visit. With no television to view or radio to listen to, the eight year old became bored and the visits dried up.

The youngest Dacey boy was in London three times that year on his own. During school holidays, at Easter and during summer, when Nan, Granddad and Terry took him on vacation to the Isle of White, and in September when he accompanied his nan on shopping expeditions she would proudly show him off to her friends. At lunch times they would call in at a pub, or meet Granddad at Russell Square Park where he was Head keeper. Mark would sit by his grandmother on one of the ornate, Victorian park benches, feeding the pigeons and enjoying the sunny weather until it was time to return home and prepare tea.

As a special treat, Mark was allowed to participate in Nell's favourite pastime, a visit to the cinema. On one particular visit to the 'Dominion', to see Lawrence of Arabia. Nell had been thrilled by the film, but it had sent young Mark to sleep.

There were times when Nell wanted Mark out from under her feet and on those occasions she would send him out to play with newly aquired friends who lived in a nearby tenement. Nell was not too keen on the kids as they were "bloody foreigners" -actually they were from Glasgow. It might as well have been Timbuktu to his grandmother. Mark and his Glaswegian friends who were brother and sister would play mostly around the bustling, Seaton Street market where Mark had become well known on his regular visits to Drummond Street. Terry would be working in Vic's Butchers and would have to suffer the presence of the three playmates as they marched up and down outside his shop window for hours. Every time they caught sight of him. "Hiya Tell,"- until the red faced older brother came out and politely told them to "Piss off." This happened three times a day.

Mark lived for the evenings when he was permitted to shadow his brother. They would meet up with the 'suvvern fairy's'- although this term for Terry's mates was no longer amusing and had been dropped some time before. Less time spent in coffee houses and more time was spent down the West End. Mark was beginning to realise that he was cramping his brother's style as the others would use assorted excuses to dump their pal when he was saddled with his younger brother.

One Friday evening, the gang were in high spirits waiting on the platform of Warren Street Tube Station for the train heading west. John, Howard, Ginger and Billy together with Terry's new friend, a live wire, happy-go-lucky, coloured youth called Bobby, and the Dacey brothers' formed the not quite so 'magnificent seven'.

Bobby's parents were West Indians, but Bobby was a Londoner born and bred. At first, Mark found the dancing accent and ebony features amusing, but after a few hours he was unaware of the difference in their colour but vert aware of the great fun it was to be around Bobby.

Ginger and Howard playfully wrestled for ownership of a pack of 'Player's Weights' cigarettes that Howard had bought earlier from the little booth at the station's entrance. Terry and John held Mark, threatening to punish his cheeky behaviour by throwing him under the next train. Bobby was standing at the platform's edge, peering up the tunnel, checking for sight or sound of their transport. A glance at the control lights told him that it was not yet due.

He was thinking how familiar the underground smell had become. The deep, smoky musk of electricity and fuel fumes, mingled with the scent of thousands of passengers who resembled incessant waves of human moles. Pushing and shoving their way through the maze of tunnels on their way to work or play, Bobby found the aromas more interesting than unpleasant.

Only Terry realised the danger. "Bobby!"

At his desperate shout the eyes of everyone on the platform turned to the space where Bobby had stood. The boisterous Howard and Ginger had accidentally barged into their friend who, caught unaware and off balance, fell flailing from the platform to the pit below.

Terry shouted at Mark to stay put. The other gang members now realised the danger that Bobby was in and started to react. By a miracle Bobby had missed the high voltage rail and though he was in a state of shock he grabbed Terry's offered hand. He felt himself being hoisted back on to the platform, then felt sudden acceleration as several other helping hands grabbed him in an effort to speed up the rescue. He heard the ominous rumbling and felt the cushion of warm air that preceded the train's rapid arrival; he felt a slight blow to his left foot, as just in time, he reached the safety of the platform.

Bobby landed in a breathless heap, as the others pulled him upright they all looked at his foot.

"Where the fak is my fakkin' shoe?" said the shaken youth.

Mark answered him. "It's ere, I got it."

The gang bundled through the open doors of the train, which closed behind them. Mark was laughing wildly the others stared to where he was pointing at the the bench on platform and where Mark had stood while the others rescued Bobby. They saw a tramp that was rubbing the right side of his head; he was looking up and down the platform in a state of bewilderment. He had been awakened from sleep by sudden violence. "The shoe it im on is ead and bounced into me arms" guffawed the youngster, and as Bobby replaced the missile on his foot the gang continued to laugh all the way to their destination.

The boys' were well aware of how close Bobby had come to death or serious injury, but they put it out of minds. For the rest of that evening, Terry held onto his brother more closely and tightly and Mark knew that it was his big brother who had saved Bobby's life that night, as did the others though it was never acknowledged.

On the Saturday afternoon Barry, Helen and Corinne had arrived having driven down to London to collect Mark. They stayed overnight and returned north after Sunday lunch.

Life had improved greatly for the residents of Saxon Place. Barry had replaced the television set with a posh new one, seventeen inches of screen encased in a roller-fronted cabinet, supported by thin, elegant, black lacquered-legs.

Barry would regularly return home with gifts, mostly for Corinne, but on one occasion he returned with a second-hand, scalextric, car racing set which Mark was not allowed to play with except under Barry's supervision, and on a second occasion, a large second-hand train set, that was set up on a board in the vacant downstairs room. Once again this was only to be played with, when Barry was present. When he found himself alone, Mark would risk Barry's displeasure and play with the trains.

It was with the privilege of operating his train set, that Mark was able to bribe Freda Connor to show him her private parts. With some badgering and promises of further opportunities to play with trains, Freda who was several years his senior allowed Mark to shag her – well, to attempt to shag her. Freda stood impassively, back against the wall, her knickers about her ankles, and Mark, with his shorts and underpants around his ankles. He found awakened animal instincts that urged him to rub his stiff penis against the girl's downy vagina. There was no penetration as the boy, was not sure where to put his manhood, while the girl, who was fully aware of where it went, had no intention of educating the boy. Becoming seriously bored by Mark's fumbling she pushed him away and pulled up her pants. "I'm going home for my tea."

Mark was convinced that he had just had his first shag but decided it might not be in his best interests to brag too loudly.

Barry regularly bought cars from the auction and did enough to them to make a profit when they were sold. Mark and Fred would always beg to be included on the test drives. The most memorable occasion was when Barry let the lads sit in the back of a grey Austin pick up truck. They whooped and yelled with glee all the way as the truck was driven through Ludbarrow, over Bleakstone Moor to the dam where Jack had worked and then back to Burnbridge.

School was a boring irritant to Mark. Every few weeks or so, he was allowed to take the bus to Castaires to see Peter. Although his father was amiable enough, Mark felt that when the clock had reached 6p.m. on a Saturday and his father had washed and dressed for the evening, his welcome had expired. Mark did not mind as the visit usually ended with a present from the shop on Denby Street that seemed to sell everything, and which was enroute to the bus stop. In fact, Mark would make those trips on those Saturday mornings looking forward more to the departure than to the arrival.

Mark had joined the church choir at St. James where his sister Mary had been a member when she had resided at Saxon Place. It was not that her little brother had notions of becoming closer to God, but that he appreciated the shilling he received for weddings and the time off from school lessons, to take the short walk to the church for choir practice.

When the Vicar found out that Mark had come from a lapsed Catholic background he soon deduced that the boy had not been christened and so it was that a visit to Helen resulted in a visit to the font for Mark and Corinne. One of Helens friend's and Barry's sister Joy and her husband Robert were drafted in as godparents. At the subsequent celebrations baby Corinne was the star of the show and Mark felt like an outsider.

Not long after the Christening the boy joined the cubs. On the Saturday, Peter took Mark to the outfitters in Richton, where his son convinced him that it was the nice blue uniform of the sea scouts he needed, not the same green that all the other members of the Burnbridge cub pack would be wearing. Akela allowed Mark to wear his eccentric uniform for a few weeks, which gave Mark the opportunity to tell the other cubs that he was a higher ranking cub scout and did not need as many merit badges as they had. Eventually Akela had no choice but to order Captain Mark to join the ranks but rather than give up his blue fatigues, he told her where she could dib, her dobs.

A few weeks later he was unceremoniously kicked out of the choir for battering a fellow chorister whom he accused of nicking his surplice from the vestry. The Vicar might have been inclined to show more leniency had not the fight which had taken place in the middle of a packed thanksgiving service, ending with Mark sitting victoriously astride his victim in front of the altar asking the boy if he had "ad enuff."

Towards the end of the summer, dark rumours circulated that the country was on the brink of a Third World War. The World sighed with relief when the Cuban missile crisis came to an end. The 'West' had gained a new, golden hero in American president, John Fitzgerald Kennedy.

On the 19th of October, Corinne became two years of age, and early in December, Mark registered the fact that he became nine years old.

Nell and Tommy again travelled north to spend the festive period at Saxon Place and this time Terry accompanied them, but he was not alone. He came with his girlfriend, Jean. They had all travelled from London's Victoria coach station, with the famous Richton coach company, 'Yelloway'. Because space at Saxon Place was limited, Terry and Jean elected to stay at Castaires with Peter, which meant that Mark saw very little of his brother that Christmas. His grandparents proudly told him that Terry had passed his driving test and had bought an old van from Jean's uncle Derek for twenty-five quid. Terry, when asked by his impressionable younger sibling wether the story was true or not, confirmed the news saying that he had christened his pride and joy, 'Fireball XL5' after a popular children's puppet show. Early in the new year Fireball landed for the last time, in a scrap yard. Uncle Derek had sold him a banger.

And at midnight on Christmas day snow started to fall and continued to fall for sixty-seven consecutive days, heralding one of the most severe winters on record for Great Britain, 'The big freeze' of '63.

Chapter 56

April 1963 in bright sunshine, Mark was busily playing with his soldiers in the dirt of the small communal yard, when his mother called him in. "Mark I wonder if you can do a very important job."

This kind of condescending request was designed to flatter the childs ego and ensured his co-operation. Intrigued, he listened as his Mother was asking if she could trust him to take a letter to his aunty Joy at the chip shop in Ludbarrow. The distance from Saxon Place to the shop was a little over four miles on the main thoroughfare. Mark was eager to ride his new bike, a metallic blue 'Raleigh Rodeo' that had been purchased as a combined birthday and Christmas present and that had only recently seen daylight when the weather had improved.

The two-wheeled pony express rider returned from his eight mile round trip without mishap, the boy puffed with pride. Putting his trusty steed in the semi-basement room, he ran upstairs to receive his praise. But all his mother said was, "Did you get given a letter to bring back?"

Mark nodded and rooted out the crumpled note from the inside pocket of his jacket. Impatiently she snatched the envelope and tore it open. Mark watched Helen's face as she read, he did not know why she smiled on the first reading but became serious as she re-read the letter to ensure that she had understood the content. When she was finally satisfied, a wide grin spread across her face. Mark asked what was in the letter but was told playfully that it was a secret but that he would be told later that night when Barry came home.

She was true to her promise and with great ceremony all the occupants of Saxon Place were assembled in the front room. Mark sat on the sofa next to Barry who had sat Corinne on his knee.

"We are moving" said the excited Helen, "to Ludbarrow."

This wonderful news had been made possible by two major events. The first event was the council's decision to compulsorily purchase and demolish, Saxon Place and the surrounding terraced hovel's to pave the way for a better Burnbridge. The Second event was, Barry's sister Joy's decision to give up their shop. Joy and her husband had found the long hours too much for Robert's failing health and they had kindly done all they could to help Barry and Helen to get the lease assigned to them. The Family were going into business.

The news prompted Mark to continuously and irritatingly hum a tune, that he had heard during a petrol commercial on ITV. "You can be sure of Shell," Mark however was no'Bing Crosby'.

Terry surprised his family up north by arriving for the weekend in his nearly new, two-tone, blue and white Ford Anglia. Accompanying him once again was his sixteen-year-old girlfriend Jean, a very pretty brunette with an infectious, happy personality. Although Mark was suspicious and jealous of this new competition for the affections of his brother, their relationship improved when Mark was allowed to miss school to accompany Terry and Jean on an outing to New Brighton, a grubby seaside resort near Liverpool.

Mark had one of the best days of his life. He enjoyed ice creams, the fair ground and the terrible scenes in the dungeon which depicted the horrors of Nazi atrocities in the holocaust.

Why children sulk when they have been given everything they desire is one of life's little mysteries. Possibly, in Mark's case it was the knowledge that his brother was leaving for London the next day. Whatever the reason, the youngster consoled himself by farting every mile or so on the return journey, prompting Terry to threaten the youngster who was giggling in the back seat, that if he stank out the car one more time he would leave him. Mark had been sat at the roadside for about ten minutes. He had been dragged out of the Ford Anglia by Terry for not taking his warning seriously. Mark continued to sulk and was unconcerned by his solitary state as he had noticed his brother and Jean were parked down the road, observing him with great amusement. Eventually they returned and Mark persisted in his sulking, refusing to return to the car.

Jean who was stood on the pavement with the door open and the seat-back pushed forward to allow access to the back seat, eventually she managed to coax the sour-faced child back in. For the next five miles the smaller boy silently and with poker-face suffered the taunts of his older brother before retaliating. "Aw Mark you dirty bastard, that stinks." Terry covered his nose with one hand and tried to drive with the other, while Jean frantically wound down the passenger window and held her nose, Mark felt his reprisal was just.

The eventual outcome of the journey was that Mark had been won over, and from that moment on would never be able to think of his Terry without adding and Jean to thoughts or conversations, loving them equally and they returned that love.

Not long after the excursion to New Brighton, it was time for the big move. Helen gave notice at Moss Mill and even though running the chippy would be a demanding venture, she was certain that she would be able to spend more time with her children. Barry had decided to give up his job at the laundry, because the old Jewish owners were retiring and he did not want to work for younger family members. He had got a job at Wilkinson haulage carriers, driving heavy goods wagons. He would be trunk driving, so there would be no weekend work, and the pay was much better.

In July it came to pass that Barry, Helen and the two children drove away from Saxon Place for the last time.

Mark did not see any of his old friends from that day forward. At twelve years of age Fred Bamber started a life of petty crime and died when the motorcycle he had stolen crashed into a parked vehicle on Whilby Road, two weeks before his fourteenth birthday. Marion France married a much older man when she was sixteen and the couple moved to Cornwall. Her eldest brother Colin joined the Army as a boy soldier and never returned to Richton. Steven, the youngest France boy, also married young and in his late teens was run over while crossing the road, leaving him severely brain damaged. His father George deserted his wife Doreen not long after his youngest son's road accident. He left town taking the poor young man's teenage bride with him. George died of a massive heart attack a few months later and Doreen France, a chain-smoker, died several years later of cancer, a bitter lonely woman.

Freda Connor and her younger sister were subject to a trial, where her father was found guilty of incestuous rape and abuse and received a sentence of seven years in prison. While alone one sunny Good Friday, Freda hung herself from the banisters of her home. She was fifteen years old.

It was as if the curtain had come down on a scene of a live stage production, except that there was no applause and so it was that this part of Mark's life was destined to fade into the realms of a distant memory.

Jack and his accomplices had been caught robbing a warehouse in Manchester and he was sentenced to two years in Strangeways, Jack had only been in the prison for one week when he battered a warden, earning him another year inside and a move to London's notorious Wormwood 'Scrubs'.

Karl had done business with most of London's underworld and preferred the ethics of Albert and Christopher Rankin's firm to the uncertain charms of the East End Brown brothers'. He had done a number of jobs where his path had crossed that of Big John Carter.

John was a hard man of the old school who had been at the peak of his power in 1960 but who was still a major force in The Manor. He, like Karl, also preferred the more intelligent approach to business that the Rankin brothers' adopted, despite the fact that as an East End boy, he was reluctantly respected by the Brown mob. John had married a girl from, 'off' The Manor and had moved to live near The Elephant and Castle. Not only did he change address, he also changed his opinion of the East End firm, from grudging respect to disdain and scorn and that would have deadly consequences.

Mary was working for the Ministry of labour in the wages inspectorate in London and was doing well. Nan, Granddad and Terry moved up-market to a bigger apartment in Hampstead, a stones throw from the famous Heath. Mary and Karl moved in to help their aged grandparents afford the prestigious new address. Karl met his future wife Linda.

Before August arrived and Mark had to start life at his new school, Ludbarrow Central, he had a week's holiday to look forward to and which was to be spent with his grandparents, Terry, Jean, and Mary in a boarding house in Clacton. It seemed to Mark that life was taking off.

Chapter 57

Chapel Sreet, Ludbarrow, was only been four miles distance away from Burnbridge, but it might as well have been a different country, as Mark would find out.

The routine of fast food commerce was quickly established. From 10.30 to 2p.m the new owners prepared for the lunch trade. After a break until 7p.m. the doors were open for the late shift, which ended at 2a.m. on Sunday morning when everything had bean cleaned and cleared away. On Sunday's the business was open 6p.m. to 11p.m. On weekdays the schedule varied, during lunchtime and evenings the workday's were almost the same as Saturday's, but finished an hour earlier. The extra teatime openings of 3.30 to 6p.m. left Helen only an hour's break before she had to start work again.

Barry would arrive home from work and after a quick tea he would wash, shave and change and donning a white coat, he prepared the raw cod that came in 28lb boxes, boning and skinning the fillets, cutting them to size and piling them onto white plastic trays. The trays were covered with a layer of greaseproof paper and a clean damp white tea towel to stop the fish from drying out. Barry filled the custom-made, stainless, steel box that was fitted to the side of the range, with a batter mix. Then he would go into the cellar which housed the ancient electric potato peeler, returning with large plastic buckets of prepared spuds.

Once the shop opened he would exchange banter and pleasantries with the customers. as he placed the potatoes into the large, iron, manually operated chipper. The sliced shapes fell into a bucket and then were immediately transferred to the hot bubbling beef dripping in the deep well of the range. One side of the range was used for fish, the other for chips. Barry was responsible for frying while Helen served.

At the busiest times Helen employed a couple of part-timers. The two young women used the earnings to supplement their husbands' low incomes. They left their men to care for the children while they worked evenings for twelve bob a night, cash in hand.

Barry still found time to visit the auctions and after being in the chip shop for only a few weeks he saw an opportunity to increase the household budget. He had noticed that every weekend, groups of his customers would hire a minibus and travel out of the village into Richton or eleven miles further to Manchester for the evening. When barry exchanged the family's Vauxhall for a dove-grey Austin minibus, Helen was not surprised. It was an astute move. Not only did he get paid for his unlicensed taxi service, but more often than not the passengers return to Ludbarrow coincided with the chip shop opening hours, this guaranteed that whatever had been left over from the evening's unsold stock of pies, chips, fish, peas, and gravy, was purchased by the ravenous inebriated revellers.

Since his return from London Mark had explored his new home and surroundings. Home was a stone-built, Victorian, terraced property' which fronted the very busy main road. The front room housed the range and shop counter. Beyond that room a door on the left gave access to two small, damp whitewashed cellars. The middle room was larger and it was filled with chairs and tables of various sizes, all covered with bright check-coloured plastic cloths. This was the dining room for customers who wished to 'eat in'. In the far corner was a door with a handwritten notice 'Private, No Entry' - for this was the stairway to two bedrooms. The bedroom over the shop was Barry and Helen's bedroom, the one over the dining room was shared by Mark and Corinne.

There was a further doorway in the dining room which led to a small kitchen on the right and a long, narrow corridor and a tiny washroom containing an old chipped sink. Off the corridor at the back of the building was a comfortably sized family room, which contained the most important family possession - the TV. At the very end of the corridor the outside door and a flight of wooden steps leading to a small dustbin shed and the brick-built toilet. These were situated in a dimly lit open courtyard, off which a lane provided parking space and allowed access to the backs of the terraces.

The living room was separated from the kitchen by a curtain of brightly-coloured plastic ribbons that reached from ceiling to floor. An identical curtain separated kitchen from dining room where another notice above the doorway announced that the area beyond was 'PRIVATE'.

Customers were not given access to the family's toilet- this did not present too much of a problem as diners were accustomed to that kind of treatment. At that time any establishment providing food, was not required to provide toilet facilities. This did not prevent drunks waking Mark and his sister by rattling the locked door, because they had failed to read the notice at the bottom of the stairs. For the same reason their television watching was disturbed if they forgot to lock the living room door, it would sometimes open suddenly and a broad Lancashire accent would inquire. "Where's tha toilet," to which Mark would reply "We ant got one," and send the laughing drunk back to his friends in the dining room, locking the door behind them.

Desperate male drunks and desperate female piddler's would disappear out of the front door, returning minutes later, much relieved. For those needing more than a pee, the ginnel which separated the terraces a few doors down, was not really an option. This encouraged the desperate to eat quickly then run for home, however they frequently failed to make it and Mark christened the ammonia-stinking ginnel as 'Piss Alley'.

Ludbarrow was a typical North-west of England semi-industrial village with its small factories numerous shops and several pubs.

At the weekend Barry took Mark by, foot, on the route he would be walking to his new school the following Monday. As they walked back to the chip shop Barry, sensed that all was not well. "First week will be a doddle, seeing as you are new and all."

The information sounded reasonable and cheered Mark up a little. Man and boy walked side by side down one of the main shopping streets, Hensley Road, it was Sunday afternoon and the street was deserted. They passed the Co-Op, the ironmongers, the newsagent's, the record shop and the electrical goods store and the clothing emporium that stocked every kind of garment and supplied the school uniforms that were compulsory in the village's four schools, three junior and infant, the Parish, the Catholic, the Central and the Secondary Modern, soon to become the Comprehensive. All the schools were within a half-mile of one another. Mark's early explorative forays had discovered ten pubs, a working men's club, the Free Trades hall, the Conservative club, five fish-and-chip shops, several newsagents, a large toy store which was opposite Mark's home and the cricket club which of course was licensed to serve alcohol. There were dozens of convenience and sweet shops, large and small. The Victoria cinema had recently been converted to a Bingo hall. There was a coffee house and car showroom that was situated in a building that had at one time been the village's second cinema, 'The Queens.'

At the centre of Ludbarrow was a small square where Edwardian, bus shelters provided protection from the elements and a turning area for buses. Just past the shelters over the small stream was the railway station. This then was Ludbarrow, the place where Mark and his family had chosen to make their new home.

Later that night the family sat in the small room on a rare moment of togetherness and Mark was told that he should really address Barry as 'Dad' to save awkward questions. Helen also asked him if he would like to change his name to Holt, which was Barry's surname as Helen and his sister had taken. Mark did not want to be known as Mark Holt and after a brief attempt to coerce her son Helen relented, she realised that Mark would not estrange himself any further from his beloved Terry, by changing his name.

From that day although Mark called Barry 'Dad', as indeed he had become, they could not play the charade of a conventional happy family and Mark found himself explaining for most of puberty why he did not share the surname as Barry, Helen and Corinne. Of course the explanation was that his mother had re-married.

Occasionally some boy who was nosier than most pointed out that meant that Corinne was only his half-sister. On such occassions Mark never failed to punch the child mercilessly, until they were bloody and repentant for their tactless observations.

Chapter 58

In the school corridor Mark scrutinised the walls. The upper parts were painted salmon-and-cream and the lower parts were covered in dark brown glazed tiles. His eyes shifted to the primitive shelves and the rows of dog-eared books. Small sections were missing from the matt-tiled floors and the gaps had been filled with cement. A line of suspended one-hundred-and-fifty watt bulbs, shrouded with dusty tin shades provided illumination. Natural light was admitted through the plethora of glazed panels. Mark had to push his way through a line of noisy bustling children who were leaving assembly, which had been held in the large centrally situated hall, the children were dispersing to appropriate classrooms.

"Mr. Lord will see you now," announced the skinny secretary.

Nervously, the newcomer entered the office-come-storeroom. "Ah Dacey, we have been expecting you."

For the next ten minutes Mark had to answer questions which were designed to determine his aptitude and social standing. His interrogation and assessment were administered by an arrogant man of medium build and an easily forgettable persona. "Right," said the self-important head teacher. "Let's get you to your class."

Mark followed The Head up narrow painted stone steps, arriving at an open corridor whose parapet looked down into the main hall. At the corridor's end was Class Three. The sign, written in crayon announced it as such.

As The Head entered the room all the class stood to attention by their desks, in a well-practised drill. In perfect synchronisation they intoned "Good morning Mr. Lord," to which he replied, disinterestedly, "Good morning children" and the children sat down noisily, opening desks to pull out books for the lesson. Mr. Lord winced then addressed a wizened little woman who was wearing thick layers of make up and an even thicker, light blue, machine-knitted, woollen, two piece suit.

"This is Dacey, the new student Miss Rhodes."

The spinster smiled back thinly at the much younger man, she still harboured bitter feelings that her own vast educational experiences had been passed over by the governors in favour of youth. "Thank you Mr. Lord."

To the ancient teacher's chagrin The Head was already closing the glazed classroom door behind him. "Children this is Mark Dacey. Now Mark tell us about yourself."

Red-faced, standing in front of the class, Mark stammered his way through the ordeal as child after child questioned him. At last the teacher pointed to a vacant chair at the back of the class next to a boy who was very-tall for-his-age. The lad was given the task of helping Mark to settle in and introduced himself to Mark as Jeff Jenks. Jeff proved to be helpful and by lunchtime the two were becoming firm friends.

It was soon the last class of the day, the arts class. Mark was sharing a painting project with Jeff, when a well-built boy with ruddy complexion and a mop of curly hair, brushed past Jeff and accidentally on purpose he knocked the jam jar Jeff was holding and which was half-filled with dirty water, over the painting and over Jeff. Leaping to his feet, Jeff grabbed some green paper towels from the desk in front and mopped his clothes, and then he tried to rescue the ruined painting. "Watch it Jinxie," said the stocky beetroot, to the flustered taller boy.

Mark studied the confrontation, moving only to escape a trickle of paint water which was running off the desk. "Jenks you clumsy oaf. What have you done now?" demanded the slim, attractive long-haired and bespectacled young Arts and Crafts teacher.

"It was an accident Miss. Gordon, sorry Miss."

On the way home Jeff explained that the beetroot was the 'Cock O' School' which meant he was the toughest kid at the Central and that all other boys' recognised him as such. "What's iz name?" asked Mark.

"Dennis Carter," said Jeff miserably, it was Jeff that suffered the most abuse from Dennis and his pals.

Jeff accompanied Mark all the way to the chip shop's front door and when he explained that he only lived 5 minutes down the road at Case Street, it prompted Mark to ask "Do you wanna play at my house after tea?"

Eagerly Jeff nodded, before he ran off happily down Chapel Sreet.

Mark banged with both fists on the shop door, when no one answered he proceeded to drub the door with his right foot, enjoying the way the bottom gave easily under his heavy kicks. "Alright, alright!" shouted his mother from a distance. "I'm coming." Helen opened the door and Mark ducked the half-hearted slap at his head. "You'll ave that bloody door off its hinges."

She re-locked the door behind them and followed her son to the living room. Corinne excitedly greeted her big brother with open arms. Throwing his satchel and coat onto the chair by the door, he picked up the impatient infant. Bouncing his giggling sister in his arms he walked to the kitchen, where Helen was preparing for opening time. Without interrupting her chores, Helen quizzed her son as to his first day at his new school and was genuinely pleased that Mark had made a new friend. She did not too much mind that he had invited the lad to call, as Mark seemed so enthusiastic about his new friendship. "He knows you can't go out to play does he?"

Mark nodded "Yeh I told im av gotta look after me little sister."

Helen learned that Jeff was sympathetic as his German-born mother, a war bride was expecting, so he too would shortly be saddled with a baby brother or sister. "Well stay in the living room and make sure you behave, and don't forget that you're looking after Corinne."

Mark promised to obey all commands and to abide by all rules.

Later, Jeff nervously called into the chip shop where he enquired after Mark Dacey. Helen left the assistant serving as she ushered Jeff through to the back room, where Mark was sat on the floor playing the games that kept Corinne amused. "Hiya Mark!" beamed Jeff and was rewarded by an equally friendly response.

The two boys' could not be more different in appearance. Mark was less-than the average height for his age and a blue-eyed blond, whereas Jeff was abnormally tall and gangly with jet-black hair and hazel eyes. In all other respects the two were perfect companions, sharing almost identical likes and dislikes.

All three children were glued to the TV when Barry came in from work. After exchanging some banter with the boys' he picked up Corinne, who was demanding her daddy's attention. Helen had just closed the shop and asked the boys' if they would like pie and chips.

Mark was ravenous as he had not yet eaten and Jeff, although he had had tea, was not going to pass up the chance of a free 'chippy'. The boys' went into the empty dining room and Helen brought them their preferred choices, leaving them to return immediately with two large glasses of pop. The lads were left to their own ministrations while Helen took more prepared food through to the living room for herself, Barry and Corinne. When Mark and Jeff had finished eating they took their plates to the kitchen, placing them on the side drainer of the small sink. "Canna go out now?" asked Mark.

Helen looked first at Barry who shrugged and then at Mark. "OK, but you must be in for half past seven."

Barry knew that he would be putting Corinne to bed soon, where she would happily drift off to sleep until morning. Mark would have to get himself ready, washing in the little washroom, where hopefully the dining room clientele would not notice him nor realise that their house had no bathroom.

The whole family had to wash daily in that tiny washroom. On Sunday mornings the tin bath was brought in from outside for the weekly scrub, which took place in the dining room when the shop was closed. Sometimes the boy would watch a little TV. Often he sat alone hoping that the adults had forgotten him. When they were extremely busy, his parent's would find him asleep in front of the buzzing blank screen. When he was not to busy, Barry would stick his head into the room. "You ad a wash?"

Sometimes Mark's pretence that he was asleep would be discovered and one of his parent's would drag him to the chipped sink with a threat that they would do the job themselves. At such times Mark rapidly saw sense and completed the job. Then trying to avoid attention he would squeeze through the dining room to the stairs that led to his bedroom.

At busy weekends when Mark was allowed to stay up later, he would have to pass through the packed dining room which he found an ordeal; he would hurry through as quickly as possible, trying to ignore the attention of drunks'. He would let out a Sigh of relief as he closed out the raucous laughter that always followed some wisecrack at his expense. Thankfully there were only four people eating that night, although, from his bed he could still hear the muted revelry below as the evening wore on and the pubs turned out.

Mark usually read for as long as he could, until either Barry or Helen peered up the stairs to see wether any light was coming from under his door. "Turn that light out NOW!"

This sometimes coincided with a part of the book that held him enthralled and it ruined the moment. He soon became acquainted with the torch- under-the-bedclothes technique. This almost solved the problem, only failing with the death of the battery, or when Barry sneaked upstairs to catch him unawares and confiscate both torch and book. The boy developed an uncanny ability to read under the covers, while listening for the telltale sound of the increased clamour occasioned by the opening of the door downstairs, on nights when the shop was quiet the telltale creak of the bottom step, enabled the boy to feign sleep by the time the house detective had arrived.

Jeff had called for his new friend to walk to school that Friday morning, as he had done all that week. Every night, once Mark had been released, the two had played in the nearby streets, where Jeff showed him about and taught him the relevance of his new territory. Jeff had bored most of the school with his tales of Mark's wealth and good fortune to own a chip shop and to be able to eat chippy every night, should he so choose. More importantly, friends could also partake of Mark's generousity, as Jeff had done twice already that week. In truth, those two occasions were the only times that Mark had eaten chippy that week, because Helen always tried to give her family a varied diet and was adamant that they would not live out of the shop.

Jeff was waiting for Mark to catch him up in the school playground after lunch when he came face to face with Dennis. "Hey Jinxie." The school's toughie used the nickname that all the kids used at Central and one that Jeff did not mind. "Where's yer mate, 'fishboy'?"
Dennis's two companions, Andy, a boy almost as tall as Jeff and Nigel, a boy similar to Mark in size and stature but swarthy in feature, laughed loudly at their leader's jest. Jeff was about to be jostled when the voice behind him caused his assailants to spin about. "What do you want, you shit-faced beetroot?"
Mark had heard the 'fishboy' insult and decided that if this insult was not to be the foundation of his new nickname, something drastic had to be done. Andy and Neil laughed again, this time at their leader's expense, but they stifled their laughter when Dennis first glared at them, then at the newcomer who was squaring up to him. "Right, a 'barney' then, after school on tha 'rec'."
With that, the stocky lad gave Mark a shove to clear his path and strutted off, chased by his minions who were already announcing the news that was taken up like wildfire by the playground's occupants.
The parks playground was two hundred yards from the school's entrance. If teachers saw a massed throng carrying combatants along, they seldom stopped what was seen as youthful exuberance and a

natural way to establish playground pecking order. That evening, the whole school turned out to see the fight between the school champion, Dennis and the 'Foreigner' Mark Dacey.

A crowd of boys' and girls' were becoming high on agitated chatter and bloodlust, heightened by chants of 'Barney. barney, barney' and 'fight, fight, fight'.

Dennis the favourite was the first to arrive at the playground. Mark, accompanied by his only friend, Jeff, followed closely behind. Mark was pensive but Dennis was loud and brash, making witticisms at Mark's expense which fueled a feeling of violent hatred in the belittled newcomer. Once or twice a spectator, or Dennis supporter ran back from the main throng to tell Mark merrily, "Yer gonna get yer ead kicked in" or, "Don't tha think o runnin away, chicken."

Running away was out of the question for Mark, as his legs had hardly managed to carry him to the 'Rec'. Mark felt that everything that others saw in him was a sham of bravado. He began to wonder what life would be like after defeat. Would it be filled with ridicule poured on the vanquished and incur unavoidable acceptance of the nickname of 'fishboy'? How would he, a newcomer, cope with the victor's sneers and his supporter's glee, most of all, for how long would he suffer the ignominy of being the new kid, the foreigner?

Jolted from his anxious contemplations Mark found himself roughhoused by a huge crowd, their numbers swollen by kids from other schools who used the popular, tree-lined Park Road to get to and from school, or to visit the playground.

Next to the 'Rec' were the football pitch's undulating mud patches. Dennis was making a show of inspecting the ground for stones and glass, kicking away any debris with the toe of a shoe. At Mark's side stood a pale and worried Jeff but if he thought that they were going to fight the lot, side by side before going down in glorious defeat, Mark was mistaken. Jeff meekly held out his hand, and then seeing his friends puzzled expression said, "I'll old yer coat."

Without the jacket, Mark suddenly felt cold and he hoped an involuntary shiver was not seen as cowardice. Dennis turned from handing his long navy raincoat to Andy. "Right then fishboy, let's av a fight."

If only the lad had not used the insulting nickname, and if only those in the noisy mob who had heard the insult had not laughed, then things and life for Dennis might have remained unchanged. The first flailing fist that caught him in the face burst his nose instantly. Wait, he thought, this is not how it goes. I go to the centre of the man-made ring, circle, the other kid and then when he is sufficiently petrified, I grab him in a headlock and pummel him until he gives in. That's what is supposed to happen, that's always what happens. It was a pity no one had explained Dennis's thesis on the art of warfare to Mark.

'Clump!' another whirling fist connected with the stocky boy's left ear, bringing a howl of pain and rage. "Right, right, Dacey, now yer for it," but the surprise and energy of Mark's attack and the sight of his own blood made it impossible for Dennis to make good his threat. "Into battle" yelled his foe, landing a looping punch to his enemy's midriff.

'OOF' wheezed Dennis and the unbelievable happened, he was down, the cold wet mud soaking into his shorts and underwear. He became aware of the baying mob, screaming for him to get up and carry on fighting for their savage pleasure. Dennis looked up at the smaller boy, legs splayed in an arrogant stance and whose arms hung at his side's, fists clenched menacingly, the wildly, glaring, blue eyes dared Dennis to get up. He felt hands grabbing him, trying to haul him to his feet, then a sudden panic that he would be hauled up to experience more pain, his shoulders slumped and that gesture silenced the crowd. Everyone heard the boy on the floor declare wretchedly. "Av ad enuff, you win."

Mark found himself being manhandled once again, but this time as the victorious hero. It seemed that all the congratulatory handshakes, slaps on the back and "that was great" came from people who assured him that they had been his friends all along. "Jinxie!" shouted Mark in the manner of a newly-crowned king.

Jeff pushed his way through the throng who were escorting the victor from the field of conflict. "Ere I am" blurted the tall lad, breathless from the frantic screaming support he had been giving his friend. He had possibly been the only genuine support until the crowd had switched its allegiance, to avoid association with the losing side. "Giv us me jacket."

Mark took the garment thrust at him and he donned it ceremoniously. "Oi, Dacey!"

Mark and the crowd looked back to see Andy. "I'm second Cock O School, so you av t' fight me next."

Mark sensed that this was a serious threat to his new found and all-too-brief status, so the jacket was already coming off. "No No not now!" "I. I.. I've gotta go 'ome for me tea," stammered the boy, taken aback by the willingness of the youngster he had just challenged.

"Monday after school then" shouted Mark at the retreating Andy.

"Yull do im easy Dacey."

Mark looked into the face of a new smiling pal. "You called me a chicken."

The smile died as the youngster was recognised as the one who had been running to and from the crowd to goad Mark earlier. 'SMACK!' If the crush of the crowd had not prevented it, the boy would have been horizontal as the punch had burst his nose and the following day would prove to have blackened his eye. Realising that he had just been made to pay for backing the wrong 'Fish,' the boy began to blubber and wail and that's how he was left, as the dispersing mob chased after Mark Dacey, 'Cock O' the School'.

The hangers on had dwindled and by the time Mark reached the main road in front of his home, only Jeff remained. "See yer later Mark?" asked Jeff.

"Yeh see yer later."

As Mark pounded on the shop door, Jeff was skipping happily down the street, returning home, a much more secure person than when he had left that morning. Was it not for his sake he told himself that Mark had fought his long-term tormentor? Was he not the best friend of the new top dog of the Central? His happy skipping almost faltered as he thought, well at least until Monday evening, when Mark would have to fight the school's number two, Andy. Jeff shook his head to dispel the thoughts and continued homeward bound, his high spirits reinstated.

The weekend passed quickly as did school on Monday. All that day the school had been a hive of excitement, as stories of Friday's scrap were embellished with extra pain and gore. Dennis had come up to Mark at the morning playtime and shook his hand announcing genuinely he had no hard feelings. Mark found himself actually warming to the boy for the gesture.

Andy sent Neil to offer a truce saying that they could be equal rulers of the playground. Mark sent back a reply that set the yard buzzing again. "I can't wait for after school, coz am gonna knock the livin' shit out of yer."

Andy had not expected to have to go through with his hasty challenge. He had regretted it from the moment he had issued it.

The battle scene was a carbon copy of the previous one except that this time Mark's theatrical battle cry was 'Excalibur,' followed by a sort of fanfare, "Ta, da da dat da dah!"

Andy, who had no stomach for the fight, surrendered as soon as his bloody nose confirmed that the first punch had landed. Within seconds of the victory Mark was again challenged, by the third Cock O School. Neil.

Although arrangements were made for the next evening, Mark again departed from all protocol when, at lunchtime the next day, he attacked his opponent without warning, saying that he couldn't wait. Neil, though he was not badly injured, sported an extremely fat lip. In shock and tears he declared that he would not be at the Rec' that night as he now acknowledged Mark as supreme commander of Ludbarrow Central School, much to the disappointment of the bloodthirsty little monsters whom adults described as playmates.

From that day Mark played his role with confidence, enjoying the importance of settling playground differences and regally distributing impartial justice, in cases where his social standing ensured instant agreement. Jeff was his constant companion and although Mark was beginning to develop an intense dislike for some of his teachers, life at school was good. This dislike of teachers turned to hatred when, one Tuesday morning, Miss. Rhodes recieved news from The Head that she had been dreading. "I'm really sorry Beryl, truly I am."

"Oh it's nothing, I was looking forward to putting my garden in order anyway," lied the woman, holding back the tears.

Sixty-two-year-old Beryl Rhodes walked back to classroom three stiffly and with a little less of her usual confidence. She swallowed the lump in her throat and mentally re-ran the recent conversation with the headmaster. Her request for an extension to her life-long career had been rejected.

Beryl felt betrayed and hurt and if she admitted to herself she was also frightened. What would life be like now that her retirement had been officially confirmed? In just over a year she would no longer be a respected pillar of the educational establishment. She would be just be another old lady living on past memories desperately hoping, that on one of her unnecessary shopping forays into the village, some former student would recognise her and stop to chat about her good old days.

She hated them all. She hated them for their youth. She hated the fact that it was they, the ignorant of society who were now embarking on life, while she with all her experience and knowledge was being cast aside, used and spent by the very system she had always strived to embody.

She hated the young. She hated the young boy who stood before her. Miss. Rhodes had dried her eyes with the embroidered handkerchief, pushing the pristine white cloth under her glasses. Pulling herself together, she had re-set her spectacles, straightened the bun in her hair and opened the classroom door to find Mark Dacey away from his desk acting the fool.

Mark had been caught in the role of class clown. In the teacher's absence he had entertained his admiring classmates with an impersonation of Miss. Rhodes. When she had entered the room the laughter died away at once and while Mark had turned bright red, the rest of the class had hurriedly banged desk lids, placing books and pencils at the ready.

Order had been restored and the elderly teacher decided that the hateful brash little peasant Dacey needed to be taught a lesson... "Dacey."

"Yes Miss?" stammered Mark, trying to retain as much dignity as possible in front of the class.

"As you wish to play at being teacher, perhaps you would be so good as to take the class for me."

Embarrassed as he was, Mark felt that not to respond in front of his grinning audience would be worse.

"Class, open your books at page eleven."

The children sitting almost cheered as Mark once again impersonated Miss. Rhodes.

"Sit down Dacey. Sit down now!" screamed the infuriated woman, who now hated youth more than ever.

Later that day the teacher had her revenge. "Try again Dacey" and once more the flustered boy stammered.

"L.U.D.B.A.R.R.E.R. Ludbarrer"

"No you ignoramus, come out to the front."

Mark slowly obeyed, smarting from the humiliation of not being able to spell out the name of the village he had moved to. Miss. Rhodes took the wooden ruler from her desktop then, standing smartly, she seized hold of Mark's hand. 'Smack' "L.U.D.B.A.R.R.O.W. Ludbarrow," each letter was accompanied by a sharp stinging crack on the boy's palm.

Beryl Rhodes' face contorted with hatred as she forcibly held open the hand that Mark was desperately trying to move in an effort to avoid or to lessen the impact of the strokes. She looked into his pale face and found herself desperately wanting to see the tears and surrender that would cause her to cease the punishment. There were none. Mark hung on to his pride precariously, but he held back his tears. With his hand under his left armpit he glared evilly at the haridan.

"You stupid cow!"

The whole room gasped in disbelief. Never before had anyone spoken in that way to a person in such position of authority. Before the flabbergasted woman could recover, Mark continued calmly. "I've only been here a few weeks and I did not know how to spell Ludbarrow." Then as the woman blustered and tried to devise an answer, the boy held his badly marked hand towards her. "Was that fair?"

The woman's rage abated when she saw the results of her excessive abuse and for a brief moment she felt sympathy for the boy. Miss. Rhodes' tone changed, she wanted to apologise, but to do so in front of a classroom of monsters, would involve a loss of face. So in a voice trembling with guilty emotion she said, "Sit down Mark," but as she looked over her horn-rimmed spectacles to the spot where the boy had been, she found that he had gone and noticed the silent pupils staring at the open classroom door. Mark Dacey had gone home.

When the bell signalled the end of the school day the elderly teacher weakly waved a hand, dismissing Class three.

The following day, after the morning assembly when they had completed registration and were about to file out for P.E. class three was held back. "Mark Dacey, stay behind please," shouted Miss. Rhodes with a voice that was firm but not threatening.

After she had shooed off the few busybodies who were trying to peer in through the closed, glazed door the woman stood in front of the boy and with an age-worn hand gently lifted his chin. "Yesterday you asked me if your punishment was fair." The boy felt compelled to look into her eyes and in them he saw the teacher she had been. He saw an enthusiasm that time had not dimmed, but which age had robbed. "Well Mark I want to answer you. No, it was not fair and I apologise deeply."

Mark had thought that such a response as that would have left him feeling elated, but it did not. He felt ashamed and humbled. "Oh it's olright Miss, I most probably deserved it for sumfink else."

Miss. Rhodes knew that the boy had forgiven her with magnanimity beyond his years. "'Something' Mark."

"What, I mean pardon Miss?"

"The word is 'something', not 'sumfink'."

"Yes Miss, sorry Miss," grinned the lad.

"Go on Mark, off you go, and we'll say no more on the subject."

Mark nodded in agreement. Later he tried to explain how he felt to Jeff. He did not want to be seen as getting the better of a teacher, he understood how Miss. Rhodes felt. He thought she was alright. Jeff did not listen or care, all teachers were 'shits' in his mind and he hated them all. This perhaps confirmed Miss. Rhodes original opinion of the young!

Beryl Rhodes inspected the immaculate, pale blue, two-door Morris Minor saloon, better known as the 'Moggy Thou'. With a well-practiced routine she climbed in, reversed from her spot and turned the car towards home, that pristine empty place in which she resided. Strangely, she felt contented and at peace. She had decided to end her career early, at the year's end. Yes, she thought to herself, at Christmas, I've always liked school best at that time.

At the crossroads she turned left, once she was in the familiar flow of pre-teatime traffic, she spared a thought for the boy who had made her come to that decision. If only she had more time, she would make it her ambition to see that Mark succeeded in life; she would have made him her project. But it was only a matter of weeks until December, not enough time even to get to know the boy.

In that instant Beryl Rhodes concluded that it was not youth she hated, it was the fact that her own youth had passed by so quickly and so uneventfully. No, Mark Dacey was at the start of his life while she, rightly or wrongly, felt that for her, life was coming to an end. The boy would encounter and deal with life's problems, victories or defeats, as and when life dealt them. So too would she have to endure whatever came her way and she hoped she would find that same resilience and defiance that young Mark Dacey had displayed. "What a pity, what a pity," Beryl said aloud, a lament for

time which had run out. And that was truly a shame for Miss.
Rhodes and for Mark Dacey.

Chapter 59

On Thursday, August 8th 1963, a mail train was stopped just South of Leighton Buzzard and robbed of two and a half million pounds. What had seemed to be a robbery of pure genius was in fact a series of cock-ups and ineptitude. Although the entire criminal fraternity applauded the audacity of the London firm involved, several major flaws marred the robbery, so that it could not be regarded as the 'perfect crime'. The gang had brutally attacked the train driver Jack Mills, thus alienating many who would otherwise have associated the robbery with a Robin Hood scenario. Part of the haul, over one hundred grand, was discovered in Redlands Wood, a beauty spot on the outskirts of Dorking. Careless talk by the firm ensured that all the criminals were eventually imprisoned for what some people considered to be unfairly long sentences, for daring to steal Crown property and in order to set an example.

The crime, the jailbreaks and daring escapades would become part of history and legend as 'The Great Train Robbery'. Sadly for the villains involved, every gang member paid for that job, one way or another. The immediate victims of that crime paid even more heavily.

During the last three months of 1963, Mark enjoyed his schooldays. He had made several friends and felt that he belonged. His tenth birthday passed as did Corinne's third. The family had been through a bad patch when it was discovered that Barry's sister and husband had decieved them into taking over a lease at a greatly increased rent, but after a solicitor had proved the illegality of such an increase, a compromise was found. Mark had been given the job of peeling the potatoes in the cellar most nights which earning him the princely sum of four shillings a week. Karl and Jack were still on holiday, courtesy of Her Majesty. In November Terry and Jean paid a short visit. Jack's wife Katy had called in to see Helen with Jack junior to inform her that she was going to apply for a divorce and that she had already sent the 'Dear John' letter to Jack, in the ''Scrubs''. Mary had started to date her boss.

On Friday 22nd of November the world was stunned by the news, graphically portrayed through the lens of an amateur cameraman that the American president, John. F. Kennedy had been assassinated.

On November 23rd Doctor Who, starring William Hartnell made its debut on the BBC. One day later Jack Ruby shot dead at point blank range, Lee Harvey Oswald, the man who had been arrested and accused of the murder of Kennedy.

By the end of November 'The Beatles' broke all British records with advance orders for 'I Want To Hold Your Hand' reaching 950,000 singles. Mark and Jeff took themselves to 'Billy Alloff', the local barber, for Beatle Cuts, and despite Barry saying that they looked as if they had worn a pudding basin on their head to guide the scissors, they were both convinced they looked the business. The annual cost of television licences rose to £4. Over twenty-one-million people tuned in on November the 10th to watch Bruce Forsyth host the Royal Variety Performance. Although the show starred Shirley Maclaine and Max Bygraves, the real stars were 'The Beatles. John Lennon announced, that for their last number they would play, 'Twist and Shout'. Then he said. "I'd like to ask your help. Would the people in the cheaper seats clap your hands? and the rest of you, if you'll just rattle your jewellery."

There were no visitors to 72 Chapel Street that Christmas and in the chip shop, the occupants felt disappointed that a year of such eventful, historical and cultural importance should come to an end, 'not with a bang but with a whimper'.

Chapter 60

January went, February came. Mark and Jeff were already wearied by the dark winter months and wished for spring to arrive with its promise of new beginnings. Potato-peeling became an onerous task. The cellars were damp and freezing and the two hours an evening needed to fill the plastic barrels seemed like a life sentence. Mark had followed his friend Jinxie's example and had got himself a morning newspaper round at the 'Roundhouse' newsagents in Ludbarrow Centre. Life became a round of never-ending chores.

When the homework started to come thick and fast, so did Mark's excuses for not completing it. Lack of concern by the temporary teacher who had replaced Miss. Rhodes allowed Mark to escape unpunished and his busy mother only remonstrated that it would be different when he got to big school.

The family's finances had improved to such an extent that the living room now boasted a new black vynil-covered suite which consisted of a three-seater settee and two armchairs with bright, orange seat cushions. The coal fire was replaced with a more convenient gas fire and a new, larger television that was capable of receiving the long awaited BBC 2 channel. A bright red telephone sat importantly on the windowsill. Thin brightly coloured cheap, nylon floor covering enabled the family to boast of wall-to-wall carpet. Compared to most of the other houses in Ludbarrow, 72 Chapel Sreet was a palace, or so Mark thought.

In February Barry bought a beautiful, American style, Vauxhall Cresta with rear wing fins and a one piece, wrap-around windscreen. He also retained the minibus for its load-lugging and passenger carrying potential.

By the time spring had finally arrived, Karl and Harry had been released from prison and after meeting up with Paddy, Karl had insisted that they all seek legitimate daytime employment to avoid attention from the police. His sojourn in H.M.P. had convinced him that he did not intend to to be caught out ever so easily again. Karl found employment driving cement trucks, Harry did the markets and Paddy ran a flower stall for his sick Uncle.

Terry and Jean announced their Easter wedding and Mary announced her engagement to Geoffrey Swift, a graduate and administrative civil servant.

On February 9th 'The Beatles' performed live on the Ed Sullivan show. On March 28th the pirate music station, 'Radio Caroline', went on air. On April 4th 'The Beatles' occupied the top five places in the singles charts and the top two slots in the LP charts. Also in April, at the Cubi Club in Richton, a crowd of fifteen hundred people attempted to see the 'Rolling Stones'. Although two of the 'Stones' were already inside, the event promised to become a disaster so the 'Stones', manager pulled the plug on the gig.

At Easter Mark travelled to London with the rest of the Chapel Street gang, they having closed the shop on Friday night as usual. Setting off in the early hours of Saturday morning they left a note in the shop door window, 'Closed for personal reasons'. Nosy regulars speculated on the first impromptu closure that Helen had allowed since taking over the business.

The wedding had been organised by Jean's parents and by Nell and Tommy. It was a day that would be remembered for the happiness of the couple and the fact that all the family were there, with the exception of Jack who still had more than eighteen months of his sentence to serve. Even Peter turned up with his new woman and as Mark and his dad had not seen one another for over a year, they barely exchanged pleasantries. Mark was informed that very soon he would be an uncle again. Karl and his gang turned up as Karl was Terry's 'Best Man'. Mary, for some reason or other became centre of attention, kicking off at the wedding then sulking during the reception.

For the first time, people noticed that Terry did not drink nor did Jean, even the wedding toast was made with lemonade. Terry would always say he had no intention of letting drink do to him what it had done to so many other members of his family. At the reception Mark had a great time bossing Jean's ten-year-old cousin Derek and dancing with his nine-year-old sister. It was another occasion when Mark felt happy.

Not long after the wedding, Mark and Jeff were taken to their first professional football match by a man called George, whom Jeff called 'Uncle', although he was actually a friend of the family. The match was at Turf Moor, home to Jeff's favourite team, Burnley. Mark had been surprised at the large numbers of fanatical spectators and while Jeff and Uncle George waved scarves and rattles, Mark felt his feet go numb and later he would look back on that nil - nil draw with Everton as one of the most boring events he had ever had to endure. The only thing he would ever remember about that game was how good the meat pie tasted at half-time.

A few weeks later, Karl and his girlfriend Linda arrived at the shop, just after teatime on a Thursday, surprising Helen and Mark. Helen insisted that they stay and that she could put a mattress in the living room for the duration of the visit. Mark was allowed to take Friday off school to accompany his brother and Linda on a trip to Blackpool, where they spoiled the boy.

Later that evening back in Ludbarrow Mark had finished peeling the potatoes and was being taught the basics of the noble art of self defence. Karl produced a pair of massive gloves from the boot of his stunning Rover 100, which had been bought with hard-earned cash.

"Hold your guard up, higher."

Every time Mark dropped the massive brown glove, Karl slapped him across the head - not too hard, but hard enough to infuriate the lad. This went on until he could stand it no longer and throwing the gloves down he launched himself at Karl. With a laugh, Karl brought his hands up to guard his face and blocked his brother's flailing arms. Mark cried out in pain but his brother grinned and told Helen that it was the boy's own fault and that he was being 'mard arse'. Half an hour later, his brother was still moaning, and Karl acquiesced to Linda's demands that Mark should be taken to the infirmary for an X-ray. Two hours later, Mark returned with his arm in a plaster-cast. Karl was penitent; he had changed his opinion of his younger brother when the doctor had shown him the two clean breaks in the boy's arm and wrist.

The next day, before leaving for 'The Smoke', Karl went into the cellar and under Mark's direction he spent four hours preparing enough spuds to last until Tuesday, he tipped them into the barrels of preservative that prevented discolouration of the potatoes - 'Dri White'. The chemical stank out the cellars and made their eyes smart. Over those few days, Mark had spent more one-to-one time with Karl than he had in the whole of his life until then and he had enjoyed every minute of it. Even the broken arm had its compensation's as he would for a week be excused peeling duties.

That July Barry and Helen, Mark and Corinne had their first, real, family vacation. It was one week at a holiday camp in Weston-super-mare on England's south west coast. Terry and Jean had brought Nell and Tommy in the Ford Anglia and they shared a wonderful week. Mark had taken with him a large pile of 'Superman', and 'Batman' comics, which he had bought at the comic exchange in Richton's covered market. Reading the American 'DC' magazines were still one of the brothers'' favourite pastimes. The comics were the cause of the only disharmony between the holiday-makers. Although the boy's enjoyed the comics, Jean did not. Part of the week was spent in sulks and minor squabbles as she sat fuming in a chalet, watching her young husband and young brother-in-law engrossed in the colourful pages. Mark lay on the top bunk bed and Terry was underneath. As they almost simultaneously finished reading the comic in front of them, they would swap with one another.

Outside the sun was blazing, but not as fierce as Jean's temper. When she finally snapped, the boys' had to compromise. After all they had to make allowances for a pregnant woman. Mark agreed to give Terry all the magazines that his brother had not read, so that he could take them back to London when the holiday was over. Secretly the small boy hoped that his brother would forget, but he did not.

The rest of the holiday was spent partly on beaches where sometimes one of their numbers would be buried up to the neck in sand. There was also time for a trip to the awe inspiring 'Cheddar Gorge', and time to spend at the funfair. Helen insisted on a cultural trip to Wells Cathedral, where Mark was enthralled to see the sign that identified the last resting place of King Arthur. Granddad spoiled things a little, when he said to the lad, "It's a load of bollocks!"

He went on to explain that it was a ruse devised by monks hundreds of years ago to bring in some ready cash, even in those far off days, the 'tourists' were hoodwinked.

Quite a lot of time was spent in and around pubs and bars and evenings always ended in the clubhouse where, on the Thursday there was a talent night. Barry amazed everyone except Helen when he got up and sang 'The heart of a man is a secret'. Helen knew that Barry had a good voice and when the panel awarded him the first prize of a 'fiver', Mark believed that they were heading for the big time.   Ever-pragmatic, Barry quashed that notion, when he said honestly with a grin; "Good job there weren't any competition."

But Mark had been suitably impressed and had a new cause to brag when he returned to Ludbarrow.

The holiday was over too soon and Mark had to console himself with Nell's promise that it would not be long before he would be allowed to visit London. September was only a few weeks away. She was right, the time passed quickly and the September break arrived. It had been arranged that Mark would be with his grand-parents and Barry, Helen and Corinne would be holidaying in Wales with Barry's younger brother John and his wife, Olive. They would be taking their two boys' John junior and Neil, aged six and four and their two-year old daughter, Annie. So there would be no shortage of company for Corinne.

Mark made the trip to London by 'Yelloway' from the Richton coach station. It was always an exciting start to the week-long holiday. On that Friday at 5a.m. it seemed that most of the world was sleeping. Mark experienced the last minute rush and checks and finally the butterflies as he waved to Barry. Helen had said her goodbyes in Ludbarrow.

Slowly the excitement dissipated, with the regular stops and starts of scheduled pick-ups, degenerating into absolute boredom. The cologne-drenched old dear next to him snored, farted and coughed all the way to the 'Watford Gap'. Here the passengers alighted for forty-five minutes, time to get something to eat, there had been plenty of opportunities, at the regular bus stops at some larger stations, for toilet breaks or to grab a magazine, newspaper or confectionery from one of the vending machines or nearby shops.

Helen had packed Mark some sandwiches, a bottle of pop, a packet of 'Golden Wonder' crisps and a bar of chocolate. When he had used the the toilet in the cafeteria, he returned to the coach to find that the farting, old stinker had stolen his prized window seat. Mark politely showed the old lady his ticket pointing to the number that corresponded to his seat and the place that she currently occupied. "Oh I've moved now, just sit there it's only a seat you know."

Despondently, Mark sat in the aisle seat. Then he tried to reason once more, "I have to have a window seat cos I get travel sick."

This was true, for some years road travel had given him a migraine and had made him feel nauseous; he found the smoke-filled top decks of public transport particularly unpleasant. The old lady gave no answer; she shuffled further into the seat and leaned against the window.

Mark had his unintentional but highly satisfactory revenge. When he had eaten and had drunk everything in the plastic bag that his mother had given him, he brought it all back and deposited onto the folded coat that the old lady had forced uncomfortably between them to stake a claim to the window seat, huge splashes of stinking vomit also landed on the sleeping woman's, turned back. She remained unconscious and oblivious to the whole event. Mark who was feeling much better, did not bother to wake her. Fortunately for Mark, the coach passengers were disembarking at 'King's Cross' by the time the woman had discovered what had happened and exploded into a furious fit. Mark, had raced to the front of the coach and was pointing to his small battered suitcase, which the driver cheerfully dragged from the boot with a long pole. Disappearing hand in hand with his grandmother he smiled to himself. Even Granddad laughed loudly at the small boy's guiltily truthful account of his journey. This made the boy feel that the old woman had got her just desserts, nevertheless thanking providence for his escape.

That week felt strange for Mark as Terry no longer lived with Nell and Tom. He and Jean had rented a two-roomed flat in North London. Nell saw her grandson and his young wife a couple of times during the week and every Sunday for lunch. Terry had reached nineteen years of age that August and had recently and reluctantly left his employment with Vic's butchers in Seaton Street. He had been offered a job at one of the most prestigious hotels in London as Butchery Manager in their famous kitchens. With a baby on the way and rent to find on the flat, the wages that were offered and that Vic could not match were reluctantly accepted. Nell found that every visit from her grandson coincided with the delivery of a paper-wrapped package, which made shopping trips to the butcher's an unnecessary assignment. Lunch times and dinner times at Constantine Road became one of the most delicious affairs in the borough of Hampstead.

Midweek, Nell took Mark to see Mary Poppins at the 'Dominion'. One day Karl, who still lived with Nell and Tommy on and off, arrived early in a huge truck, a concrete mixer and asked if his brother would like to spend the day with him. While Mark hurriedly got ready, Nell made breakfast for Karl and by the time he had eaten he found his young sibling was ready to go.

"Ow's ya arm now?" grinned Karl.

"It's ok," replied the youngster, twisting the limb around to prove the point.

It had registered with the youngest Dacey that his older brother now had a London accent which impressed him almost as much as the way, in which he expertly drove the giant vehicle to and from the cement depot, delivering the loads to a building site. At several times during the day they made short stops for cups of tea and then they were off again. The day passed pleasantly and when they arrived back at Constantine Road, Mark sat down to eat and Karl took a bath, changed and left for the city, before his brother had finished eating.

That night, Mary and a girlfriend from work took Mark to see a film about ancient Egyptians, which starred Joan Collins as a femme fatale. This prompted the small boy to ask his older sister a multitude of eager questions about ancient civilisation.

The arrangement was that Barry, Helen and his little sister would arrive to pick him up on Sunday. Saturday was the last day of his holiday, so as a special treat Terry and Jean took Mark down the West End, where they kitted one young Dacey in the latest gear, before dining in the Leicester Square 'Wimpy'. After eating they decided that they would go to see the film 'How the West Was Won," in 'Cinerama' and 'Surround Sound'.

That night, back in the little bed at his grandparents', Mark felt both elated and depressed, elated at the wonderful week he had had and depressed that he was going home the next day..

The journey home seemed to take forever, and when eventually they were unpacking the car at the back of the chip shop, Mark thought that after the vibrant city life of London, Ludbarrow at 8p.m. was the nearest thing to a cemetery you could get without actually dying. With the knowledge that school restarted on the following day, it was difficult to find anything to be cheerful about.

During the year Mark had made friends with Amy, a girl of the same age that lived nearby. In the times when Jeff was not around, Mark enjoyed her company. One Sunday morning Barry, Helen and Corinne had gone to visit Barry's brother on the other side of Richton. Mark was alone, watching TV. There was a knock at the back door, it was Amy. "Wanna come in?" asked Mark.

The girl nodded and followed him into the familiar living room.

With nothing worth watching, the television was turned off. How the conversation had turned to sex was a mystery, but it had Mark's limited knowledge coupled with Amy's equally sparse education, had brought the surprising request for Mark to show Amy his 'willy'. Mark responded with that age old cliché 'show me yours and I'll show mine'.

Mark dropped his pants and stood patiently while Amy closely inspected male differences, noticing how it excited the boy when she touched his now erect 'willy'. Mark corrected the deficiencies of her education; its real name was a 'dick' or 'nob'. When at last she announced that she had seen enough, she kept her part of the bargain, dropping her knickers. Mark complained that he could not look properly with Amy standing up, so she lay on the floor. Mark became more and more agitated as he opened her legs and inspected every detail, thinking to himself that's it, that's where it goes.

Mark and Jeff had often slyly consulted the encyclopaedias in the school library, looking at the drawings of human reproduction, which did not help much, as they did not represent any part of the anatomy that they recognised. But in the playground, in-between smutty jokes and tall tales of 'shagging' prowess came the occassional serious discussion when opinions were split into two factions. One faction believed that the dick went up the girl's 'arse 'ole' and nine months later a baby miraculously appeared, by the belly button. The second faction believed that there was a separate wee hole, which was big enough for the nob to be pushed up, with the baby arriving soon after via the rectum. Here was an opportunity to settle the dispute and Amy was the living proof, legs apart, Amy's almost bald minge and arse 'ole when scrutinised, revealing a poo hole, pee hole and there in between in the pink fleshy folds, a separate orifice. Mark explored this making Amy jump and complain as he gently pushed the tip of his finger in, but as she lubricated and his finger penetrated fully she seemed to actually enjoy it, relaxing and allowing the boy to do as he wished while she looked away. Emboldened by the way things were going, he climbed in between her legs and looking down guided his member to the enlarged hole. He had managed several small thrusts that made the girl gasp then the one instinctive thrust as full penetration was achieved.

Amy allowed a few moments of thrusting before she pushed Mark off her. Rolling sideways and standing shakily, she pulled on her discarded underwear. Mark guiltily hoisted up his pants that had been around his ankles. Amy announced that she had to go home. "Don't tell anyone will you?" Mark shook his head, he would be happy to oblige, he had thought of making the same request of her. "Promise?" urged the girl.

"On me mother's life," said Mark.

Amy came to call as usual and on the rare occasions they were left alone she needed little persuasion to allow Mark to play with her private parts and was easily coaxed into fondling his. However her mother had noticed blood in her pants on washday and had told her about things called 'monthlies' and the horrors and pain of sexual reproduction. Amy had learned a lot more about sex than he had. Whatever the reason no matter how he pleaded or reasoned, Amy never again allowed penetration.

Amy and her younger sister and Jeff, joined Mark and Corinne on a Sunday afternoon in early December for Mark's eleventh birthday. Helen no longer opened the shop on Sundays, so they were able to play games and to enjoy the partyfare sandwiches, cakes, sweets and jellies. As the visitors prepared to leave, Amy, unseen by the others, kissed Mark on the lips before she rejoined the other guests who were departing.

For the first time the family spent Christmas in London that year of 1964, at Constantine Road where Mark enjoyed the best Yuletide celebration's he could remember. For three day's the whole family was present, except for Jack who would have to face one more festive season in prison.

Chapter 61

On January 24th 1965 the Nation lost one of its greatest heroes - Sir Winston Churchill. He was ninety years old. Mark and Jeff had watched the sombre, black-and-white television coverage of the state funeral and later that day they mooched around the forlornly silent neighbourhood. Both boys' felt that something terrible had happened, and that the whole British way of life had changed forever.

They were on the verge of graduating from childhood to youth membership of the, 'Swinging Sixties.'

With the worst of winter over, conversation at school centred entirely on the forthcoming eleven-plus examinations, that would be taken in late spring. The results would determine which Central pupils would be destined for the ignominy of the secondary modern and which brighter sparks that would be off to various grammar schools. There was very little doubt that day-dreaming Mark was not in that select band of swots.

Terry and Jean had a new baby boy, whom they named Ian. They had also moved from their small apartment to a larger one in Mornington Crescent, a short walk from the BBC theatre.

Mary informed the family that she would be married later that year to her fiancé Geoff. The wedding was to be held at his parents' home in Bradford at the Catholic church that his mother and father attended.

Karl had re-organised his shady business and as he had completed the probationary period allotted by the parole board, he immediately ceased employment at the concrete company, vowing never to work for anyone else again. He controlled several club doors and disposed of vast qauntities of the stolen goods that were endlessly available in the city's pubs, clubs and workplaces. The more important 'faces' now accepted him as a major player, they trusted and were prepared to do business with him on a regular basis. As a result Karl became a wealthy young man. His hand- made suits and shirts were tailored in Saville Row and his shoes were hand crafted by most skilful Italian cobblers. Silk ties and numerous pairs of solid gold and diamond cuff links and tie pins contributed to his absolute immaculate presentation. To those who knew him, he represented a 'gangster of the new order' - organised crime with class.

It was at this time Harry-the-Axe disappeared. At first Karl and Paddy thought nothing of it, as Harry often went on drinking binges for a day or two. They began to be concerned after three day's had elapsed and they experienced a sinking feeling in their stomachs. Nothing fully prepared them for the news they eventually received that Harry's dismembered torso, had been identified through its tattoos. It had been found minus his head and hands signifying a professional murder and a deadly warning for Karl and Paddy.

The man whom Karl was talking to in the small pub in Camden was Big John Carter, a 'face' well known as a vicious thug, who had once slashed a woman's cheeks for what he saw as an insult. Nearly everyone kept his or her distance from this bull-neck, six-foot bruiser when he was on the lash. Without the drink he was totally fearless, with it he would reveal himself at his savage, sadistic worst. "Nah Mank, naffink to do wiv the Brown boys', that's for sure. Mad Martin says to 'ave a word wiv Albert an' Chris."

Karl knew that Mad Martin Meehan like John was a 'face' and enforcer, for the powerful Rankin Brothers'. They contested hotly with the Brown brothers' for total control of London's gangland, especially the lucrative West End. "Yeh thanks John; can you fix that up for me?"

"No problem my son." Karl politely refused John's offer of another drink explaining that he had a bit of gear to shift. Carter shrugged then said "I'll see you at the boozer on Saturday night, 8 o clock, an let yer know what the boys' say about a meet an' what I can turn up."

"Thanks John yer a pal."

"Like fucking no way are you a mate, you nutter," said Karl to himself, as he moved the Rover through the evening streets of Camden Town. Looking at his wristwatch he compared it with the clock in the Rover's dash. He was a little late for his meeting with Paddy, and that was bad, as he had made sure that all his plans were military-like in precision. Paddy had moved gaffs a couple of times since Harry's body had been found. He had been living for the last week with a cousin in Holloway, leaving the house only occasionally and nervously to meet Karl.

Paddy was just about to leave the little Italian restaurant when the Rover pulled up outside. He threw a ten bob note at Toni the owner

for two coffees and told him he would see him later for the change. The passenger door slammed and Paddy gave a nervous smile. "You alright" the driver nodded. "Sorry I'm late, but you know what its like tryin to get away from Carter."
"An ow is that line goin?"
"Ee is gonna set up a meet wiv the Rankins."
"Good," nodded Paddy. "What that firm don't know, they can find out."

John Carters discreet investigations had confirmed what the pair had already deduced, that the East London firm had nothing to do with Harry's demise, but whoever had done the hit was good, very good. Now, the most worrying questions facing Karl and Paddy were, "why, who" and "Were They Next?" Both had racked their brains for events and deeds relating to past jobs or 'rucks' that could have prompted such a deadly response. Nothing had come to mind but they conjectured wildly to the possible and probable causes. There was no clue to the identity of the killers and no one was talking or bragging. The bent coppers had admitted that the 'filth' were totally in the dark.
"We gotta make a call at Pauline's."
The young lady in question was a bright twenty-four-year-old, who sold bent gear about 'The Manor' for Karl. Living as she did in a gaff in Kentish Town, she was ideally placed to sell to the new middle classes who were moving into Hampstead and outlying districts and who had plenty of spare cash and who found it difficult to resist a bargain. As knock off gear went for a third of its normal price, there were certainly bargains to be had.
Pauline had started to become fairly affluent as a result of her career in merchandise disposal, thanks to Karl who paid her good commission and ensured that no one else encroached on her patch or tried to muscle her for protection. In turn, Pauline controlled a dozen girls' and women who sold for her. They were either young, single mothers', or older wives of lags who were in the 'nick' and prostitutes looking to boost income. Karl's relationship with his employee was purely business, although they were more like brother and sister than friends.
"Allo, I was wonderin where you was hidin."
Karl and Paddy followed the slim brunette through the door and into the kitchen of the two-bedroomed apartment.

"You alone?"

"Ooh! I bet you says that to all the gals," mocked Pauline, then observing that Karl was not in the mood for banter, she soberly added.

"Yeh the kids are at me mums."

" Pauline had two children Vi, short for Vivian was a precocious six-year-old with a mop of curly auburn hair which made her resemble Shirley Temple. Sean, a shy four-year-old boy with dark hair and sad eyes, was so spoiled that his sad countanence was puzzling. Pauline had been ensnared by his handsome father, also called Sean, when she was only fifteen. The Camden Irish villain had been the love of her life, until at the age of twenty-one, she had discovered the reason for his reticence whenever marriage was mentioned. He was already married!

The events that brought their ill-fated relationship to an end started one morning at 5a.m. when a police special squad, sledge-hammered the front door and arrested Sean McAvoy, for armed robbery and membership of an illegal paramilitary group, the IRA. Sean somehow managed to get out of the local police station after one days incarceration and told Pauline and his friends that they had let him go due to lack of evidence. Over the next few weeks the Irish cell was decimated and most members of the unit were arrested. Rumour had it that they had been fingered. Whether the rumours had any truth Pauline would never know.

Pauline had just put the kids to bed when the phone rang. The thick Irish accent told her with no emotion that she need not bother waiting up for Sean as he would not be coming home - ever. The voice went on to explain that were she to assist the police it would be detrimental to her health and to the health of her her children.

Karl had been a godsend, Paddy had known Sean from schooldays and sometimes as adults they had got drunk together. It was Paddy that had intervened one night, when a well known pimp was most insistent that Pauline have a drink with him later that night when she had finished her job as a barmaid.

The young woman, who was struggling to make ends meet told him, "go fuck yourself, what do you take me for, one of your 'brasses'?" The furious Maltese pimp had threatened to slash her face. Paddy's timely appearance at the bar prevented any unpleasantries.

"You 'avin a problem wiv my sister, you Maltese slag?"

Maltese Joe instantly recognised Paddy and though he didn't give a shit about the 'dip' (pick pocket), he did care about the giant bruiser who was standing behind him.

"Problems av we Paddy me old china?" said 'Harry the Axe'.

"Nah no problem pal, this cunt is just goin, aint you?"

Joe was not afraid of a 'ruck' but he knew he was out of his league with Harry. "Yeh there's been a mistake I'm on my way anyway, I got business."

Karl's sudden arrival behind Maltese Joe hindered his departure. "Not until you buy the lady a drink and apologise to her, I fink a 'pony' should do it."

Joe had no wish to be in the company of this lunatic Mank, or to enter into a row with his little firm. "Look am sorry Mank I, I made a mistake. I didn't know she was a friend of ... I mean Paddy's sister."

"She aint his sister, she's my sister."

Joe understood the claim not for the lie it was but what it signified. Pauline was under the Mank's protection and even though the Maltese prostitution and drugs ring of which Joe was a senior 'face', was deadly in its own right, this Mank had connections. "Yeh right, got it, sorry love." With apology made, Maltese Joe turned to leave, Karl did not move and Harry spoke. "Not sorry enuff you slag," and in a flash he had produced his deadly toy.

"NO!" shouted Karl and the machete blade stopped inches from the terrified pimp's face. "I fink we said a 'pony' would be fair."

Joe fumbled in his pocket and brought out a wad of money. Undoing the elastic band, he peeled off a 'pony' and threw the notes, twenty-five-pounds onto the bar. Harry looked at the wad of cash, then at the pimp and lastly at Karl who gave a slight shake of his head. With an exaggerated sigh, Harry shrugged his shoulders and slipped the tool back into the specially-tailored inside, pocket of his mid-length, black, leather coat.

Karl looked into Joe's eyes and noticed with satisfaction, that the Maltese pimp could not hold his gaze. "This is an end to fings Joe ain't it?" The man nodded, understanding that he was not to approach Pauline again. "I mean we wont be avin any problems with your little firm will we?" The meaning of Karl's words became even clearer. "No it has nothing to do with business, everything is sweet."

Karl thrust out his hand and in surprise Joe shook it, when Karl stepped slowly aside the Maltese pimp hurriedly left.

"Well an' what do you fink your gonna get fer yer Sir Galahad routine?" sneered Pauline in relieved, mock indignation.

Karl looked her directly in the eyes and she too could not hold the steely grey-blue gaze. She felt ungrateful and frightened to think that perhaps she had escaped one deadly dilemma only to be caught in another. "Well I don't fancy fuckin' yer bony arse, if that's what you mean." Flabbergasted, Pauline lifted her eyes to the ones that moments before she had avoided. This time they sparkled without menace and Karl grinned mischievously like a naughty school boy. "So I guess it will 'av to be a cuppa tea, sometime."

The woman laughed, not just with relief but because something about this man suggested that he was not a threat to her. "Well, I owe you a cuppa then."

What she didn't understand, was the reason for Karl's intervention. Paddy had pointed Pauline out to Harry and Karl as they had sat in a peaceful corner of the pub. He had acquainted them with the rumours about her common-law partner and his subsequent death. When events unfolded at the bar, Karl had sent Paddy to intervene. The Maltese pimp did not seem to be co-operating in the manner envisaged, so Karl had ordered Harry to 'sort it'. He had himself decided to become involved for very personal reasons, Pauline reminded him of his sister.

It was two years since that night when Karl had interviened on Pauline behalf. Apart from the time that Karl had spent in 'Wandsworth', Pauline had supplied his daily cuppas. "I've ad a few problems" explained Karl. "Harry?" Karl gave a gentle nod. The three adults were seated on glossy black plastic chairs at a bright yellow Formica covered kitchen table. Each took turns to sip from the floral beakers, in what appeared to be a practised ritual.

"Fing is, we ain't even 'eard a whisper, naffink."

"Yeh naffink," reiterated Paddy.

"Well I've got the girls' being slippy an' keeping there ears an eyes open," offered Pauline.

"You av told em to be clever about it ant you?"

"Course I fuckin' av, wot you take me for, a fuckin mug?"

Karl smiled at the show of false indignation. "Talkin of mugs" he grinned, "fill that up then."

Pauline stood up and took the beaker and as she noticed Paddy downing the last mouthful of his own brew she collected his cup as well. Returning to the table, she wished she had made a cup for herself, then as if she had had a sudden thought she stood up again and crossed the small room. She opened the fridge and stooped to search the icebox. Where she found a plastic bag which was folded to make a small package, she closed the flap of the icebox and the fridge doorand rejoined the men. She tossed the packet to Karl. "There's a 'one'er there."

Pauline imparted the knowledge that the packet contained one hundred pounds with an air of nonchalance and was a little disappointed that Karl said nothing in return but pushed the cash over to Paddy, who put it in an inside pocket. After all, who better to carry the cash than a 'dip'? "You should change yer hidin' place for the moolah, every fucker uses the fridge."

Pauline ignored the remark and took the upheld cup to fill for Karl's third cup of tea. "You must piss for England."

Karl ignored the flippant remark.

Taking the steaming mug, he threw her the packet that he had just taken from Paddy. "These av gotta go for ten bob each, they will fetch more nearer the time."

Pauline took out the stack of green and mauve watermarked tickets and read the description aloud.

"Empire Stadium, Wembley.

The Football Association Cup Competition.

FINAL TIE. Saturday May 1st Kick-off 3p.m.

West enclosure, entrance 64, standing.

Seven-shillings-and-sixpence. ."

She let out a whistle, "FA cup tickets are they kosher?"

Karl almost choked on his brew. "Yeh they're kosher alright, I got 'em from the White Heart Lane Yid."

It took her a moment to recognise the intentional pun. The bent Tottenham official had acquired two hundred tickets in a manner that Karl was not about to disclose. Karl continued. "You keep two bob a ticket and we split anything over ten bob each, fifty - fifty.

Pauline was already calculating the Cup final between Liverpool and Leeds United was expected to be a sell-out. There would be close to one hundred thousand spectators. She anticipated that with strong demand from last minute buyers, her share could be over thirty quid, not bad at all, when her last working wage as a shop assistant had been less than eight pounds a week.

Karl and Paddy left after a fourth brew and headed out of town, northwards to meet some villains from Newcastle who were offering a truckload of whisky which had not yet been missed, but which soon would be, once the deal had been done. The rendezvous was at an all-night transport café just off the A1.

Chapter 62

Mary's wedding had been arranged to fall one week after the FA Cup, not for the love of sport, but for convenience. The news that she and Geoff would be moving to Leeds where they had transferred to live and work delighted Helen, as it was less than an hour's drive from Ludbarrow to their new home in the Meanwood district of Leeds. The couple had stayed at Chapel Street one weekend and Mary had been kinder than Mark could ever remember before. He was even more impressed when she promised that he could come to stay with them in their new home whenever he liked during any weekend or school break.

Mark met Jeff on Prince Street at the back of the chip shop. Jeff had the football and together they walked up the street towards the village square, stopping at the Conservative Club car park. There the two of them re-acted that day's Cup final, during which an animated Mark had sat in front of the TV shouting support for his sister's new hometown team, the white shirted Leeds United; unfortunately the Yorkshire side had been defeated 2-1 after extra time. Jeff automatically assumed the role of Liverpool and Mark was Leeds United. At the car park there was no extra time, the boy's game lasted only twenty minutes because the rat-faced club steward chased them off.

"See yer tomorrer Jeff."

"Yeh, see yer," and Jeff ran kicking his ball all the way down the narrow road.

"Hey Jeff!"

"What?"

"We get told about the eleven plus tomorrer."

"So what!" laughed Jeff and waved once more before disappearing down a back street.

By lunchtime every child at Central knew which school they would be attending in that year's new term. They had been given a brown sealed envelope that carried the typed words, 'FOR THE ATTENTION OF THE PARENT OR GUARDIAN OF' and the child's name. Of course, hardly an envelope reached its destination unopened. "Bloody 'ell I've passed!" All eyes turned to Jinxie, who rolled his eyes and draped an arm across his forehead in a mock swoon, before farting loudly. "Passed wind that is" and the whole playground shared the joke.

Mark had said nothing all day, ignoring inquisitors by telling them "I don't know an' a don't care."

That afternoon during arts and craft, Mark gazed out of the large classroom window during arts and craft class at the sky, he drifted into wishful day dreaming that he was none other than a lost, alien prince of immense power and was disappointed to be brought back from his reverie by the school bell, just as he was receiving the adoration and accolades of the whole world. Daydreaming was a form of escape that came easily to Mark.

Later he relayed the truth of the exam results to Jeff on the walk home. "I passed the tests with the best marks ever seen," said the boy. "But I'm gonna tell 'em to stick it, cos I wanna go to secondary modern wi' my mate Jinxie."

Mark looked at Jeff, who broke into a big grin. "Great, you failed as well."

Mark nodded and knew that's just how Helen would see it.

Barry said it was only as he expected. Helen said she was disappointed and that she could not understand why he did not have an ounce of his bigger sister's savvy. "Well get changed and get to it. Those potatoes won't peel themselves."

Mark sullenly obeyed, looking back briefly to Barry who was throwing the chortling Corinne into the air and each time he caught her he said. "Well we won't be…. A big dunce… when we grow up… will we?"

Mark changed his clothes and descended the cellar steps. Standing on the wooden pallet, at the side of the ancient machine, he threw the large metal lever. There was a brief blue flash and the internal carbon-coated drum slowly picked up speed, then he turned on the tap to allow water to enter the drum, turning it down when the force was too strong and splashing everywhere. He threw the dirty potatoes, taken in handfuls from one of the many paper sacks, into the noisy rumbling contraption until the machine was full and any more potatoes would have quickly been converted to missiles. The boy expertly judged the timing before he opened the levered door and the peeled potatoes were deposited into the large ceramic Belfast sink, which allowed the water to drop through the grid below.

While a second load was rumbling, Mark skilfully removed the eyes and any blemishes, tossing the finished spuds into one of the large plastic barrels, part filled with 'Dri-White' chemical and water. Later, he thought to himself, he would point out that he was not a dunce and that if most of his free time were not taken up with the family business, chores and baby sitting, then maybe, just maybe, he would have understood some of the questions on the exam sheets.

The next day he did mention it to Helen who scoffed that Barry's remarks had only been a joke and that he should stop being a soft sod. However, when she heard his thoughts of the subject on free time she said that she could not spare him from the jobs and that if he was having trouble learning then he would have to stop playing out. But in what might have been a pang of guilt at this theft of his childhood, she did raise his pocket money by one shilling, to five bob a week.

Mary's wedding to Geoff went well until the church service started. The happy couple got spliced inside, while Karl was outside, drunk as a lord, throwing empty beer bottles at passers-by. Later at the reception, Geoff's parents told him exactly what they thought of him and instead of verbally attacking them, as those who knew him well, expected he grinned in drunken stupidity and said in his loudest voice that they were most probably right, but that he had found it difficult to understand why his sister was marrying a girl's blouse like Geoff. Mary promptly told him to "fuck off" and when one of Geoff's relatives offered her his support, she told him to go fuck himself as well. Karl drove back to London despite his drunken state. Terry and Jean, who had brought their two month old son, Ian, gossiped with their grandparents, while Helen alternately tut tutted or broke into bouts of uncontrollable laughter. Mary eventually went over to the table where her family were seated and told them all to 'fuck themselves'.

The minibus carrying those who had been advised collectively and individually to commit impossible acts of a carnal nature, weaved erratically as it crossed the Pennines from Bradford. Barry's inebriated state alarmed the teetotal Terry and Jean who took turns to hold onto their baby son protectively. "Well," piped Mark, "I don't suppose our Mary will want me over for a visit now."

This time it was Nell who, hugging her grandson closely, her eyes streaming and her ample frame racked with chortling spasms said, "Nah, go fuck yerself."

Even Barry who had never and never would use profanities, burst into a fit of laughter causing the vehicle to behave more erratically.

Chapter 63

Vietnam dominated the news, the prime minister agreed in principal with the furtherance of democracey, but believed it was not in Britain's interests to become involved in what was seen as an American excersise. None of this concerned Mark. Several weeks before, Jeff's dad had deserted his family. Jeff's mother far from being heartbroken, had never been happier, she found solace in the sympathetic arms of Uncle George. Who had since taken the whole family camping, leaving Mark alone. His friend Amy had been accepted at grammar school and that summer she rarely visited Chapel Street. It seemed that by autumn she had disappeared off the face of the earth.

Mark visited his grandparents at Constantine Road. For most of a the week he remained with them and the rest he spent with Terry, Jean and the baby. That weekend Karl, who had some news for Helen, took Mark back to Ludbarrow. "Jack is getting out in two weeks." Somehow Jack had been put on parole four months early and the news cheered Helen and Mark.

Karl did not stop over, he immediately returned to 'The Smoke'. The journey on the motorway would not take long. Parliament intended to enforce a seventy-miles-an-hour speed limit by June. But until then Karl could brag that he would be home legally in less than three hours.

In Mark's absence, Helen had bought the uniform and other items that she had been advised would be required in a letter from the 'central' school's office, for commencement of term at the 'big school'.

"Lets 'ave a butchers at yer then."

Mark stood resplendent in his new, school uniform, dark blue blazer, long grey flannel trousers, white shirt and navy and claret diagonally-striped school tie. Helen cocked her head to one side scrutinising the badge and eventually decided that it was not crooked enough to warrant unpicking and re-sewing.

Jeff met his friend on the door step and together they walked exactly the same route that they had always walked on their way to school, except that when they reached the 'central' school gates, they did not stop but bypassed them, continuing up the lane past the 'Rec' and onto the carriage drive that led to the big school's gates. Mark had felt a pang of regret when they had passed the excited clamour of his old school, where he had been fairly happy there. He had ruled the roost as 'Cock O' the School' and the teachers had become pleasant enough and were mostly undemanding. Jeff, however bent double, lifted his jacket and showed his arse to the children and teachers who were in the playground.

The first impression the boy's had was its physical size and then they were amazed by the number of students- almost a thousand Jeff said. The two new boys' were swept along by the crowd to an assembly hall that seemed as large as a football pitch.

For the whole of the morning they wrote out timetables in their allotted form rooms. Mark and Jeff had been separated, Mark was allocated to Mrs. Bannister and class 1M and Jeff was at the other end of the school in class 1B with Mr. Clark.

The two boys' met in the vast playground at breaks and lunchtime, where they swapped stories and opinions. They looked around nervously, Mark understood that he might have been top dog at 'Central' but here, with the big kids he was just like all the other newcomers - an arse wipe and fair game.

Chapter 64

At the prison gates, Karl opened the passenger door of the Rover saloon. "Get in, you ugly fucker"

"Nice motor" said Jack, not really sure of what to say now that the long awaited moment of freedom had arrived.

"What you got planned?" chuckled Karl.

"I though I'd visit the Queen for tea, seein as she's been providing it for the last two years," grinned Jack.

"Come on then, I know exactly where to go."

"So where are you takin me then? a brothel I hope."

"No! next best place, Hymies," replied Karl, studying his older brother, by one year.

Prison had hardened him, his sinewy body was deceptively powerful, he reminded Karl of a giant cobra and was just as deadly.

Several suits had been tried off the peg. Jack eventually turned from the long mirror to face his brother who sat in a small armchair. Karl nodded his approval. Paying the short, rotund, Armenian Jew in cash, Karl asked, "You won't forget that he needs those two suits in the material we picked for next week, will you Hymie?"

"Alright already!" and Karl took that for a 'No I won't'. "They'll be ready for next Thursday afternoon; you can pick them up then my boy." Karl grinned. He liked Hymie, but most of all he liked his craftsmanship. "Well who's a pretty boy then?"

"Well it ain't no short-arsed, big chinned, ugly fucker anyhow," railed Jack.

"Now, now, no need to get personal you lanky streak of piss."

The two men looked at one another, Jack threw his arm round his smaller brother's shoulders and they walked off, down the shop-lined London thoroughfare. "Ere, do you think these honest citizens think we are a couple of Nancies, Jack?"

The question was spat at a couple who had interrupted their window-shopping to stare at the brothers'. "Nah," said Jack, "After the ''Scrubs'' I'm a fuckin' expert on Poofters an' we definitely don't fit the bill."

When the window shoppers had meekly scurried off, the brothers' carried on their way in a more sober fashion. The Sir Thomas was their first stop and just before they left the car, Karl took out a wad of cash that would have choked a donkey. Peeling off five ten pound notes he put them into Jack's top pocket. "That should see you through the night me old son." At a loss for words, Jack just mumbled his embarrassed thanks. "Come on, let's surprise Somers Town."

Paddy and a couple of other minor villains were waiting inside to welcome Jack home. "You do know young man, that you are on parole, and associating with lags like what we are could get you sent back inside," sniggered one of the old jail birds.

Jack laughed and said that they would have to hang him next time, "Well you had better get a move on son, they are talking about abolishing hangin' this year," at which the whole of the pub's afternoon clientele laughed and cheered.

The drinks were flowing freely and as news spread that a 'face's' brother was out and on the town, very soon The 'Thomas' was packed and in a party mood. "Ere Karl, did you hear about that firm in Kensington last night?"

"Course I did, I told you, you silly bleeder."

Paddy, a little tipsy, looked puzzled then laughed. "Oh yeh so you did."

"What was that then?" asked Jack.

This allowed Paddy to go into great detail about a raid that had been a set up by the police and the firm doing the blag had shot at the coppers injuring several. "Pity they didn't kill the fuckers," growled Jack evilly, at which the group cheered again.

They had been in the pub for about three hours and the clock showed it a little after six thirty when Desmond, the landlord, caught Karl's eye and beckoned him to the bar. "It's a call for you, some bird din't give 'er name but say's it's important."

Karl picked up the receiver, making sure that there were no nosy bastards to overhear. "Hello."

"It's me," said the excited voice. Karl instantly recognised the caller as Pauline. "The gentlemen you are seeking 'ave made themselves known."

Karl had trained the girl well. No names or details were ever used on telephones, especially boozer phones like the one at the Sir Thomas. Landlords were not averse to allowing the 'old bill' to tap phones for a favour or two. "Is everything clear for a cup of tea?"

"Yeh, sweet as a nut."

Thirty minutes later the two Dacey boys' and Paddy had extricated themselves from the party, promising the revellers that they would be back later.

Breathlessly, Pauline welcomed the men, giving each of them a quick peck on the cheek and welcoming Jack a little more warmly as it was their first meeting. The tea was poured, this time from a huge teapot. "OK lets 'ave it," demanded Karl.

"Well you know big Linda, one of my girls'?"

"That short arsed-brass with the enormous knockers?" interrupted Paddy. "Yeh that one," Pauline continued. "She was wiv a punter and ran into that cunt Maltese Joe. He tells her to get rid of the punter cos ees her job for the night."

"So what?" said Karl irritably.

"She does as he tells her an' takes Joe back to her gaff, but she gets frightened cos ees comin on strange, so she fixes 'im a scotch an slips 'im a mickey."

Karl asked the excited woman to make her point. "Alright 'ang on to your wig, I'm tryin to tell you ain't I?" Karl shrugged. "It's like I was sayin, she slips him the Mickey Finn and he passes out before ee gets on the job. She lies there waiting for 'im to come round when she intends to tell 'im ee was the best fuck she ever had, when ee starts mumbling in is sleep like."

"What did he mumble?" asked Karl, becoming more interested.

Elated that she now had his full interest, Pauline continued. "Ee starts goin on about it not bein so funny now and couple of times mentions Harry's name."

Karl and Paddy twitched and adjusted their position slightly, while Jack listened impassively. "Go on," urged Paddy

"Well ee also rambles on about how he should 'ave listened more carefully and laughed about his wallet an' other stuff she couldn't make sense of."

"That it?" asked Karl.

"No, she gets nosy an' goes through his pockets, finds 'is wallet an' only goes an' finds a human fuckin' ear."

"What 'appened when ee came round?"

"Well like the pro she is, she pretends to be asleep; ee thinks ee did the business and fucks off without payin her."

"Can she be trusted Pauline?"

"On my life she can," swore the woman earnestly.

"It may come to that for all of us," whispered Karl hoarsely. "It's the fuckin' Maltese firm that done the deadly on Harry."

"What we do now?" asked Paddy.

"What we do now my son, is go to fuckin' war."

Karl and Paddy looked towards Jack who in all this time had sat expressionless, but was now grinning like a crocodile. "Am I invited to this party or are you intendin' to keep the fun for yourselves?" Then between them a council of war convened, while Pauline made another pot of tea.

Chapter 65

School life was endured and so far Mark had managed to escape physical harm. His social life, however, was on the up, he had been spending less time with Jinxie and his football and more time with an older group of kids from the next street and one girl in particular, a long-legged buxom fifteen-year-old called Pamela O'Shay. Mark had become besotted with her and had even started smoking with the gang to impress them. Things took a turn for the worse when he started to steal from his mother's purse and the shop till, to take the girl to the pictures and keep her supplied with fags. Although he spent restless guilt-ridden nights, in Pamela's company he continued to ham it up as the 'big I am'.

His reward for becoming a thieving Thespian braggart was that the older and more experienced girl would ridicule him in front of the other older boys' and make him jealous as she flirted with them, scolding them while laughing, as they were forever trying to thrust hands up her skirt or down her blouse. The eleven year old was no match for the older lads and had to feign indifference. Pamela would provoke the younger boy until he could take no more. When he was about to make an excuse to leave, she would grab him by the arm saying aloud. "Come on Mark, let's get away from these idiots" and as she dragged him away the boy was aware that although he felt jubilant at being the chosen one, he also felt emasculated by the backwards glances Pamela made to check who was watching their departure. If she had the attention of any or all of her admirers, she would flounce away holding onto Mark even more intimately.

This Saturday evening was different. Earlier that day the pair, along with several hangers on and friends, had been to the pictures, to see 'The Beatles' second major film, 'HELP'. Mark, like thousands and thousands of other kids, had been uplifted, not only by the vibrant music, but in the hope it gave the working classes, that in some way no matter how small, they could emulate their heroes.

A host of Richton's youth's had run and jumped in excitement bordering on frenzy, down Mallard Street from the picture house. Pamela was still in that state of euphoria when she arrived with Mark back at her home. She opened the front door with her Yale key and went through the short hall into the kitchen where she found the note from her mother, which said that both her parents had been called away to tend a sick relative and that they would not be back until very late that night. The note went on to explain that she was expected to feed herself and not, under any circumstances to have other children in the house. Several crosses conveyed her mother's love. "Well, what are yer standin' at the door for? Come in!" Pamela shouted at Mark, more irritably than angrily.

The boy slightly abashed wiped his feet and closed the door behind him, then he went into the back room as directed. Pamela was putting a stack of Beatles 45 rpm singles onto the red and cream record player. "I'm just getting changed" said the girl and she disappeared out of the door and up the stairs.

'I Want To Hold Your Hand' had just finished, the mechanical whirring and clunks of the arm releasing the next single, preparing the pair for the imminent burst of sound from the next selection. 'That Boy" might have been the song, but all Mark could think about as Pamela flopped beside him on the tapestry settee, in a pale yellow party dress, was 'that girl'. The room was lit by a forty-watt bulb in the ugly table lamp, with a shade that was meant to match the suite. There was no window in the room and that added to the subdued lighting that Mark found welcoming and exciting.

Pamela first snuggled up to Mark, then kissed him as though she were performing a screen test in Hollywood. Although it seemed a little false, Mark responded in the manner he considered would please her. "Get yer dick out."

Hesitating momentarily, shocked at the sudden command, the boy, in embarrassment obeyed. In the dimly lit room, Pamela was confident, almost aggressive. At her insistence he removed his trousers and underwear completely. "Ave a wank, I want to watch."

The boy now caught his breath and hesitated, he had not expected anything like this and felt he was about to be subjected to ridicule of the most personal nature. "No wait, lie back. I'll do it."

The lad was in no state to offer to participate in the procedure and the girl took a delight in his shocked submissiveness. Taking his erect member in her fingers she started to perform the rapid but rhythmic wrist movements that caused Mark to arch his back in an effort to increase physical contact. Sometimes the girl was a little too enthusiastic and her hand slipped, causing the boy pain but the pain was not severe enough to halt his pelvic thrusts. As Mark convulsed with the final euphoric spasms of his climax, Pamela studied his vulnerable shuddering and watched carefully for the imminent ejaculation. None came.

"You aven't cum!" announced the puzzled girl.

Mark had felt the griping in his testicles that usually followed masturbation, but as in all previous occasions there was no sign of ejaculated sperm. He was spent and embarrassed and wanted to get dressed and leave, but as he watched Pamela he saw she had lifted the frilled dress, revealing she had not been wearing underwear. He was shocked at the thick bush she was parting with her fingers and at her boldness and the delight she was exhibiting in performing for him her own masturbation routine. Feeling encouraged by her lack of inhibition, Mark grabbed at her ample breasts and she allowed him to pull them free of the low neck of the dress. It was her turn to feel the pain caused by clumsy fingers twisting and rubbing her hardened nipples. "Not so rough!" she hissed then as the boy was about to stop she demanded, "Put your finger in."

Impatiently she grabbed his hand and he did as he was told. He felt the wetness and was erect once more, his throat was dry and he found himself in between her splayed legs. "NO!" hissed the girl, almost stopping her actions. "I'll get pregnant if you put your dick in, just use your fingers." Then she said, "But you can't come yet."

She knew from the other lads whom she had allowed to do everything except full intercourse, that it was a sin to spill the seed that Catholic priests ranted on about. Sin it might be, but she had been mesmerised at their excitement and then had shown indifference to the grey-white mucus that had spurted over her hands and clothes, while the stupid looks on the boy's faces when they ejaculated amused her. When she had been examining too closely one of the older boys' with the largest penis she had seen, he had climaxed so strongly and copiously that great globules had jetted over her bare breasts and into her face.

But the sexual experience presenting itself now was unique. She knew, from talks with the boys' and her equally sexually active girlfriends, that boys' under a certain age did not ejaculate. "Alright," said the girl huskily, "put it in."

Mark scrambled into position, his engorged boyhood slipping into its offered partner easily. For several minutes the two rutted violently, the boy would look up now and then to hide a victorious smirk, only to see a picture of the crucifixion hanging on the wall and our Lord seemed to be glaring with rage at the pair.   The girl arched and quivered while Mark erratically thrust as deeply as possible and hung on as securely as he could in case she suddenly changed her mind and cut short the state of exhilaration that he was achieving.

The familiar gripes occurred almost in unison with the whimpers that the girl emitted. This time, was different, he came. Pamela felt the difference, as the pulsing spasms of the ejaculation made her jump a little in surprise. She was so spent that even the heat of the semen could not induce Pamela to immediately throw the sweat-soaked boy from her.

As he slipped from inside her she jumped more animatedly and then found the reserves to push him from her. "Just get the fuck off me yer stupid bastard."

"Why?" asked the boy, "What 'ave I done?"

"Yer cum in me, that's what you done!" snapped Pamela as she brought her legs together.

Mark looked down and saw a milky dribble, the remnants which confirmed his ignorant first procreative attempt. As he pulled on his underpants and trousers, he watched smugly as the temptress put her breasts back into the crumpled dress. She looked anything but refined and worldly. "Just fuck off yer stupid bastard!" and any thoughts of asking about the possibility of a repeat performance disappeared when the door slammed behind him.

As he walked home, he tucked his shirt in and felt like telling the world what had justhappened, but he knew that it would be a big mistake. Even bragging to the others would incur disbelief and ridicule for the pair of them, besides, he did not want to jeopardise prospective visits to that glorious back room.

Pamela would not be her arrogant, cruel self for three weeks, until her period arrived. She resolved to take more care in future.

Once things returned to normal, Mark was treated with the usual disdain only more so by the older girl. Then one Friday evening, Mark was invited to the backroom as Pamela's parents had again been called away to her aunt who was seriously ill. This time they got down to business in a more restrained manner and there was a lot more foreplay, it all seemed more erotic as they practiced kissing in different ways. Although they were both aroused to fever pitch, Pamela wriggled and twisted to prevent penetration, and when Mark's advances became stronger and almost threatening, the girl relieved the boy before performing the same service for herself.

Although he was dispassionately thrown out once again, Mark was walking on clouds. This, he thought, was love. They did not meet that weekend and when he met up with the gang of older boys' and girls' the following Saturday, he was heartbroken when he discovered that Pamela's aunt needed permanent care, so the O'Shay's had moved to the Midlands, to share the large house that would be theirs on the aunt's death. In the space of one week Mark had felt the pangs of first love, born of lust and the bitter sweetness of love lost. He was never to hear from or about Pamela again.

School became more of a drag than ever and shortly after the departure of his girlfriend at his lowest ebb, the bullying started.

Chapter 66

"You sure you can trust 'im?" asked Jack.

Karl nodded. "Ee's a diamond keeps is mouth shut, he does business with me for a lot of money. Ee's sweet as a nut."

It was with those few words that Karl confirmed to Paddy and Jack that their intimate corps had been increased by one.

Later that day the Dacey brothers' and Paddy met Reggie Sheldon, a well known East End 'face,' who was commonly known as 'Digger'. "Alright boys'?"

There followed almost half an hour of banal chatter. Eventually Jack became bored and as he could not start drinking seriously until the meeting had finished, he gave proceedings a push. "For fuck's sake Karl, we all know why we're 'ere, lets get on with it."

Digger grinned. 'I like this geezer already,' he thought.

Over the next three hours the four men considered strategy and options, both positive and negative. Finally Karl said that he would inform the South London firm, that the deadly was about to begin and at the last moment out of respect, Digger, who had no love for the Browns, agreed to alert the East End faction that there would be serious happenings in West London that weekend. This would prevent their business being compromised by events that could bring the law on to the streets in force.

"There is no problem with us Mank; your business is yours as far we are concerned, with one exception." Karl had thought his meeting with Albert and Chris was going too well and he now found himself preparing for the bad news. "There must be no straights involved."

Karl relaxed and smiled at the big man in front of him and at his younger brother. "Goes without saying Chris."

In all gang wars it was an unwritten rule that no harm was to come to any innocent member of the public. "So all we can say is, be lucky Mank."

Karl left the office of the scrap yard, when he reached the gates he jumped back startled when the huge German shepherd launched itself at him. When it stood on its hind legs the short chain choked the animal back with a violent snap. "Get down you crazy facker," Chris Rankin bawled and the cringing cur obeyed. "Mank, lets go for a drive."

Karl climbed into the driver's side of the Rover, telling Chris that the passenger door was likewise open. "Don't you lock your motor Mank?"

"What outside your offices, I don't fink so. only a crazy fucker would steal your motor."

Chris liked the answer. "Mank I need to know if you are gonna be a pain in the arse to my firm."

Karl's brain raced, if he got his response wrong it could well prove to be a fatal error. "Not intentionally Chris."

Again the big man appreciated the honest answer, so refreshingly different from the grovelling or brash bravado answers he normally got to his direct questions. "No offence Mank, but if this little party of yours facks up, then I ain't got a problem. But if you pull it off, that leaves you in a pretty strong position on 'The Manor'." Chris paused to see Karl's reaction but the driver was listening. "I want to know right now if you intend to try and build your little firm up at my expense."

Karl did not answer immediately, but left sufficient pause to make his inquisitor a little uncomfortable. He had considered that this might be a hit but he knew that it would have been easier to do the deadly back in the office. No, this he thought is simply business, a marking of boundaries and rules of future commerce. "Look Chris, we ave never 'ad a problem, we 'ave done business and all made money and I don't want to fuck up a good thing. The way I see things is, if all goes well on this bit of business, then it would mean I could come to you with a deal to make a lot more money."

Karl's passenger interrupted. "Fack me Mank, a bit o' business, for one fing the Maltese firm is big, rich and fackin deadly, for another, what deal can I possibly expect from this war of yours?"

Karl asked wether Chris would mind if they pulled in as he could not drive and look him in the face. The big man nodded his approval. Karl pulled on the handbrake but left the engine running, he turned in his seat to face his passenger. "I have no intention of losing this one, and no intention of taking over the Maltese firm's prostitution racket."

Chris exhaled and rubbed his chin as if deep in thought. "So let me get this straight, you are goin to war, an' if you win, your gonner frow away a fackin' fortune?"

"Not a fuckin' chance" laughed Karl.

"What then?"

"I intend to put the business out to that little firm that 'ave 'ad bad blood wiv the Maltese for years."

"What, the Cypriots?"

Karl nodded then continued.

"They get control of the business and we get thirty percent."

"We?" asked Chris, now smiling.

Karl nodded. "We split our end fifty-fifty."

"Very generous of you Mank, but what do you expect from us in return?"

"Simple, I need your firm to make the Cypriots realise that it would be in their best interests to do business with us."

"So they don't know about your little plan then?"

"It would be a mistake to let anyone know what I'm about to do, now wouldn't it?"

Karl's passenger grinned and nodded. "I suppose you are goin' to let that firm over the water know something is in the offing?"

"Yeh, but as far as they are concerned, it's just revenge for what they did to Harry."

"So what you gonna offer them if they come on strong?"

"Fuck all." Karl grinned back at Chris. "Way I look at it, if our three firms become partners in the deal, then there is no need to do business wiv em."

Ah so that is the real reason Chris thought to himself.

His South London firm had already experienced a run-in with the 'East End' gang over a parking scam the Rankins operated at Heathrow. They had not said directly that they wanted in on the lucrative business to Albert and Chris, but had spoken to big John Carter and Mad Martin Meehan in a chance meeting in a boozer off the Caledonian Road. Martin had been diplomatic and had said that there was no reason that he could see why the firm should give anything to the East; while John had been a little blunter, saying that it was a liberty for anyone to expect anything from an enterprise that was nothing to do with them. The Brown boys' and their firm had swallowed and had had to accept that line of reasoning.

Contrary to popular belief and newspaper reports, there was no ongoing war between the firms, but now and then one of the Rankin soldiers would kick off and perform or visa versa. It was just macho bullshit by young men out to make a name for themselves – something that was not uncommon in their line of business.

Thinking in greater depth, the big man considered the scrap yards and the other businesses that his firm owned. The fruit machine empire was raking in the money, as was the airport scam. These ventures had made possible a vast accumulation of wealth. The Mank would be a valuable ally should war ever break out, between East and South, threatening his firm's lifestyle. "You gotta deal Mank."

Karl took the offered hand and shook it firmly.

On the short drive back the Rover got caught in mid-afternoon traffic.

"That Franco came visiting us a couple of days ago."

"Oh yeh" replied Karl, trying to sound unconcerned.

"Yeh apparently he heard a whisper that your firm were planning to sort one of their boys' sometime next week."

"I know."

It was Rankin's turn to pretend he was unsurprised.

"Know what? That he came to see me or that they know you intend to ave a go at em?"

"Both."

Chris knew that there was always the chance that his meeting with the Maltese firm had not gone unnoticed, but he was taken aback that his disclosure that the Mank's plans were known to the pimp's firm had not raised even an eyebrow.

Back at the yard Chris rested his right arm on the car's roof and poked his head in through the closed passenger door's open window. "Well I 'ope everything goes sweet."

"So do I!" laughed Karl and when Chris rounded the rear of the car and disappeared through the gates, Karl turned the Rover towards town and the meeting with the others.

Karl talked aloud to himself. "Course I knew you fuckin' met em. I also know they gave you five grand to stay out of the frame and I know that they think that we are gonna hit Joe next week, that's why there's a Scots cunt comin down from Glasgow to shoot me next Friday. Only problem with that, is that Friday will be too late."

The first thing Karl had done was to put a permanent watch on every member of the Maltese firm, using Pauline's girls' and a couple of kids Paddy knew. It was one of these sixteen-year-old boys' who had reported that Maltese Joe had met up with a geezer in a 'speeler' and when the geezer had left the illegal drinking club, the youth had followed him home, while his mate had followed Joe.

The boy had followed the small man back to Holloway to a nondescript groundfloor council flat. When he thought the geezer was settling in for the night, he ran to the corner and telephoned Pauline. The youth returned immediately as ordered, to take up sentry duty. He had been there for over an hour when he witnessed how the geezer was pleasantly surprised on answering his door to a good looking woman and then several men had pushed past her and into his gaff. The girl, who he had never seen before was a heavily made-up Pauline, who like the young sentry having played their parts quickly disappeared.

Digger had held the red hot, electric, flat iron to his face, but he had not talked until Jack had cut off one of his fingers with the large pruning shears. Even though they had extracted the information about the hit man from Scotland, the knowledge he had imparted had not saved the man, he knew too much.

Maltese Joe had told him that since his job of arranging the hit man was done, he should take his money and disappear for a few weeks. Jack gave a broad grin. "Oh you're goin to disappear alright."

By their acts of torture, the wretch had confirmed that the false information leaked by Karl, had had been swallowed hook line and sinker by the Maltese firm,

"Yes," said Karl, "You've got everything right you Bastards except the deadly is not next week and it's not just Joey that's getting it, it's every fuckin' one of you, including the cat, the dog and the goldfish."

Karl chuckled to himself and was filled with a feeling of intense pleasure as he made his way to the meeting place where the others were waiting, in readiness for his return. In twenty-four hours it would all be over and he would either be dead or a prince of the city.

The waiting was the worst part for the gang. Jack paced up and down and every now and then he grimaced and threw imaginary punches, or rehearsed the stabbing of some invisible enemy. Before he could speak to Digger and Paddy, they left the room and he continued to pace the floor.

In the other room Digger was trying to catch the odd word from a conversation between Karl and the tall, slim, moustachioed man in his mid-fifties who was dressed in a long, caramel raincoat, belted tightly at the waist. "Do we need to go over it once more or ave you got it?"

"Fuck me Mank, I've got it. I'm not as thick as the slags you usually keep company with."

Karl ignored the insult and continued. "OK Just for my stupid sake once more please."

The mackintosh man sighed exaggeratedly. "I will be in 'the speeler' with the Maltese slags at the meet I arranged yesterday with just Joe, Franco and the other fucker whose name I don't remember."

"Riz," reminded Karl.

"Yeh whatever," snapped the tall man, annoyed at the interruption. "I do my bit convincing them to take the bait then when a geezer comes in an' asks if anyone called a cab I've got exactly five minutes to leave. On my way out I meet y..yo..Someone," he corrected himself, "at the door and give them the gen on where bodies are sat. Then I fuck off sharp, OK?"

"Yeh, fuckin' spot on, especially the bit about bodies."

The much taller man was disinterested in the Mank's humour and sensed that the meeting was at an end, but business was unfinished. "Ahem. I do believe you have something for me."

Karl was already handing over a large buff envelope to the man. When he saw that the man was about to count the cash Karl said tersely, "Two grand, it's all there, I wouldn't fuck you over, Sanderson."

"Oh I know that you slag, I just like to look at the means to buy my dream retreat in Spain."

'Raincoat' left and Karl opened the dividing door and addressed the others. "Ok it's time."

All four men climbed into the back of the dark blue Bedford CA van which had blacked out windows and Paddy closed the double back doors. Digger gave a bang on the inside of the vans metal body and the motor, already running, revved up and sped away. "Your cousin knows what ees doin' Paddy?"

"Ee does."

Forty-five minutes later the van parked on the small patch of waste ground just behind the drinking den owned by the Maltese firm. Each of the men checked the other's disguises. In wigs and beards they aped Disney characters and looked strangely comical in the yellow, low voltage battery light of the blacked-out van. "We look like four fuckin' Fagins," quipped Paddy and all four laughed nervously.

"What time is it?" asked Karl.

"Don't know" replied Jack. "You told us to leave everything back at the gaff and to wear this shit."

"Just checking," said Karl.

He knew that to get away with this job they would have to make sure that no evidence was left to provide clues for the law.

'BANG,' a single thud at the back door, then two more in rapid succession told the men that the driver, who had left them five minutes before had returned. Paddy opened the door slightly, when he saw his cousin in the darkness, he held his breath in anticipation. "You're on." The doors were fully opened and the four men climbed out, their long gabardine coats swinging about their shins exposed the one-piece navy boiler suits and each mans allotted weapon. "What time is it son?"

"The clock above the speeler's bar said 10p.m."

"How many did you see in there?"

"Three of the firm are there, two at the bar talking to Sanderson and one sat at the table nearest to them. Nobody was on the door and nobody locked it when I left, I waited a bit to make sure."

"Did any of the fuckers seem suspicious of you when you went in?"

"Nah the two at the bar hardly looked up from talking to Sanderson and the other one told me to fuck off when I asked if anyone had called a cab, they thought I was touting for a fare."

"Well done son, you wait here, keep your head, an' don't panic." Karl turned away from the young man and faced the others. "OK let's do it."

"Well to what do we owe the honour of your important cannot-wait-til- tomorrow visit, CID sergeant Sanderson?"

Franco was deliberately sarcastic he had been forced to cancel business and at the policeman's insistence had put himself out, arranging things so that only the three senior gang members would meet the bent copper in absolute secrecy. Sanderson was expensive but, thought Franco, he's worth his weight in gold. "I mean it's not another wage increase negotiation is it? No, no of course not, that was last week." The long coated policeman smiled. "Just a friendly visit to warn you, that very soon you are going to get a visit; from vice."

"Fuck me Sanderson, that doesn't give us much notice does it?"

"Fuck you, you slag cunt, I'm serious crimes not fuckin' vice. I only found out the exact time of the raid myself a few hours ago, I had heard a whisper a couple of days ago that it was gonna be tomorrow."

The three Maltese thugs sprang into action. "Joey, hide the tools and any gear in the safe place. Riz, get a pack of cards from behind the bar and sit at the table calm like." As Riz obeyed, Franco opened the peep-hole in the back door that led to the waste ground and there, in the darkest corner was the black shape of the Bedford van. "Sneaky bastards are already ere, there's a cop van hiding out back," growled the stocky ex-wrestler. "Well looks like you 'ave earned your crust this week Sanderson, we had quite a bit of gear lined up for tonight's dope heads."

The CID man was checking his watch. "Yeh well it's what you pay for, but you will excuse me if I make myself scarce now. We wouldn't want to be recognised associating with shit like you now would we?"

With that, Sanderson made his exit, pausing momentarily at the entrance to the small foyer, to look back and salute the gangsters mockingly. What had really taken place was a final check of the game board. Clearing the foyer, he passed the four men at the door. "They put the drugs, shooters and a lot of money behind a false panel in the cupboard at the back near the door to the car park. Franco, Joe and the other cunt are sat at a table near the bar pretending to be playing cards, they're the only ones in the gaff," whispered Sanderson.

Once he had imparted that knowledge, the policeman entered the street, looked about and pulling up his collar, he made great strides to put as much distance as possible between himself, the 'Speeler' and the Maltese firm's visitors.

If only they had not been so smugly looking at their cards or one another, they would have noticed the heavily disguised marauders sooner. "Evening officers," said Franco, turning to face them from his chair. "What the fuck…"

Panic stricken, the Maltese who were seated at the table tried to stand but the heavy blows that rained down on their heads from the pick shafts forced them back down. Their screams of amazed protestation were silenced as the Maltese fell into a terrified stupor or unconsciousness. It had taken Karl and his boy's just two minutes from entering the 'Speeler'. "Dopey, you sure you locked the front door behind you?"

"Yes Doc."

They had rehearsed the only names that were to be used, those of 'Disney's' famous dwarves. 'Doc' was Karl, Paddy as 'Bashful' was already stashing the money and drugs, three hand guns and a sawn off into the sacks that had been hidden under his long coat. Dopey, alias Digger, had savagely clubbed Riz, who had stirred into semi-consciousness.

Seconds later Paddy's cousin saw the lit match at the 'Speeler's' back door, this signalled that he was to back the van close to the exit of the club. Before the vehicle had stopped the dwarves had opened the doors and while the driver watched for witnesses, the bound and unconcious Maltese were dragged and flung into the back of the van.

"What a Fuckin' doddle that was," said 'Grumpy', or Jack.

The van trundled away slowly, not picking up speed until it was well out of the area. "We ain't in the clear yet, we got thirty minutes before we get to the lock up."

By the time the late evening drinkers, well-heeled drug addicts and lesser gang members were banging on the front door of the drinking club for access, Franco and his gang were coming round to find themselves trussed like chickens in the soundproofed, lock-up warehouse under the railway arches. There was not much noise to worry about as all the chickens were gagged. Doc dragged one of the Maltese gang members into a sitting position. "Right now Riz me ole china, I'm going to remove this plaster from your mouth and you are going to oblige me by not screaming or making a fuss, besides there is not much point as you could explode a bomb in here and outside they wouldn't hear a thing."

"You stupid bastard, when I get free I'll kill you." The heavy-accent of the largest gang member spat venom and menace. Karl still in disguised looked sideways and nodded. Grumpy swung the wooden shaft with full force onto the top of the snarling mobster's head. Bone splintered and his left eye came free of the shattered socket and cheekbone, killing the victim instantly. The other two gang members screamed silently, their eyes stared wildly at the casual way in which their friend and cousin had been dispatched.

"Now, as I was saying." Karl had moved onto the next in line and was removing his adhesive gag, tearing it roughly. "That was not what I was opin to hear. I do hope you won't disappoint me."

Doc was now talking in hushed child-like tones to the second man. His presence was evil incarnate. The false beard and boiler suit were spattered with blood that was soaking into dark blotches, turning the navy cotton black. With his red-streaked face he now resembled a blood soaked 'Mephistopheles'.

As soon as the sticking plaster had been ripped from his face, the second trussed chicken babbled information. "Slow down Franco sunshine, slow down." The unaturally calm manner of the gory villain who was staring into his eyes, only served to increase the gang's leader terror, but he sensed that his only hope lay in his willingness to provide immediate answers. "Now who was in on the job to sort out the Mank?"

The miserable captive named the three men who had been kidnapped earlier. Then he named the go-between who had already been taken care of and who had been the only man known to the paid killer. Finally he provided the name of the Glaswegian hit-man, including his intended arrival time at Euston and the passwords to be exchanged when he was met at the station. "Well done son, almost finished, just one more thing." Behind the mask Karl's face contorted briefly and then he was calm once more, but that brief agitatation was sufficient to ensure enthusiastic responses from the man he was interrogating. "Who did the deadly on Harry the Axe?"

"Me and Joey."

"Who else?"

No one. We 'ad no choice, I swear it on my mother's grave."

In soft tones Doc falsely promised the wretch that Harry's death was of no real consequence. Although the man knew that this was a game that very soon he would be killed, he clung to life a little longer in the only way that was possible; he talked and prayed for a miracle. Over the next ten minutes he related in detail how they had followed the 'Axe' to a quiet pub and spiked his drink when he had gone to the toilet and how the big man on feeling violently ill, had called a minicab and how unbeknown to Harry, Joey and Riz intercepted the one called and had arranged the private taxi that arrived for him. Snow White's posse listened in silence to the details of the degradation and torture of their friend Harry, drugged and helpless in the final hours before his death.

There followed a long pause, during which the inquisitor studied the wretch's face,

"Fuckin' 'ell, my legs ave gone dead."

The sight of their leader hopping and lurching about the room, trying to lessen the cramp and painful pins and needles broke the silence and caused the three dwarves to break into hysterical laughter. Even Franco, his face bleached white forced a false smile.

"Now you av told us the truth, an' I agree in our line of business you din't 'av a choice cos your brother Joey 'ated Arry's guts. "Naffink personal Franco."

'SMASH'…. The man felt nothing; his nervous system could not relay the pain inflicted by the terrible sideward swipe of the scaffold pole, which destroyed bone and brain in that life-ending stroke. It had struck his left ear and smashed a splintered path from one side of his skull to the other. Black blood mixed with red, were diluted with clear cerebral fluid and large particles of matter exploded like a macabre firework.

The speed of Karl's action caused the three dwarves to jump visibly and to gasp obscenities. Recovering their wit's, they followed Karl's example and removed disguises. They then turned their attentions to the remaining pimp, Maltese Joe.

Karl was looking at Franco's lifeless body, silently mouthed words that were witnessed by none but himself and the deceased. "Sorry pal you an' me never 'ad a quarrel, but that's the game innit?"

Karl had shown the only mercy he could, ending the mobster's life with such surprising speed that the man did not realise what was happening.

"Allo Joey, there's only you left old son. What a to do eh? Well anyway, you do realize that all this is your doin now don't ya?" As Karl chatted away cheerfully, he toyed with something in his right hand. "What did yer fink of me planning then? Good eh?"

The job had been executed exactly to plan. When the van had arrived at the lock-up, the driver had been sent on his way. Before the young man had left he had been told to forget everything and had been made aware aware there would be a price to pay for as much as talking in his sleep.

Paddy had reversed the van into the small 'lock-up' and the full-length doors of the warehouse had been closed and locked. Once inside the Maltese firm had been hauled to the huge wooden box that formed a room within a room. The box was lined with thick waterproof sheets and had been built to suggest its purpose was a paint spray booth for vehicle panels, doors, wings, bonnets etc. In reality however, it provided an abattoir that could be easily cleaned, to leave no clues.

"So you see you don't ave to worry about anyone grieving over yer coffin, cos you ain't ever gonna be found." Karl's chilling words were accentuated when he theatrically produced his plaything - Harry's severed ear. "Found this in yer wallet while you were avvin a little kip in the van. Oops silly me, 'ow the fuck can we ave a chat when your gob is all taped up?" Joey shrieked as the plaster was ripped as painfully as possible from his face. "Now if you as much as make a sound you'll wish you hadn't."

"You go fuck your mother you fuckin' Mank bastard. Kill me, I don't be afraid of a cunt like you, go on finish it."

Karl ignored the defiant accented curses and stood back to allow Jack to pass him, Digger following.

The violent thrashing was similar to a shark attacking a seal and was over in about the same time. While Digger held Joe's head, Jack rammed the steel tyre-lever into the captive's mouth sideways, shattering several teeth in the process. Then with a savage wrench dislocated Joe's jaw, Karl returned to thrust the fang like pliers into what had been a mouth and after a brief tussle dragged out the man's quivering blood-and-spittle-slimed tongue. No sooner had it appeared, than Jack with a swift, slicing stroke from his cutthroat, severed two thirds of the muscle, causing Karl to fall backwards as his pulling actions became unnecessary. Jack had to jump back to escape the gushing blood and released the mans head. Joe was making animalistic noises, the pain-racked man made more noise than any of the gang could have thought possible, Karl stuffed a rag into a bloody hole that had once been a mouth. "Thank Gawd for that" sighed paddy, as Joe's screams became restrained mewling and then whimpers.

Karl had the severed tongue in the wet, slippery grip of the pliers and Harry's ear in an equally bloody right hand and he was holding them up in front of Maltese Joe's bulging eyes. "I told you not to make a sound you naughty boy, now eres what we are gonna do. Jack 'ere is gonna slice off your ears, then ee is gonna take those two dinner forks in his top pocket and rip out your fuckin' eyes like pickled onions."

Joe did not have enough wit left to consider that it all might be a sick bluff, because Jack was about to slice off his second ear. "Ang on yer silly fucker, if you slice off his ears too soon, ee won't 'ere what we got planned for 'im" said Karl.

Jack chuckled. "I fink ee will still be able to ear a bit wiv out his flappers."

"Oh, ok carry on then."

The gruesome banter between the two brothers' continued as the muscle and tissue parted easily from the victim's skull. Jack took the metal forks from the zippered, top pocket of his blood-soaked, boiler suit but Joe suddenly stopped struggling and was silent. "Aw fuckin' bastard, ees gone an' fuckin' dropped dead on us," moaned Jack, genuinely disappointed.

Maltese Joe's heart had given way under the terror and the agony, sparing him from any further suffering.

Joey died at about four in the morning; by seven Karl and the boys' had separated. They had all of them washed in the large metal tank and when they had scrubbed themselves clean and had dried off with paper towels, they dressed in garments taken from a stack of clean clothes. The four had drawn lots to decide who was to dispose of the bodies and who was to clean the lock up of all evidence. It had fallen to Jack and Digger to get rid of the corpses. The van, the booth and warehouse had been thoroughly inspected for any signs of the killing. The bloody, bath water had been rinsed down the drain with copious amounts of water and two, twenty-gallon drums of pine disinfectant and bleach. The tank had been dried and filled with dark pungent degreasing fluid. When it had been unanimously decided that they were as 'clean as a whistle', the big doors had been opened allowing the stench of butchery, masked by bleach and disinfectant, to waft into the early morning London air. Paddy had remained at the warehouse where he was later joined by his cousin; together they dismantled the large wooden booth. It had been decided that the firm would not be going into the car spraying business after all. In the rough, dirt-hardened yard the panels were stacked up several at a time and the two men cheerfully chatted about nothing of importance while they enjoyed the bonfire. By the time night arrived, all the timber and sheeting had been reduced to a pile of ash and the lock-up stank of wood smoke and a slight smell of disinfectant. "Come on, lock the place up an' we can go for a drink."

Happily, Paddy's younge cousin complied.

It was noon and the blue van that had travelled at a very sedate pace, arrived with its grisly cargo, at the remote farmhouse in the Norfolk countryside. The old pig breeder was expecting them. "Back it up to those doors and then go over to the house, my missus will make you cup of tea," ordered the man.

Two hours later the farmer walked through the door and without any show of emotion told the men that the van was sparkling clean, everything had been taken care of and that all that was in the back of the Bedford now, was the three polythene sacks which awaited separate disposal. Jack handed the old man the large envelope containing a 'grand,' receiving nothing but a polite nod for the thousand pounds, the pair took their leave.

The drive back to London was just as tense as the first part of the journey, the two men in the van realised that the longer they were on the road the greater the chance that someone would discover the three macabre parcels in the back. "Its pigs you see, once a carcass is all chopped up and boiled, them pigs eat everything, bones an' all. And there aint no change from inspecting pig shit."

"Yeh every thing except heads, hands an' feet," replied Digger sullenly. "Just the 'eads they can't manage, the feet an' hands, well they 'ave too many small bones an' its better not to risk one of the little buggers being overlooked now inn'it?" said Jack.

"Yeh I suppose it is" and Digger forced a grin.

When the van reached Hemel Hempstead they brought it to a halt at the deserted building site. They waited until the driver of the cement mixer had left, followed soon after by the night watchman. At a little after six, Karl who had also been waiting unseen at the site, appeared through the opening gates and waved them in. The foundations were huge and it took only minutes for the packages to be removed from the van and thrown into the centre of the still-liquid concrete. Karl walked across the plank and used a long-handled rake to push the bags, containing head, hands and feet, under the grey mass. As he raked and tamped the surface he felt heat rising from the curing concrete.

"Fuckin' good job you two were not late, this stuff will be rock 'ard in half an hour."

They left the scene a good hour before the drink-sodden night watchman returned to the post that he had deserted. He always left the site unguarded after the last delivery of the day, after all, there was nothing on site to nick and the company did not pay him enough to be conscientious.

Earlier that night he had met a nice young bloke who had bought him a couple of drinks and who had seemed to be interested in the importance of the watchman's job. Paddy had been waiting in the pub for the arrival of the old soak and had made sure that he did not leave early. On his return, the watchman tripped over a plank that had not been there earlier. "Fuckin' kids."

He then went into his hut and slept until he was awakened by the first concrete delivery of the day. The impatient driver was already pouring the truck's load into the foundations. The old night watchman leaned against the outside of his hut and estimated that the trenches would be completely full by mid-morning and set solid enough for the builders to start erecting the office block on the following day.

As he made his way home, his shift over, he wondered how long he would remain employed and how many years the police station, when built would stand after he was dead and gone.

Later that evening three men watched the Bedford van in silence. Jack and Digger knew that the machine operator would ask no questions. They were the only people present at the scrapyard at that time. Within a few minutes the massive iron jaws of the crusher reduced the vehicle into a cube and the men separated, going in different directions, one to his office to stash the fifty quid, his unexpected bonus for getting rid of what he surmised was probably a stolen motor that had been used in a blag. He got one or two of those. The other pair walked wearily to the gates where Karl was waiting.

"You two fancy a cup of tea?"

"Nah take me home I need a kip. I'm fuckin' knackered," said the exhausted, but relieved Digger.

"Fuck the tea. I 'ad a kip in the van on the way back, lets go down West an av a beer. An' I hope your buying supper, cos I'm fuckin' starving," said Jack.

Sergeant Sanderson C.I.D. looked down at the body that had been discovered in the side street near Euston. It lay half-in and half-out of the stolen Ford Zodiac. A single shot to the back of the head had dispatched the Glaswegian. In the vehicle they found a selection of firearms that, he knew on forensic examination, would prove to be covered in the Maltese firms' fingerprints, allowing him to make an eventual report that, in his opinion, Franco and his gang had serious issues with the Jocks and that they had done this one. Perhaps that was why the Maltese had mysteriously disappeared.

Well, at least it would give the newspapers another angle and perhaps they would pay less attention to the bleating relatives.

The front pages would read. 'Maltese trio wanted for questioning in Gangland slaying.' There would be reports of misleading and spurious sightings, all fabricated by Sanderson himself. In a few months, it would only be the whining relatives who cared and as soon as they realised that their protection had disappeared with the firms disappearance, they too would shut up and get on with life as best they could in this 'shit hole' of a city.

The Cypriot gang would take over the Maltese firm's rackets and he would receive his increased cut of the action as agreed. 'Yes', he thought, I like doing business with the Mank, he is a cut above the others, but still a piece of slag shit.

In July that year, capital punishment had been abolished except in cases of piracy and treason. By November, Karl and Jack's little firm were doing lots of business and Karl was moving more and more into financing blags, funding criminal ventures and loan-sharking rather than performing more risky capers. Karl's often stated philosophy was, 'why have dogs and bark yourself'?

The good life had arrived and in the comfort affluence brings, Karl decided that perhaps it was time to think of marriage; to the girl who looked the spitting image of Dusty Springfield and with whom he had been living with since he had left prison. Her name was Linda Briggs. Most of all, from now on, he was 'The Mank', a serious 'face' in London's underworld.

Chapter 67

Mark and Jeff watched the fireworks explode into a multitude of garish colours above their heads. "So what do yer think of our 'bommy' then?" Jinxie was first to speak. "Hiya beaver."
The lad was the same age and about the same height and build as Mark but with dark brown hair and sharp features. His front teeth protruded, not very noticibly but unfortunately for the boy this feature had earned him the nickname of a dam-building rodent. "Hiya Jinxie, hiya Mark."
Mark nodded coolly, "Olright Ron"
Ronnie Costin grinned, "'Av yer 'ad any black peas, or tater 'ash yet?" The lad's shook their heads. "Come on then."
Ron pushed his way through the small group of neighbours, family and friends who were crowding around the flaming bonfire now that the firework display had ended. Each family had set off their own selection or box of fireworks, while the others had watched and admiringly 'oohed' and 'ahhed', or if they considered the offering too poor they had hissed and booed. "Av yer got any peas or pie left mum?"
The short, skinny woman looked at her eldest child. "You have already had some Ron" "It's not for me it's for me mates."
It was the normal practice for almost every street corner to hold individual 5th of November celebrations. While neighbours all joined together to provide food and fireworks, the children would collect wood for the fire over many weeks, and guard it jealously. Mark and Jeff had helped to collect the timber, though their particular collecting expertise lay in raiding other kids' woodpiles. The theft had made this bonfire the largest in the district. The stack had been erected on ground where a row of back-to-back terraces had once stood, there were a plethora of levelled sites in the locality awaiting private or council development.
"Oh I'm sure we can find something," With a big smile Ron's mother doled out some congealed black peas into two small bowls, then smothered them with vinegar.
"There's no potato 'ash left, sorry boys'." The two lads thanked Mrs. Costin and said they were fine. The woman, who was impressed by Mark's politeness added, "There will be some baked potatoes later, when the fire dies down."

The boys' thanked her again and promised to bring her bowls back when they had finished eating.

"So what you doin' tomorrer Costy?"

Mark preferred this nickname to the crueller version. "Me dad's takin me to see Man City."

"Shit team," said Jeff.

"Better than shitty Burnley," responded Ron.

Mark interrupted before the two started their usual routine of slagging each other's team off, player by player. "Just give over you two," and for a few minutes, there was peace.

After the bowls had been returned, the three friends watched the fire burn slowly down. "I'm off home, you comin' Jinxie?"

"Nah I'm waiting for a baked tater, arn't you?"

Mark loved the smoked taste of potatoes charred black in the fire's embers but he had already overrun his allotted playtime. "Nah I gotta go 'ome, or I'll get dun', See yer later" Mark left them to their late night, fire-watching vigil.

When Mark arrived at the chip shop entrance, he gently pushed his way through the customers. His mother smiled at him as she busily went about her business of serving fish and chips, Mark crossed the noisy dining room to reach the back corridor and living room, where he sat in front of the television.

Later, when his mother called in with a pie and a few chips she asked if he had, had a good time at the bonfire. "Yeh it was great," he replied. That was the only conversation he would have until the early hours of the morning when, if he was still awake, he would help tidy up at closing time. He was pleased that 'A Christmas Carol' with Alistaire Simm, was showing on TV. The black and white masterpiece captivated the lad and at its end he was left feeling joyous and excited in the anticipation of another Christmas.

When he arrived at school the following morning, he was reminded of 'Charles Dickens' classic tale. The three brutes who were teasing and bullying him called to mind, 'Scrooges Christmas past, Christmas present and Christmas yet to come. "You think yer 'ard don't yer, yer little dick 'ead?"

Mark tried to ignore them and walk past, but one of them put out his foot and tripped him. Getting to his feet, he carried on into the school by way of the playground door that the three now jeering louts had been hanging around, waiting for their victims. Once satisfied that he was unseen, he inspected his knees that had borne the brunt of his forced landing. "Oh no!" he gasped in dismay, the gash in the right knee was nothing to him, but the tear in his nearly-new trousers was a serious cause for concern.

"Me mum will kill me."

After months of increasingly abusive treatment by his tormentors, the boy's anger erupted. When Mark burst back through the door the three fourth-formers were in the process of stealing another unfortunate wretch's dinner money. THWACK! Mark furiously punched the nearest thug in the side of the face and then watched as the bully yelled in shock and pain. "You ripped me pants an' you 'ad better pay for 'em."

As they realised that one of their regular victims had dared to retaliate, all three prepared to pulverise the much smaller boy. Fortunately for Mark the arrival of the history teacher, who had been on yard duty, saved him a certain beating and he used the timely interruption to make good his escape. Jinxie and Ron sat in the main hall at that first morning break and commiserated with their friend. "Even you can't beat all three of them bastards," said Jeff.

"Yeh they 'ave got all the school shittin' themselves," joined in Ron. Mark was regretting his foolhardy loss of temper because the three thugs had tried all that day to corner him, each time he had evaded them by sheer luck or by the sudden appearance of a teacher. On those occasions they had mouthed silent threats, leaving him in no doubt that the earlier incident was not going to be overlooked.

At lunchtime Mark had volunteered to help put up a collage showing the achievements of his 'House'. Four 'Houses' competed during term times. Handel, Shore, Stubbly and Mark's 'House' Schofield. The 'Houses were named after famous, old local, great Houses and Halls. They were also represented with the identifying colours, blue, green, yellow, and red. As he helped two of the class swots affix the material to the wall of his classroom, he felt humiliation, hiding as he was from confrontation.

At the afternoon break, Jeff and Ron reported that it was all over the school that Binksy, Hollins and Marsh, or as the bully's were referred to behind their backs' 'The Three Stooges', were going to wait for Mark on the carriage drive after lessons. Most of the school would be turning out to witness the beating that they intended to give to Mark.

At the end of the school day Mark waited until most of the students and the stooges had disappeared from school, to await his appearance on the carriage drive, but they were all to be disappointed. With pounding heart Mark took the long way home and once more avoided injury. That night he was sent to bed early, by his mother who had exploded at the sight of his torn trousers. Mark had not tried to explain, as his Mother was in no mood to listen. Fear of physical injury was bad enough, but it was the fear of being called a coward that was keeping him awake.

On the following morning the miserable boy was deliberately late for school. He had tried the "I'm feeling sick" routine but Helen had placed a hand on his forehead and pronounced him fit and well. When he arrived at school he was met by Jeff at the entrance to the main hall. Making their way to assembly Mark's misery was compounded. "They were waiting for you this morning and they said you are a shitty coward, and they are definitely gonner get you today."

Mark noticed that both Jeff and Ron had chosen not, to sit next to him in one of the packed rows of canvas chairs. He knew that with the 'Three Stooges' only five rows in front, the idea had occurred to Jeff and Ron that to be a friend and associate, of the unwilling sacrificial victim could have repercussions for them.

In the noisy bustling time, before the teachers entered the hall, the three stooges continually turned in their seats to pull faces and sneeringly draw fingers across throats, to suggest that they would only be satisfied when they had killed their victim. The teachers climbed the steps leading to the stage in Indian file, the headmaster was last. Mark did not hear a single word of that morning's speech, nor did he have any awareness of its religious significance. His head was full of other things as the whole school was ordered to rise and sing hymn three-sixty-four.

They had managed to get to the chorus of Holy, Holy, Holy when Mark suddenly lost all self control. He dived and scrambled over the rows separating him from the 'Stooges', scattering children and chairs in all directions. The bullies froze; as did the entire teaching staff and student body. The temporary state of rigor-mortis only lasted seconds, during that time Mark landed several cracking punches on Binksy's face, forcing him to retreat and fall backwards. As students started to scream support and encouragement for the rash little boy who was attacking the much bigger and feared school terrorists, the teachers were finally stirred into action. However it took too long to get down the steps of stage for them to prevent all three stooges from being battered with elbows, knees and fists.

Mark was transformed from aggressor to defender as two of the male teachers grabbed him roughly by the hair and arms and when one of them hit him across the face Mark punched the French teacher right on the nose, causing him to topple onto his colleague. Mark was now demented, kicking the 'Stooges' and teachers alike until his body could no longer function. Then, as he panted like an animal, he became aware that the whole school had become silent as they surveyed the scene of devastation. All who had been involved in the fracas were battered and bloody. Mark had the beginnings of a black eye, courtesy of one of the teachers, a split second before Mark's elbow had done a much better job in retaliation closing his right eye instantly. "Dacey, hold still now."

The voice was one of great authority and belonged to the school's deputy headmaster. 'Stormin' Norman Booth' or 'Batman' as the kids called him on account of his master's gown that flowed behind him like a cape, when he stormed up and down the school, like a regimental sergeant major. "Dacey, I said that is enough boy."

Exhausted, Mark could not have continued even if his life had depended on it.

Batman a giant of a man held the pathetic figure in a vice like grip as he dragged the boy along. There was no animosity in his action, just a determination to deposit the boy at the headmaster's office as quickly, and as quietly as possible.

There he threw his charge onto a chair in the corner. The boy surveyed his surroundings, the huge windows and glass dividers, the secretary and other staff members who were crowding round to catch a glimpse of the wild animal. The lad felt as if he were a fish in a tank and as his situation became clearer, he felt as if he were drowning. The headmaster, Casper Lorimer, burst through the glazed door and scattered loose papers from the desk and screamed. "You....you bloody animal, you flaming stupid Hun."

'Batman' stood between the purple-faced Head and Mark. Casper in looks and stature was the likeness of William Hartnell, the first 'Doctor Who', with one important physical difference - Casper Lorimer was bow-legged. This made his strutting walk somewhat comical to the cruel children under his control. Slowly the headteacher's blood pressure dropped, his complexion regained its unhealthy pallor and his boiling anger reduced to a simmer. "You my lad are for the high jump, and that is for sure."

"I would like to get to the bottom of this debacle, headmaster." Stormin' was serenity personified.

"Ahem.. yes.. of course as I, Mr. Booth." Casper thought quickly, now that his deputy had reminded him that it was unseemly to reveal such emotion before the onlookers who were gathered outside the office windows. "Mrs. Adams, please be so good as to disperse that rabble outside. You can tell them from me there is nothing to see, it is all over."

The secretary obeyed demurely. Finally satisfied that he was now in control of the situation, Casper again faced the boy who was seated in the high backed chair, his head-bowed. "My first instinct is to call the police Mr. Booth, eh.. What do you think?"

"I think that is your prerogative as Head, Sir," replied Norman, staring at the boy, trying to ascertain if The Head's threat had any affect. It had none. Mark looked at the floor and his shoes.

"Look at me boy!" shouted Casper.

Slowly Mark raised his bruised face, which now looked a sorry sight. The blow that the Religious Studies teacher had given Mark had been delivered at full strength. Blood was trickling from both nostrils and his eye was also closing to a puffy slit. "Now you thug, let me tell you what the police do to delinquents like you, once they get you to the police station......."

Casper went on into detail and explained that it was just a matter of hours before the officers of the law would have been summoned, Mark would be taken him away and beaten to within a hair's breadth of death. Without trial, or recourse to his parents he would be locked up and the key would be thrown away, perhaps one day he would be released, when he would be old, infirm, socially ruined and miserably repentant. This was Casper's tried and trusted method of striking fear into children who dared to challenge the harmony and authority of his little empire.

"Call them then." The defiant youngster replied. Batman stiffened to attention and Casper gasped in disbelief.

"An' when they get 'ere I'll make sure they know who punched me face in. A teacher that's who."

Flustered, the Head was suddenly on the defensive. "But you attacked the teacher!" he stammered. Then with his composure regained he added triumphantly, "He was only defending himself."

"No ee want, I din't know it were a teacher grabbing me, but ee knew I was only a kid."

Flabbergasted, the bow-legged man sat back into his own black, leather-bound chair. "You are an incorrigible heathen, and if you have anything worthwhile to say in your defence, before I cane you severely, let's have it now."

"No, I want you to call the police."

Casper's face was once more bilberry purple. Norman Booth cut short the Heads spluttering indignation. "Mark I want you to tell me why you went berserk, and no lies mind."

It took all of the lad's pride and resolve to hold back the tears as he poured his heart out to the deputy Head, while ignoring the presence of the bandy-legged headmaster.

When Mark had finally finished, his body crumpled and he again looked at the floor. "Head, can I see you outside for a moment please?" Surprised by the request from his deputy, Casper got up from the leather chair and though wearing a puzzled frown he followed him outside, along the corridor to the vacant staff room. "What is it Norman?"

"I think the boy has suffered enough." Then before his superior could speak he added, "If he insists on the calling the police, we could have a potential problem regarding his injuries and the fact that they were inflicted by an adult."

"But it would be that brat's word against ours."

"Not that simple I'm afraid, with several hundred witnesses."

"Ah yes I see….. ahem. What do you suggest Norman?"

"I think it would be best if you were to tell the boy that in consideration of - mitigating circumstances, you think that he has suffered enough and that if only he had come to you sooner, this unfortunate scenario could have been avoided." "Yes. Yes.. of course it would have been, wouldn't it?" Stormin' gave an imperceptible sigh of relief. "But will it not seem to the other children that Dacey has got off scot free?"

Pausing for a few seconds, the deputy Head suggested a compromise. "Yes of course, you are right, Head, so what if I were to supervise the boy's detention every breaktime and lunchtime for a fortnight?"

"And evenings," said Casper, his old brashness returning.

"I would appreciate your indulgence on that issue, as I have other commitments for the evenings. What if we had the wretch clean the staff room during his detention?"

"Yes, very well, capitol, that is settled then."

Mark had cleaned his face as best he could at the small wash basin in the boys' toilets and with as much confidence as he could muster; he walked into the room to join his classmates.

The detention was a pleasure for Mark as he was amazed by the friendliness of Mr. Booth. At the completion of his punishment he was disappointed to be deprived of the personal interest that the deputy Head had appeared to show him. That Friday lunch-time, 'Stormin' Norman called Mark to his desk. "Dacey, your period of penance is over my boy, but before you disappear I want you to know this. I understand why you did what you did, and I sympathise."

"But Sir..."

Mark sensed the magnitude of what the man was saying and as he had come to respect him greatly over the last weeks, he wished to lessen the task. "No. Let me finish. When I was a lad of your age, I was a beanpole of a thing and I too suffered terribly at the hands of similar bullying morons. Eventually, I settled things with each of them, one by one, but not, and I repeat not, in the sight of any other living sole, especially not in front of hundreds of witnesses. Do I make myself clear boy?"

Mark grinned, his face now showed little sign of injury and his brilliant white smile brought a similar response from Norman."Yes Sir, thank you sir."

"Well then, be off with you and I'm sure I will not be seeing you in detention again."

"I hope not sir" and as directed by the deputy's waving hand Mark headed for the classroom door, which he opened then hesitated. "Sir?" Norman looked up from marking the papers on his desk. "Sir it's a good name for you."

"Oh and what name might that be boy?"

"Batman sir."

"Batman?" said the teacher intrigued.

"Yes, they call you Batman, an' the way I see it, you pretty much 'elped me out of a tight spot, an' I won't forget it sir. Thank you."

"You are welcome Mark Dacey, now sod off and leave me to my marking." Mark turned to leave. "Mark!" The boy halted. "I suppose Batman is a step up from 'Stormin' Norman, eh?"

Mark nodded, grinned widely and left a far happier child than he had been since he had started at the senior school.

Over the next couple of days Mark made it his business to ambush the 'Three Stooges' separately and he battered each of them in turn. The job had been far easier than he had expected it would be, as the bullying trio considered him insane and now wished that they had never met him. After that weekend, the Stooges' days of bullying were over and Mark was recognised as a 'nutter,' best left alone.

When Helen had first seen the effects of the confrontation that had taken place in assembly, Mark had explained that he had sorted the lads that had ripped his pants, no more information was offered. The next day his mother called in to the school's out-fitters, 'Vernon Haigh' in the village and bought him a new pair, of grey, flannel school trousers.

December, Beatlemania was coming to an end and Mark was twelve years of age. A quiet Northerners-only Christmas celebration merged, and then 1965 blurred into a new year.

Chapter 68

On 8th, January 1966 in Vietnam eight thousand American GIs launched the biggest attack of the war on a Vietcong stronghold near Saigon. On the 10th, British prime minister, Harold Wilson arrived in Lagos, for talks on Rhodesia. In India Mrs. Indira Gandhi came to power. On the 17th after a mid-air collision, the American air force lost a hydrogen bomb somewhere over Spain. On the 21st Beatle George Harrison married model Patti Boyd.

In February, Watney's increased the price of a pint of beer by one penny to one shilling and eight pence and on the 14th, America found its lost H-bomb intact off the Palomares.

March and World Cup fever was beginning to take hold of the nation's and of Mark's interest. Barry had rented a small, lock-up greengrocer's in the village and he was opening it at night times and at weekends, to increase the family income. The minibus had been sold and the Vauxhall Cresta was the only vehicle that Barry then owned.

Mary and Geoff had settled into married life in the Meanwood district of Leeds. Mary had decided to go to University. She had also passed her driving test and Barry had found her an immaculate black, Austin A35, two door saloon. The Ludbarrow gang had been over to Leeds several times for Sunday dinner and although Mary was stressed when she prepared lunch, she always seemed more relaxed once it had been served and she was very considerate to everybody.

In the April school break, Terry came north by coach with his livewire son Ian, and collected a spotless two-tone blue and white Ford Consul that Barry had sourced for him. After parting with one-hundred-and-ten pounds of his hard earned cash, Terry returned to London with Mark and fourteen-month-old Ian sat on the back seat. Mark was to spend the week in London with Terry and Jean.

Terry had changed jobs again, this time he had joined London transport as a bus conductor and on reaching twenty-one later that year he would automatically be trained for the driving job he so desired. It was compulsory for all would-be bus drivers to have to complete from three to six months probation as a bus conductor in order to learn the bus routes. The pay and working hours were much better than he had enjoyed when he had been employed in hotel kitchens and he was able to work overtime, or spend time with his young family as finances dictated.

Jack had moved in with a young woman called Vera who had two infant daughters.Vera and Jack and Vera's mother and brother all lived just a short distance from Terry's apartment. Vera was an expert shoplifter and she thought the world of Jack.

Karl announced that he would be getting married to Linda in spring the following year.   It would be a flashy affair in London. His business was going from strength to strength, although there had been a major hiccup on the 9th of March. Big Joe Carter had been drinking in the Nelson pub, when one of the East End firms, John Brown had arrived to settle an old score, catching him by surprise and shooting him in the head, at close range, with a hand gun.   An accomplice had fired several shots into the air as warning for the pub's punters to keep their heads down, and then they had casually strolled away. Joe Carter was one of one of the Rankin's leading soldiers and so the stage was set for a deadly show down.

Karl and Linda brought Mark back north and on the way the younger brother enthused about that Summer's up and coming World Cup, so much so that it prompted his big brother to say, "Olright, for fuck's sake Mark, if you shut the fuck up I promise to take you to the final." The boy was ecstatic and instead of shutting up, he became more vociferous as he asked Karl and Linda if they thought it might be England in the final. "Fuckin' doubt it, them Brazilians are pretty good."

Unperturbed the young boy started dreaming from that moment that England could be champions of the world.

At school, Mark was the envy of his pals when he finally convinced them that his brother would be taking him to the final of the greatest sporting event that the world had to offer.   There was the added excitement of the theft of the famous Jules Rimet trophy and coverage of the crime dominated the media. Fortunately for the football world, rescue came in the shape of a mongrel by the name of 'Pickles' who sniffed out the trophy where the thieves had hidden it in panic, making the dog, overnight a Global hero.

In May Myra Hindley and Ian Brady, the moors child murderers, were sentenced to life imprisonment.

July was a wonderful month for Mark and his pals, as the world came to Britain. Supporters from every corner of the earth travelled to and around England to watch their teams. England was in group one and England matches were watched enthusiastically by the whole nation.

July 11th   England 0   Uruguay 0
July 16th   England 2   Mexico 0
July 20th   England 2   France 0

England went through to the quarter finals top of their group.

QUARTER FINAL

23rd July   England 1   Argentina 0

Now the whole country believed that their team could do it.

SEMI FINAL

26th July   England 2   Portugal 1.

And that was how at 3p.m., on Saturday, 30th July, 1966 at Wembley Stadium, the four Dacey brothers', Paddy and Digger werte waiting for the referee's whistle to start the World Cup Final against West Germany.

Mark held the bright blue programme with its picture of the Jules Rimet trophy and big red letters proclaiming that this was the 'FINAL', in the corner was the rip-off price of two shillings and sixpence.   Karl had got the best, stand tickets for under two quid each.

The passions that poured out that day were of the kind that once experienced would be remembered for a lifetime by the fortunate spectators. Mark was in tears when the West Germans snatched victory from them, when they scored with a goal-mouth scramble from a free kick moments before the final whistle, had made the score 2 - 2.

Extra time brought euphoria, but also doubts as the England team appeared to be the most exhausted of the two.   Then, after the first half had been underway for only eight minutes, Geoff Hurst fired a shot that hit the underside of the German crossbar, bouncing down and out and despite frantic objections from West German players, the Soviet linesman was insistent. 'GOAL'.

The agony of the remaining time was almost unbearable, even more so as the final whistle was only moments away. Again Geoff Hurst was running for the German goal.   Whistles echoed round the ground and some fans were already on the edge of the pitch ready to be the first to congratulate their heroes. Hurst launched a thunderball of a shot. 'GOAL' he had scored a hat-trick, which added to Martin Peter's earlier goal, gave England four goals to two and making them the world champions.

It also sent young Mark Dacey into insane celebration for the next twenty-four-hours. His three brothers' had indulged Mark and in the evening they had took him to Trafalgar Square, to share the occasion with thousands of rejoicing fans. The next day the brothers' stayed together, as if they were reluctant to let the moment go, travelling in Karl's Rover up the M1 late on Sunday afternoon they escorted Mark back home.

The shop was crowded with happy, hung-over customers. The four brothers'' ate in the dining room of the chip shop that had been opened especially for the still-celebrating public. Mark begged his brothers' to stay overnight. Helen tried several times to send Mark to bed, but her other son's partly to annoy her, refused to give him up.

Jack iced the cake of that glorious weekend for the youngest brother, when he obtained permission from Helen and Barry for Mark to accompany his brothers' on a midnight ramble on the heath, on the ancient Roman Road at Bleackstone Moor.   The walk in the company of his siblings was magical. After forty minutes of chatter and ambling up the steep incline of the road and even steeper approach to the monument, they found themselves sitting on the cool, grey, ancient cobbles, absorbing the peace of the moor and the warm summer's night.   Mark lay back and looked at the stars, a huge grin across his face. Could anything in life ever be this good again?

.

The next morning, Mark eventually surfaced at 10a.m. in a state of total exhaustion, he missed school and was devastated when Helen broke the news that his brothers' had already left but had asked her to pass on their farewells.

Mark and his mother sat side by side in the dining room, sharing the little leisure time that was available before lunchtime opening. "Mark, don't be upset love, at least I've let you stay off school. Anyway I've got some great news." the boy's mood lifted a little. "We're going to move in six weeks."

Helen went on to explain, they had a buyer for the business and had found another on the other side of the village.   It was a convenience store which sold a wide variety of goods. In addition to the shop, a living room, a small kitchen, cellars, three bedrooms and joy of joys, a bathroom. At the back a small private yard completed the busy main road enterprise. The park, playing fields and 'rec' were at the top of the street. Mark was now truly excited but he was puzzled by the huge grin on his mother's face, "That's not all." When she felt she could contain the news no longer she said, "Nan and Granddad are coming north to live in Ludbarrow."

Since Nell and Tommy had been left alone at Constantine Road by grandchildren who had moved on in life, they had given more thought to how they wished to spend the remaining years of their old age. When their Hampstead landlord doubled their rents, they decided to move near their daughter, where they hoped to enjoy a slower pace of life. Helen and Barry had found them somewhere to rent just around the corner from the new shop.

These were turning out to be the best days of Mark's life, for surely if his beloved grandparents and big sister Mary could leave the attractions of London, surely his equally well-loved Terry would follow, and if Terry, then why not his two remaining siblings? 'Yes' thought the boy, it was going to be inescapable, fate had so obviously decreed that his family should be one again.

With heart beating wildly, Mark made a token effort to wash and to make himself presentable. Finding his mother was preoccupied with his little sister, he used the diversion to escape any requests for him to complete his chores "See yer later." The boy grabbed his football and rushed out to play. On the street he found Jinxie, who had also ducked school. When he shared his news his euphoria was contagious. Then together; as they would many times that late summer and autumn, the two friends battled heroically to win the World Cup all over again.

Mark found life full of hope. But he would learn that there could be no going back, his childhood was almost over and in a few months he would be a teenager. Future events would bring him closer to his brothers' in ways that no one could have envisaged. Indeed had they possessed the ability to see into the future, would they have wished to do so?

The great Rankin - Brown gang confrontation never escalated into a full scale war because that summer, Sergeant, soon to become Inspector Sanderson of the serious crimes division, raided the headquarters of the Rankin brothers' firm. Albert, Chris and most of the gang were arrested and charged with extortion, torture, and murder. Nearly all would very shortly be serving life sentences.

"And I," said the policeman aloud to himself, "will see to that." For Sanderson had more ambition than any of the players could have dreamed. When he had taken care of the Rankin's, with the help of the Brown brothers', he would consolidate the London underworld. Once that was done, he would take care of the Browns. Sanderson rubbed his unshaven chin between thumb and forefinger, as if it were an afterthought he murmered to himself, "And Karl Dacey. Well, we will just have to wait and see what happens. Time will tell if there is going to be a place on my Manor, for that... *'Norvern Monkey'.*"